The Palestine Exchange

a novel

by
Stephen Lewis

authorHOUSE®

AuthorHouse™
1663 Liberty Drive, Suite 200
Bloomington, IN 47403
www.authorhouse.com
Phone: 1-800-839-8640

First published by AuthorHouse 1/10/2008

ISBN: 978-1-4343-3473-2 (hc)
ISBN: 978-1-4343-3472-5 (sc)

Printed in the United States of America
Bloomington, Indiana

This book is printed on acid-free paper.

ACKNOWLEDGMENTS

I would like to thank my wife, Brona, for her computer skills, sister, Janet, and mother-in-law, Cyril, for their support; for editorial assistance on the first draft, the AuthorHouse editing team; my college roommate, Chuck Loomis; my daughter, Lindsay, for helping to construct my synopsis; Marc Lieberman, Attorney at Law, for his photographic services; Barry Kluger, media consultant and columnist, for his editing and commentary; Barry Zwick, contributing editor, for his commentary; and Pastor Eddy Paul Morris, Scottsdale First Assembly, for his advice and support. A special thanks to family friend Dr. Barry Chandler for his last minute book doctoring. Finally, I would like to thank William J. Wolf, radio host of Middle East Radio Forum (available on the Internet and on KKNT radio 960 in Phoenix, Arizona) for his invaluable historical editing and assistance. Lastly, I dedicate this book to Generation X and Y, with the hope that some of you will read *The Palestine Exchange*.

THE END OF THE BEGINNING

July 18, 2007

Kremlin, Moscow

Destroy the International Space Station (ISS) and all of its crew members and make it look like an accident. His orders came from high up in the Kremlin. The former KGB agent had another issue to deal with as well: a traitor in the Kremlin. Igor looked forward to that challenge. He was a specialist in torture and painful death from the old days of the Soviet Union.

When Yuri returned from lunch, he knew something was amiss when his computer password was rejected. Then he saw a detail of the Kremlin's secret service approaching his office. He quickly asked a favor of his friend Nickolai. He scribbled down his brother's e-mail address and password on a sheet of paper and quickly handed it to Nickolai. "Take this and e-mail my brother. Tell him I've been arrested."

The detail arrived. "Yuri Kafelnikoff, you are under arrest," said one of the secret service officers.

"On what charges?" Yuri asked.

"Treason," said the officer, and Yuri was taken away in handcuffs.

Cathedral at Reims, France

"Father," begged the man in the confessional booth, "Let us pray for those brave souls who sometimes are sacrificed for the 'greater good.'" Father Gauthier immediately connected the voice to the confessor.

"Good evening Archbishop, what brings you to my confessional booth so late this evening?"

"Father, I am a sinner."

"We all are sinners," Father Gauthier replied. "Do you wish to confess your sins to me?"

"Another time, Father. Right now just pray for me," requested Dominique Clement, the Archbishop of Paris.

"God forgives."

"I hope you will forgive me too." The archbishop quickly exited the confessional booth.

Chapter 1
AFTER THE CEASE-FIRE

June 7, 2007
Jerusalem, Israel

Israeli Prime Minister Ehud Olmert was in his office when he heard a familiar voice over his intercom. "Mr. Prime Minister, there is a call from Abu Mazen on the secure line," reported the aide. The Palestinian territories, in the post-Arafat era, had become lawless societies, with gangs and thugs patrolling and fighting each other for local turf, corruption still rampant. While President Abbas appeared to be weak and unwilling to crack down on the militant factions, Hamas, the newly elected government in the Palestinian territories and its proxy Islamic Jihad, remained steadfast in its ongoing war against Israel. They launched rockets and, to a lesser extent, sent suicide bombers into Israel, usually from the West Bank. Fortunately, most were caught at the border checkpoints.

Abu Mazen, also known as President Mahmoud Abbas, was considered an ineffectual leader of his people. He had been with Arafat from the early Fatah days, when the duplicitous Arafat often proclaimed to the Western press that peace and coexistence were possible among Israelis and Palestinians. At the same time, he told the Arab press the Jihad must go on. Perhaps Abbas was a sheep in wolf's clothing, perhaps not, but he was all Olmert had to work with now.

"Good afternoon Mr. President. And I hope your family is well," said Prime Minister Olmert.

"Well, indeed," replied Abu Mazen. "And yours, Mr. Prime Minister?"

1

"Well, thank you."

"Please give my best to the Sharon family. Such a tragedy."

"Of course," responded Olmert.

"Mr. Prime Minister, it is most urgent that we meet."

Ehud quickly reviewed his appointment book.

"Tomorrow is good, at 9 PM, at the usual place."

"Yes, of course," agreed Abu Mazen.

It was after 11 PM when the meeting broke up. The Palestinian president and his bodyguards discreetly left in a bulletproof black Mercedes Benz. Accompanied by a security entourage, the cars sped away through the winding streets of Arab East Jerusalem toward Ramallah. *Politics is strange in the Middle East*, he thought to himself. Only minutes earlier, he revealed the following information to Olmert.

"Mr. Prime Minister," said Abu Mazen, "we have reliable information that a convoy of trucks containing 100 converted Russian rockets with a range of fifty kilometers is en route from Damascus to the Bekka Valley, where the Lebanese contingent of the peacekeeping force is stationed. This is an Iranian-funded operation. The rockets are mounted with chemical warheads, and the agent is nerve gas. Our intelligence believes that these are the first of its kind in Hezbollah's arsenal."

"Why are you telling me this?" asked Ehud.

"Mr. Prime Minister, Hezbollah is an extremist Islamic Shiite terrorist organization. Their success against your forces last summer only radicalizes the Palestinians and Hamas. Conditions in Gaza are worsening, and Iran is becoming bolder. To introduce chemical warheads into Israel's northern border is a recipe for disaster. Hezbollah's arsenal is still intact, and they have been resupplied with Fajr 3, 4, and 5 rockets that have a range from twenty to seventy kilometers that can be mounted on a 6 by 6 chassis for launching. Can you imagine what will happen to the region if chemical weapons on Katyusha rockets are fired indiscriminately into our neighborhoods? Mr. Prime Minister, this convoy has the cover of the Red Crescent. The missiles have been disassembled and secretly hidden in the vehicles. They will be taking the following route into Lebanon." Abu Mazen opened a map. "The vehicles also carry medicine and medical supplies for the Lebanese. You will be accused of breaking the cease-fire when you destroy them."

"Of course," replied Olmert.

"Mr. Prime Minister, I am requesting your assistance in obtaining vaccination for the Palestinian people against a possible biological or chemical attack. We are not certain that war won't come to the region again." There were other reasons, too, but Abu Mazen kept silent.

"We will see what we can do. If war does come, you bear as much responsibility as Arafat. Your press is inflammatory, as your schools prepare the next generation to hate us. You squander the money you receive and blame your lifeless economy on us. Your failed policies and corruption led to this Hamas-controlled government. The Israeli-Palestinian conflict continues to incite the Arab street. Mr. President, you never took any risks for peace."

"There is truth to what you say Mr. Prime Minister. Anwar Sadat and your Rabin took risks and it cost them their lives, but we all die anyway."

He didn't bother to share his epiphany with the prime minister, but Abu Mazen was preparing to accept Israel's generous offer for the two-state solution that Yasir Arafat walked away from in 2000 and set into motion the second intifada or Palestinian resistance.

Predicated on the peace models created by previous negotiations with the Israelis, under the auspices of the Clinton administration and with assistance from moderate Arab leaders, Abu Mazen was willing to accept a portion of East Jerusalem as the Palestinian capital. He was also ready to postpone for now the dream of the Palestinian "right of return" and acknowledge the reality that Palestinian refugees and their offspring could only return to a new Arab Palestine, not the Jewish one. There were many more details to hammer out of course. In spite of an occasional IDF incursion, the Gaza Strip was already in Palestinian hands due to the unilateral Israeli pullout, but Abu Mazen appeared to be powerless to stop the militants from moving in after the Israeli pullout, and from launching the hundreds of homemade rockets into Israel, most falling short of population centers. If Abu Mazen could come to terms with Israel on a two-state solution, he needed help to eliminate Hamas from the Palestinian government.

Abu Mazen had been against the second intifada orchestrated by his predecessor Arafat. Although Arafat was dead, his blunder emboldened Israel to fence off the Gaza Strip and much of the West Bank to cut off the suicide bombers. Israel's economy grew rapidly and the tourists came back. The Palestinian economy was still in shambles, and, except for humanitarian needs, essentially all funds had been cut off to the Hamas government. Palestinians hated the fences, but were powerless to take them down. Abu Mazen believed he could negotiate a swap of Israeli land as compensation for West Bank land Israel took, but only if Hamas was out of the picture. Tomorrow he planned a meeting with his closest advisers on the Palestinian Executive Council. He collected his thoughts.

Empathy was not an attribute of Arab Muslim societies. Abu Mazen knew Jews were also evicted from Arab countries after World War II. But this fact bore little political significance because that bit of Jewish history was rarely recalled, as was the history of the Grand Mufti of Jerusalem who actually conspired and plotted with Adolph Hitler to exterminate the Jews of Palestine. It was good fortune for the Palestinian cause that both of these events had sunk to historical oblivion.

Skeletons from the past did not worry Abu Mazen; he was concerned only about what the future portended. Time, he recognized, may no longer be on Palestine's side. Iran had changed the geopolitical landscape by attempting to smuggle in chemical weapons to Israel's northern border. Abu Mazen had no way of knowing that, when he left his meeting with Olmert, Israeli fighter jets over Lebanon had already destroyed the Red Cross convoy and all its vehicles. The death toll would not be confirmed until the next day. To avoid being charged with violating the UN cease-fire and breaking international law (as they were in 1981 when Israel destroyed Iraq's only nuclear reactor), the Israelis would submit proof they acted defensively. Israel certainly didn't want to take the spotlight off Iran at the United Nations. Abu Mazen learned about the raid on his return from that meeting.

Chapter 2

DAMAGE CONTROL

June 9, 2007
Tel Aviv, Israel

Richard H. Jones, U.S. ambassador to Israel, had taken Olmert's phone call minutes after Abu Mazen had departed. Apologizing for the tardiness of the call, Olmert proceeded to explain the Israeli mission in Lebanon that destroyed the convoy.

"Yes, Richard. We have seen this one coming for a long time. We have it all: photos and a documented paper trail that leads back to Tehran through Damascus."

"Thank God for that," said Jones. "The world press, especially the Europeans, will have you for lunch in the morning. Call a press conference as soon as possible and present your proof. Of course, the Arab street will go nuts for a while."

"Of course," agreed Olmert.

"Mr. Prime Minister, we should plan to meet within the next couple of days. I have to call Washington about this development."

"I understand. But before you go, there is something you should know. Yesterday I met with Abu Mazen, who provided me with information about the convoy and its chemical weapons. In return, he asked Israel for gas masks and vaccine for the Palestinians, but we're not capable of any more production at this time."

"Good to know. We'll meet soon, Mr. Prime Minister."

The following day there were protests in Cairo. Iran's Islamic government organized a hundred thousand-man march through the streets of Tehran. Even Shiites and Sunnis in Iraq took the day off from killing each other to join in protest. In France, England, and Germany, Muslims and non-Muslims took to the streets, burned tires, and ransacked cars. In Saudi Arabia, security was on high alert, while in the West Bank, Palestinian youth threw rocks at the fence, and a suicide bomber was killed at an Israeli checkpoint. It took two weeks for things to simmer down, even though by all credible accounts, the Israeli press conference the day following the operation proved their actions were defensive and justifiable. The American press focused on the collateral damage, ignoring the bigger picture as usual.

Chapter 3

A HISTORY LESSON

June 9, 2007
Ramallah, West Bank

Abu Mazen sat down and faced a few trusted members of the Palestinian Authority still on the Palestinian Executive Council. They included Hussein Agha, an academic and adviser to Abu Mazen; Abu Ala, lead negotiator at Oslo; Hasan Asfour, Palestinian negotiator; Hanan Ashrawi, Palestinian spokeswoman; Mohammed Dahlan, head of Palestinian security in Gaza; Saeb Erekat, Palestinian negotiator and Minister of Local Government; General Amin al-Hindi, head of Palestinian secret police; Yasser Abed Rabbo, Minister of Information and Culture; Jibril Rahoub, head of Palestinian Security in the West Bank; Mohammad Rashid, former finance adviser to Arafat; and Nabil Sha'ath, Minister of Planning and International Cooperation.

Abu Mazen began by asking, "Is there any one on the Council who does not remember Abba Eban, former Israeli ambassador to the United Nations?" He paused. "Mr. Eban once said that the 'Palestinians never miss an opportunity to miss an opportunity.' Would anyone like to critique Mr. Eban's perspective?"

A moment of silence befell the group, followed by inaudible grumbling. Finally, Hanan Ashrawi, supremely confident with her Ph.D. in medieval literature from the University of Virginia, replied, "Maybe he was right some of the time, and maybe he was wrong some of the time."

Abu Mazen responded, "For a moment, let us forget our own rhetoric. We shall take a vote. In front of each of you, is a sheet of

7

paper. There is one question as you can see. The question is: Should Arafat have taken the deal in 2000? There are three boxes for three choices, yes, no, and not sure. Each of you, one at a time, go into the other room, check one of the boxes, and drop the paper into the ballot box. No names, please." When the votes were in the ballot box, the Palestinian president tallied the votes and read them. Three voted yes, five voted no, and four voted not sure.

"This vote affirms that most of us still believe that Arafat should not have taken the deal for eventual statehood in 2000. Who among us believe that if the Jews lost the war in 1948, there would be a Palestinian state today? Eleven hands are raised. Hanan, you didn't raise your hand, and you are a student of history. Please share your thoughts with us," said Abu Mazen and he sat down. She stood up.

"From a historical perspective, the occupation of Arab Palestine from 1948 to 1966 was Arabic, Egyptian, and Jordanian to be sure, but not Israeli until 1967. I actually think there were two wars in 1948. The first war was for the Arab armies to destroy the new Israel. That war was lost by the Arabs and won by the Jews, who earlier had accepted our right to have an Arab Palestinian state adjoining their state. That we can agree on. It is part of history. The second war was for Arab Palestine, the state we rejected. And since most of us left to have others do our fighting for us, Arab Palestine was lost by default to the Egyptians and Jordanians for eighteen years. And during those eighteen years, Palestinian grievances were not addressed because the world didn't care. We outsourced our own war, and who is so kind to die for you and then hand to you the spoils? Stateless Palestinians will find a thousand-fold more receptive ears when you complain about Israeli injustice, but if we complain about other Arabs, those complaints fall on deaf ears. Since 1948, our best chance for statehood has been and will always be with the Israeli occupation, not the Arab one." She sat down.

Abu Mazen rose again and said. "Thank you, Hanan, for your perspective. Are there any further comments on this subject or should we move on to other business?"

They all agreed to move on.

"As we are all aware, Israel destroyed chemical rockets from Iran coming in through Syria to Lebanon's southern border. I met with

Prime Minister Olmert the night of the Israeli air attack to actually inform him about the Iranian convoy. I wasn't aware he already had that information. The Israelis have no doubt improved their intelligence along the borders. You might ask why I provided this information. What I wanted was something in return: gas masks and vaccine to protect Palestinians against a biological or chemical attack."

Saeb Erekat asked, "I don't believe the Israelis have the production capability to make vaccine and gas masks for us all." Abu Mazen agreed, but believed that Olmert could get the necessary supplies from the United States under circumstances that he was about to explain.

Abu Mazen continued. "Once upon a time the phrases 'the liberation of Palestine' and 'armed struggle' meant the same thing, but now I think these phrases can be separated. I believe we can have our own Palestinian state with East Jerusalem as its capital, or we can have the 'armed struggle,' but not both. The question is which one do we want? Not an easy answer perhaps. It is often difficult to change direction in midstream."

Abu Ala, lead negotiator at Oslo, asked Abu Mazen, "Mahmoud, with all due respect, there can be no progress as long as Hamas controls the government."

"Exactly. We have to rid our government of Hamas, because time is no longer on our side. Listen to what Hanan said. I agree with her logic. The best deal we will ever get is only if Fatah can engage the Israelis. Israel unloaded Gaza on us like a family unloads an unwed spinster. The world witnessed the Palestinians receiving a Gaza Strip and using it as a base to launch unprovoked rocket attacks on Israel. For Sharon, it was another masterstroke that boosted Israel's prestige. He proved that the Palestinian security forces were powerless to control the militants from firing Quassam rockets at Israel from the Gaza. World sympathy for Palestine is now being replaced by the Lebanese crisis. I fear the world is tiring of Palestine, and if we lose our victim status, we no longer have Israel to blame, only ourselves. The political horizon brightens for Israel because Iran is an easy target to despise, especially after the war with Hezbollah. The Persians don't give a crap about Palestinians. We are a lightning rod for Iran, who uses our cause to bring the region to the brink of uncontrollable war. Palestine will not be Iran's stooge.

In a chemical and biological attack on Israel, Palestine will be Iran's collateral damage. But Israel will survive and make Iran rue the day. Let us choose our side, not the Iranian side of this dispute. Remember when Arafat sided with Iraq after the Kuwait invasion, Palestinians all over the Middle East were evicted from Arab countries. Arafat paid a heavy price for that support.

If deadly chemical or biological agents are dispersed in the airspace over Israel, they are likely to move with the wind currents. It is probable that those deadly agents could blow east to the West Bank or south to the Gaza. There is no way to guess how many of us will die a horrible death if such an event should take place because we have no protection for germs or gas. The Israelis have protection. And remember this: it couldn't matter less to the rest of the Arab world that Palestinians die this way. We would be seen as sacrificial lambs and martyred forever. Is that the place we want to be in history? Lest you forget, Iran and Iraq both used gas on each other. Iran even martyred their children, sending them to the war front to detonate Iraqi mines and save the lives of Iranian soldiers. Their children were told they would ascend to paradise and handed symbolic keys, not unlike our homicide bombers when they are photographed. Would Iran not hesitate to sacrifice us?"

Nabil Sha'ath spoke. "Mr. President, how can we rid ourselves of Hamas?"

Abu Mazen replied, "I will handle that, but only after I have a majority approval from this committee to accept, on behalf of the Palestinian people, the principles for peace established in year 2000 by the Clinton administration as a basis for a two-state solution."

"We weren't walled in in 2000," said Saeb.

"These are the new realities that we will have to deal with," replied Abu Mazen.

"Mr. President, that Israeli fence has added about 3 percent of the West Bank to the Israeli side. That is 3 percent less land than originally offered," Saeb noted.

"I intend to get an equal swap of Israeli land. The difficult part will be reaching an agreement on which land. But there is a bigger issue here. After Gaza and Lebanon, the Israelis are not likely to leave the West Bank anytime soon. In my opinion, the only way to get them out is to accept the accords of 2000. Before voting, remember, when Israel defines its borders, it will define ours."

The vote passed ten to two. Mohammed Dahlan, head of Palestinian Security on the Gaza Strip, and Jibril Rahoub, head of Palestinian Security in the West Bank, immediately requested a private meeting with Abu Mazen. Abu Mazen, like the late Egyptian president Anwar Sadat, was placing the bet of his life.

Chapter 4
DIVINE INTERVENTION

June 9, 2007
ISS, Space

My name is Ari Ben Ora, and I am one of four international scientists conducting experiments aboard a Russian-built International Space Station orbiting at 300 kilometers above the earth's surface, completing a full orbit every 96 minutes. Mission control, located outside of Moscow, coordinates communication with the ISS and the other space agencies. The other crew members are Sanjay Bushar from India, Andre Dubois from France, and Alexander Kafelnikoff from Russia. We have been in space for five weeks. At the end of August, our mission will be complete, and we will be replaced by a new group of scientists who will be shuttled to the station. Returning on the shuttle, we hope to safely land at a strip in the Russian steppes, then to board a bus to Moscow International Airport for flights to our countries of origin. Mine is Israel.

Ari had just finished his two hours of mandatory exercise for maintaining normal muscle tone and fitness on the ISS when the call came in from his wife, Rachel.

"Ari, this is Rachel. Honey, did you receive my e-mail?"

"Hi, Rachel. I did."

"Then you know what happened in Lebanon," Rachel said.

"It's very ominous, Rachel. I feel so badly that I've left you and the children alone."

"It's okay, Ari. We'll be fine."

"How are the kids doing?"

"Good. Life goes on. David made the soccer team. His grades are still good, and Rebecca attended her first bat mitzvah celebration, Ariel Cohen's, down the street. Rebecca's growing up fast. You should be back just in time to celebrate her thirteenth birthday."

"I wouldn't miss it for the world," Ari said. They spoke for another ten minutes until Ari told her he had to perform some light maintenance outside the station that required him to "space walk" for several hours.

The thought of her husband floating in space tethered to the craft did not sit well with her that night. On more than one occasion Rachel had planned to surprise Ari with the news of her pregnancy, but the timing never seemed to be right. Ari would certainly welcome the news, but Rachel feared his moment of elation would soon dissipate and be displaced by feelings of self-guilt and remorse for not being with her. She wouldn't take that chance. Modern science did not fully comprehend how living in space for long periods affected one's physical and emotional well-being, especially in a controlled micro-gravitational environment. But she planned to tell him before his mission was over for the simple reason they both knew: Ari may never come back to his family, or to his mother, Sarah.

Sarah's family illegally immigrated to Palestine in 1941 from Odessa. They first arrived in Turkey and then boarded a fishing boat that breached the British blockade, getting out of Russia in the nick of time, just before the Germans invaded Russia and launched Operation Barbarossa, which sent over three million of its soldiers including death squads, to exterminate the Jews of the Soviet Union.

Ari's father, Yoram, was a Sabra, a Jew born in Palestine. Yoram grew up on a kibbutz near Tel Aviv. Kibbutzim are economically self-sufficient collective farms. Children like him were educated there, and they worked the land to grow the food they ate. They also learned how to help defend their community from attack. Living on a kibbutz was no picnic; Ari had heard when he was young.

When his father was in his twenties, he moved to Tel Aviv and met Sarah. They married and Ari was born in 1958. Sasha, his sister, was born in 1959. When Yoram passed away in 1999, he was seventy-seven.

Ari became fluent in English, Hebrew, Arabic, and Russian, and was admitted to the Israel Institute of Technology specializing in mechanical engineering. Both sets of grandparents came from the Soviet Union, and Sarah's father, Yefim, often spent time with Ari, sharing stories of their exodus to Palestine. The Jewish Agency in Palestine was established to assist the legal immigrants. Covertly and with the Agency's assistance, Yefim and his wife, Serafima, received forged British identity cards, known as legal certificates, and began their new lives in Palestine.

Ari returned to the space station after the maintenance was completed and decompressed for another two hours. Ari was living proof that appearances can be deceiving. At forty-five, he was the oldest of the crew. He was five feet ten, with a swarthy complexion that belied his actual age, a medium build with good muscle tone. His salt-and-pepper hair, cut short, was beginning to recede, but his blue eyes stood out, especially when he smiled. Like his crewmates, Ari spent countless hours getting in great physical shape.

Sanjay, the scientist from India, performed the perfunctory physical for Ari for health-monitoring purposes. Sanjay was Ari's closest friend on the ISS. At five feet nine inches tall, he was slight in stature, with a dark complexion and black hair. They occasionally played chess together and often engaged in relaxed conversation. Although all four of the scientists spoke in different native tongues, English was the official language aboard the ISS.

They both were scheduled for their meals. Their food was pre-cooked in a little bag, ready with a little water and heat from the oven. Strapping a tray to their laps, they each used a scissors to open their bags and forks and spoons to remove the contents. There were no tables on the station.

"Ari, I can tell something is wrong from your face," Sanjay noted.

"Sanjay, I am worried for my family in Israel. You heard about the nerve gas and the rockets that were destroyed by Israel in Lebanon."

"I did. I hope you take some comfort knowing those rockets were destroyed," Sanjay replied.

"Some comfort, but the Iranians are clever. I'm sure they have a back-up plan."

"Don't underestimate your own people's resourcefulness. Israel probably has more nukes than India."

"Maybe, but Iran could still survive multiple nukes attacks because it is such a large country. Israel couldn't absorb one."

"Ari, I do understand what you are going through, because my family and my country have been threatened by a nuclear-armed Pakistan. The hatred between India and Pakistan has brought us to the nuclear brink also, but both countries stood down with the help of the United States."

"Sanjay, Israel and India have much in common. Both were founded on democratic principles, achieved independence from Britain within months of each other; we have fought wars against Muslims, and each country became the haven for our peoples fleeing from hostile Muslim countries."

"That's true, Ari, but there is a divergence to our histories. India was always here waiting for a Ghandi to liberate us, but Indian liberation would have happened anyway, sooner or later. World War II finished off the British Empire, and India, with its hundreds of millions of people, would not be denied its independence. It was just a matter of time."

"You make a valid point, Sanjay. Ghandi was such a great man, such a great leader. I had never thought about your independence happening without him."

"But Ari, your Israel was re-created by dreamers facing overwhelming odds against them. Ari, to reconstitute a Jewish state that had ceased to exist nearly two thousand years ago required a confluence of events to occur. The Jewish population had to be imported to Israel in the face of Arab opposition and their threats of another Jewish genocide. The political path to Arab oil had to be rerouted. There had to have been a Hitler and a Holocaust to provide the moral imperative. Even more was needed: an endless stream of homeless refugees that no other country wanted, FDR's timely death and Harry Truman's presidency, Winston Churchill's tenacity, and Stalin."

"It is true that Stalin provided Israel with weapons during our War of Independence, not the United States."

"And then for Israel, with no outside help, to be able to defend itself against a massive Arab invasion from surrounding Arab countries, including the British-trained Jordanian Foreign Legion, is beyond belief, something out of a motion picture. Do you wonder why evangelicals in the United States line up behind you? They believe Israel could only have come from divine intervention. Who could say they're wrong, Ari?"

The two friends, so animated a moment before, were lost in thought. Something Sanjay had said had stuck: no Hitler, no Holocaust, no Israel. Sanjay was probably right.

"I say we play a game of speed chess," Sanjay said.

"Later, perhaps. Right now I am going to take a nap," the Israeli replied.

"You leave me no choice. It's Rhett and Scarlett O'Hara again." Sanjay took out his iPod, put on his earplugs, and selected *Gone with the Wind* from several movies he uploaded into his mp3 player.

They were not aware that Andre Dubois, the French scientist, had overheard their conversation. Dubois silently agreed with Sanjay's long-shot assessment of Israel. But rather than attribute Israel's creation to divine intervention, Andre preferred to think of it as a curse on mankind.

Chapter 5
GET OUT OF JAIL CARD

June 9, 2007
Ramallah, West Bank

After the vote, Abu Mazen adjourned the meeting of the Palestinian Executive Council to meet privately with Mohammed Dahlan, head of Palestinian Security on the Gaza Strip, and Jibril Rahoub, head of Palestinian Security on the West Bank. Also in attendance were Yasser Abed Rabbo, Minister of Information and Culture, and former Palestinian Prime Minister Ahmed Queria, who had just arrived. Abu Mazen had briefed Ahmed on the vote just taken.

"Yasser," said Abu Mazen, "if our political calculations are correct, soon I am going to have to prepare the Palestinian communities here and abroad for peace with Israel, which is something Arafat never bothered to do. As minister of Information and Culture, your emphasis should be to gradually transform the Palestinian relationship with Israel from one of confrontation to one of cooperation. This spirit of cooperation should be reflected in the newsprint articles, television coverage, radio, and changes in our school textbooks, with the assistance of the Education Department. Eventually, you need to coordinate with your Israeli counterpart. In other words, if this accord is going to be accepted by the Palestinian people, we have to stop demonizing Israel, and hopefully, we'll even receive a boost in the polls. Order our press and television news to distance us from the Persian devils. Expose their war crimes, and convince the Palestinians that Iran would destroy Palestine and Jerusalem in order to destroy Israel."

"But Abu Mazen, the Israelis still refuse to meet with us," exclaimed Rabbo.

"Don't worry, Yasser, they soon will. Mohammed and Jibril, during Israel's war with Hezbollah, Israel imprisoned much of the Hamas government, especially on the West Bank, for ties to terrorism. You will coordinate with Israel a massive arrest of all Hamas elected officials in Gaza and the West Bank. We will make a legal case that Hamas has been an illegitimate government and call for new elections."

"Yes, Mr. President," said Jibril. Mohammed nodded his approval.

"The Palestinian Constitution authorizes me under the emergency provisions to maintain order, and that's what I intend to do. Are there any questions?"

"I have a question," said Mohammed Dahlan. "If we are going to sell a two-state solution to the Palestinian people here and abroad, I think we could face an uphill battle in any future elections. Truthfully, the Palestinian people know we're corrupt. Our past strategy to blame the Israelis for the poor living conditions of our people was very effective. If we can no longer blame Israel, the people's discontent may fall on us. Having said that, I believe there is a way for your strategy to work." With eyes and ears on him, he took a deep breath and said, "Convince Israel to free Marwan Barghouti."

"Mohammed is right," Jabril exclaimed. "Marwan is still a very popular guy among Palestinians, and although he is serving consecutive life sentences in the Israeli jail for a conspiracy conviction on multiple murders, I have a feeling the Israelis will free him to counter Hamas. Marwan's a natural leader. He brokered peace among the militant groups in the past and challenged Arafat on alleged human rights violations and corruption charges. In 1996, he was elected to the Palestinian Legislative Council. On the Palestinian 'street,' Marwan was considered the people's candidate for going after the 'Old Guard' in the PA. He speaks fluent Hebrew and English, and has even garnered support from liberal Israelis."

Abu Mazen agreed. The deal with Israel would have to include Marwan's imminent release and his endorsement of any peace agreement. It might just work. Mohammed Dahlan could have been the prophet Mohammed at that moment. He was hugged and adored, and Abu Mazen politely excused himself. He had to make a phone call.

Abu Mazen would try a bluff to gain Marwan's release. Dahlan's perspective was incontrovertible, and Marwan could perform well in his new role. That could lead to trouble for Abu Mazen down the road. But now the problem for Abu Mazen and the PA was more of a financial orientation.

The Palestinian Authority had been the recipient of hundreds of millions of dollars a year, primarily from the European Union and for the benefit of the Palestinian people, but much of that had been scammed by Arafat, when he was alive, and allegedly by members of the Palestine Authority including Abu Mazen. Now that money was spent, and no more was coming into Palestine, thanks to Hamas, still sworn to destroy Israel. Couple that with a hemorrhaging economy and an unemployment rate approximating 50 percent, Abu Mazen needed money now.

Chapter 6
VIEWS FROM ABOVE

June 11, 2007
ISS, Space

Andre Dubois, the French scientist, was thirty-two, with hair still blond and very fine to match his fair complexion. He wasn't too tall at five feet eight, but well proportioned and handsome in a European way. Andre may not admit to it, but to be French was sometimes to be condescending to other nations and cultures. And to be French was to dislike England and Germany. It would have suited him if the two countries had never been around because, in the years past, France had often been at war with them and not fared well.

On the streets of Paris, Andre once encountered an American tourist who said he had two weeks to see all of France. Andre politely suggested to the tourist, "You can't go through all of France in only two weeks." The American laughed and said, "Why not, the Germans did," referring to French Army's almost immediate defensive collapse in World War II. So to be French means having to live with the jokes usually associated with that humiliating defeat suffered by the French Army.

Andre's problem with Israel was not only personal. The Jewish state's existence flew in the face of many things French. French history may be rooted deep in anti-Semitism, but that was France. From a cultural perspective, France and Poland were likely the two most Catholic countries on the continent, even more so than Italy. They were also the most anti-Semitic. Original Catholic dogma was grounded on displacing and supplanting Jewish theology. The Jews fall from God's grace when the Romans destroyed their Temple and marched them out of their homeland almost two thousand years ago was once considered theological proof that their rejection of Christ would eternally damn them to the four corners of the world.

But with the resurrection of the nascent Jewish state, emerging out of the desert like a biblical David and Solomon crushing their Arab enemies, Andre believed that the consequences of a powerful Israel was an ongoing challenge to Catholic dogma that forced the Vatican to further revise and scale down scripture, as it did at the Second Vatican Council. To Andre it was simple. The Second Vatican Council removed the Jewish blame for the Crucifixion. Israel was an assault on the Catholic Church. Still, he did not want to see Israel perish in a ball of fire. The thought of a second holocaust was anathema to most French people. A better fate to befall Israel would be that its Jewish identity be immersed and lost within the faster populating Arab culture. That could happen, but it would take time.

Alexander was the tallest of the crew at six- feet two-inches tall. He had a muscular build with broad shoulders and large hands. His hair was thick and light brown and matched the color of his small eyes.

Alexander and Andre had been observing and photographing weather patterns over Earth for analysis. At the other end of the station, Sanjay and Ari were conducting experiments with flames, fluids, and metals in a zero-gravity environment. In the absence of gravity, flames burn differently, thereby reducing convection currents that allow warm air or fluids to rise or cool air and fluids to sink on Earth. This study of zero microgravity utilizes changes in combustion to enhance metal mixture in order to create different combinations of molten metals that couldn't be created on earth's environment, lending itself to potentially better materials for computer chips as well as other industries.

When Alexander and Andre finished for the day, Andre asked Alexander if he wanted to play a game of hearts. Alexander declined and reached for his Bible.

"What book are you reading?" Andre asked.

"I'm reading about the prophet Ezekiel and the first exile of the Jews to Babylon, around 580 BCE."

"The only exile of the Jews I know about is the Roman exile in 70 CE, after the Romans destroyed their Temple."

"That was the Jews second exile. In 586 BCE, the Babylonians destroyed Solomon's first Temple and exiled them to Babylon. But the Jews returned seventy years later and rebuilt the Temple. Do you ever read the Old Testament, Andre?"

"No. I was instructed in the New Testament."

"Andre, the Old Testament is filled with prophecies that have come true, especially for the Jewish people."

Andre instantly recalled Sanjay's earlier conversation concerning the evangelical Christians of America and their belief that Israel was divinely inspired. The Frenchman was surprised that Christian Zionism had found adherents in Russia. Alexander offered Andre his Bible.

"Andre, read this passage." The passage was from the ancient prophet Ezekiel, from the Book of Ezekiel, in the sixth century BCE, when the prophet Ezekiel and the other Jews were captured and taken from Jerusalem and exiled to Babylon.

"For I will take you out of the nation; I will gather you from all the countries and bring you back to your own land. ...You will live in the land I gave your forefathers, you will be my people and I will be your God. I will save you from all your uncleanness.

I will call for the grain and make it plentiful. ...I will increase the fruit of the trees and the crops of the field, so that you will no longer suffer disgrace among the nations because of famine.

On the day I cleanse you from all your sins, I will resettle your towns, and the ruins will be rebuilt. The desolate land will be cultivated instead of lying desolate in the sight of all who pass through it. This land that was laid waste has become like the Garden of Eden; the cities, that were lying in ruin, desolate and destroyed, are now fortified and inhabited.

Then the nations around you that remain will know that I, Jehovah, rebuilt what was destroyed and have replanted what was desolate, I, Jehovah have spoken, and I will do it."— Ezekiel 36:24

After reading this passage from Ezekiel, Andre was obfuscated. In literature he read the radical traditionalist Catholic dogma associated with the Society of St. Pius X, the international order founded by the late and excommunicated French archbishop Marcel-Francois Lefebvre. Andre believed the Roman destruction of the Jewish Temple in 70 CE, and the Jewish exile from the Holy Land had been incontrovertible proof of God's final punishment for the Jews' rejection of Christ and their complicity in his death. The fact that Rome wouldn't be officially Christian until Constantine arrived a few hundred years later mattered little to Andre.

What troubled Andre was what he learned from Alexander - that the Roman destruction of the Jewish Temple and subsequent exile, two events that the Society's theologians had offered as evidence against the relevance of Jewish theology, were not unique to Christianity, but a repetition of the earlier Babylonian exile. And neither of the two exiles had prevented the Jews from returning to their homeland; and because they did return, Andre's father was dead and Michelle might as well be.

Chapter 7
IRAN PLANS

June 12, 2007
Tehran, Iran

"In my judgment, we have at least two years before we are attacked either by the United States or Israel," said Iran's president Ahmadinejad to Iran's Supreme Leader Ali Khamenei. Khamenei was the real power in Iran, but Ahmadinejad was the public face. "We passed the UN deadline and we are in defiance, but Russia and China will block any punitive UN sanctions against us. When that lengthy process is exhausted, it will take a coalition of the willing headed by the United States or a surprise attack by Israel," Ahmadinejad reiterated. "I have a plan that could change the coalition of the willing into the coalition of the unwilling," he continued. Last night an Iranian oil tanker departed from the Iranian seaport of Bushehr in the Persian Gulf on its way to Kuala Lumpur, the Malaysian capital.

Tel Aviv, Israel

Ambassador Jones awakened this Wednesday morning at his usual wakeup time of 5:30 AM. His plan was to drive to Jerusalem to meet with Prime Minister Olmert. It is about an hour's drive from the coastal city of Tel Aviv to the hills approaching Jerusalem. Jerusalem would be cooler this time of year, which was a good thing. Jones had a lot on his plate. Israel had foiled the Iranians, and the United States intended to use Iran's complicity with chemical weapons to bolster the case against Iran at the UN Security Council emergency meeting on July 2.

Called for by the IAEA, the International Atomic Energy Agency, the emergency meeting was to warn Tehran to suspend its program for nuclear fuel production. In open defiance, Iran violated its agreement with the NPT, the Non-Nuclear Proliferation Treaty, by removing seals at three of its sites, the first step to enriching uranium essential for producing nuclear fuel for energy purposes or nuclear fuel for bombs. Iran insisted its nuclear program was only to develop nuclear fuel and for peaceful purposes, but no one was convinced.

Although only about fifty-five kilometers or thirty-six miles apart, Tel Aviv and Jerusalem were a study in contrast. Tel Aviv was very secular and modern. Jerusalem felt ancient, traditional, and ethnically culturally diverse. Its buildings were faced with Jerusalem stone, as required under the old British Mandate, giving the city a uniform look and reflection against the sun.

The Old City of Jerusalem, under Israel's control since the Six-Day War, was divided into four quarters: Jewish, Armenian, Muslim, and Christian. The Christian quarter was further divided into sections representing Greek Orthodox, Syrian Orthodox, and Coptic Christians.

In 953 BCE, King Solomon built the First Temple, but in 586 BCE the Babylonians destroyed it, sacked Jerusalem, and exiled its people. The Hebrews returned, and in 19 BCE, King Herod commissioned the Second Temple to be built, and it was completed in the year 63 CE, just seven years before its destruction by the Romans. In the third century, Jerusalem became a center of Christian pilgrimage. The Church of the Holy Sepulcher, which commemorates the hill of the Crucifixion and the tomb of Christ's burial, was built by Emperor Constantine in 330 CE. The eastern part of the city was filled with neighborhoods occupied by Muslim and Christian Arabs.

On a typical day the vendors compete on the narrow cobblestone streets for the attention of tourists, Christian monks can show up at anytime chanting their Gregorian hymns, Arabs displaying their kafiyeh walk by Hasidic Jews dressed in their traditional garb, and the smell of ethnic foods fills the air. Very holy to the Arabs in East Jerusalem is the architecturally beautiful Dome of the Rock, built in 685 CE, where, legend says, Mohammed once ascended to the heavens.

Most holy to the Jews and also in East Jerusalem is the Western Wall, the only remnants of the Second Temple. The Wall is about 28 meters in length and consists of twenty-four rows of stone.

Despite competing claims, Jerusalem is considered the ancestral home to Judaism, Christianity, and Islam. The city has been fought over and contested since recorded time. In West Jerusalem, one can view fine art collections and see the Dead Sea Scrolls at the Israel Museum or spend a solemn day at the Yad Vashem Holocaust Museum. There are archeological digs and tunnels to explore, evidence of prior civilizations.

Jerusalem also has great restaurants featuring many different kinds of ethnic foods, and Richard H. Jones, U.S. Ambassador to Israel, had enjoyed many of them. But today he was heading to 3 Kaplan Street in West Jerusalem to meet with Prime Minister Olmert. As he drove by the government district, Ambassador Jones glanced at the Knesset, impressive and perched high on a hill in West Jerusalem. The Knesset is Israel's legislative body. Other government offices in the area include the Central Bureau of Statistics, the Government Press Office, the State Archives, the Government Names Committee, and the Atomic Energy Commission. The ambassador had arrived.

After exchanging greetings, the U.S. ambassador sat down next to the prime minister. The ambassador began to reveal the full extent of the Palestinian peace offer, including operations to arrest the entire membership of Hamas, followed by negotiations on unencumbered land for the purpose of defining the West Bank border. After the arrests and new elections, a peace summit was planned at the Egyptian seaside resort of Sharm el Sheikh in the presence of Egyptian President Mubarek, U.S. President George Bush, and perhaps King Hussein of Jordan. The ambassador also shared with Olmert that the United States intended to provide the Palestinians the vaccines and equipment for protection against chemical or biological weapons after the peace deal was signed.

"Mr. Prime Minister, how will you expect the Palestinians to react to this accord?"

"That depends on how Abbas handles the situation. He is ineffectual, but Abbas believes if nothing tangible is reached with Israel, then he will have to contend with the militants again. As you know, we plan to fence the entire border, agreement or no agreement."

"And that will play into his enemies hands," responded Jones.

"We have no choice."

"This is what Abbas proposed," the ambassador said, "and I think it makes good sense, although on the surface, it appears risky. Place Marwan Barghouti on probation." Olmert frowned. "Mr. Prime Minister, his probation will be subject to his full endorsement of this peace both publicly and privately. Anything less, he goes back to prison. He will have to sign off on this. Abbas considers him a political rival, so he will be watched very carefully. Marwan can check the influences of Hamas, Martyrs' Brigade, and Islamic Jihad. The Palestinian people will listen to him, making an easier job of arresting the Hamas membership. If we make it to the peace agreements at Sharm el Shiekh without suicide bombings and without an implosion in the Palestinian territories, he'll want to run in the 2010 Palestinian presidential election. That will be the carrot and stick I think he goes for. What do you think Mr. Prime Minister?"

"I think there is chaos in the Gaza Strip. Israel pulled out unilaterally to give the Palestinian Authority a chance to fix their corruption, to see if they could begin the process to function as a normal modern state. But instead, the PA security forces refuse to control the area; the militant forces are free now to use Gaza for launching rockets into Israel. They are closer now to our population centers. Every agreement Israel ever signed for the last fifteen years only happened because the PA's charter to destroy Israel was officially disavowed. All of this has been undone by the Hamas government."

"And that provides Israel the legal justification for jailing them and removing them from office," Ambassador Jones noted. "Even the European governments despise Hamas. Europeans don't want an Islamic Palestinian state. Contributions from the EU, the United States, and the United Nations have dried up faster than spilt milk in the desert. International funds will now be going to Lebanon, not Gaza. The Europeans and the Arabs are still angry as hell at the PA for siphoning off their money, but you and I know that Abbas is a better alternative than Hamas. He needs help. He is no Arafat, and he doesn't excite the masses."

"Abbas may not excite the masses but Marwan Barghouti does," said Olmert.

"That is why this I feel this gambit is worth the risk. Put Marwan's public face on the side against the militants."

"We don't even know if he'll go for it. I'll sleep on it and give you my answer tomorrow," but Olmert had already made up his mind. "Let's talk about Iran."

They spent the final hour talking about Iran, and both of them acknowledged what every head of state knew but would never publicly say. No economic sanctions passed by the United Nations would dissuade Iran unless its regime was overthrown.

U.S. ambassador Richard H. Jones was fully aware that Israel could never tolerate a nuclear-armed Iran, nor for that matter, would the European countries that could easily be blackmailed by Iran. But Israel was in the most immediate danger. The ambassador only hoped that the UN Security Council would show a united front against the Iranians. The recent month-long war between Israel and Hezbollah, and the ongoing war in Iraq, only seemed to be a prelude to what was coming. In the event of any future sea blockade of the Persian Gulf, the question remained: Who would be hurt worse, an Iran where oil can't get out or a world where oil can't get in?

Chapter 8
COMPLIMENTS TO THE CHEF

June 13, 2007
Jerusalem, Israel

It was before dawn on Saturday when a crack team of five Israeli security officers entered a Jerusalem detention center. Using surprise and deftness, the Israeli team apprehended a very drowsy prisoner, taped his mouth shut, bound his hands, placed a white hood over his head, and quickly made their exit to a white van. The prisoner was forced into the rear of the vehicle and joined by three of the security guards. The other two guards entered the front of the van. A driver was already in place, and the van's engine was running. The van sped away from the detention center through the empty streets of Jerusalem until it arrived at the back of Arnold's Deli, one of Jerusalem's more popular kosher restaurants. With the sun beginning to rise, the three security guards quickly removed their prisoner and ushered him into the restaurant. Marwan Barghouti would be placed in a semi-circular booth with a security guard on each side and one directly across from him sitting in a chair.

This quartet plus one would be Arnold's only patrons eating breakfast today, because this Saturday, like all the others, the restaurant was closed for breakfast to commemorate the Jewish Sabbath, which lasts until sundown. Although the lights were on, Arnold's windows were boarded so that passersby would be unable to fathom that the restaurant was catering to a private event. Inside, the pleasant breakfast smells, the aroma of fresh coffee and smoked whitefish, emanated from the kitchen and permeated throughout the dining room.

Although Marwan was not in a position to talk, his sense of smell slowly began to crack his armor as thoughts shifted from survival to filling his empty stomach with delicacies that long ago were given up for prison. The guards had spoken very little, and he surmised they knew he spoke Hebrew. Abruptly, his hands were untied and the hood removed. He was staring into the face of Mohammed Dahlan, head of Palestinian Security on the Gaza Strip and the brainchild of this prison break. Dahlan let his eyes gaze upon the prisoner for what seemed like an eternity to Marwan. Then Dahlan not so pleasantly ripped the tape from his mouth.

"Hello Marwan," said Mohammed. "You look well. Let's talk after we eat," and at that moment Jibril Rahoub, head of Palestinian Security on the West Bank, walked out of the kitchen carrying a huge tray of piping hot food, fresh breads, eggs, smoked fish, and spreads. Marwan was as surprised as he was speechless and decided Mohammed was right to eat first.

Barghouti was born in the West Bank, in the city of Ramallah, and became actively involved with Fatah when he was only a teenager. In the mid-1970s, when he was eighteen years old, Israeli authorities arrested him and deported him to Jordan. After seven years, he was permitted to return under the conditions set out in the Oslo Accords in 1994 between Israel and the Palestinians. Two years later, he was elected to the Palestinian Legislative Council and assumed the position of General Secretary of the Fatah in the West Bank. During this time, he advocated accommodation with Israel, often coming into conflict with Yasser Arafat. Their ongoing conflict did not abate, and in the summer of 2000, the younger Palestinian accused Arafat and the "Old Guard" of corruption and the police of human rights violations. Arafat had planned to dismiss him but changed his mind soon after the second intifada began. Barghouti became too popular as the leader of al-Aqsa Martyrs' Brigades, a terrorist group that killed and maimed scores of Israeli civilians usually through suicide attacks or drive-by shootings. Barghouti claimed that he was always against the killing of civilians; he stated that his intent was to kill Israeli soldiers.

He was captured and arrested by Israel in early 2002 and charged with conspiracy to murder and attempted murder in a civilian court instead of a military tribunal, which is the usual procedure for militants.

Although he was acquitted on many counts due to insufficient evidence, he was convicted of five counts of murder, including the murder of a Greek Orthodox monk. In the summer of 2004, Marwan was sentenced to five life sentences for the five murders and forty years' imprisonment for the attempted murder.

From his prison cell in late 2004, he announced his candidacy for president of the Palestinian Authority. He eventually abandoned his candidacy and Abbas won handily.

Many liberal and pragmatic Israelis joined with Marwan's Palestinian supporters in a campaign to gain his freedom. As a member of the Palestinian Parliament, his supporters argued that he had diplomatic immunity. It was also argued that Israel didn't have proper judicial authority in the Palestinian territories.

In December 2005, from prison, Barghouti announced that he would form a new political party, al-Mustaqbal (The Future), and include the members of Fatah's Young Guard, including Mohammed Dahlan and Jibril Rahoub, two of the people he was having breakfast with. Marwan knew that Dahlan was acting out a machismo role for the Israeli guards. Dahlan and Jibril remained two of his very best friends.

"Give my compliments to the chef," Marwan spoke in Hebrew as he sipped his coffee and chewed his food.

"Mine, too," said Jibril in English.

The chef and current proprietor of Arnold's Deli was Meir Goldstein. He had heard the compliment but stayed in the kitchen as instructed. He was told that this breaking of bread might help his country a great deal.

Arnold was born in Russia in 1900, but religious persecution prompted his father, Yossi, a tailor by trade, to move the family first to Germany in 1920, where Jews were a lot safer than in Russia. The family settled comfortably in Frankfort. Arnold met Yetta while both were attending evening courses at the university. They were married in 1922. Arnold left his studies and accepted a job as a butcher in a meat-packing plant in Frankfort. But in 1932, Jews were no longer safe in Germany, and the family emigrated to the United States.

The extended family moved to Boston and shared a large apartment in nearby Brookline. Arnold worked as a cook in a Jewish deli until 1936, when he and Yetta decided to do an "Aliyah," a term applied to Jews who move to Palestine, leaving the Diaspora, or Jewish exile, behind. They took their two children, David, twelve, and Meir, ten, but Arnold's parents, Yossi and Edith, didn't make the trip. They decided they were too old to move from Brookline. Neither Yetta, whose parents remained in Germany, nor Arnold would see their parents again. In three years, German Jews would painfully discover that the task of getting out of the Fatherland would be as difficult as getting into British-occupied Palestine.

But in 1936, with assistance from the Jewish Agency, Arnold, Yetta, and their children began their new life in British Palestine. Arnold had money saved, and he opened up Arnold's Delicatessen in April of 1936. Meir and David both worked at the restaurant as teenagers. The restaurant's early patrons were mostly Jews of Russian descent.

The two boys had both joined the Haganah, a Jewish paramilitary organization that was formed during the British Mandate. During Israel's War of Independence in 1948, the IDF defended West Jerusalem against the invading Jordanian Legion and other Arab volunteers attacking from the West Bank. Meir would never forget the sadness in his parents faces on learning that David had been killed in the battle for Jerusalem during Israel's War of Independence in 1948. Meir fought in the 1956 Suez Campaign and again in the 1967 Six-Day War. To mirror the national exuberance on the aftermath of the Six-Day War, Arnold's expanded to validate the country's feelings of great expectations that were never fulfilled.

In 1973, Israel's feeling of invincibility was quickly eroded as both Egypt and Syria launched a surprise attack on the most holy of Jewish holidays, Yom Kippur. Eventually, Israel's improvised tactics and a U.S. airlift of supplies turned the tide of the battle in Israel's favor and led to formal relations with Egypt in exchange for the return of Sinai.

In 1968, Arnold died, and in 1970 Yetta died. Meir had married Brona Rothstein in 1962. She was a strikingly beautiful Sabra, whose parents emigrated from Germany in 1936. Brona was born in 1938. Meir and Brona had only one child, a daughter named Rachel born in 1964. Rachel was married with two lovely children, a son named

David after Meir's brother and a daughter named Rebecca. Meir and Brona loved and often doted on their grandchildren, and they were especially proud of their son-in-law, Ari Ben Ora, a trained scientist from Tel Aviv University, a decorated IDF officer, and expert military tactician who was currently orbiting Earth aboard the International Space Station.

In the summer of 1980, when Rachel was only sixteen, she met nineteen-year-old Ari, who was on summer break from Tel Aviv University. He was hired as a waiter at her family's restaurant and stayed until the fall began.

During the 1980s, Israel began the process of absorbing waves of thousands of Russian immigrants. Many settled in the Jerusalem area and frequented Arnold's. Although Ari had no previous experience as a food server, he learned quickly and was able to practice speaking the Russian language he learned as a child. Rachel was also a food server but spoke and understood very little Russian. In addition to waiting on his own tables, he would act as her interpreter much of the time. Her father was hoping she would master the language by the end of the summer.

The Goldsteins owned and occupied a three-bedroom apartment above the restaurant. Ari boarded in their small converted room in the garage behind the restaurant. It had a pullout bed, shower, and bathroom. He would eat his meals in Arnold's kitchen and take some leftover bread or bakery products to his room at night in case he became hungry. From the beginning, there was a spark between Ari and Rachel that evolved into a lasting relationship. Then Ari was called up for military service in 1982.

Arafat and his PLO, the Palestinian Liberation Organization, had found refuge in Lebanon after King Hussein expelled the organization from Jordan in the war called Black September. Arafat had failed to overthrow King Hussein's government in the fighting that began in 1970 and lasted until July of 1971. The PLO proceeded to use Lebanon as a base from which to stage raids into northern Israel. Israel retaliated and launched an offensive to eliminate that threat; it marched its forces all the way to Beirut. During the campaign, Ari was a tank commander and displayed a gift for military tactics that proved decisive in Israel's entrapment of Arafat's forces. Fortunately for Arafat, an agreement was brokered that allowed him and many of his fighters to relocate to Tunis. The Israeli army eventually withdrew from Lebanon. Ari came back to Israel and resumed his studies, and in 1986 Ari and Rachel were married.

Meir came to realize that he might be the final generation of his family to operate Arnold's. He had no sons to take over the business. Rachel, with two children and one on the way, had no interest. Arnold's was more than a family restaurant. The restaurant had been around to witness Israel's rebirth as a nation in 1948, and often to facilitate backdoor channels between high-level Israelis and Palestinians. Today's encounter was not the first to take place at Arnold's, nor would it likely be the last, though he wondered what good ever came out of these secret meetings. They never put a stop to suicide bombings. Arnold, like most Israelis, had lost friends to those bombings, and it turned his stomach to know the architects of many of those homicides were sitting in his restaurant and had just given him a compliment.

Marwan Barghouti was half way finished with breakfast when Dahlan took a document from his attaché case. Still chewing his food, Dahlan said, "Sign this Marwan and you're free." The Israeli guards were listening, but remained silent and continued eating. As a matter of security, both Palestinian security agents were checked for weapons before entering the restaurant. Before dawn, the two Palestinians each arrived at different Israeli checkpoints, one at Gaza and the other on the West Bank, and met with their Israeli counterparts. They arrived at Arnold's within five minutes of each other and remained in their respective vehicles until Marwan arrived; they silently followed him into the restaurant.

The day after the meeting, the Israeli prime minister called the U.S. ambassador to inform him of his decision to release Marwan subject to the terms discussed. Olmert's office quickly faxed the document containing the terms and conditions of release to Abbas for his signature, and within thirty minutes, Abbas signed the document, affixed the presidential seal, and faxed it back to Olmert, who then faxed it to the U.S. Embassy in Tel Aviv. Hard copies would be received later that day. The prime minister signed the authorization and assumed responsibility for any political fallout for Marwan's prison release. A plan was coordinated between prison officials, Israeli security, and Palestinian security and went off without a hitch.

Marwan picked up the document and read it. He had a Master's Degree in International Relations from Birzeit University in the West Bank. He read it over twice and asked in Arabic? "What's this all about?" He directed the question to either Jibril or Mohammed still in the presence of the Israeli security team.

"It is what it is," Dahlan replied in Arabic. "Iran needs to be checked and Hamas needs to be purged before it can turn Palestine into an Islamic state. Abbas has agreed to sign off on the 2000 peace accords. The signing will take place at the Egyptian resort of Sharm el Shiekh with or without you. You are needed to help Abbas- no, actually to help Fatah, and sell this to the Palestinian people. It won't be a hard sell. The people are starving. European countries don't recognize Hamas. No recognition is tantamount to not receiving money, and the world feels sorry for the Lebanese, not the Palestinians."

Marwan knew well that the U.S. and European governments couldn't recognize Hamas, whose charter called for a one-state solution in Palestine and the total destruction of Israel. He believed Fatah would achieve a moral equivalence with Israel once the organization officially renounced violence, and it was not held particularly accountable when acts of violence were perpetrated against Israel by any of its affiliated or nonaffiliated militant groups. Nor was Fatah held responsible for its inaction or failure to stop these groups from attacking Israel. As long as Fatah endorsed a peaceful solution, they seemingly could strike out at Israel with impunity, but that was becoming more difficult. Israel was securing its borders with high-tech fences and barriers.

Fatah and the Palestinian Authority were secular in nature and vehemently opposed a Hamas endorsed Islamic state in the Palestinian territories. That would be a civil war worth fighting for. There was much work to do and many fences to mend. The Old Guard had been corrupt and diverted much of the money for their personal wealth. Marwan had made up his mind. He dreamed of being president of Palestine to settle old scores with Abbas and the rest of the Old Guard. Until then, he would take this deal and reach out to the other militant groups. He signed four times on four of the same documents, one for Israel, one for the PA, one for the Americans, and one for Marwan.

"Marwan, you are my friend," said Dahlan, "but if you violate the terms and conditions of the agreement you signed, I have no choice but to hunt you down and return you to the Jerusalem prison." Marwan understood his friend was only grandstanding for his Israeli counterparts. "You will be Abbas's puppet and be on probation until 2010. That means if you are caught defaming Israel or the PA anytime before your probation ends, you go back to that prison. Is that understood?"

"Agreed. When am I a free man?"

"Right now. You'll be dropped off at a West Bank checkpoint, and your clothes and personal items will be returned. Palestinian security will meet you and take you to your wife," said Jibril. Marwan smiled and left unencumbered, walking by his own free will to the van at the rear of Arnold's. The day was sunny and cool and his stomach was full.

Chapter 9

PREPARATIONS

June 15, 2007
Tel Aviv, Israel

Richard H. Jones, U.S. Ambassador to Israel, was finishing his breakfast and sipping on his coffee. Just yesterday, he had informed the Secretary of State of the good news from Israel; the peace agreement would be signed after the new Palestinian elections, and after Hamas's removal from the Palestinian government. Marwan Barghouti had signed on and pledged to support the peace agreement and assist Abbas's effort to isolate Iran. Barghouti's release made front-page news in both the Palestinian and Israeli morning newspapers. There was no mention that his release was subject to probation.

Abbas needed a peace agreement with Israel to remain financially solvent and to hold onto power. The devil was in the details. News coverage was planned to show that Israel—not the United States— would provide the needed gas masks and vaccines for Palestinians. Palestinian editorials were gearing up to criticize Iran and Hezbollah, accusing them of insensitivity to Palestinians. Scheduled for print were scores of articles and cartoons in order to drive a wedge between the Palestinians and Iran. Iranians were Persians, not Arabs, and Iranians were Shiite and not Sunni. Similar messages were planned for radio and television stations including Al Jazeera and other Sunni Arabic stations. Isolate Iran and hopefully reverse a disturbing trend in the region: the election of Islamic parties to political office in Egypt, southern Lebanon, and Iran.

Until Hamas was removed from power, anti-Israel propaganda would also continue in the classrooms, in the newspapers, and on television and radio. Ambassador Jones sipped his coffee. He thought about the age-old fable about the Scorpion and the Turtle at the banks of the Nile River, and applied its relevance to the twenty-first century.

> A scorpion asked a turtle for a ride on him to cross the Nile. The turtle backed off and said "No, I don't want you to sting and kill me." The scorpion replied, "If I stung you and killed you, then I would die because I can't swim." The turtle agreed, and the scorpion climbed on the turtle at the edge of the water. Halfway across, the turtle felt the fatal sting and said to the scorpion, "You killed yourself by killing me. That makes no sense." The scorpion replied, "This is the Middle East, nothing makes sense."

A wire sent by the State Department just crossed his desk. President Musharraf of Pakistan had been suddenly deposed by the Pakistani military, which also began moving troops into the province of Kashmir. The ambassador thought the Pakistani coup was too fortunate and timely for Iran to be coincidental.

Chapter 10
WE GET MAIL

June 18, 2007
ISS, Space

During a ninety-minute orbit, the ISS receives forty-five minutes of sunlight to charge its solar batteries that provide its electricity during the forty-five minutes the ship is in the dark. The atmospheric pressure within the station is similar to Earth's, and the temperature is well maintained. Water is brought in from the outside and used sparingly; much of it is recycled.

The scientists aboard the ISS are actually on a tight schedule. They have to perform daily chores and maintenance operations in addition to the scientific experiments. They must exercise a minimum of two and a half hours every day, using resistive exercise equipment to increase muscle tone; in the absence of gravity, muscles are used less and atrophy. Exercise is not recommended either immediately before or after meals. In addition to self-examination, they are given frequent checks for physicals by one or more of the other scientists. Space walk decompression can exceed five hours. The scientists must find time to communicate with their respective agencies about the nature of experiments and living in space; they must be cognizant of satellite operation and corresponding time zones on Earth. They need time to sleep in their sleeping bags suspended in air, but when there is free time, there are phone calls to make and receive from family and friends, and lots of e-mail to be checked.

Sanjay received an e-mail from his wife, Harpreet, and it disturbed him. The president of Pakistan had been deposed and put under house arrest. Additional Pakistani troops had moved to the Pakistani side of the "line of control," which separated Indian and Pakistani troops in the province of Kashmir. Pakistan's new military government declared it would conduct a nuclear test in July. He e-mailed her back and told her not to worry, and that the Indian-Pakistani conflicts had always resolved themselves.

Ari received an e-mail from his wife, Rachel. She said that Israel had released Marwan Barghouti, and, though it wasn't common knowledge, he was actually released on probation. The details of his release were hammered out at her dad's restaurant while Marwan was there. Once the news of his probation was revealed, Israelis were initially divided, but more interested in the Palestinian newspapers that published articles chiding Iran for attempting to arm the Hezbollah Shiites in Lebanon with chemical weapons that could kill Palestinian Sunnis.

The Israeli public was taken by surprise at the release. They did not realize this was part of a plan hatched by Abbas to outflank Hamas. Ari e-mailed Rachel that he sensed it was part of something bigger. When Alexander checked his e-mail, he found a message from his brother Yuri, who was on the foreign policy team that advised Russian president Vladimir Putin on Middle Eastern and Near Eastern affairs. Yuri was of the opinion that the coup in Islamabad and the Pakistani troop movements to Kashmir were reactions to the negative fallout and deaths surrounding the recent U.S. missile attack on a gathering of Pakistanis and Al Qaeda members in the mountain regions. Yuri finished his e-mail by saying that he believed Russia and America together would be successful in diffusing the potential crisis looming between the two nuclear countries of India and Pakistan.

As an astute observer of foreign affairs, Yuri marveled at the dichotomy that inherently challenged American foreign policy. In Iran, the United States was opposed by its Islamic government but not by the majority of its people. In Pakistan, the reverse was true; the government was not opposed to the United States, but most Pakistanis were.

Although the majority of Pakistanis preferred an Islamic government, most Iranians wanted Islam removed from the Iranian government. Pakistan would be more dangerous to U.S. interests if an

Islamic government ever took power there with a ready-made stockpile of nuclear weapons.

Two other phenomena didn't go unnoticed in Moscow. One was that the Palestinian newspapers were criticizing Iran. The other was that there was a likely connection between the current Pakistani crisis and Iran.

"Sanjay, if it's any consolation, my brother Yuri believes that Russia and America will defuse the crisis in Pakistan. He thinks it's a reaction to the recent American missile strike on Al Qaeda that killed innocents."

"That may be true," said Sanjay, "but why provoke India by moving troops and announcing a nuclear test next month?"

"It may be that Pakistan is grandstanding," said Alexander. "They will probably pull those troops back, and a test—well it's just a test. A lot of countries do it."

"I think it's a ploy," said Ari. "I think Musharraf will soon be back in power and still may be. I think the crisis was premeditated to take world attention off Iran."

"For all we know," said Andre, "this might be a cover-up of something sinister, and Musharraf is being set up as the fall guy, or maybe he's behind the plot."

Ari thought if anyone knew about cover-ups, it would probably be someone French. And when Ari thought of something French, it wasn't cuisine; it was the Dreyfus Affair of 1894, a French scandal of epic proportions. Captain Alfred Dreyfus, from a wealthy family and the highest-ranking Jewish artillery officer in the French army, was wrongfully convicted of treason in 1894.

He was charged with passing French military secrets to the German Embassy in Paris and sent to prison on Devil's Island. The evidence against Dreyfus was circumstantial, and his innocence later proved by a French intelligence officer who discovered evidence implicating Major Ferdinand Esterhazy in the treason. Esterhazy was deep in debt, which provided motive, but the military higher-ups decided on a cover-up. Eventually the evidence made its way to Dreyfus's brother and his other supporters, and in 1898 Esterhazy was tried by a court martial. It took only a few minutes' deliberation before he was acquitted.

For more than a decade, the Dreyfus Affair created a schism within France. Against Dreyfus were the French nationalists, monarchists or royalists, the clergy, and militarists. Supporting Dreyfus were the anticlerical elements, republicans, and socialists.

In 1898, it was proved that Colonel Henry of army intelligence had forged much of the evidence that had been presented against Dreyfus. Henry later committed suicide, and Esterhazy later escaped to England. In 1899, Dreyfus was retried in a court of appeals, which upheld the military court's conviction. Dreyfus was returned to Devil's Island, where he spent another ten years.

In 1906, President Loubet of France pardoned Dreyfus, and the Supreme Court of Appeals exonerated him. The formerly disgraced officer was reinstated as a major and decorated with the Legion of Honor. His innocence was revalidated with the publication of the Schwartkoppen papers in 1930. Dreyfus was alive and fought for France in World War I.

The political fallout from these trials led to the official separation of church and state in France in 1905, brought the political left to prominence, and precipitated the decline of the military and the Catholic Church's influence on public policy. The passions surrounding this case affirmed how deep anti-Semitism was in France at the end of the nineteenth century. The Dreyfus Affair was only one example of constant slander directed at Jewish officers in the French military. And anti-Semitism was not limited just to the French Army. In 1895, anti-Semitic resentment was stoked when a Catholic banking consortium, Union Generale, failed in its attempt to overtake the Jewish financial establishment. In 1886, Edouard Drumont published the book *La Fance Juive* (Jewish France). Drumont helped publish *La Libre Parole* (Free Speech) in 1892, which suggested that all Jewish officers were French traitors. Several pistol duels involving French Jewish officers ensued, with one being killed and Dumont being wounded.

A Jewish Austrian journalist by the name of Theodore Herzl witnessed the trials surrounding the Dreyfus Affair and the virulent anti-Semitism exposed by it. Herzl wrote a book in 1896 called *The Jewish State*. He is considered the founder of Zionism, the political movement for the modern state of Israel. Sanjay once said, "No Holocaust, No

Israel." Sanjay might have been wrong. Perhaps he didn't know about the Captain Dreyfus Affair. Ari wondered if Andre did.

Despite political ambiguity, Pakistan scheduled a nuclear-missile launch into the earth's atmosphere on Wednesday, July 20, 2007, from the Kharan desert, 10 AM Pakistani time. Messages of the pending event were communicated by radio frequency and e-mail from the space agencies involved with ISS mission with instructions to keep the space station as far away from the detonation as possible

"What are they worried about?" asked Sanjay. "We are orbiting at 260 miles a minute at 186 miles above the earth. Pakistan's nuclear blast should occur in the lower atmosphere within the 20- to 25-mile range above the earth's surface, and we are more then 160 miles above that."

"Depending on the explosive yield of the blast and its occurrence it the atmosphere, a nuclear blast wind can travel several hundred kilometers, or at least 160 miles. So I think we should pay close attention to our orbit path on that day, just to make sure we are not within that range. Better to be safe than sorry," said Alexander.

Chapter 11
YOU WOULD DESTROY JERUSALEM

June 19, 2007
Tehran, Iran

"Now we know that some Palestinians don't want to die for Jihad, and Marwan Barghouti is one of them," said the president of Iran, Mahmoud Ahmadinejad. He was commenting on Al Jazeera's satellite television special *You Would Destroy Jerusalem*, narrated by Marwan and directed at Iran. "Just as Barghouti made a deal with Israel, so must have Abbas. The Palestinian newspapers are asking Israel for gas masks and vaccines. Do the Palestinian idiots think we would only fire chemical weapons into Israel, when Israel can fire back nuclear bombs on missiles from submerged submarines? Do they think we Iranians would miscalculate just because their Arab brethren do? We need to assure them. Contact our Hamas representative in Damascus and set up a meeting in Gaza."

"With Abbas?" asked Rafsanjani.

"No with Barghouti," said Ahmadinejad. "One day I would like to kill him."

As a member of the Iranian Council of Experts, former president Rafsanjani was summoned for a private meeting with Ahmadinejad. "One day he may be president of the Palestinians," replied Rafsanjani. Rafsanjani believed that his successor had made a monumental mistake sending nerve gas to Lebanon, only to have it destroyed by Israel in their typical fashion: precision bombing and very little collateral damage. But more significant, and as a result of Ahmadinejad's miscalculation, the Palestinian Authority, once an ally, was now turning into Iran's adversary.

"Ali, I have been staving off the Pakistani ambassador's attempts to reach me. Saheed. He likes you, Ali. Perhaps you can convince him."

"To let us keep their nuclear bomb?" asked Rafsanjani.

"Yes. Tell them we'll provide Pakistan with even more petroleum."

Rafsanjani took a moment to think. Ahmadinejad's increasingly threatening rhetoric to destroy Israel, and his recent fiasco in Lebanon, were unsettling the Pakistani government. Iranian scientists were working around the clock to master the technical challenges of mounting a nuclear warhead onto an Iranian missile. With world attention on Iran, Pakistan could ill afford to be exposed. Rafsanjani instantly tried to put together the remaining pieces. It was under Pakistani president Musharraf's watch that the nuclear scientist A. Q. Khan allegedly and illegally sold Pakistani nuclear technology to Iran, and he had never been brought to justice. It was not inconceivable that Pakistan was preparing for damage control in the event that its complicity was revealed. Blame for any future political fallout was obviously intended to fall first on Khan, second on President Musharraf, and if necessary, on the president of Iran and his mullahs. Jailing Khan was risky. The Pakistani government's announcement of additional troop mobilization to Kashmir and another nuclear test was timed to deflect the public's anger and ignite the passions and national pride that comes with having the only Islamic nuclear bomb.

Ahmadinejad said to Rafsanjani, "Ali, sit down and watch this Al Jazeera tape. This is airing all over the Middle East, but will soon be forgotten. Soon Muslims all over the world will rail against the Danish cartoons that defame our prophet."

> Arab brothers, how can we Palestinians achieve our political goals and destiny if the strategies to reclaim what is rightfully ours is to destroy what is rightfully ours. Jerusalem and its holy sites of Islam could vanish if weapons of mass destruction are allowed to rain down on the Dome of the Rock, where our prophet Mohammed once ascended to heaven. Iran's threats to wipe Israel off the map, if successful would wipe Palestinians

off the map and Jordanians and Muslims in Lebanon and Syria as well. Are we Arabs here to hand over our land to Persians assuming there is any land worth living on? We will win what is rightfully ours. Time and demographics are on our side. We waited out the Crusaders and we waited out the Turks. We can wait out the Jews as well. Let us make sure that we win for ourselves, that the win will be for all Arabs and Palestinians, not Persians.

Ahmadinejad and many Arabs knew, but kept silent about the fact that Palestinians were expendable, and Jerusalem was not all that important as a holy Muslim site. The idea of a Palestinian state was a twentieth-century idea, because a Palestinian state had never existed. And without an Israel, the Arab world had little need for Palestinians or their state. Jerusalem was not even mentioned in the Koran. Mohammed never ventured there, and Jerusalem had never been a capital of any Arab state. There are no daily prayers for Muslims to make to Jerusalem. Not in four hundred years of Ottoman control, from the sixteenth century to the early twentieth century, and not under British or Jordanian control that followed was there ever a Muslim pilgrimage to Jerusalem. Only when Muslims had to compete with Christians and Jews for the city did the Arabs consider Jerusalem to be an important religious center or future capital of a Palestinian state.

Ahmadinejad felt in his heart that Palestinian deaths would be considered "noble deaths" by other Arabs, who would tolerate the destruction of Jerusalem if Israel were destroyed in the process. He only had to look at recent history to prove his point. Arab countries were insensitive to Palestinians needs when Jordan and Egypt controlled the Palestinian territories from 1948 to 1967. He was confident in the Shia tradition of martyrdom and Jihad to pave the path for the glorious appearance of Imam Mahdi, the mystical twelfth imam who will rule just before the end of the world.

Later that evening Rafsanjani drove to Le Sans Souci, his favorite French restaurant in Tehran, for a private meeting and dinner with the Pakistani ambassador Saheed.

Chapter 12
GETTING READY FOR TOMORROW

June 22, 2007
Tel Aviv, Israel

U.S. ambassador Richard H. Jones was waiting for a call from the Israeli prime minister. They had last spoken three days ago, and both were pleased with Al Jazeera's airing of Barghouti's speech. Unknown to most viewers, Abbas and Prime Minister Olmert had pre-approved the speech for its content, which contained nationalistic messages to encourage Sunni Arabs to oppose Iranian meddling in the region.

Ambassador Jones had several topics to cover with Prime Minister Olmert. The first was coordination between the Palestinian Authority and the Israeli government on their joint operation against Hamas. Negotiators from both Israel and the PA had been working and meeting discreetly for nearly two weeks to finalize and resolve disputed territories, including the land exchanges to define the borders, security arrangements, shared administration of Jerusalem, and the final wording concerning the Palestinian Right of Return. Each negotiator was instructed to report on the daily progress, including any impasses or anticipated ones.

Unresolved issues had to be mutually resolved no later than midnight June 23, or there would be no announcement of peace. The good news was that, with less than thirty-six hours until the deadline, there were yet no impasses, and most of the serious issues had already been addressed. Planning would soon begin for the peace summit.

Any terrorist's fantasy would be to infiltrate the Egyptian sea resort at the time of the peace signing. Sharm al Shiekh had not been immune from previous terror attacks. In the summer of 2005, there were several coordinated suicide bombings in the Egyptian resort that took nearly one hundred lives and wounded many more.

"Ambassador Jones," said the phone operator at the U.S. Embassy, "Prime Minister Olmert is on the line."

"Thank you, Doris," replied Ambassador Jones. "Good morning, Mr. Prime Minister."

"Good morning, Richard," replied the prime minister.

"I hear the negotiations are going well," Mr. Jones replied.

"I can't be excited Richard. All the promises the Palestinians made at Oslo to fight terrorism were promises never kept. I don't expect this one to be kept either."

"At least you can disengage from them and define your borders. After Israel's borders have been defined, the accusation of 'occupied territories' becomes irrelevant. Even within Jerusalem, you can separate your Jewish holy sites from the Arab neighborhoods of East Jerusalem. You've sealed off Gaza. No terrorists have snuck into Israel from that location. Mr. Prime Minister, the growing emergence of militant Islam is showing its ugly face in Iran, southern Lebanon, the Palestinian territories, and even in European cities. I sense that much of the civilized world now sees the Israeli-Palestinian conflict as part of global struggle and cultural war waged against Western values and way of life. The once-shared European view that defined Israel's conflict with the Arabs as one-dimensional is rapidly falling into disrepute. The Palestinians have spent their political capital."

"I should have you in my cabinet."

"You couldn't pay me enough, but thanks for the compliment. Another matter concerns Marwan Barghouti. He has been contacted by Hamas, and they want to set up a meeting. Hamas wants Barghouti to tone down his anti-Iranian rhetoric."

"Abu Mazen has assured me that Barghoutti is not merely acting," the prime minister revealed. "Like most of the Fatah intellectuals, he is secular and opposes Sharia law for any future Palestinian state."

"I agree with Abu Mazen," Jones replied. Most of the Palestinian students attending Birzeit University are typically fond of Western jeans, especially many of the female collegians. The thought of these liberated Palestinian women having to submit to a social and religious dress code imposed on them by Hamas is anathema to them."

"It's not the students at Birzeit University that Hamas wants. It's the little children—the next generation—that Hamas wishes to indoctrinate into Sharia, the families with little children who require the services Hamas has been providing at the grassroots level. They will become the next generation of homicide bombers."

Ambassador Jones couldn't have agreed more. The Islamist governments that sponsored terrorism were gaining popularity and through the process of democratic elections. There was Hezbollah to the north, Hamas on the east and on the west, as well as the Egyptian Brotherhood in Egypt, all making electoral gains and looking to Iran for direction.

"Richard, what's your take on Pakistan?"

"The truth is we really don't know. On the surface it appears suspicious, a ploy to divert world attention away from Iran. The United States has been assured by the new military government in Pakistan that there will be no changes with respect to U.S. policy in the region, and the war on terrorism will continue as it has. The successor to the presidency, the chairman of the Pakistan Senate, Soomro, is very pro-Western. The Pakistani military told us that no harm would come to Musharraf. Also arrested in Pakistan was A. Q. Khan, the nuclear physicist, who is revered by the Pakistani people for his work on Pakistan's nuclear bomb program. Musharraf didn't dare arrest Khan in spite of very solid evidence that his assistance unlawfully aided Iran's nuclear program. This begs the question, "Why did they arrest him now?"

"Your government must be concerned with Pakistan's additional troop movements into Kashmir and the announcement of their nuclear-missile atmospheric test," the prime minister noted.

"Very definitely. Our State Department believes that they were designed to please the 'Pakistani Street' and mitigate the public's anger about Khan's arrest. With a little help from their mosques, it seems to be working. The Sunni imams are playing the Shiite card and telling their faithful that Khan made millions by trading Pakistan's nuclear secrets to a Shiite Iran. Eighty percent of Pakistan's population is still Sunni."

"Richard, this may be an opportunity for the United States to drive a wedge between Pakistan and Iran."

"We hope so."

Chapter 13
WHAT A DIFFERENCE A DAY MAKES

June 23, 2007
Tel Aviv, Israel

Like the stroke of an artist's pen, the world had changed. U.S. ambassador Richard H. Jones, President Abbas, and Prime Minister Olmert suddenly agreed to delay the joint Palestinian-Israeli directive to arrest the Hamas government that had been scheduled for tomorrow. In fact, all negotiations were put on hold bracing for the Muslim onslaught.

On this very day, it was revealed throughout the entire Muslim world that a series of cartoons published in a Danish newspaper that demeaned and likened the prophet Mohammed to terrorism were republished in other nations, including Germany, France, Spain, and Belgium. The political fallout could not be contained. Because depictions of the prophet are considered blasphemous, Muslims protested in all parts of the world. Outside the Middle East, where the protests were typically nonviolent, Muslims defiantly marched and burned primarily American, Danish, and Israeli flags. There were also protests in Europe. In Kuala Lumpur, Malaysia, police held firm at the Danish Embassy as ten thousand Muslims tried to force their way in. The Malaysian government subsequently banned any newspapers from reprinting any of those cartoon caricatures. Protesters also demonstrated in Sri Lanka, Bangladesh, and India, but in the Middle East, people died and property was destroyed.

In Beirut, Lebanon, the Danish Embassy was torched when troops and police couldn't prevent the thousands of protesters from breaking through the defensive lines. A Christian neighborhood nearby was ransacked by the same mobs. Hundreds of angry protestors threw stones and rocks and Molotov cocktails at the Danish Embassy in Tehran, Iran, as the mob broke through the safety perimeter. Due to the imminent danger, Denmark issued instructions for its embassy staff to vacate their embassies in Iran and Indonesia.

The Iranian press had a field day calling the cartoons a Zionist conspiracy. They offered a prize for the best cartoon of the Holocaust and challenged the European presses to do the same. A Catholic priest was shot dead in Turkey by a Muslim fanatic. In Damascus, Syrian mobs attacked both the Danish and Norwegian embassies, and in Gaza, masked gunmen broke into an EU building demanding an apology. The Danes and other Europeans remained steadfast. They would not apologize for their right to free press, no matter how distasteful or controversial the subject matter.

It was a reality check and several steps back for those optimists who thought democracy would be the social cure for the region. Free elections within the Arab world had proved to be popular, but not for the democratic ideals that are cherished by so many other cultures— the freedom of speech, assembly, and religion—but instead to elect Islamists sworn to destroy those very freedoms. Without Islam, the concept of freedom of religion simply meant freedom from religion. For years, Muslim presses and newspapers had published false accounts, inflammatory editorials, and cartoons degrading to both Christian and Jewish faiths, a double standard the Western world had tolerated and the Muslim world did not want to concede.

Chapter 14
LET'S TRY TO GET ALONG

June 27, 2007
Gaza City

Marwan understood the Israelis needed him even more as a stalwart against radical Islam, which had just showed its contentious side when confronted with an unpopular cartoon image. He was amazed how easy it was for Muslims to stop most of the world's printing presses from depicting the demeaning cartoons. Deference and fear had been exacted by the followers of Islam, so full of their own sensitivities but blatantly devoid of others. Marwan had seen sermons on Palestinian TV that described Jews as the sons of pigs and monkeys. He knew that Syria ran a prime-time TV series that showed rabbis murdering non-Jewish children and drinking their blood. Even Egypt, the first Arab country to establish diplomatic relations with Israel, was running a TV series based on fabricated anti-Semitic conspiracies to take control of the world.

Marwan considered the cancellation of the Israeli-Palestinian summit his bit of serendipity. Without a peace summit, he didn't have to endorse one. The Mossad and Mohammed Dahlan urged him to wear a bulletproof vest, but Marwan chose not to. If the vest was discovered, Hamas would see it as a sign of weakness. He calculated it would be political suicide for Hamas to try to end his life now. Hamas knew he was very popular on the streets of Gaza and the West Bank towns, and his death at the hands of Hamas would strip them of their political gains in those areas. Still, Dahlan insisted that he drive him to the evening meeting and wait for him. Marwan agreed.

They drove up to a house to meet the Hamas leaders, and Mohammed Dahlan accompanied Marwan to the room, but he would not stay. The head of Palestinian Security in Gaza decided to make an entrance as well, and he signaled Hamas that he was waiting outside. Inside were Hamas leaders Khaled Mashaal and Mahmoud Zaher, along with Hamas spokesmen Ismail Haniyah and Masheer al-Masri. After exchanging embraces, they all sat down, except for Ismail who went into the kitchen to bring out a tray of coffee and cookies.

"It is so good to see you again, Marwan," said Mahmoud.

"Yes, it is good to be free again," replied Marwan.

"Marwan," Mahmoud continued, "you have nobly fought corruption within Fatah and have challenged Arafat and Abbas when they stole from the Palestinian people. You are admired for your courage. Hamas was elected not because our charter calls for Israel's destruction, or that all Palestinians want to adopt Sharia, but because the Palestinian people were crying out against the corruption."

"Marwan," said Khaled, "you are misinformed about Iran. Just because Hezbollah might one day have chemical warheads means no more or no less than Syria's stockpile of chemical weapons only one hundred miles away from Israel's population centers. Our shared goal is to apply as much psychological pressure on Israel as we can. This we can agree on?"

"Yes," replied Marwan, "this we can agree on. Can we also agree that Palestinians are capable of miscalculation?"

"We have made our share of mistakes, probably no more than other Arabs," replied Khaled.

"Excellent point, Khaled," Marwan responded. "How far should the Arabs go back to recount their miscalculations-- to Al-Naqba, the birth of Israel, the Six-Day War, intifadas, or to Arafat and Saddam Hussein? You remember that Arafat supported Iraq in the first Persian Gulf War, and that decision was disastrous for us. Palestinians were not only evicted from Kuwait, but the rest of the Gulf region as well. In my judgment, the Palestinians will make another colossal miscalculation by siding with the Shia Iranians."

"So what would you have us do?" Khaled appealed.

"Reject Iran's policies in Lebanon, reject Hezbollah," replied Marwan. "Work with Fatah to recover lost Palestinian land. Yes, the wars against Israel were just, but they cost us our land. Look at our history. We reject peace offers and then fight again. When the fighting ends, we are offered less than before. We reject and fight again, reject and fight again; each time there is less and less land for the Palestinians to have."

"That is why we must never stop fighting. No recognition of Israel, ever. We must have all of Palestine," said Masheer.

"We can recover more of our land sooner by not waging war," declared Marwan.

"That is not all of Palestine," Khaled replied.

"Eventually Israel will give us the land. They will have to if they want to remain a Jewish state. Israel's Arab population numbers over a million and is growing faster than their Jewish population. Soon Israel's Arab citizens will comprise 25 percent of its total population. Israel's dilemma is that it has to be both democratic and Jewish. One day Israel's Arabs will constitute 51 percent of the population, and it will cease to be a Jewish state. Without a substantial Jewish immigration, Israel's only recourse will be to separate from its Arab population centers, not an easy task."

"I beg to differ, Marwan. Israel's disengagement from Gaza was not so difficult," said Masheer.

"It is easy to disengage from Palestinians," said Marwan, "because we are not Israeli citizens. Israeli Arabs are. Israel will be compelled to cede land and bribe much of its Arab population to separate from Israel. Israel will be forced to withdraw from land, or be faced with a demographic nightmare of epic proportions. Each time Israel cedes land, they become a smaller state. And when Israel becomes smaller, Palestine becomes larger. Just as the Berlin Wall came down, so will the Israeli Walls come down. But Palestine must first become a state, and you must look at Palestine statehood as a more immediate goal than the destruction of Israel. One is attainable and the other is not, at least in the near future. Even as a pretext, the goal of statehood must compel Hamas to revise its charter and accept Israel's right to exist."

"What if the Israeli Arabs don't want to leave Israel? And what if we don't want them in Palestine?" asked Mahmoud.

"Of course we don't want them. This dilemma will tear at the very fabric of Israeli society, pitting democratic values against the desire to remain a Jewish state. By evicting its Arab citizens, Israel risks becoming the pariah of the world, a racist state, an apartheid state. There would be Muslim riots that would make the ones we have just witnessed seem pale by comparison. I don't think Israel will choose to evict; rather, I think they will come to the Palestinians to try to work something out. There are only two eventual options. Israel either loses its land or its Jewish majority."

"If there were no wars waged against Israel, how long will it take for an Arab majority to form?" asked Khaled.

"It could take up to several decades or more, probably not in our lifetimes," replied Marwan.

"What could speed this process along?" asked Khaled.

"Emigration or a declining Jewish birthrate," said Marwan. "On the other hand, Israel's economy is strong with a high-tech industry that is creating jobs and that may encourage more immigration, especially from France and Russia. It is difficult for me to predict. I am not a prophet."

"Marwan, you may not be a prophet, but you are very convincing. I was surprised the Israelis released you from jail. Were you surprised?" Mahmoud asked.

"Yes, but I don't think Israel thought its case against me was ever on solid ground. Many legal experts deny Israel even had jurisdictional authority to make my arrest in the West Bank, which is under the jurisdiction of the Palestinian Authority, let alone the legal authority to transfer the trial to Israel. I was an elected member of the Palestinian Legislative Council, and that should have afforded me diplomatic immunity from prosecution as it did Arafat."

"Marwan," said Mahmoud, "I have heard from many sources that you learned to speak fluent Hebrew at the Israeli jail, and that you have acquired Israeli friends. You are in a sense an agent of Israel, because you do their bidding. You could have refused the freedom they offered you."

"Let's not be hypocritical," said Marwan, "Your group Hamas has been cozy with Israel when it suited your purposes, and even the Ayatollahs in Iran accepted assistance from Israel in their war against Iraq."

There was a moment of silence, and then Khaled said, "Enough talk. Let the Palestinian people decide their future and there will be a great future, Allah willing."

They finished drinking their coffee. They bid Marwan goodnight, and he left with his security detail. Ismail Haniyah spoke very few words that evening but listened intently as he recorded the entire meeting.

Chapter 15
RESTORATION THEOLOGY

June 30, 2007
ISS, Space

The most recent space weather outlook bulletin forecasted no disruptive space weather for the next seven days. The crew was mindful that weather predictions could be unreliable. Weather-alert bulletins were immediately issued when imminent changes in space weather were expected to occur, or to signal the end of a current weather disruption. Solar flares and storms were very dangerous and had the potential to emit harmful radiation capable of permeating spacecraft and exposing the scientists. The ISS had equipment to measure radiation levels, and in the absence of solar storms, the space station, orbiting low, was generally well protected from deadly radiation by the Earth's magnetic field. Yet outside the ISS lurked other potential dangers, including possible encounters with space debris or tiny meteorites that traveled through the galaxy at lightning speeds. Ari's wife's concerns were not unfounded.

"Alexander," Ari said. "Both sets of my grandparents originally came from Russia, and my mother was born in Odessa."

"When did your family arrive in Israel?"

"They arrived in 1941. Israel was called Palestine then."

"They were fortunate to escape Hitler's death camps."

"Lucky twice. They actually ran the British blockade."

"I have studied the British blockade. The British 'White Paper Policy' restricting Jews from Palestine was an illegal, unilateral violation of the Palestine Mandate. But Israel's legitimacy is from God, from the scriptures, not the Palestine Mandate," Alexander said.

"Where did you study?"

"At the Christian College of St. Petersburg, during a summer semester with my twin brother Yuri. The college was founded by American evangelicals."

"Evangelicals have been very in interested in Israel's future," Ari said.

"That's true. For two hundred years evangelicals were eagerly waiting for the Jews to return to their ancient homeland and reclaim Israel and Jerusalem."

"That's not so long. We Jews have had to wait almost two thousand years," Ari blithely replied. "Why do evangelical Christians want the Jews in Israel when other Christians either don't care or would rather that we weren't there?"

"It has to do with biblical interpretation," Alexander responded. "Evangelicals are waiting for Christ to return to Jerusalem, but that requires the rebirth of the nation of Israel and a Jerusalem in Jewish hands. And these things have happened. Our interpretation of the scriptures is known as Restoration Theology. To many, John Darby was considered the early leader of Restoration Theology in the early nineteenth century, but William Blackstone of Chicago was considered the major catalyst in the late nineteenth century. Blackstone worked closely with Jewish Zionists, and at the 1918 Zionist convention in Philadelphia, he was hailed as the 'Father of Zionism.' In 1956, Israel memorialized Blackstone by naming a forest after him."

"I have never heard of John Darby or William Blackstone," Ari admitted.

"Early Christian Zionism's basic message remains credible with contemporary Christian Zionists," Alexander continued. "When Israel was created in 1948, Christian Zionists thought it was the greatest event in centuries, even though Israel was without its ancestral capital, Jerusalem, and it was a mere fraction of its size during biblical times. In 1967, when Israel won its Six-Day War and captured all of the territory of ancient Israel and all of Jerusalem, Christian Zionists couldn't contain themselves. For the first time in nearly two thousand years all of Jerusalem was in Jewish hands."

Alexander opened his Bible and read from Luke 21:24, "Jerusalem will be trampled by the Gentiles until the Times of the Gentiles are fulfilled."

"I am amazed," replied Ari. "Only days ago Sanjay, a Hindu, told me he understood why evangelicals believe that Israel could have only have been created by divine intervention. He even went so far as to suggest that if there had been no Holocaust, there would have been no Israel."

"Sanjay might have been right, Ari. Many in Christendom adhere to some interpretation of Replacement Theology, that Christianity has replaced Judaism in God's plan. They believe the Jews have fallen out of God's grace, that the Church replaced Judaism, the New Testament replaced the Old Testament, and Vatican City replaced Jerusalem as the City of God. But Ari, the continued and thriving existence of the Jewish people in spite of numerous attempts to destroy them, and the revival of the state of Israel, debunk Replacement Theology. If Israel were condemned by God, how can they explain the twentieth-century reappearance of Israel after nearly two thousand years?"

"That may have been the Church's theology long ago, before the Second Vatican Council. Today the Vatican recognizes Israel," Ari insisted.

"After forty-five years, the Vatican recognizes your country, but not your right to Jerusalem," Alexander noted. "Ari, there are still some very powerful, conservative Catholics who reject the changes of the 1965 Second Vatican Council's Nostra Aetate, which officially ended the charges of deicide against the Jews. A Jewish Israel and Jerusalem raises the issue as to whether Replacement Theology was ever legitimate, and definitely weakens Vatican claims that Jerusalem is no longer God's city. This is an ongoing dilemma for the Church as long as Israel remains a Jewish state and claims Jerusalem as its exclusive capital. If Israel should no longer function as a Jewish state, or if Jerusalem were internationalized or to become part of a future Palestinian state, then the Vatican is better positioned to reassert its theological claims. This is my opinion, Ari; the Vatican does not want the Jews to get Jerusalem back. The fact that most countries do not recognize Jerusalem as Israel's capital and house their embassies in Tel Aviv has as much to do with religious realities as political ones."

"Alexander, when Israel was granted statehood in 1948, Palestine was partitioned into two states, one Jewish and one Palestinian. Jerusalem was designated an international city to be administered by the United Nations for the benefit of Jews, Christians, and Muslims. You know the story. The Palestinians rejected their state, thousands fled, and subsequently Israel was invaded by Arab armies from Jordan, Syria, and Egypt. Israeli forces captured West Jerusalem, but the Jordanian army captured East Jerusalem, including the Old City, and closed it off to Jews and Christians."

"Not only did the United Nations do nothing to intervene militarily on Israel's behalf, they did nothing to reclaim Jerusalem from Jordan's illegal occupation," Alexander posited. "Even the Vatican remained silent during this illegal occupation; that is, until the Six-Day War in 1967, when all of Jerusalem came under Israeli control."

Andre had been listening, and could no longer contain himself. "I also know something of Israel's history," the Frenchman said. "Israel's occupation of East Jerusalem was just as illegal as Jordan's was. The city belongs as much to Muslims and Christians as it does to Jews, and it should be internationalized."

"Andre, in 1947, Israel accepted the terms of the UN partition and conceded Jerusalem's international sovereignty to its governance," Ari replied. "Although we would have preferred Jerusalem in Israel, we were comforted knowing that an international Jerusalem would guarantee our religious freedom to the city. In 1948, when Jordan invaded East Jerusalem, very few people from Europe, America, or the United Nations were concerned enough to force the terms of that partition. The Jordanians evicted Jews and desecrated holy sites. Because the international community failed to intercede and force an international status on Jerusalem during that nineteen-year period of Jordanian rule, the international community conceded the moral high ground. Since 1967, Israel has guaranteed freedom to all religions in Jerusalem. We were even prepared to share parts of East Jerusalem with the Palestinians, but they rejected that offer again. And still France is not happy with Israel."

"Ari, it isn't just France," replied Andre. "Much of America is not happy either. Alexander may talk about Israel's support from Christian Zionists, but there are other Christians, liberal Protestant groups, and even Jews who have advocated disinvestment from Israel because of the way the Palestinians are treated. Israel has put up a fence and grabbed Palestinian land for future settlements. The Muslim world is angry and takes its frustrations out on the rest of us, and you still blame the Vatican."

"Andre," Sanjay interceded, "the Muslim world is angry, but for many reasons. There are no Jews in Kashmir, the Russian province of Chechnya, the Philippines, or Malaysia, but there are still Muslim insurgencies. In Africa, there is religious war in the Sudan between Christians and Muslims, as there is in Nigeria. In Indonesia, the province of Ambron is a source of conflict between Christians and Muslims, and Christians have been driven out of Halmahera and churches burned. Catholics have been murdered in East Timor by Muslims. In Macedonia, Cypress, and Kurdistan, there are ongoing Muslim and Christian conflicts. In all of these places, there are no Jews, none left in Iraq to blame for the Sunni and Shiite Muslims sectarian violence. In Lebanon, there were years of civil war between the Christians and Muslims and no Jews. Why do so many in the West focus selectively on the Palestinians and not the plight of the persecuted Coptic Christians in Egypt? The Palestinians have been offered a state more than once, and they have refused. Their militia groups send suicide bombers to kill Jews indiscriminately, and I don't blame Israel for putting up a fence. Look what Hezbollah did last year. Perhaps European culture has been so immersed in anti-Semitism that it cannot separate from it."

"Europe can separate from its past, Sanjay," responded Andre. "America has a past, too. The American government slaughtered the Native American tribes, then forced them onto reservations, and a century later forced Japanese Americans into detention camps. And America's treatment of its black citizens was atrocious. Your criticisms of Europe and the Vatican are no less selective than my criticisms of Israel. Mayhem in Africa and the Muslim world does not excuse Israel's mistreatment of its Arabs."

"Israeli Arabs have full citizenship and are protected by laws of the state of Israel," replied Ari. "They have their own political parties that operate in the Knesset."

"They are still second-class citizens in your country, Ari," replied Andre.

"As are French Jews in France," responded Ari. "Or if you disagree, perhaps you would agree French citizens of Moroccan or Algerian extraction are second-class citizens in your country."

"On that point I cannot disagree with you," said Andre. "I don't dispute that Europe has had a history of anti-Semitism, and admittedly it still exists. Don't you find any comfort or consolation that the late Pope John Paul II went to Israel and apologized for the sins of the Catholic Church, and said that there is no place for anti-Semitism in the Catholic Church?"

"Of course I do, but why hasn't any pope excommunicated Adolf Hitler?" asked Alexander.

"I cannot answer that," replied Andre.

"Please explain why *Mein Kampf* was never even placed on the Catholic list of banned books. Vatican silence only encouraged the Nazis, a tacit approval."

"Alexander, the Vatican never approved of the Holocaust. The Holy See was very afraid of Hitler," replied Andre.

"Then why not excommunicate him after his death?" asked Alexander

"Alexander, you are implying that the Holy See is conspiring to take Jerusalem away from the Israelis," responded Andre. "Christians have holy sites in Jerusalem too."

"I believe the evidence supports that implication. Ironically, the Vatican and the Arabs line up as unlikely allies. The Palestinian position has always been that Israel should retreat to the pre-1967 borders, and that would effectively remove East Jerusalem from Israel, a position not inconsistent with Vatican policy, but they will both find themselves to be on the wrong side of history."

Andre came to realize that much of what he had learned in France about the Jews controlling the media and Hollywood paled compared to the power of the Christian Zionists. They were prepared to duke it out with the Catholics or any other entity they perceived would act against Israel's interests, including France, Russia, or the United Nations. Israel was often held to a double standard, but the Christian Zionists could play on a level field and on their own terms.

"So your side of history is the restoration of Israel and its Jews, Christ returns, the Jews are converted, and there is some final battle between good and evil. Conversion is just another form of Replacement Theology," replied Andre, feeling as if he scored some late debating points.

"If the Jews are converted, it will be by God's plan and not by an inquisition or torture," Alexander replied.

Andre was developing an intense dislike for the Russian Alexander. Andre had read about the evangelical interpretation of the "end times." Many of them believe the European Common Market or Russia will usher in the anti-Christ. What nonsense he thought. Then he thought about that day when he was a little boy, June 7, 1981. Andre's father was the French engineer who had the misfortune to be the only one working at Osirak, the Iraqi nuclear reactor, on that morning. He was also the only one who died from the Israeli bombing raid. Andre remembered the loud blasts over Baghdad. That was the day he became an orphan.

Chapter 16
PAKISTAN MAKES DEMANDS

July 3, 2007
Tehran, Iran

The time was 3:10 PM. Pakistani ambassador Saheed arrived at Tehran University with his bodyguards, who remained with the vehicle after they escorted him into the building where he was greeted by President Ahmadinejad. Looking more like a slovenly UC-Berkeley professor than an Iranian politician, a smiling President Ahmadinejad and his entourage escorted the ambassador down the hallway to the president's office as students looked on.

"Please have a seat," said Ahmadinejad. The two of them were now alone in his office. Saheed sat down in a leather chair.

"Ambassador Saheed, Iran needs your bomb for only another two weeks," said Ahmadinejad.

"Only two weeks. Can you guarantee that Mr. President?"

"Only Allah makes guarantees," replied Ahmadinejad. "We have hidden the weapon from Israeli and American satellites, and due to precautions, two weeks is necessary. As you know, Iran is now in front of the Security Council."

"You are obligated by our agreement to tell me where the bomb is. Where is the weapon Mr. President?"

"Not even close to Israel. Look, Ambassador Saheed. The Western press wants to make me out as a madman, but I am not so stupid as to try to sneak an 8-kiloton bomb into Tel Aviv. Look how easy it was for Israel's agents to discover our nerve gas hidden in the Red Cross convoy on its way to Hezbollah in Lebanon. If that was a test for Mossad, they passed. Iran could ill afford the risk of having the Israelis discover an Iranian provided nuclear weapon in southern Lebanon. The Security Council is looking for evidence Iran is seeking a nuclear weapons program. And neither one of us wants to provide that proof."

"Mr. President, you recall that our agreement imposes strict limits on Iran's use of this weapon. There is no detonation permitted under any circumstances. The weapon was to provide your country with a framework for solving technical problems with missile application."

"Mr. Ambassador, what is the urgency? You are receiving oil payments to help your economy?"

"This decision to remove the weapon is for your protection as well as ours. Your country has received too much unwelcome attention, and is now in front of the UN Security Council. Mr. President, you have provoked the Israelis and most of the world by denying the Holocaust, and that Israel should be wiped off the map. Need I say more? Mr. President, as you know, President Musharraf and A. Q. Khan are under house arrest. The CIA is trying to figure out what prompted these arrests, because they know that A. Q. Khan is very popular in Pakistan. I will tell you. Mr. Khan was arrested as Pakistan's guarantee you will return our weapon, and when you do, he will be released on insufficient evidence. President Musharraf's arrest, the announcement to test, and the troop mobilization to Kashmir were politically necessary to satisfy the Islamists who are angry over Mr. Khan's arrest. Mr. Khan is the father of Pakistan's nuclear program, but if necessary, Pakistan will bring him to trial on charges that he illegally assisted Iran's nuclear weapons development program and provided your country with a nuclear bomb. We will prove the charges, and the world will know that Iran has a Pakistani nuclear bomb. A. Q. Khan will go down as a traitor, and Musharraf will be blamed for letting it happen under his watch. The UN Security Council will finally have proof. The unforeseen consequences I wouldn't even want to imagine—none of which could be good for Iran. Of course this is avoidable if you return our weapon promptly."

"Give my best wishes to your new president." Ahmadinejad stood, signaling the meeting was over. The Iranian president walked the ambassador to his car, shook his hand, and smiled for the benefit of all those looking on, then returned to his office. He had recorded the meeting and began dictating into the recording device.

> The ambassador's not-so-veiled threat to Iran, including a willingness to implicate his own country's culpability, I do not consider a credible threat. Pakistan, a beneficiary of U.S. aid, is held to higher standard than Iran. To be caught in a swindle of this magnitude could lead to unforeseeable and nefarious consequences for Pakistan. Setting up Musharraf and Khan as scapegoats would not contain the fallout, or conceal the trail to free oil that leads all over Pakistan. At a time when many countries' economies were hemorrhaging because of expensive petroleum and tight supplies, Pakistan could ill afford to expose itself as the country that opted to transfer an illegal nuclear weapon to Iran to obtain free oil. The political price to be exacted would be too high even for Pakistan.

Chapter 17

TO HELL WITH THE NPT

July 4, 2007
Tehran, Iran

The UN Security Council had deliberated for two days without revelations. The IAEA's charges against Iran were predicated on evidence of Iranian NPT treaty violations, and that, for at least two decades, Iran deliberately failed to disclose a program for developing key techniques necessary for nuclear weapons development. Uranium enrichment and plutonium separation from spent fuel were secretly carried out on a limited scale. Iran did not deny the accusations but dismissed them as insignificant. The nuclear watchdog agency had adopted a resolution that demanded Iran totally suspend all enrichment and uranium reprocessing activities, including research and development. Iran did not comply with that request. These were the known facts as the president of Iran was about to address the Assembly of Experts, comprised of eighty-six learned Iranian clerics.

"Thank you all for attending this meeting of the Assembly of Experts." Ahmadinejad continued on. "We are here today to discuss our country's options. At this moment, Russia, China, America, France, and England are discussing what, if any, sanctions will be imposed against Iran. We are hopeful that the Russians and Chinese will be our advocates and distance themselves from the Europeans and Americans at the Security Council meeting, but we cannot be certain. What we can be certain of is that the Supreme Leader Ayatolla Khamenei will authorize Iran to withdraw from the NPT if sanctions are threatened.

And if any sanctions are actually imposed, Ayatollah Khamenei and I agree that Iran will place an oil embargo on those countries that support the sanctions."

"A partial oil embargo might be reason enough for the United States and Great Britain to blockade our ports in the Persian Gulf. Our economy, which is suffering now, will only get worse," said one of the clerics.

"If sanctions are imposed, Iran's economy will suffer anyway. Ahmadinejad is right. If Iranians have to suffer, let the price of oil rise so the rest of the world suffers too," replied another learned cleric.

"Iran can still pump oil to Turkey, Pakistan, and north to Asia, and maintain revenues. We can use other countries to broker the oil and resell at higher prices on the spot markets, and purchase necessities on the black market through the Russians, the Chinese, and some of the Europeans. When the oil-consuming countries feel enough pain at the pump, they will be more accommodating to Iran."

"What if the Security Council doesn't impose sanctions but issues a warning?"

"We will still considering withdrawing. What do Pakistan, India, and Israel have in common?" Ahmadinejad answered his own question. "Each one of these countries has produced its own nuclear arsenal, each is or will be the beneficiary of U.S. aid, and none of these countries has ever signed the NPT Treaty. In fact, the United States is likely to provide India nuclear assistance for the first time without requiring India to sign the NPT."

"If Iran withdraws from the NPT, might that be the justification that the U.S. or Israel needs to attack our nuclear facilities?"

"A good question. In 2003, North Korea withdrew from the NPT and has not been attacked."

"But North Korea allegedly has a nuclear deterrent," responded Rafsanjani.

"So I have heard," responded Ahmadinejad.

When the meeting ended, the Iranian president believed he had achieved a general consensus from the Assembly of Experts to withdraw from the NPT Treaty. The decision to exit from the treaty and respond to any future sanctions would be rendered by the supreme leader, not

Ahmadinejad. Privately, many of the Experts had sincere doubts about Ahmadinejad's ability to govern as president, but on one issue there was no disagreement: Iran's inalienable right to become a nuclear power.

"Ali, may I have a word with you?" requested Ahmadinejad.

"Of course," replied Rafsanjani.

"I'd like to meet with you for a few minutes in my private quarters." At that moment, Ahmadinejad's secretary walked over and whispered something in his ear.

"Ali, I have to take a phone call. Make yourself comfortable here for a few minutes and I will send for you." Rafsanjani poured himself some coffee and sat down to chat with some of the other clerics.

Ahmadinejad picked up the receiver. The phone call was from the captain of the oil tanker *Shooting Star*.

"Mr. President," said the captain," we are only a day away from Bushehr."

"Arash, what is your closest port?"

"Aden in Yemen," replied the captain.

"Take the *Shooting Star* to Aden and refuel."

"And go where Mr. President?"

"Your next port of call will be Jakarta, Indonesia."

"Yes, of course. But I will have no fuel to deliver," said the captain.

"Fudge the paperwork. Tell them your tanker recently departed from Kuala Lumpur and is in need of repairs. Then request permission to dock," Ahmadinejad commanded.

"Yes Mr. President."

"Please await further instructions."

"Thank you, Mr. President"

"Goodbye, Arash, and Allah be with you."

Chapter 18

MORAL EQUIVALENCE

July 4, 2007
Ramallah, West Bank

   Marwan Barghouti contacted Israeli intelligence at the gas station near his house. He pumped gas and delivered payment inside to a cashier, who was an Israeli informant. With the exchange of money, Marwan received instructions. He suspected his phone lines were tapped, but was unaware Israeli agents had inserted a listening device into his watch during his interrogation at Arnold's Deli. Marwan felt trapped between a rock and a hard place. The warmer relations between Abbas and Olmert had cooled since the Danish cartoon and continued on a downward spiral. An Israeli raid into the Palestinian territories to hunt for terrorists was seen as another slap in the face of the weakening Palestinian Authority. Marwan Barghouti was cognizant of the changing political dynamic as he played his role of an Israeli pawn, the price for being free. He still considered the Hamas elected government to be a disaster, and a retraction from the secular Palestine and independent Palestine he envisioned. Ironically, he believed the benefits he provided to Israel, he was also providing to Fatah.
   The next day Jibril Rahoub, head of security in the West Bank, drove to Marwan's home and honked his horn. A few moments later, Marwan walked out his front door and joined Jibril on the front seat. The old Mercedes took off. Before they started talking, Jibril intentionally turned up the volume of his radio, which was playing Arabic music, just in case there was a bug planted in his car. They were on the way to the offices of the Palestinian Authority, just a few blocks away.

"It's not only about ideology. The Palestinian government is broke, and under Hamas, there is no money to pay the government workers," said Jibril. "I believe the idea to sign on to this peace deal with Israel was as much about getting a pipeline to new money as it was about getting vaccines and gas masks. Fatah needs another opportunity to show the Palestinian people that the Palestinian Authority can deliver for them now. Look what the stupid Danish did with their cartoon. They converted millions of moderates to extremists."

"We only have ourselves to blame. Too much corruption and for too long," Marwan replied. "Besides, any peace deal we ever did with Israel was nothing more then the promise of peace."

"Exactly," responded Jibril. "That was Arafat at his best. He could easily satisfy the Europeans and the Americans by simply saying he wanted peace. He signed a peace agreement, and then sent homicide bombers to cross the border to kill the Jews. Arafat correctly assessed that the West, especially Europe, chose to view our conflict as one of 'moral equivalence' that denied both sides the higher moral ground. With moral equivalence, the homicide bomber's death is considered as tragic as his victim's. Questions of motives, morality, right and wrong, are readily dismissed. The resulting death is considered egregious, not necessarily the perpetrator. The greatest advocate of moral equivalence is the United Nations. The answer for the United Nations is usually to say 'we regret the loss of life on both sides. Please stop the killing.'"

"But with Arafat dead and the Hamas election victory, don't you think the Palestinian people have lost the moral equivalence?"

"Without question," Jibril replied. "Hamas has no moral legitimacy, and its theological underpinnings are repugnant to the secular Europeans. Israel will have a free rein to grab even more of our land and unilaterally define the borders. Our protest will fall on deaf ears. The world is crying for the Lebanese, while the Palestinians are now considered another tribe of angry Arabs engaged in sectarian strife. We must reclaim our cause and once again take away the moral high ground from Israel, even if it means doing their bidding."

"The enemy of my enemy is my friend, but hopefully not for too long," Marwan finished the conversation as Jibril pulled onto the parking lot of the Palestine Authority's headquarters.

They entered, cleared security, and walked to a private room on the other side of the cafeteria. Marwan speculated that he was being tailed, and the last place Hamas would expect to find Israeli agents would be at the offices of the Palestinian Authority. The agents were there to see if Marwan were trustworthy. They planned to ask him questions concerning his recent meeting with Hamas. Agents Shimon Levi and Ariel Garon had listened in on the conversations through the device embedded in Marwan's watch. The Mossad agents arrived and were escorted by Palestinian Security forces from a West Bank checkpoint. They entered through the rear of the building as Marwan and Jibril arrived. Handshakes were exchanged, and Jibril left the room. Marwan sat down.

"Marwan, I have a bet on you that you will succeed Abbas as the next president. Ariel doesn't think so, but we will have to wait several more years to find out."

"I appreciate your vote of confidence," replied Marwan in fluent Hebrew. "You may win the bet, but you might not enjoy the result." The three of them laughed.

"Marwan can you tell us about your meeting with Hamas?" asked Ariel.

"Of course," he replied. Ariel and Shimon took turns asking Marwan questions about his meeting. Marwan had proved to be trustworthy.

"OK, we're done here," Shimon said. "You are looking well, Marwan. Freedom apparently suits you." Marwan offered no reply, and he left. As the two agents drove to the border, they again listened to the slightly audible discourse between the two Palestinians as well as the loud Arabic music emanating from the car radio.

"I agree with their assessments," said Shimon.

"As do I," replied Ariel. "For Israel's sake, you better pray that you lose that bet to me."

Chapter 19

INCLEMENT WEATHER

July 6, 2007
ISS, Space

Since he arrived on the ISS, Sanjay had maintained a daily journal documenting how the crew members were getting along. After months of living in confinement within the space station, and working within a microgravitational environment under constant stress, he began to see visible signs of psychological stress for Andre and Alexander. He had witnessed them rail against each other over theology and politics. Even though the crew members had prepared for space by passing rigorous physical and psychological testing in a simulated environment and engaging in daily exercise aboard the ISS, Sanjay recognized the human need for privacy. The constant interruption of sleep eventually took a physical and psychological toll on all of the crew members, some more than others. Neither Andre nor Alexander was married. Did matrimony impart a sense of well-being that enabled Sanjay and Ari to better resist the stress of space? Sanjay put his pen down and closed his journal. In the weightless environment, he meandered to the communications center aboard the ISS and received a late transmittal of a weather alert.

The satellite communication they depended on had been disrupted by unexpected solar storm activity. On the ISS, there was a designated area called the storm cellar that would afford the crew members as much protection from solar radiation as was humanly possible. Sanjay read the message.

Unexpected solar storm flare in your vicinity, erupting with the force of millions of hydrogen bombs traveling at warp speeds, emitting waves of radioactive particles. Storms have shut down some satellites and communications. Take precautions now.

"Andre," Sanjay echoed, "we are in a solar storm." Andre moved as quickly as possible to the storm cellar, but Ari and Alexander were too late. They were spacewalking when the storm came upon them.

"Ari, Alexander. Return immediately. Solar storm around you. Repeat, come in right now."

"We hear you," said Ari. Sanjay immediately opened the decompression module for them. They came in and sat there until the compression had risen to the level inside the spacecraft. They waited to take off their suits until they reached the protected area of the spacecraft. When the storm threat subsided, Sanjay initiated the process to determine what levels of radiation Alexander and Ari sustained.

Chapter 20

BACKDOOR CHANNELS

July 6, 2007
Tehran, Iran

Rafsanjani arranged the meeting between Ahmadinejad and Saheed. Now he would listen to what was said. He went to a private room, rewound the tape, put on the headset, and activated the play button. Rafsanjani understood Ahmadinejad wanted so much to believe that the Pakistani ambassador was bluffing with his threats and was seeking affirmation. When Ali finished, he walked down the hall and knocked on the door.

"Come in," said the Iranian president. Rafsanjani returned the recording apparatus and the tape.

"Thank you," responded Ahmadinejad. "Ali, you know Saheed. Is he bluffing?"

"No he's not bluffing Mr. President."

"Ali, not so long ago you were the Iranian president. The one issue that most Iranians agree on is that Iran should have a right to a nuclear weapon."

"Yes, that is true," Rafsanjani said.

"Under the best of circumstances, we could wait three to five years to develop enough centrifuges and processed uranium to produce a low-grade nuclear weapon, and that estimate doesn't account for a military strike against our nuclear facilities."

"Mr. President, we could return the bomb to Pakistan. The Russians and the Chinese are doing a wonderful job stalling the UN Security Council at this time. Perhaps they can buy us a year or two before we face the possibility of military sanctions. As you assured the Assembly of Experts, Iran can deal with economic sanctions."

"Ali, my scientists tell me that in a year or less, they will be able to solve the technological problems of fitting this bomb to the nose cone of our Shahab missile."

"Mr. President, a nuclear-armed missile has to be tested before launch. Tel Aviv is 1,800 kilometers from Iran and presents a formidable challenge even for our conventional missiles, which have a much lighter payload than a 1,000-kilogram nuclear bomb placed on the Shahab. Even if we solve the technological problems of the missile launch, Israel's anti-ballistic missile system is one of the best and could easily intercept this one nuclear missile, exposing Iran to a full-scale retaliatory attack. For all we know, our missile could even break up over Iran."

"I never said I would launch a missile at Tel Aviv. I would have preferred to truck the bomb to Hezbollah through Syria, but the war was ill-timed, and UN soldiers are patrolling the border. Ali, I intend to deliver a blow to Israel that will be more devastating than 100,000 Hezbollah rockets, a blow that will render them defenseless and unable to retaliate."

"That would be quite an accomplishment, and one that the Arab armies have failed to do," Rafsanjani responded.

"We are not Arabs. We are Persians. Ali, imagine that Iran's first nuclear-missile launch comes from the South Pacific. Our nuclear bomb mounted on a Shahab missile fires into the sky and detonates over the Indian Ocean, far away from Israel."

"I can imagine the world will believe that Iran has a nuclear arsenal," Rafsanjani added.

"Yes, an unpleasant surprise. And as the newest inductee into the nuclear club, we will demand special treatment. Membership has its privileges. We can expect less intrusion and interference in our affairs, and an engagement policy that is more to our liking. Our country should be able to proceed with its nuclear-development program rather unimpeded."

"What a dare," Rafsanjani patronized. "Still, to conduct a nuclear test that is entirely unexpected will be considered an extremely unwelcome event in Washington and Jerusalem, and it could lead to unintended consequences. A preemptive strike against Iran is not out of the realm of possibility, Mr. President."

"I beg to differ. Any plan to strike at Iran is to prevent the nuclear option from becoming real, as was demonstrated by the Israeli destruction of Iraq's only nuclear reactor in the early 1980s. Once the nuclear option is in place, it is too late for such an attack. Has any country dared to attack North Korea, or any other country that is thought to have a nuclear deterrent?"

"No, Mr. President."

"Countries that have nuclear weapons do not fear being attacked by other countries, except for Israel."

"Because they are too small a country to survive a nuclear exchange," Rafsanjani posited.

"Yes, one nuke over Israel and it disappears. Iran is a big country with many cities and distant regions. We could absorb multiple nuclear strikes and survive. Ali, the beauty of this ruse is that Iran doesn't have to nuke Israel, only threaten to. Israelis will never learn to live with a nuclear Iran, or the perception of a nuclear Iran. Expect the following to occur after we successfully test. Arab governments friendly to the United States will switch alliances, or risk being overthrown. The United States will be perceived as the loser in the region. Arab countries will clamor for an alliance with Iran, and a noose will tighten around Israel."

"Mr. President, one million Israelis are already dealing with post-traumatic symptoms from the Hezbollah rockets that exploded in northern Israel. When Israelis learn of our nuclear launch, they will be so traumatized that those who are able to emigrate will likely choose to do so."

"But Ali, we could have the same problem as Hitler. No country wants them."

"Mr. President, this is a bold vision. We need someone to bring pressure to bear on the new Pakistani government, and I think the Russians can help us. I'll work the backdoor channels."

"And what can we offer the Russians?" Rafsanjani thought for a minute and a smile came to his face.

"Jews," he responded.

Chapter 21

A WALK IN SPACE

July 6, 2007
ISS, Space

The following day, when the storm had passed, Andre suited up and decompressed before his inspection spacewalk to report on possible storm damage to the exterior, including heat shields, solar panels and optical surfaces. The inspection would take several hours.

On the day of the storm, Ari had no sooner donned his space suit when he began to feel nauseated, one of the early symptoms of radiation poisoning. An hour later, Alexander also complained of nausea. Sanjay used medical devices to measure both chronic and acute levels of radiation. Chronic radiation exposure came with the territory, usually from radiation emitted from space that had to be monitored within the ISS to ensure the levels didn't exceed the norms. Yesterday's solar storm emitted acute radiation, and Sanjay tested everyone, including himself. He and Andre were fine, but Ari and Alexander were sick. Sanjay used the Extravehicular Activity Radiation Monitoring device, also known by its acronym EVARM, to measure the dosage of radiation Ari and Alexander received to their eyes, skin, and internal organs. This information registered on silicon chips inserted inside several badges sewn into the different areas of the space suits worn by the two scientists during the storm. Sanjay then connected badges to a storage reader box in the EVARM, which read the radiation levels from the chips and transmitted the information to ground control. They would wait for the RAD count, a number to quantify radiation exposure. The lower the RAD number, the better the chance for their survival.

Sanjay knew that the faster the onset of the vomiting the more deadly the dose.

Ari began his vomiting spells three hours after exposure, while Alexander began vomiting in the fourth hour, and that was the good news. Had the vomiting commenced within the first hour of exposure, death within weeks would have been a certainty for the Israeli and the Russian. With proper medical treatment, they might have a decent chance of survival. The results from ground control came across the wire: Ari's RAD count was 245, and Alexander's was 230. They had a better then even chance to survive if they could receive hospital treatment. But if treatment were delayed, their odds of survival would get progressively worse. Sanjay took the pair aside.

"Tell me how you are feeling, Ari."

"Weak and still sick to my stomach," responded Ari.

"Me, too," responded Alexander.

"You guys have taken some radiation. Your RAD counts are below 250. Both of you can survive this, but we need to get you home. For the next few days, you will be experiencing some nausea and diarrhea. Please suspend all activities aboard if you start to feel ill and go to your attached sleeping bags."

"Sanjay, I don't want my family to know about this yet," Ari requested.

"Ditto for me," said Alexander. "I don't want either my mother or Yuri to know right now."

"Understood," responded Sanjay. "I would, however, suggest you notify your loved ones before you depart on the shuttle."

"When will that be?" asked Ari.

"Within two weeks," replied Sanjay. "We have to stabilize you until then. The ISS is equipped to monitor your radiation levels, but ill suited to treat them, and our microgravitational environment actually impairs your immune system from healing itself. Don't worry about the workload. Andre has been reassigned to outside maintenance, and when the shuttle arrives, two astronauts will take your place."

After two days of vomiting, fatigue, and weakness, Ari and Alexander could expect to feel better for up to two weeks. Later they could experience internal bleeding, hair loss, and a curtailment of white blood-cell production necessary to fight infection. In a hospital environment, they both stood a good chance to recover, but not aboard the ISS.

Andre looked forward to his private time outside the ISS. Technically, there was no such phenomenon as spacewalking, because there is nothing to walk on in space. In the absence of gravity, one simply floated in space, tethered to the space station. Andre's space suit came with a jet pack, so he could propel himself back to the station in the event the tether attachments broke off. There were many accessible handles welded to its exterior, which provided him with additional safeguards as well as access around the station.

At night, he often shed a powerful light on the ISS from his helmet until sunrise came; that was no less then sixteen times a day. For Andre, being in space was surreal, but it didn't make his thoughts of Michelle go away.

Chapter 22
PERCEPTION IS REALITY

July 6, 2007
Tehran, Iran

"Jews!" exclaimed Ahmadinejad.

"Yes," replied Rafsanjani, "a million Russian Jews who have settled in Israel within the last twenty years, the ones who couldn't get into America. They know that no Hezbollah rockets or Iranian nuclear bombs will be aimed at Russia. Given the opportunity and a little incentive, they might gladly return. These recent groups of Russian Jews aren't Zionists. They were political refugees from the former Soviet Union, who had Jewish bloodlines. They didn't even grow up with religion. I tell you Mr. President, tough talk from a nuclear Iran, coupled with recent memories of the last war, may send a million Jews into voluntary exile if they had a place to go. Perception is what creates the reality. As you said, an Iran perceived to have nuclear weapons will not be attacked."

"If we're not attacked then in few short years, we'll actually be able to produce the real nuclear bombs and delivery systems," Ahmadinejad said excitedly.

"Israel will fear a nuclear exchange. In the war with Hezbollah, a million Israelis were forced to underground shelters. Now they will fear their own holocaust. Israelis will doubt their ability to survive as a Jewish state through the twenty-first century."

"Ali, at the Hamas meeting, Marwan Barghouti was prophetic when he said Israel was built on shifting sands. He said in time, demographics and democracy will implode the Jewish state."

"Mr. President. We can make his prediction happen in our lifetime. Let's discuss the Americans and the Europeans for a moment. After the launch, they will want to engage us, like North Korea, except North Korea has no oil to bargain with. We can link our good behavior to Israeli concessions and compel the Jews to relinquish more land to the Palestinians in return for the promise of peace. As Israelis flee in droves, the fences will come down like the Berlin Wall. Imagine that Iran sponsors an international plan that recognizes a bi-national Jerusalem and a bi-national state of Palestine in place of Israel. On this issue, you will even get the support of Western Europe."

"If the Jews go to Russia. But Ali, what makes you believe Russia would even want these Jews? Russian governments have persecuted Jews, and introduced the *Protocols of the Elders of Zion* in 1905, available in our own bookstores. Are they growing soft and stupid like the French and British?"

"No," responded Rafsanjani, "the Russians are smarter. Let me tell you why."

Chapter 23
A SENSE OF ENTITLEMENT

July 7, 2007
ISS, Space

The previous day, Andre conducted a full inspection of the ISS and the small space capsule attached and discovered slight damage to the heat shields. The good news was that the ISS had all the equipment necessary to make the repairs. The bad news was that Andre had to do it himself. The task would be a lot easier with two working, but Ari and Alexander spent most of the time in their vertically attached sleeping bags either sleeping or experiencing nausea.

Not only did Andre work away the many sunrises and sunsets that occurred in a day's work, he also had a lot of time to reflect about conditions in France. A few weeks ago, it was the Muslim French, children of immigrants, who were burning cars and trashing their neighborhoods to protest alleged job discrimination. This week it was the native French youth who were protesting vehemently against a government-proposed jobs bill that would eliminate job security and the sense of entitlement the French had grown accustomed to. The French government was caught between a no-growth economy and a young workforce that rejected "cowboy capitalism." The socialistic system that seemed to work effectively in France since the 1980s was now out of sync with the onset of global economics, outsourcing, in-sourcing, and offshoring.

Andre had seen the published studies by the think tanks that predicted the world's future economic leaders would include the United States, China, India, Japan, Indonesia, and to a lesser extent, Russia.

Although Russia was blessed with natural resources (including oil and gas) to help its economic growth, the country shared an affliction with many other European countries: a declining birthrate. Countries with declining birthrates typically do not join the ranks of the economic elite. Fewer native French having fewer children did not bode well for France, especially when that shortfall would be offset by a higher birthrate among immigrants from North Africa and other Third World countries that often depended on generous French welfare benefits.

Sanjay represented an India with its billion plus population, eager to embrace capitalism, millions who were technologically adept and capable of creating new technologies for the twenty-first century. Alexander represented a Russia tearing out the remnants of an old and failed communistic system in order to propel itself into the new economic century, but facing uphill challenges of wide-scale corruption and Islamic terror in its southern provinces. Those two countries stood in contrast to France, whose youth were resisting even the smallest steps toward a more market-based economy. Ari represented Israel, the Silicon Valley of the Middle East, diminutive in size and relatively small in population, but so overachieving. It was a country Andre had never visited, but one with which he would become inexorably intertwined.

Andre was thirteen when his father died. They were living in Baghdad, just the two of them. As an orphan, Andre spent the rest of his teen years at a Catholic orphanage outside of Reims, France. He excelled in school, and even once thought of becoming a priest. Sensing that Andre was in need of a father figure, Father Gauthier gladly assumed that role, even throughout Andre's university years. Andre was a very religious boy but equally interested in the studies of science. He received a scholarship to INSA at Lyon(s), one of France's highly rated universities in the science field. After completing his undergraduate degree, Andre was accepted at the University of Paris Sorbonne where he continued his studies in science and became fluent in English and Russian. Mastering English was almost second nature, but acquiring fluency in Russian was much more difficult.

Upon his graduation, Andre enrolled in the French Air Force Academy, Ecole de l'Air, and graduated with an advanced degree in engineering. He went to Russia for advanced training in EVA, or extravehicular activity, also known as spacewalking. He returned to

Paris and accepted a teaching position at the Ecole de l'Air until he was offered an opportunity to fly in France's space program. Andre received the good news in April of 2006. After summer, he would intensely train for his scheduled liftoff in March to the International Space Station. Andre would join three other astronauts from three other countries to replace the four astronauts who had been in space for the previous three months.

This was the news he had been waiting for, a chance to make Father Gauthier and the citizens of France proud of him. It was time for celebration. Andre collected a few of his close friends and went clubbing at Montmartre. Overlooking the city of Paris, the main attraction at Montmartre was La Basilica du Sacre Coeur, a church devoted to the Holy Virgin built at the end of the nineteenth century. On this perfect spring evening, with a slight breeze blowing through his hair, Andre relished the opportunity to stand next to this famous basilica and its statues of Joan of Arc and St. Louis peering over the city of Paris, the City of Lights. With the Eiffel Tower in the distance, he imagined nothing could be more beautiful—until he saw the face of that woman walking with her friends in the adjacent village square. Andre watched her disappear into a crowd. The village district of Montmartre attracted many tourists from around the world, and they walked, but never hurriedly, often gazing into the windows of the many shops before entering.

Andre and his friends walked around the square for a while before deciding on a restaurant that featured Italian cuisine. The maître d' escorted the four of them to a street-side table. There were sounds of music, conversations from tourists, and clatter from the kitchen, busy waiters going in and out of revolving doors. Andre and his friends had just been seated when they heard young women at the next table speaking French. The subject was archaeology, and the conversationalists were obviously students. Out of curiosity, Andre turned around. He saw that face again, the girl who had disappeared into the crowd. She and three other girls were sitting at the table behind him. This time he would not let her get away. He fixed his eyes on hers, and she returned the gaze.

"Bonjour. I am Andre."

"Bonjour. I am Michelle."

Andre soon learned that Michelle attended the University of Paris Sorbonne, where she was an archaeology major. She was pursuing an advanced degree, and planned to be a teacher. Andre was thirty-two years old, and Michelle was only twenty-five, but he swept the younger student off her feet and a relationship began to develop. Michelle was Andre's intellectual equal, and they could communicate on many levels. She was as interested in his field as he was in hers. They had many things in common and fell deeply in love.

In the middle of June, Michelle had finished her studies for the semester and Andre was teaching one summer class. She surprised him when she showed up at the French Air Force Academy. They met at the cafeteria.

"Andre, I have wonderful news. I have just been accepted to Tel Aviv University's archaeology program for the summer. I will receive full credits and graduate sooner."

"What about our holiday in Spain this August?"

"This program covers July and August. We can go in September instead."

"My training for the space flight starts in September. You know that."

"Well then, come to Israel with me."

How vivid the memories were. Andre looked at his watch. He had been outside for hours and witnessed the sun rise and set at least three times. He finished repairing this last heat shield.

During July, Michelle called Andre as often as she could, usually at the end of the day or on a Saturday, the Jewish Sabbath. The rest of the time she was working on a dig at the ancient seaport of Ashkelon, the ancient site of the Canaanite kings and the Philistines. She had her laptop computer, but preferred using the phone to hear Andre's voice.

In August, Michelle called Andre. He remembered hearing a sense of desperation in her voice. "Andre, please come. I need to see you. Please come?"

"Michelle, you'll be back in only six weeks. I signed up for another four weeks of teaching summer school. I can't make it."

Michelle then asked, "Tell me honestly, Andre, had you not signed up for teaching, would you come?"

"I can never go to Israel," he responded.

Michelle began to phone less, and so Andre began to phone her more. Her e-mail communications became more perfunctory and less special. Toward the end of August, Michelle called him. She had applied for transfer to Tel Aviv University to complete her graduate studies. Andre tried to play down its significance.

"I understand," he said defensively. "I will be on the spaceflight beginning in March for six months. Perhaps you can come back to France after your summer session, before you start your new semester? We can be together for at least a few weeks." And then she told him. She had fallen in love with an Israeli university student she had met at the dig. She wasn't coming home.

Andre was in a state of shock. Michelle represented the best of France: beautiful, sensitive, intelligent, Catholic, and admiringly aloof. She belonged to him. Michelle was as much his entitlement as job security was to the French. They were fighting to hold on, and he would too.

"Michelle, I am going to take the next Air France jet to Tel Aviv."

"Andre, please don't make this more difficult. I will always have a special place for you in my heart, but your life is in France, and my life will be in Israel for at least a year on this dig. I have a love for this land and its people, the Ethiopian Black Jews, the Arab Druze, and Christian Arabs and Greeks.' Andre asked her what her new Israeli friend was called. She said Ari. He followed up the call with an e-mail and told her he would still be waiting for her when she came back to France. She did not reply.

Chapter 24
THE CONVERGENCE

July 8, 2007
Tehran, Iran

The timing of Russian president Putin's planned trip to Turkmenistan this week could not have been more fortuitous, thought Rafsanjani. He contacted the Russian ambassador to Iran and requested a most discreet meeting with President Putin outside of Ashgabat, the capital of Turkmenistan and only a few miles away from the Iranian border. Rafsanjani's request was granted, and the meeting was planned for late evening at a mountaintop retreat often used for matters of state. Rafsanjani would cross the border under the cover of darkness at 9 PM on July 8.

Only the day before, Rafsanjani had wrung a major concession from Iranian president Ahmadinejad. For their nuclear caper to succeed, Iran needed both Russia and Pakistan to be on board, and just as Russia had been Egypt's insurance policy against the Israeli Army's march into Cairo in 1967 and 1973, Rafsanjani hoped that he could also play the Russian card.

President Putin's visit to Turkmenistan had everything to do with the business of energy cooperation. Turkmenistan's president Saparmurat Niyazov was hosting the Russian president for the purpose of acquiring Russian investment for the development of Turkmenistan's gas reserves for export to Europe. The joint venture would allow both countries to profit, and for Russia to expand its influence in Central Asia. Putin didn't come alone. He brought with him top Russian business executives and his foreign policy team, which included

Alexander's brother, Yuri. The agreements were signed on the morning of July 8 followed by handshakes, photo opportunities, and a lunch at 1 PM. President Putin returned to the mountaintop villa to spend his last evening in the Turkmen province before he and his team left for Moscow in the morning. Rafsanjani felt very fortunate that he would be able to meet with the Russian president on the last evening of his trip.

Ashghabat, Turkmenistan

Former president of Iran Ali Rafsanjani and President Putin exchanged quick handshakes—no cameras and no reporters. Then they parted. Rafsanjani came in through the servant quarters after he arrived in a nondescript van, dressed in local attire.

"Thank you for seeing me on such short notice," said Rafsanjani through his Russian interpreter.

"This must be important for you to cross the border in disguise."

"I'll come right to the point, Mr. President. Pakistan has provided my country with a small nuclear bomb through a complex arrangement that provided much needed and very cheap oil to Pakistan. The bomb was to be studied by our scientists, but never intended for offensive purposes."

"Iran is playing a very dangerous game," Putin replied. "If word gets out, we will be compelled to halt our efforts to help Iran at the United Nations."

"Mr. President, our agreement stipulates that Pakistan can cancel the contract unilaterally and demand the return of its bomb. Pakistan has elected to do so. My country is petitioning your assistance in this matter to influence Pakistan to withdraw its demand for its bomb. Ambassador Saheed has threatened to go public if the bomb isn't returned promptly."

"And the blame will fall on A. Q. Khan and the deposed President Musharraf."

"Yes," responded Rafsanjani, "they are the designated scapegoats. They would prefer to release Khan because he is so popular among the people. I'm certain the new government will do so as soon as they get their bomb."

"What do you intend to do with this bomb?"

"With Russia's assistance, we would like to fit this bomb to an Iranian missile and launch and detonate harmlessly over the South Pacific—but only after we withdraw from the NPT. We have an ingenious plan, one that will benefit Russia. Imagine, Mr. President, that Russia could hijack Israel's high-tech industry. Here is how it could work."

Rafsanjani paused. "The benefits for Russia would be many." And in the next half hour, Rafsanjani shared his epiphany concerning global economics and geopolitics, but Putin understood the cleric's real purpose, to become the North Korea of the Middle East and stave off the "coalition of the willing," who were prepared, if necessary, to destroy Iran's nuclear facilities. The Russian president saw that Ahmadinejad was in hot water and didn't want any part of his diabolical scheme.

"Mr. Rafsanjani, Russia and Iran are wonderful trading partners, but Russia also trades with the West. The scenario you describe is only based on untested assumptions that are very difficult to gauge. For the sake of argument, assume you are correct and most of the Russian-born Israelis are told they can return to Russia. They'd receive subsidized housing and other financial incentives for their businesses. The costs to repatriate a million Jewish repatriates would be so staggering that real-estate prices, already off the charts, would skyrocket beyond comprehension. And that's just economics. I can't even begin to fathom the social ramifications that would ensue from the arrival of a million Jews, but I assure you, it wouldn't be a pretty picture."

"And that is why Ahmadinejad is willing to subsidize Russia with as much as 100 billion euros for relocation—if you can convince Pakistan to drop its demands."

"A hundred billion euros can create a lot of infrastructure and government projects, but it can also cause a lot of inflation."

"Maybe in the beginning, but Mr. President, you and I both know what tempers inflation in a global economy."

"Economic growth," Putin replied. "Mr. Rafsanjani, I will talk to the Pakistanis. Let me notify you within a couple of days."

"Thank you, Mr. President, and I hope your trip to Turkmenistan was a productive one." They shook hands, and Rafsanjani departed through the kitchen.

Chapter 25
BACK IN THE USSR

July 9, 2007
The Kremlin

The following day, President Putin returned to the Kremlin. He called a meeting. Russia's ambassador to Pakistan was present

"Thank you all for being here on short notice. The foreign policy team has just returned to Moscow with me and must be very tired. We had a successful trip to Turkmenistan and signed contracts that will increase Russian business significantly. Give yourselves a hand of applause." They all clapped.

"The purpose of today's meeting is to brainstorm the pros and cons of providing nuclear assistance to Pakistan of the sort that the United States will hope to provide to India. The ambassador and I will return in ninety minutes. Yuri you take the notes for me."

"Certainly, Mr. President," Yuri thought, *If Russian nuclear technology was on the table for sale or trade to Pakistan, something huge was in the works.* Why would his country even consider transferring its nuclear technology to an Islamic country with fanatics and an unelected government that had taken power by a coup? President Putin and the Russian ambassador to Pakistan returned. Yuri handed over the notes he had taken during the brainstorming session. The five members of Putin's foreign policy team unanimously agreed with current Russian foreign policy: no to nuclear assistance in spite of warming relations between India and the United States.

President Putin thanked them and said, "Yuri and Nikolai, I have assignments for each of you. Nikolai, your assignment is to report on global economics, and what that portends for Russia and competing countries. Yuri, your assignment is to evaluate Israel's economy."

"I beg your pardon, Mr. President," Yuri responded.

"In the last twenty years, over a million Russians, most of Jewish extraction, emigrated to Israel. Some became billionaires. They represent almost 20 percent of the Israeli population, excluding Arabs. Israel exports a lot of high technology and creates a lot of software products. Can you extrapolate what portion of Israel's economic growth comes from Russian émigrés?"

"I can try Mr. President." Yuri was blown away.

"Have your reports completed for our next meeting in two days, same time. Meeting adjourned."

When the meeting concluded, Yuri and Nickolai decided to frequent a popular watering hole near the Kremlin to have a drink or two. The first beers went down very quickly. They ordered another. The waitress brought over two more. Halfway through the second beer Nickolai said to Yuri.

"What are these assignments really about?"

"I have no idea."

Chapter 26
BALI HAI

July 10, 2007
ISS, Space

Sanjay Bushar was happy the cell phone rang for him. He needed a diversion from his stressful regimen of submitting reports, maintenance, and doctoring his two sick crew members. His brother was on the other line, and he was happy to hear his voice.

"Yatin, it is good to hear from you. How is life in India?"

"You tell me brother. I am on the island of Bali."

"How nice. I should have been a missile engineer like you, brother."

"To be in space, I'd gladly trade places with you Sanjay."

"Not these days. I have two sickly crew members who were exposed to radiation during a solar storm. I am making plans to send them home for medical treatment. My only other capable crew member is repairing damage to some of the heat shields. Do you still want to trade places with me?"

"I think you've changed my mind. I am lying on the beach admiring the beauty, and listening to the ocean roll up to the beach."

"I wish I were on the beach."

"You won't believe this Sanjay. As we speak, I recognize a group of Russians walking out of the hotel lobby."

"You do. Who are they?"

"They are missile engineers like me. I've seen their pictures from the science magazines. Sanjay, I am going to avoid them like the plague. I do not want to engage in shoptalk. I just want complete anonymity—and to lose myself in island booze and schmooze."

"You better hope they don't recognize you. You've been in those magazines, too," replied Sanjay

"I don't think they will. I have a huge hat on and dark sunglasses. Besides, I look very much like the natives."

"Well, enjoy and thanks for the call. Tell Mother and Father I will be calling them soon."

"I will. Take care and be safe Sanjay."

It was a good day for Alexander. He was feeling better and decided to check his e-mail, his first attempt to communicate since the onset of his symptoms.

"How are you feeling?" Sanjay asked

"A little better," said Alexander. "Now it's time to inform my family that I will need medical treatment."

"Good idea. When Ari feels better, we will also encourage him to tell his family. Incidentally, my brother Yatin called. He is vacationing in Bali and recognized a group of Russia's best missile engineers at his hotel."

"That's a coincidence."

"Looks like Ari is getting up," said Sanjay. "Ari, call your Rachel. She called yesterday, and I told her you had the flu. Yesterday, you and Alexander were in no condition to take phone calls." Sanjay handed him the cell phone. Ari dialed home.

"Hi Rachel. Sorry I couldn't talk with you yesterday."

"You sound terrible. Are you all right?"

"Listen Rachel, Alexander and I will leave the station soon on the return shuttle. We were caught in a solar storm and exposed to some radiation, but not too much. Our prognoses are good, but we need to be hospitalized." Rachel started to cry. She composed herself.

"I'm glad you're coming home. I'm pregnant ... five months."

"Why didn't you tell me?"

"I didn't want you to worry," Rachel said.

"I can't wait to see you and the kids," said Ari. "We have so much to celebrate."

"I love you, Ari. Shalom."

"I love you too, Rachel."

Originally he was going to e-mail Yuri but changed his mind. Alexander's mother answered the phone. Alexander did not tell her about his sickness, only that he and Ari were being rotated out early. Anna was very excited and happy to hear that news, and gave the phone to Yuri.

"Hi, Alex."

"Yuri, don't tell Mother yet. I am coming home because I was exposed to radiation during a solar storm. My prognosis is good, but I need medical treatment. A supply ship will be here in a few days to take us down. My crewmate Ari is also sick like me. We are both coming down."

"I will meet you both at the landing strip."

"That would be great. By the way, a group of our top nuclear engineers were spotted having a little fun in the sun on the island of Bali."

"No one told me," Yuri said.

"Who saw them?"

"Sanjay's brother. His name is Yatin, also a renowned Indian nuclear scientist."

"Is there some kind of international symposium at the resort?" Yuri asked.

"I doubt it. Yatin is in Bali for a vacation only. In fact, he told Sanjay, he is afraid of being recognized by them, and he doesn't want to talk "shoptalk.""

"Don't blame him. Call me when you get more details of your flight, and take very good care of yourself, no spacewalking or exertion. Look forward to your safe return."

"I will. Goodbye, Yuri."

Chapter 27
FROM RUSSIA WITH LOVE

July 11, 2007
Moscow, Russia

When he arrived at the Kremlin the following morning, Yuri was told the Russian nuclear scientists in Bali were attending a symposium in Bali. For a symposium, Russian scientists abandoned vital work on Russia's first nuclear stealth missile. Yuri had his doubts. Nonetheless, at 11:00 AM, he joined the rest of the foreign policy team. Accompanying President Putin was Russian Economic Minister Greff.

"Nickolai," said Putin, "please share with us your evaluation of today's global economics."

"Mr. President, Mr. Greff, the two topics of my discussion are global economic trends and the relative role of population growth or decline with regard to economic growth. Global economic trends suggest a larger role for the multinational corporations, but at the expense of the nation-state. The multinationals frequently choose to relocate offshore businesses once reserved for local employees, because the talent pool abroad is often better educated, harder working, and less expensive.

"An American company that employs more foreign workers, and therefore creates more foreign revenue that generates more foreign taxes will be thought of as a global company. National identification and nationalism will weaken in the face of global economics, at least in the industrial world. Multinational corporate tentacles will spread out to increasingly obfuscate political ideologies so profound in the twentieth century. Outsourcing requires cultural collaboration, synergy, and empathy, and these are forces that cannot be reversed.

"Finally, let's examine the correlation between economic growth and population growth. Any country's economic growth is very difficult to sustain without a corresponding growth in population. Russia's economic competitors, India, China, and the United States are in good shape. Japan and Russia are not in good shape, because each is facing a severe population decline. If the United States faces a labor shortage in a specialized field, an administration can easily fill the talent shortage by simply issuing more H1-B Visas."

"Our government is exploring financial incentives to be awarded to Russian families that have additional children. Don't worry. Russia is not going to disappear," Greff added.

"That's an excellent idea Minister Greff. Some reputable statisticians have suggested that on the present course, Russia's population could decline by as much as thirty million people by mid-century, or one fifth of the current population. If a situation develops where there are not enough young workers to replace the old, a crisis in health care and pensions usually ensues. Most of Europe faces a similar predicament. Europe, including Russia, was once home to nearly a quarter of the world population. Today it is down to only 11 percent, and by the end of this century, it could be 7 percent," Nickolai added.

"Russia also needs to be creating more industries that create more jobs," Putin said. "Economic growth begets population growth."

"Our president is correct," Nickolai responded. "Let me demonstrate with the tiny country of Ireland, an island nation. Ireland is Europe's bright light, hi-tech oriented with the lowest unemployment rate, at 4.2 percent. At least a hundred thousand U. S. citizens of Irish ancestry have moved back, primarily for business reasons. That is an amazing statistic. Ireland is also attracting bright Poles, Latvians, and citizens from the Czech Republic, hundreds a day. American companies like Intel, Dell and Apple, Pfizer, and Microsoft have set up shop there. Ireland is proof that economic growth begets population growth."

"A great deal of Ireland's growth appears to be from American companies," Putin said.

"The American companies have gone to Ireland because the Irish did what was necessary to lure them there: tax incentives and homegrown talent. In Ireland, Intel is considered as Irish as American."

"Countries that cannot serve the needs of the multinational corporations are likely to gradually lose the economic benefits provided by these corporations as productive assets are shifted to other countries that are more sensitive to their needs," said Greff.

"Excellent point, Minister Greff, take France."

"No thank you, Nickolai" Greff replied. "I don't think the Americans would appreciate that." A quip from the minister and, suddenly, laughter filled the room. Nickolai laughed the loudest. "Continue, Nickolai."

"Recently, the French government wanted to deregulate the labor market by allowing employers to fire employees younger than twenty-six years old without reason. It was the right move, but the French government retracted because most of the French disapproved. There was so much resistance from the unions and the students. To survive, French multinational companies will have to outsource jobs. Eventually, these French multinational companies will be considered global companies."

"Europe, Ireland, China, India are politically stable," Putin interceded. "Taiwan and South Korea are economic juggernauts that live precariously in dangerous neighborhoods, both next door to a stronger military neighbor."

"In my judgment, if Taiwan no longer had U.S. military protection, it would eventually merge into mainland China," responded Nickolai. "With the economic collapse of communism, ideology is not that important anymore. The two Koreas would probably unify like Vietnam. It would be a difficult adjustment, but Koreans still have a shared culture and language."

"I agree with that assessment. Ideologies come and go, and nothing is more powerful than a shared culture and language," said Russian economic minister Greff.

"Nickolai, it takes time to grow babies into workers. Is there a way for Russia to reverse its population decline now?' inquired Putin.

"If it were possible, Mr. President, to emulate the Irish model," Nickolai responded. "Can you offer incentives to foreign multinational corporations to locate to Russia? Talented Russians are available to work. Growth begets growth. Unfortunately Russia does not have a huge source of expatriates to woo back to the mother country as Ireland has with the American Irish, but there are Poles, Lithuanians, Latvian, and Estonians nearby."

"Are you sure that Russia has no expatriates, Nickolai?" President Putin wryly stated. Yuri's light turned on.

"Twenty percent of Israeli Jews speak Russian. A million Jews left the former Soviet Union to settle in Israel during the last two decades," said Minister Greff. "With their children, these Russian Jews constitute 40 percent of the Jewish population in Israel."

"With all due respect Mr. Greff, while the American Irish hold Ireland dear to their hearts, I sincerely doubt that most Russian Jews think fondly of Russia," said Yuri.

"I agree," said the economic minister," but there are other considerations. East and West Germans were separated by the Berlin Wall, but now Germany is one nation. Once there were two Vietnams at war with each other, and now they are one country. What is the lesson to be learned, the common denominator?"

"That shared language, shared customs, and common culture can not be understated," Yuri answered.

"Exactly," Greff replied. "During last summer's war, nearly one million Jews were under attack from Hezbollah rockets. Many of them had to move to underground bomb shelters for days. One has to wonder how many dreamed of returning to Russia. Certainly, Russia is afflicted with endemic anti-Semitism, but tell me, who outside our borders would dare launch rockets into Russia."

"Minister Greff, are you suggesting Russian Jews desire to return to Russia?" Yuri asked. Minister Greff looked at President Putin first before he responded.

"Who knows? We haven't asked them." Again they all laughed, Yuri, for the sake of political correctness.

"There was a time not long ago," said Putin, "when India's most valuable export to the United States was its scientists and engineers. Now many Indians have returned to the high-tech city of Bangalore. Yuri, what's your read on Israel's economy?"

"Gentleman and ladies," responded Yuri," the following statistics are from the January, 2006 edition of FinFacts, an Irish business Web site. Israel has seventy-one companies on the American NASDAQ exchange; Ireland has seven. Israel is second to America in the number of companies listed on NASDAQ. The *Economist* magazine states that Israel attracts twice the amount of venture capital as the whole of Europe." Yuri paused and looked at the faces around the room. They revealed a look of astonishment that such a small country, surrounded by mortal enemies committed to its destruction, was so capable. Yuri continued. "Fifty-five percent of Israel's exports were in high technology. Intel developed the Centrino chip in Israel. The *Economist* says that Israel has 135 engineers for every 10,000 employees, compared with 70 in America, 65 in Japan, and 28 in the U.K. There is a synergy between the innovation of Israeli civilian and military technology that would be difficult to duplicate elsewhere."

"Many of those engineers and scientists came from our Soviet Union," replied Minister Greff.

"In as much as Taiwan and South Korean are dependent on the U.S. fleet and armed forces for their protection, Israel has the military advantage in its neighborhood and is, in fact. increasing it."

"What about Iran?" asked Nickolai.

"Still a few years away from being a nuclear threat," replied Yuri. "Excellent information, Ari and Nickolai," said Putin. "I will commission this team to prepare economic and educational plans for horizontal collaboration, including outsourcing and in-sourcing, between Israel and Russia. Break up into two groups: one to research companies not sensitive to Israel's national security and the other to research study-abroad programs for Israeli university students. Any questions?" There were no questions, and Putin and Greff immediately left without a mention of what was soon to be breaking news—an announcement that Russia had agreed to provide civilian nuclear energy to Pakistan.

The following day, General Musharraf was released, but not reinstated as president. He did retain his position in the military. Charges were also dropped against A. Q. Khan. Yuri returned to his office. There was absolutely no reason to offer nuclear technology to Pakistan, a country with nuclear bombs that could be conceivably overthrown by Islamic militants, and there was no reason for Russia's scientists to be in Indonesia. He sent Alexander an encrypted e-mail.

Chapter 28
CATCH A SHOOTING STAR

July 12, 2007
Tel Aviv, Israel

Richard Jones, U.S. Ambassador to Israel, just hung up on Secretary of State Condi Rice. Many foreign policy experts, including Ambassador Jones, were asking the very same questions after hearing the news of the Russian-Pakistani nuclear-energy agreement. Why on earth would Russia provide that kind of expertise to Pakistan? Pakistan couldn't even control its own borders, and the country was filled with Islamic fanatics, many in high places. Ambassador Jones was informed that Prime Minister Olmert was on the line.

"I'll take the call. Hello Mr. Prime Minister."

"Richard, good morning, our agent in Iran was able to eavesdrop on an interesting conversation, one I'm certain you would like to hear."

Tehran, Iran

Ali Rafsanjani knocked on the door.

"Come in Ali," Ahmadinejad said. Ali walked in and saw a smile on Mahmoud's face. Ali smiled back.

Rafsanjani said, "The convergence is on. Pakistan has accepted; Russia has accepted. The Russian scientists are in Jakarta and will board the *Shooting Star* this evening."

Bali Hai Resort, Indonesia

"Hi, Brother," said Yatin as he picked up his room phone at the Bali Hai Resort. "Is everything all right up there?"

Hurriedly Sanjay said, "Yatin, can you do me a favor"

"If I can."

"Are the Russians still there?"

"I haven't seen them for two days."

"Can you let us know if they're still there?"

"I'll see if they're still registered here and get back to you."

"Thanks, Yatin." Sanjay hung up.

Chapter 29

THEORIES AND DEDUCTIONS

July 13, 2007
ISS, Space

Sanjay's cell phone rang. "Hello, Yatin."

"Brother, the Russians flew to Jakarta yesterday."

"Can you find out why?" asked Sanjay.

"Probably not. Is this something I should report to our embassy in Bali?" Yatin asked.

"No, we're actually doing a favor for someone in Russia. Let's keep this only to ourselves for right now. I'll keep you informed. Goodbye Yatin." Alexander and Ari were asleep. Sanjay grabbed Alexander's phone, located Yuri's private number, and called him.

"Hello, Alex," answered Yuri.

"Can you speak English please? This is Sanjay calling from the ISS. Alexander is asleep. Your friends in Bali have flown to Jakarta today. That is all we know."

"Thank you, Sanjay."

"How is Alex feeling?"

"Better, but the next two weeks is as good as it's going to get. I'll tell Alexander I spoke with you." Sanjay ended the call, sensing Andre's presence.

Moscow, Russia

Yuri was still holding the cell phone as he was thinking. Finding these Russians in Jakarta, a city of ten million, would be like finding a needle in a haystack. They could be anywhere. A thought came to him. Yes, Jakarta had over ten million people, but he had high-resolution satellite photography at his fingertips. He activated the program, and his monitor screen became his window to the world. Clicking his mouse on Indonesia, and again on Jakarta, he began his search at the first location that came to mind: the Russian Embassy. For forty-five minutes, his eyes were riveted on the embassy, but he noticed no unusual activity. Nickolai walked into his office.

"It's Friday night and time to go. Let's walk to Leone's for Italian." Yuri looked at his watch. It was 6:00 PM.

"Great idea," Yuri said, and he quickly turned off his monitor. It was a balmy July night, and Leone's was only a ten-minute walk from the Kremlin.

"Yuri, did you see any of this coming?"

"See what coming?"

"The nuclear agreement with Pakistan and this Israeli business."

"No," Yuri replied.

"Yuri, I bet you didn't know Putin met secretly with Ali Rafsanjani in Turkmenistan."

"I didn't know."

"Angelina, my assistant, went into the kitchen for a late-night cup of coffee. She saw Rafsanjani leaving through the kitchen."

"Very interesting," Yuri said. They arrived at Leone's and only had to wait a few minutes before being seated.

Jokingly Nickolai said, "Yuri, too bad you and I aren't Jewish. We could emigrate to Israel, find good jobs, phone Putin or Greff, and get a sweet deal to come back to Russia, maybe at twice or three times our current salaries."

"I'm almost positive if we both go back far enough in our lineage, we'll each find at least one Jewish relative." The waiter returned with the drinks, and they placed their orders. Nickolai noticed two attractive women, a blond and a brunette.

"Check this out," said Nickolai. Yuri, nursing his drink, had other things on his mind, like returning to his office as soon as he finished his meal. After dinner, the two friends parted company. Nickolai joined the two women for a nightcap, and Yuri walked back to the Kremlin.

No one was on his floor, except for the cleaning crew. Immediately, Yuri booted up his computer and activated the satellite system; still no activity at the embassy. He clicked his mouse a few more times and beamed down on Jakarta harbor. He surveyed the waterfront, identifying ships in the harbor and looking for unusual activity. He identified a vessel bearing a Swedish identification, a European cruise ship, and two oil tankers from Saudi Arabia. Yuri took out a notepad and began jotting down possible theories about recent events, his eyes still riveted to his monitor.

> Russian missile scientists are in Jakarta to provide assistance to another country or regime with or without the approval of the Russian government.

> Russia has offered nuclear technology to Pakistan. Could this agreement be connected to the Russian scientists in Jakarta?

> Why would Russian scientists operate discreetly in Jakarta for Pakistan? Russia is open with its proposed assistance for Pakistan, and Russian scientists can easily operate within Pakistan.

> If not Pakistan, who are the Russian scientists assisting in Jakarta?

> Pakistan arrested its president and renegade nuclear scientist A. Q. Khan for selling nuclear technology to Iran and then released them.

> Why did Pakistan release them? Why were they arrested in the first place? Every intelligence agency in the world knows that for years Khan, with impunity, sold nuclear technology. Why would he be arrested now? What if it were deeper? What if Khan actually sold a nuclear bomb to Iran? He couldn't do it without Musharraf's knowledge. What if Pakistan got spooked with the UN investigation of Iran and set up Khan and Musharraf to take the fall as part of damage control by Pakistan if the United

Nations discovered Pakistan's complicity. But Pakistan released these two men, suggesting that Iran disposed or returned the nuclear bomb to Pakistan, or the new government of Pakistan permitted Iran to keep the bomb. Yuri had studied the Iranian leader. Ahmadinejad would not willingly give up a nuclear bomb, nor would the ayatollahs.

Rafsanjani met with Putin a few days before the announcement to offer Russian nuclear assistance to Pakistan.

Russia offers Pakistan a bribe, a nuclear-technology agreement similar to the program the United States offered India. Pakistan allows Iran to keep the bomb. What is Russia's payoff?

Russia is trying to recruit Israeli business and lure Israeli Jews to Russia.

Why would Russia be complicit with a nuclear-armed Iran that could use its nuclear bomb or bombs against Israel? Why would Russia wade into such dangerous waters and risk involvement in a future nuclear war between Israel and Iran?

Fatigue began to set in. Yuri thought of returning to Leone's. His eyelids began to close, and he leaned back in his chair. Then, like an epiphany, it hit him, and he continued writing.

Russia wants to hijack the million plus Russian Jews living in Israel to offset an immediate population decline. What Russia wants is for Iran to successfully test a nuclear missile to create an international crisis, creating mass hysteria in Israel and a mass exodus from Israel to Russia. As America once said, "Give me your tired, your poor, your huddled masses….." Russia's message will be "Jews come back and bring your high-tech brains." Tiny Israel could ill afford to be involved in a nuclear exchange with a much larger country in population and land size. Israel would have few military options. A threat of nuclear annihilation could bring another national psychosis to bear upon the Israeli population, in addition to their collective post-traumatic syndrome from the Lebanese war last year. Israel would naturally seek help from an international community that despises it.

Would the Israeli Russian Jews return to Russia? Maybe; no country is going to attack Russia. As Minister Greff said, a shared culture and language is a uniting and compelling force. Russian Jews who return would discover a much freer and capitalistic Russia, no longer communist. On the other hand, a fiscal nightmare of epic proportions could ensue as a consequence of relocating hundreds of thousands of Jews to Russia. Classic inflation when demand exceeds supply. The strain on the Russian economy could be so severe with a Jewish absorption of that magnitude. Russia would need to be bankrolled to provide the needed capital for this massive relocation. Iran has the ability to discreetly fund the billions of dollars Russia would need.

Yuri stopped writing and looked at his watch. He was exhausted. It was 8:35 PM in Moscow, and three hours later in Jakarta. He was looking for proof of an Iranian connection to the Russians in Jakarta.

Using his mouse, he continued his virtual patrol of Jakarta harbor, searching for any kind of movement. Coming into the harbor was an Iranian oil tanker named the *Shahab* or *Shooting Star* (highlight, click, copy, save to documents). The tanker's large italic letters were scripted off the bow in Farsi. Yuri immediately zoomed in for a closer look. For thirty minutes, he focused his attention on the tanker as it stopped and anchored in the harbor. Yuri almost missed the dingy heading toward the starboard side.

A ladder came down from the *Shahab*, and eight of the nine people on the dingy climbed up and onto the ship, then disappeared aboard (highlight, click, copy, save). The one person who remained in the dingy, motored back to the slip (highlight, click, copy, save). Yuri zoomed in. The man was tall and Caucasian and wore dark glasses, a hat and overalls (highlight, click, copy, save). The man secured the dingy, stepped out onto the dock, and sped away in a dark van (highlight, click, copy, save).

Yuri went back to the *Shooting Star*. The Iranian tanker had lifted its anchor and was heading out to sea (highlight, click, copy, save). Yuri had a hunch and zoomed into the Russian Embassy again. His hunch paid off. The dark van that left the port slowly stopped at the embassy's back entrance (highlight, click, copy, save). The man wearing dark glasses and a hat (highlight, click, copy, save) was quickly escorted in. Yuri had found his missing Russian scientists, and they were on the *Shooting Star*.

Promptly, he initiated a search through the World Wide Web for Web sites that track and publish statistical data for commercial sea vessels. Yuri narrowed the search to the *Shooting Star* and brought up its timeline, where the tanker had been and where it was going. Again using the keyboard functions, Yuri copied and saved the information to his documents.

Next Destination: Bushehr, Iran
Arrival: Jakarta, Indonesia, July 12, 2007
Departure: Jakarta, Indonesia, July 12, 2007
Cargo: none
Previous port: Aden, Yemen, July 05, 2007

Next Destination: Jakarta, Indonesia
Arrival: Aden, Yemen, July 05, 2007(unscheduled stop)
Departure: Aden, Yemen, July 06, 2007
Cargo: none
Previous port: Kuala Lumpur, Malaysia, June 28, 2007

Next Destination: Bushehr, Iran
Arrival: Kuala Lumpur, Malaysia, June 28, 2007
Departure: Kuala Lumpur, Malaysia, June 28, 2007
Cargo: unrefined petroleum
Previous Port: Bushehr, Iran, June 23, 2007

On June 28, the *Shooting Star* arrived and unloaded its oil cargo, but instead of returning to Bushehr to refill its empty coffers, the tanker stopped in Yemen for a day and uncharacteristically reversed direction, heading east again to Jakarta without cargo. Tankers don't exactly crisscross the oceans without cargo to deliver. The *Shooting Star* arrived in Jakarta on July 12, long enough to pick up some Russian missile experts and ship out again. Its next destination, according to the itinerary, was a return trip to Bushehr, Iran, and back to Bali, Indonesia. *Why*, Yuri wondered, *would Russian nuclear scientists board this Iranian tanker, and how long would they be on it?*

> Arrival: Bushehr, Iran, July 19, 2007
> Departure: Bushehr, Iran, July, 20, 2007
> Cargo: unrefined petroleum
> Destination: Bali, Indonesia

Long enough to engineer a nuclear bomb to an Iranian missile he concluded. Was it coincidence the name of the tanker was named after the Iranian missile Shahab-3? Yuri thought not. The missile launch pad is concealed in the tanker; the launch and detonation would take place over water and far away from Israel, but Yuri had no idea where or when. Certainly not before Iran withdrew from the NPT and the Russians got off the tanker. The good news was that the *Shooting Star* could be tracked by satellite. The bad news: he was on a slippery slope.

Yuri thought of e-mailing Alexander to warn the Israelis, but to do so would be seditious. There was no denying Yuri was proud he had been chosen to be on Putin's foreign policy team, and proud of Alexander's accomplishments, too. Russia had been kind to him and his family. If he were caught, his mother would lose her deceased husband's pension, and he and, possibly, Alexander, could be imprisoned for years. He continued writing.

> What if Russia and Iran are wrong in their assumptions? Could these miscalculations trigger a nuclear confrontation? Perhaps Israel would lash out with scores of nuclear attacks on Iranian military facilities.

Yuri finally put down his pen. He locked his notes in his desk drawer and shut down his computer. He took the elevator down to the Kremlin garage and drove home.

At home, he quietly went into his room, not wanting to disturb his mother. Yuri wrestled with a troubling thought. The plot he uncovered was all too familiar, mirroring the millennium-old Judeo-Christian eschatology of the "end times" prophesized in the biblical passages he had studied. It was to be a time when God's final judgment is rendered, a final battle when Satan and his armies are destroyed by God as they descend on Israel, the land God promised to the sons of Abraham, Isaac, and Jacob as the prophets dared to say. Like his twin brother, Yuri was an evangelical and shared a view held by millions of other evangelicals: the rebirth of Israel was the greatest miracle of the last millennium, a revelation of God's final plan. Yuri felt despondent. His silence could only aid and abet those who would dismember Israel piece by piece. He turned on his reading light and reached for his Bible on top of his nightstand.

Chapter 30
WE COULD CHANGE THE WORLD

July 14, 2007
Tehran, Iran

Ahmadinejad went to sleep last night reading his Koran, praying he was doing all that was possible to bring on the end times and usher in the return of the lost child Messiah Mahdi, the twelfth Imam. And during the seven years of the Mahdi's return, Israel would cease to exist, and the world would submit to Islam. Ahmadinejad took comfort in preparing himself and his country for that eventuality.

When Ahmadinejad awakened, he opened his curtains to let the sunlight come through and brewed some Turkish coffee before he read some of the world's newspapers. He was in good spirits and anticipated his meeting with Ali Rafsanjani.

Jerusalem, Israel

On this Thursday morning, Ambassador Jones awakened early, showered, and left Tel Aviv at 6:30 AM. Jones drove to the prime minister's residence in Jerusalem in time for coffee and breakfast. The ambassador was hungry. The topic of his discussion with the prime minister, now that the clamor over the Danish cartoon controversy had seemingly waned, was to jump-start the Israeli-Palestinian peace talks, including preparations for dissolving Hamas in the Palestinian government.

Olmert personally greeted the ambassador at the door. They walked to the study and sat down. Breakfast was on the table. The ambassador poured himself some coffee and orange juice, and Mrs. Olmert brought a platter of poached eggs, smoked fish with onions, capers, and spreads with bagels and toast in from the kitchen.

"Ambassador, before we discuss the Palestinians, I believe we have an even more acute problem with Iran. Mossad believes that Iran has at least one nuclear bomb provided by Pakistan."

"Mr. Prime Minister, what is your evidence?"

"Photos and conversations," and Olmert handed over a large envelope containing pictures and a compact disc. The ambassador removed the contents. The first set of pictures was dated June 19, and included pictures of Ambassador Saheed, the Pakistani ambassador to Iran, entering the French restaurant Le Souci in Tehran, with Ali Rafsanjani, former Iranian president and adviser to Ahmadinejad.

"So they like French food," said the ambassador. "What else?"

"Keep the photos, Mr. Ambassador." The prime minister turned on his recorder. "We were able to plant a listening device in Saheed's car and record his conversation on his cellular phone following his meeting with Rafsanjani." Olmert turned on the recorder.

> The Iranian president refuses to understand the gravity of the situation. I don't believe he wants to honor our rights to this agreement. He wants to meet, and if he does not comply promptly, then in the strongest terms, I will threaten to expose the arrangement to the United Nations. Our discomfort will be that of a mere mosquito bite, while Iran will experience the unbearable pain of a thousand scorpion stings.... I'll be sure to use those exact words, good-bye.

The Israeli prime minister handed the ambassador a second group of photos.

"These were taken on July 8. Ali Rafsanjani crossed the border into Turkmenistan and met with Putin late in the evening. We have been tailing Rafsanjani for a while. A few days later, Russia signs a nuclear-energy agreement with Pakistan, confounding intelligence agencies worldwide. From Saheed, there is no more chatter on Iran, no more discussion of Pakistani rights and demands. Now when Saheed talks, it's about food and money, his bank accounts, etc."

"When did Iran acquire this bomb?" asked the ambassador.

"Our best guess is before Ahmadinejad became president. Before the lunatic tried to smuggle chemical weapons into Lebanon, before he threatened Israel with extinction and denied the Holocaust, and before he ran afoul of the NPT. If you look, I bet you'll find a trail of cheap oil to Pakistan."

"Mr. Prime Minister, after Iran's chemical weapons gaffe in Lebanon, do you think Musharraf got spooked, and demanded that Iran give the bomb back to Pakistan?"

"Yes, and deposed himself to neutralize the militant wing of his party that was angry over Khan's arrest. Khan may have been set up to take the fall if and when the new government was prepared to go public."

"And the nuclear-test announcement and troop movement to Kashmir?" Richard inquired.

"All designed to relieve domestic pressure."

"Rafsanjani meets with Putin, who subsequently offers a politically unstable Pakistan a nuclear-assistance program to match the U.S. offer to India. If all this is true, Mr. Prime Minister, what's in it for Putin?"

"We don't have an answer yet."

"Let me know when you do, but until then, the president recommends that you take no unilateral action."

"Would you like some coffee, Mr. Ambassador?" Mrs. Olmert asked from the kitchen.

"Yes, Mrs. Olmert. Thank you." She brought him a fresh cup, and he took three fast sips and looked at his watch.

"Mr. Prime Minister, I think it's time to discuss the Palestinian crisis."

Tehran, Iran

"Ali, come in please. A beautiful morning, isn't it?"

"Yes. Mr. President, the Russians need approximately two weeks to prepare the missile for launch."

"An hour before launch, instruct our ambassador to notify the Secretary of the United Nations that Iran is unilaterally withdrawing from the NPT, and to order the observers to immediately leave Iran.

And be certain that no Russians are on the *Shahab* at the time of launch. Then make the first call to Al Jazeera, then the BBC, then CNN. I don't have to tell you, Ali, your expertise is handling the foreign media."

Chapter 31

TRUST IN PROPHETS

July 15, 2007
Moscow, Russia

Still unable to sleep, Yuri continued reading from his Bible. He had uncovered Putin's plot to aid in the dismemberment of Israel and set into motion the third exile, a coming home of Russia's lost Jews (with their intellectual assets and property) set free by Gorbachev two decades earlier, during the final days of the Soviet Union. Yuri believed in the scriptures, and God's message concerning the Jewish people and Israel was unambiguous. Yuri wondered if Putin had ever read Ezekiel or any part of the Bible.

> Thus says the Lord God: Surely I will take the
> Children of Israel from among the nations, wherever
> They have gone and will gather them from every side
> And bring them into their own land.

Ezekiel 37:21

> Behold, I have set the land before you,
> go in, and possess the land which the
> Lord swore unto your fathers,
> Abraham, Isaac, and Jacob,
> to give unto them and to their seed after them.

Deuteronomy 1:8

> As for Me, behold, My covenant is with you,
> And you shall be a father of many nations. ...
> I will establish my covenant between Me and you
> And your descendants after you in their generations,
> For an everlasting covenant, to be God to you and
> Your descendants after you. Also I give to you and
> Your descendants after you the land in which you are
> A stranger, all the land of Canaan, as an everlasting
> Possession; and I will be their God.

Genesis 17:4, 7–8

These passages affirmed to Yuri that God's covenant with the Jews was eternal, that the promise of the land of Israel was forever. The implications of Israel's rebirth on May 14, 1948, were enormous, especially to its detractors, who could take some solace that Jerusalem was intentionally kept out of the new Jewish state, not withstanding that over 100,000 Jews lived in Jerusalem, more than the number of Muslims and Christians combined.

On May 14, 1948, Jerusalem, the ancestral home of the Jewish people, was designated to be an international city administered by the United Nations. Israel, separated from Jerusalem, was strategically left indefensible and was expected to crumble against the numerically superior armies of Egypt, Syria, and Jordan. Israel prevailed, however, and even captured additional territory, including West Jerusalem. When the fighting stopped, the Jordanians conquered East Jerusalem, sealed shut the Old City—including the Wailing Wall, the remnant of Solomon's Temple, and the Church of the Holy Sepulcher, believed to be the site of the Crucifixion—from Christians and Jews.

The fighting ended with an armistice. Egypt kept the Gaza, and Jordan retained the West Bank, territory the Palestinian Arabs rejected for a state of their own. Jerusalem's de facto status as a divided city did not prompt Christian Europe, the United States, or a United Nations to take concerted action to impose the UN mandate on the Jordanians, not until the conclusion of the lightning Six-Day War in 1967, when the Israeli forces destroyed the combined Jordanian, Egyptian, and Syrian armies and recovered all of Jerusalem, the Golan Heights, Judea and Samaria, and the entire Sinai. For the first time in nearly two thousand years, the Jews reunited Jerusalem as prophesized, and the world took notice. Yuri continued to read.

> I have chosen Jerusalem, that My name
> Might be there.... For now I have chosen and
> Sanctified this house that My name may be
> There forever; and My eyes and My heart
> Will be there perpetually.... In this house and in
> Jerusalem, which I have chosen.... I will put
> My name forever.

2 Chronicles 6:6; 7:16; 33:7

> If I forget you, O Jerusalem
> Let my right hand forget its skill upon the harp.

Psalm 137.5

> May my tongue stick to the roof of my mouth
> If I fail to remember you,
> If I do not make Jerusalem my highest joy.

Psalm 137.6

> Jerusalem will be trampled on by
> Gentiles until the times of the Gentiles are filled

Luke 21:24

The 600,000 Jews in the new state of Israel grew in population to 2.4 million by 1967. During those two decades, they came from war-torn Europe, North Africa, and Egypt. Evicted and dispossessed, they streamed in from Iraq and Iran and from a hostile Soviet Union. Thousands were airlifted from Yemen. They came from the east, west, north, and south.

> Fear not, for I have redeemed you ...
> I am with you:
> I will bring your descendants from the east,
> And gather you from the west;
> I will say to the north, "Give them up"

And to the south, "Do not keep them back"
Bring My sons from afar.
And My daughters from the ends of the earth.
Isaiah 43:1, 5–6

In the 1980s, Yuri was alive to witness the next miracle. The Soviet Union let its Jews go, and a million left, mostly to resettle in Israel. A decade later, thousands of threatened Ethiopian Jews were airlifted to Israel. And even that miracle was foretold.

Again, I will bring you, and you shall be rebuilt ...
Behold, I will bring them from the north country,
And gather them from the ends of the earth,
Among them the blind and the lame,
The woman with child, and the one who labors with child,
Together, a great throng shall return there.
Jeremiah 31:4, 8

I will gather you from the peoples, assemble you
From the countries where you have been scattered,
And I will give you the land of Israel .... I will give them
One heart and I will put a new spirit within them.
Ezekiel 11:17, 19

Yuri contemplated what think tank in 1948 would ever have believed that fledgling Israel would have outlasted the Soviet Union, then second in power only to the United States. Perhaps the Soviet Union's demise was a punishment from God. Yuri recognized he might have a chance to save Russia from God's certain wrath if he could keep his country on the right side of God as it was foretold.

I will gather all nations, and ... enter into judgment
With them on account of My people, My heritage
Israel, whom they scattered among the nations, they
Have also divided up My land.
Joel 312, 14

I will bless those who bless you
And I will curse him who curses you;
And in you all the families of the world will be blessed.
Genesis 12: 3

In the wee hours of Friday morning, July 15, Yuri sent Alexander an encrypted e-mail with photo attachments. The subject line of his e-mail was prefaced "urgent," and attached to that e-mail was an automatic return receipt request to notify the sender when it had been delivered and received. Yuri turned off his laptop and did something he was unable to do previously. He went to sleep.

Chapter 32
RETURN TO SENDER

July 15, 2007
ISS, Space

For two days Andre Dubois had been waiting for a time when the remaining crew members would be asleep at the same time. The moment had arrived, and he decided to avail himself of the opportunity by hacking into Alexander's e-mail, hopefully to uncover the mystery of Bali and the Russians.

Andre guessed correctly that Alexander's password was Ezekiel 3624, because the biblical reference was penciled in out of sequence on the last page of Alexander's Bible. Andre had snooped close enough to Alexander and counted eleven keystrokes at the password prompt. Quietly, Andre entered the user name that all crew members had been assigned, *ISS in space.com,* typed in the biblical password, and gained access. He clicked on Alexander's e-mail account. Andre could barely contain his enthusiasm. An unopened e-mail from Alexander's brother, prefaced "urgent," was a good place to start. His enthusiasm quickly turned to anxiety after he read Yuri's e-mail and saw the attached photos.

Alex.

The missing Russian scientists boarded the Iranian oil tanker the *Shooting Star* in Jakarta, Indonesia, on the evening of July 12. They were transported by a driver at the Russian Embassy in Jakarta. The *Shooting Star* departed later that evening destined for its home port of Bushehr, Iran, and is scheduled to arrive on or about July 19. The arrival date is important, because the *Shooting Star* is a floating missile lab masquerading as an oil tanker crisscrossing the Indian Ocean with Russian and Iranian scientists preparing to fire Iran's first nuclear missile. Review the enclosed itinerary and notice many of the *Shooting Star*'s trips were made with no delivered cargo. Ahmadinejad has kept the tanker out of the Persian Gulf to circumvent any potential naval blockade. The tanker needs to be watched, especially when it leaves Bushehr for Bali.

When Iran plans to launch a nuclear missile I do not know, but probably not before the Russian scientists are removed from the *Shooting Star* to avoid any proof of complicity. If the Russians don't get off at Bushehr, they will probably get off at Bali, but who can be certain? Some background information: Pakistan provided the bomb for Iran, and Russia the nuclear-missile expertise. The purpose in the launch is to mislead the Israelis into believing that Iran has a viable nuclear option. By virtue of its population, land size, strategic military superiority, Iran intends to ratchet up the pressure to attack Israel. At the same time Russia intends to offer financial incentives as part of a generous right of return for Israel's Russian Jews, with hopes that fear of nuclear attack will precipitate a mass exodus of Israel's population to Russia. What does Russia get? Probably billions of untraceable euros from Iran, but what Russia wants is its Jews back, the ones that Soviet Premier Gorbachev allowed to leave, the ones who seeded Israel's high-technology industry. Russia is prepared to offer extremely generous financial incentives to lure back the Jews. As absurd as it sounds, Russia is betting last summer's Hezbollah rocket attacks into Israel and threats of a nuclear attack by Iran will traumatize Israeli citizens.

Who knows what the Israeli response will be? Israel may feel justified in attacking Iran after Iran successfully tests a nuclear missile, considering Iran has threatened to wipe Israel off the map. The Iranians have a different view. They believe the Israelis will seek the help of the international community to contain Iran. Given time and minimal interference, as the North Koreans have proved, the Iranians expect to develop their own nuclear weapons and delivery systems. Russia's non-Muslim population is declining at an alarming rate, and returning Jews represent Russia's only immediate immigrant source to draw upon. Russia hopes to emulate or even surpass the Irish economic miracle; more on that later. Right now you must warn Ari to warn Israel, because to save Israel is also to save Russia.

"I will bless those who bless you and I will curse him who curses you."

Genesis 12:3
Hope you're feeling better
And call me when you can speak freely

Yuri

Chapter 33
ON AND OUT OF LINE

July 15, 2007
Moscow, Russia

Yuri's digital alarm clock awakened him at 6:00 AM. He booted up his laptop and checked his inbox: two unopened e-mails. The first was the receipt request and the second was his brother's reply. Something didn't feel right. Yuri hopped into the shower, hoping the warm water pouring over his head would calm him. After he dried himself, he reread his brother's e-mail. It just didn't sound like Alex.

> Yuri, to speak freely on the ISS regarding this matter will be difficult. I will inform Ari and update you as needed, but we need to be careful. For your safety, please refrain from e-mailing me about this matter. I'm feeling better and hope to be home soon.
>
> Alexander

ISS, Space

After Andre replied, he deleted Yuri's correspondence from Alexander's inbox, but not before he moved the e-mail and attachments to his own inbox. Sanjay had gradually awakened, hearing the sound of keystrokes, not terribly loud but still audible. It was no big deal that Andre was up and working on his laptop; after all, sleep on the ISS was hardly regular for any of the other crew members let alone him. Sanjay tuned out the pitter-patter of typing sounds and reentered the world of sleep.

Dear Father,

I am in a quandary, so I come to you for direction. Enclosed please find an e-mail with photo attachments that has come to my attention. Until I receive further instruction from you, I am the only one on the ISS who has seen or will see this explosive e-mail. A few days ago I became suspicious of activities on the ISS. The author of this e-mail works for the foreign policy team at the Kremlin, and he sent this to his brother. As a young boy, my life was placed in your hands, and through you and the Church, I have received guidance and the blessings of our Lord. I place this e-mail in your hands with the same conviction. I look forward to hearing from you.

Andre

Reims, France

Father Gauthier stayed on his side of the confessional booth until he was certain the last sinner had left the church. He listened for the door to the cathedral to close. Friday afternoon was time for leisure.

He quickly scanned the church, then made his exit out the side door. Mounting his bicycle, and with a knapsack on his back, Father Gauthier proceeded to pedal to his favorite café, only two miles away.

Today was a bit more humid than usual, with threatening clouds above. Rain was okay with Monsignor Gauthier; he enjoyed riding in it. His timing was good, as the Friday lunch crowd at the Café Voila had come and gone, leaving the makings of a quiet and relaxing afternoon. Chai sat him at a table and brought the monsignor his favorite red wine and a basket of baguettes.

"Bonjour, Father. Shall I order you the usual?"

"Oui." The waiter poured a little red wine into the glass, and the monsignor lifted the glass for a quick sniff and taste.

"Magnifique."

"Merci," the waiter replied and immediately left to place his order. The monsignor grabbed a baguette, buttered it, and sampled a bite. It was delicious and fresh. He took a sip of wine and pulled his laptop from his knapsack on the seat next to him. Monsignor Gauthier preferred to check his e-mail first, then play his computer games. Today he was in the mood for chess.

"An e-mail from Andre," he said to Chai.

"How nice. Please give him my best."

"Certainly," and Father Gauthier opened the e-mail. Chai attended to some Americans who were waiting to be seated.

"Bonjour, would you prefer inside or out?" Chai asked.

"Outside, please." Chai sat the couple several tables away from the monsignor. He knew the priest valued his privacy and wasn't particularly fond of Americans. The Moroccan waiter quickly glanced at the monsignor when he finished seating the Americans, and noticed how pale the monsignor had suddenly become. Chai quickly came over to his table.

"Monsignor, are you all right. Did anything happen to Andre?"

"Andre's fine. It's me. Some wine went into my windpipe. I'll be okay in a few minutes. Perhaps you can bring me some water."

The monsignor shut down his laptop and placed a call to the archbishop on his cellular phone. A receptionist answered.

"Hello, this is Monsignor Gauthier of Reims. It is urgent that I speak with the archbishop right away. Is he there?"

"Yes, Monsignor. He is in a meeting with the apostolic nuncio from France and asked not to be disturbed. Shall I interrupt the archbishop?"

"Yes."

"Please hold Monsignor."

"Father Gauthier, so nice to hear from you," said the archbishop.

"Archbishop, I apologize for my interruption. This is a matter so important I would rather not talk on a cellular phone."

"Where are you now Monsignor?"

"I'm at a café in Reims."

"I will wait for you."

"Thank you Archbishop. Goodbye." The monsignor called to his waiter, "Chai, please bag my lunch and call me a cab." In a few minutes, a cab pulled up and Father Gauthier stepped in, holding his lunch bag in one hand and his computer case in the other. The driver put the monsignor's bicycle in the cab trunk.

"To Paris, please."

Chapter 34

THE NIGHT HAS A THOUSAND EYES

July 16, 2007
Jakarta, Indonesia

"Mikhail, so nice to see you again, and thank you for seeing me on such short notice," said Leopoldo, Indonesia's apostolic nuncio. They shook hands outside the ambassador's office at the Russian Embassy in Jakarta.

"I was supposed to be on a jet to Moscow."

"Yes, the weather is indeed a bit bad. Typhoon season is approaching," Leopoldo replied. The two emissaries walked into Mikhail's office.

"Please sit down, Leopoldo." The Vatican emissary was only too happy to oblige. He sat and poured himself a glass of water from the pitcher next to his leather chair. He took a drink then opened up his attaché case and removed a large envelope.

"This is for you Mikhail." The ambassador emptied the contents of reprinted e-mails and satellite photographs.

"What do we have here?" asked Mikhail.

"I would suggest reading the e-mail first," Leopoldo said and remained silent.

"Who sent this? This is ridiculous, nothing more than the ranting of a crazed individual. This has no credibility. How did you come by these, Leopold?"

Bingo, thought the astute Vatican emissary, who had been trained in the nuances of body chemistry and facial expressions. Mikhail was clearly stressed.

"The night has a thousand eyes," the nuncio said. The Russian ambassador stood.

"I have no idea what this is about. It's ridiculous. Even more, it's dangerous. Is there anything else, Leopoldo?"

"No, thank you for seeing me," and Leopoldo rose from his chair and shook the ambassador's hand. "Mikhail, you still might want to check this out."

Mikhail waited for his visitor to leave, then immediately placed a call to his superiors in Moscow and sent off a fax. Like a chain letter that comes full circle—and stops in Paris, Rome, and Jakarta—Yuri's e-mail was back in Moscow, on President Putin's desk. Putin, a former KGB agent, placed a call to internal security. Leopoldo returned to his office and finalized the report of his meeting. He faxed it to the office of the Vatican's top foreign policy official, Archbishop Giovanni Lajolo.

Chapter 35

COME MONDAY

July 18, 2007
Moscow, Russia

"Igor."

"Good morning, Mr. President."

"Place Yuri Kafelnikoff under immediate arrest."

"What shall I charge him with, Mr. President?"

"Let's start with treason. Igor, immediately start to monitor all communication to and from the ISS, including satellite phones. Only nonsensitive and essential e-mails should be allowed to go through. Assign someone good on this." The Russian president hung his phone up on Igor then buzzed his assistant.

"Call Foreign Minister Lavrov. He can be reached at our embassy in Vienna."

Vatican City

The archbishop's cellular phone vibrated softly in his pocket. "Hello, Mr. Lavrov. How is Vienna? Yes of course, Mr. Lavrov. I look forward to your visit."

Moscow, Russia

Yuri made it through the weekend. Saturday he joined his friends for dinner and a movie. On Sunday, he and his mother spent the afternoon at Gorky Park. Today was Monday. Central command confirmed the

130

supply shuttle was scheduled to launch on Thursday and dock at the ISS early Saturday. Its cargo of food, water, and two new astronauts—one American the other Japanese—would be unloaded. After inspections were conducted, it would return with Alexander and Ari.

Both astronauts had received a fair amount of press coverage about their medical problems. Israel requested and received permission from the Russian government to fly in a medical team to attend to Ari when he returned on the shuttle. A potential fly in the ointment was the Pakistani nuclear-test launch scheduled for Tuesday. A launch delay, due to inclement weather or some other reason, would likely ground the shuttle for another few days and delay their medical treatment.

Yuri left his apartment about 6 AM and stopped for breakfast at a McDonald's near the Kremlin. He ordered his usual, an Egg McMuffin, and a cup of coffee. He ate his breakfast while reading the newspaper. He put the paper on the seat and logged onto his laptop and his inbox. There was something about Alex's e-mail that didn't seem right. And then it hit him like a lightning strike. He was jolted when he discovered that e-mail was signed *Alexander*. His brother always signed *Alex*.

ISS, Space

"Hello," said Alexander, his voice faltering.

"Alex, this is Yuri. I have a question about the e-mail you sent me Saturday."

"I didn't send you an e-mail on Saturday." Yuri felt his adrenaline surge while driving his car. He was three blocks from the Kremlin. He pulled into an empty space on the side of the street, turned off the ignition, and locked his doors. He took several deep breaths before resuming the conversation.

"Alex, I sent you an e-mail. Whoever intercepted it did so around 3:00 AM Saturday morning, replied to me, and signed off as Alexander."

"I always sign off 'Alex'."

"I know. It didn't dawn on me for a few days."

"Hold the line, Yuri. Sanjay, please bring my laptop." Ari began to awaken from his slumber after hearing bits and pieces of the conversation. Sanjay handed Alex his laptop. For the moment, Andre had settled into a very deep sleep.

"Is there a problem?" Sanjay asked.

"Sanjay, hold my phone please." Using both hands, Alexander logged onto his laptop. There was a new message in his inbox. He opened it. It was a return receipt. Sanjay handed him his phone.

"Yuri, all I have is your return receipt in my inbox on Friday at 6:05 AM." Suddenly, the signal was lost, and the line went dead, not an uncommon occurrence in space. Alexander tried, but was unable to reestablish the connection.

"There might be a weather disruption out there," Sanjay said. "Yuri will call back. I'll check for weather-alert bulletins in the meantime."

"Do we have a problem?" Ari asked.

"Friday evening Yuri sent me an e-mail that was intercepted, replied to, and deleted from my computer. Unfortunately, I don't even know what the original e-mail was about. Yuri didn't get a chance to tell me."

"I remember briefly waking up Friday around 3.00 AM. Andre was on the computer then."

"Before we start accusing Andre, let's do a search of your hard drive. Maybe we can recover that e-mail," Sanjay said excitedly. "I can install the software in about fifteen minutes."

While they anxiously awaited the results, Andre slept. "Bingo! Two deleted e-mails have been recovered, but forwarded to another Web domain, one registered to Andre Dubois. Now we can start accusing." Sanjay handed the laptop to Alexander.

"Yuri explains why the Russians are in Jakarta. Ari, Sanjay, take a look at this e-mail and attachment."

"I have to inform my government immediately," Ari insisted.

"Wait, a new e-mail in my inbox," Alexander said. "It's from Nickolai, Yuri's friend in the Kremlin." He opened it. "Yuri's been arrested by internal security. He asked me not to reply; it's too dangerous. Sanjay, are the phones working?"

"No."

"Our communications may be compromised. Ari, hold off on that e-mail to your government. We need to find out what Andre's part in this caper was."

Sanjay went to the medical supply cabinet and took out a new syringe. He opened a bottle of clear Valium, inserted the needle into the Valium, and drew out some of the drug. He shot a few drops out to clear the air bubbles from the syringe. Sanjay approached Andre and gently squeezed his arm. Startled, Andre opened his eyes.

"We know you hacked into my computer. We recovered Yuri's e-mail on the hard drive, and your footprint. Who did you send the e-mail to?" Alexander demanded.

"I don't know what you are talking about."

"Andre, my brother has been arrested by Russian authorities. I'm almost certain we'll be monitored. Our phones are down. You need to tell us what you know." Sanjay applied a little more pressure on Andre's arm. Andre thought if he could only get out of his sleeping bag, he could overpower the slight Indian.

"Tell us, Andre," Alexander demanded. "Who did you send this too?"

"I sent it to my priest. I suspected something. Russian scientists were in Bali, and nobody was telling me anything. So I snooped."

"Not only are you a thief, but you had a responsibility to inform Ari of this hideous plot."

"I owe Ari nothing, and Israel less. Israel killed my father, at Osirak, in the bombing raid." There was momentary silence.

Finally, Ari responded, "If your father was the French engineer who died, I am truly sorry. Andre, your father wasn't even supposed to be in the reactor that Sunday; no one else was. He was the only casualty of the raid."

"Ari, it only takes one dead father to make an orphan."

"That must have been tragic for you then. Still, it doesn't excuse your behavior, Andre," Alexander said. "I would like to read what you sent to your priest. What is your password?"

"What's between me and my priest is my business only." Andre felt a prick on his arm. "What are you doing?" Andre glared at Sanjay.

"I'm giving you a little tranquilizer to make you less combative. If you don't reveal your password, you'll continue to receive more until your muscles atrophy." A few minutes passed, and Sanjay put him in handcuffs. Finally, the Frenchman relented and gave Sanjay his password.

Stephen Lewis
While Sanjay was logging on, Andre said. "I e-mailed my priest, because I wanted him to tell me what to do. He wouldn't tell anybody. What's between a priest and his confessor is private."

"I found it," Sanjay said.

"Did he reply?" Andre asked.

"Not yet."

"He will," Andre said.

"I just received a wire from ground control," Sanjay said. "Until further notice, all cellular satellite communication has been disrupted, probable cause, weather disruption working on a fix, estimated time to repair, unknown."

Vatican City

It was late afternoon when the Russian foreign minister's jet landed on a private landing strip in Rome. He was met by an aide to the archbishop and driven the short distance to Vatican City. The Swiss Guards opened the gate, and Mr. Lavrov stepped out of the car.

"Welcome to the Vatican," said the archbishop, and he held his hand out to extend his greeting.

"Thank you," the minister replied and shook his hand. "This is my first trip here."

"Shall we walk privately?" the archbishop suggested. "After dinner we have planned for you a private tour of the Sistine Chapel. This way, Mr. Lavrov, to my office." Once inside, Lavrov sat on a leather upholstered chair and poured himself a glass of water from a pitcher on a silver tray. Giovanni Lajolo sat across from him in what appeared to be a handcrafted leather-stitched chair. On the walls were beautiful paintings of the ages, depicting Jesus, Mary, and the Apostles. Silk draperies lined the window panes that stood guard over St. Peter's Square.

"Archbishop Lajolo," the minister began, "I want to assure you that this renegade at the Kremlin has been held to account for his improper conduct. I need your assurance that this e-mail and attachments will remain within the confines of the Vatican."

134

"You have my assurance, Mr. Lavrov, as long as there is no truth to what this so called 'renegade' purports. It is rather diabolical." Lavrov remained silent for a few moments and leaned forward in his chair.

"Archbishop, what is true is that Russia has leverage with Iran. President Putin believes that Iran will act more responsibly if it no longer fears a preemptive attack from Israel or a 'coalition of the willing.'"

"Mr. Lavrov, if the e-mail is true, Russia is providing technicians to construct a nuclear warhead provided by Pakistan for an Iranian missile, to be launched from an Iranian oil tanker. The world will falsely believe that Iran has joined the ranks of the other nuclear powers."

"Perception is reality," the minister responded, sensing his arguments were falling on unsympathetic ears.

"And what of the Jews?"

"Two decades ago, when the Soviet Union was in a freefall, Premier Gorbachev permitted nearly a million Soviet Jews to emigrate to Israel. Russia, like much of Christian Europe, is experiencing a population decline. Russia, as you know, is an entrepreneurial country now, very capitalistic. Russian Jews have made Israel a technological powerhouse, the Silicon Valley of the Middle East. Russia needs those Jews to inspire economic and population growth; one follows the other."

"So the one arrested for treason was right. Let's be honest, Mr. Lavrov. Had the Soviet Union been decent to its Jews, they would have stayed."

"It's true. The Jews were treated badly under the czars, worse in Europe, the Spanish Inquisition, and the German death camps. Perhaps your Church could have done more to save Europe's Jews."

"We should have, and we have apologized. The Vatican's Second Council in 1965 was a start to eliminating anti-Semitism from all of the Church."

"True, but in doing so, the Church has weakened itself in the process."

"Explain," insisted the archbishop, rather disdainfully, from the man who was reared in atheism.

"There are always those who resist change to centuries-held dogma. Many of your faithful still believe that the Jews should forever carry the burden for their treachery against our Lord. How can Christians be the new people of God, led by the Vatican in the new city of God, when many Christians believe that Bible prophesy revealed itself with the resurrection of the Jewish state and the return of the original people of God to their ancestral home and their ancestral capital Jerusalem, the original city of God? Archbishop, for nearly two thousand years your Church claimed there was only one city of God; now you have to explain there are two."

"Mr. Lavrov, in 1948 there were hundreds of thousands of displaced Jews, mostly concentration camp survivors. British Palestine was the only place for them to go. Jerusalem was not part of the nascent Jewish state. You may remember in 1948, the United Nations designated Jerusalem to be an international city it would administer. Unfortunately, the Arabs initiated a war and lost West Jerusalem to the Jews. We never thought the Jews would grab any part of Jerusalem, let alone survive the assault, but they prevailed."

"And now all of Jerusalem is under Jewish control," responded Lavrov.

"You act as if this is the Vatican's fault. Jerusalem is open to all faiths now," responded the archbishop.

"You miss my point. Everything your Church has done to keep Jerusalem out Jewish hands has failed. In 1948, the Vatican should have protested the illegal Jordanian occupation of East Jerusalem."

"The Jordanians would not have left East Jerusalem, and the Israelis would not have left West Jerusalem. Your country was on the Security Council. The United Nations had a legal mandate to force both countries out of Jerusalem. Look, Mr. Lavrov, the Vatican has tried to marginalize the Jewish impact on Jerusalem. Ever since 1994, we recognized both Israel and the PLO. We almost succeeded in making East Jerusalem the capital of a new Palestinian state, but Arafat walked away. The Vatican does not enjoy competing with Jerusalem, or being tweaked by fundamentalist Christians who are devoted to an exclusively Jewish Jerusalem. Why do you think virtually all embassies are located in Tel Aviv, Mr. Lavrov?"

"To render Jerusalem's status unresolved," responded Lavrov.

"It's the best that we can do," the archbishop answered.

"Archbishop, the Vatican is in a zero-sum game with the Jews. You can't win when they win. Their victories are your losses. Do you realize that in 1948 Israel only had 600,000 Jews, and now they have over

5,000,000. It is likely to get hundreds of thousands more from France in the next decade. France, as you know, is rife with anti-Semitism, especially from their Muslims. All biblically predicted and proven, if you ask the world's evangelicals. The Jews and the evangelicals have their miracle in Israel. Where is your miracle, Archbishop?"

"Mr. Lavrov, our Church is doing very well, especially in Eastern Europe."

"But Western European Catholics are drifting away, embracing secularism, gay marriage, and abortion rights. Church attendance is abysmal. You are becoming insignificant, and eventually that trend will find its way in Eastern Europe," responded the Russian minister.

"And Israel is to blame for nonobservant Catholics?" mocked the archbishop.

"No, the Second Vatican Council is. Your miracle is within your grasp: take back your flock and reinstate Vatican City as God's only city."

"You are suggesting that Israel be destroyed."

"Dismantled as a Jewish state, and in the process, Russia intends to offer refuge and save Israel's Jews. If our plan is successful, Israeli Jews will emigrate by the thousands. The United Nations will take notice. As Israelis leave, Russia will invoke the Palestinian 'right of return.' Israel will not be able to hold onto its Jewish majority.

"Mr. Lavrov, are you discounting the possibility that Israel will strike Iran after its launch?"

"Israel won't, for the same reason Russia never attacked the United States, China, or Europe. Countries that have or are perceived to have nuclear weapons are not attacked by other countries. North Korea is another example."

"Israel is perceived to have nuclear weapons. If what you say is true, why should Israel fear Iran?

"Because Israel is a tiny country and because its enemies are Muslims. Muslims embrace death and martyrdom. I promise you that Russia will contain Iran's nuclear ambitions during this deflation of Israel. Russia considers Israel's Jews to be its future. For the remaining Jews, they can be part of a tri-national state consisting of Jews, Christians, and Muslims. Jerusalem will again be designated an international city under the auspices of the United Nations, and UN troops will be deployed at the borders. For over nineteen hundred years this land was called Palestine. Let it be known as Palestine again. Archbishop, help us to reclaim your miracle."

The archbishop studied the Russian foreign minister. "Mr. Lavrov, do you really think that you can pull this off? Surely you have considered the possibility that your plan may come unhinged, that the Mossad or CIA will uncover it."

"There is always that risk. And you could expose us, but then your Church wouldn't receive all the confiscated Catholic property that is now in the hands of the Russian church."

"The property we lost to the communists?" exclaimed the archbishop. The Russian minister presented a document of property transfer to the Vatican. The archbishop was euphoric, but not for long. True, the offer was nothing short of magnanimous, signed not only by the Russian secular leaders but by the Russian Orthodox patriarch himself. But it came with a steep price as the details were revealed. The transfer of title would happen only after the successful launch of the Iranian nuclear missile. There would also be a human cost exacted that tore at the archbishop's conscience; Moscow planned to destroy the ISS and all its crew members as part of its containment policy. Although Lavrov regretted having to destroy the ISS and its crew, any evidence that could implicate either the Vatican or the Kremlin had to be eliminated.

"We've isolated the ISS, allowing no phone communications and carefully controlling their outgoing and incoming e-mail."

"Andre the Frenchman was orphaned by the Israeli bomb strike in Baghdad and grew up under Father Gauthier's tutelage. Can't you make an exception for him?"

"We can make an exception for them all. We have a submarine trailing that tanker. It is in your power to enjoin us to remove the nuclear weapon and the scientists to the submarine. Just say no, and the author of the e-mail will be released from prison and charged only with unlawful correspondence. The charges will be dropped to avoid publicity. The worst thing to happen would be a spawning of conspiracy theories. It's your choice, archbishop. Save them and forfeit your properties in Eastern Europe."

"How will you destroy the ISS?"

"An explosion in space, and they will feel no pain. It will look like an accident."

The archbishop was suddenly alerted by the sound of bells ringing. Dinner was being served in the Vatican dining room. He looked at his watch.

"Dinner is ready. Unfortunately his holiness will not be in attendance, but in his place will be the Vatican secretary of state, the archbishop of Paris, and myself."

After dinner, Lavrov was escorted for his private tour of the Sistine Chapel. The archbishop and the secretary of state went to private quarters to discuss the Russian minister's proposal. When the Russian returned, he received the answer he was expecting. Letters of intent were executed and exchanged.

"Archbishop, I understand that Monsignor Gauthier is very close to Andre, and that is naturally of some concern to us."

"Mr. Lavrov, I assure you that you have nothing to worry about from Monsignor Gauthier. I will take care of this. You have my word." The archbishop and the other Vatican officials waved goodbye to Sergey Lavrov as he sped away from the Vatican.

Chapter 36

THE BEGINNING OF THE END

July 19, 2007
Cathedral at Reims, France

The Vatican wasted no time. Hot off the presses in today's bulletin of the Holy See offices was the following announcement:

> The Russian government and the Russian Orthodox Church have agreed in principle to restore to the Roman Church all former dispossessed Vatican properties confiscated by the previous communist regime in Romania and other parts of Eastern Europe.

Sergey Lavrov called the archbishop and strongly protested. Not mincing words, the Russian foreign minister reminded the archbishop that the unauthorized release of the announcement violated the terms of the agreement. Archbishop Lajolo apologized profusely and accepted blame for the timing of the press release. He promised to publish a revised bulletin immediately, recanting any notice of previous agreements.

Father Gauthier read the announcement. The great news was troubling to him in light of the strange confession by the Archbishop of Paris just hours earlier. He recalled vividly the archbishop's very words:

Let us pray for the brave souls who are sometimes sacrificed for the greater good

I hope you will forgive me, too.

He deciphered the hidden meaning. The "greater good" had to do with serving the needs of the Church, and "those brave souls to be sacrificed" were none other than Andre and his crewmates, perhaps even himself, in exchange for silence and property rights. Tears began to fall down his face. How he disdained this unholy conspiracy between his Church and Russia. For two days he had tried to e-mail Andre to warn the French authorities, but each time he received a notice of nondelivery. Unable to reach Andre by phone, Father Gauthier suspected foul play.

Father Gauthier threw caution to the wind and called a taxi to meet him at the Café Voila at 8 AM for the long ride to the Israeli Embassy in Paris. They might be the only ones who would believe him. If they did, there was still time to save Andre and the others. He left the church, mounted his bicycle, and began peddling. The sun had just come up when he approached the Café Voila. He had not slept, and he looked rather disheveled as he dismounted and parked his bicycle in front of the café.

"Good morning, Father," said Chai. You're early today. Coffee?"

"Yes, Chai, and an orange please. I'll sit inside today."

"Of course, Father," said the Moroccan waiter, and the monsignor took a table by a window. Chai returned with a cup of black coffee, hot and steamy. The priest took a sip. It was good and fresh, and the caffeine worked its magic from his head to toe. Feeling more relaxed, he unzipped his windbreaker and placed it on the chair where there was a newspaper. The monsignor took the paper and scanned the headlines. He had thirty minutes to finish his breakfast. His cellular phone rang.

"Hello," he listened for a few moments. "I'll be waiting."

The black limousine displaying the Vatican flag pulled in front of the café, its engine still running. A tinted window on the passenger side partially opened.

"Chai, check, please." Father Gauthier left his chair and walked to the vehicle. He peered in.

141

"Good morning to you, Archbishop Clement and to you, Archbishop Lajolo."

"Please join us," said the Vatican's foreign policy adviser, "and don't forget to collect your personal belongings. You can pack your bicycle in our trunk."

"Of course," responded the monsignor. He quickly returned to gather his attaché case and laptop.

"See you tomorrow, and Father, don't forget your windbreaker on the chair under the newspapers."

"You keep it, Chai. I have outgrown it. Please apologize to the taxi driver. Au revoir." The young Moroccan watched the monsignor fold up his bike and enter the limousine before it sped away.

"Monsignor Gauthier," said Lajolo, "in this life, sacrifices sometimes have to be made. We are concerned with your attachment to the boy Andre, so your archbishop has decided to reassign you to a Franciscan monastery in Bolivia. You will receive additional details on your flight. Your plane leaves Paris tonight. All your personal belongings have been packed, and you will no longer have need for a laptop, phone, or attaché case." The archbishop handed the monsignor an airline ticket, "Monsignor Gauthier, your ticket to La Paz."

"Am I a prisoner?" asked the monsignor.

"Of course not. You are free to go, but we are being shadowed by some despicable people who would gladly do you bodily harm. We have some time before your flight. Perhaps you'd like to pray with us somewhere in Paris," Archbishop Lajolo suggested.

"As long as we are going to Paris, I would like to visit the Basilica Le Sacre Coeur."

"Montmartre," said Lajolo, "is an excellent choice, the most scenic part of Paris."

The Vatican driver looked into his rearview mirror before pulling out. A taxi was waiting for his space. The Vatican car slowly pulled out as the taxi pulled in. Chai delivered the message.

"Pardon Monsieur, the gentleman waiting for you wanted me to offer his apology. He is a priest, and while waiting he was called away and left in a Vatican car.

The taxi driver shook his head and said, "That's too bad. It isn't every day a Tunisian Jewish cab driver gets to take a Catholic priest to the Israeli Embassy in Paris."

"I'm a Moroccan Jew. Come into the café and have breakfast on me."

"Thank you. A cup of espresso sounds good."

Paris, France

It was a three-hour trip. They arrived at the village of Montmartre, located 130 meters above the city of Paris. The Basilica Le Sacre Coeur was perched high above the city. Its main attraction, the bronze equestrian statue of Joan of Arc, still remained defiant and impervious to the scores of visitors who were snapping pictures of her. July brought visitors and tourists from everywhere. The three clergymen exited the vehicle. As they made their way to the front steps of the basilica, they caught the attention of a television cameraman conducting a photo shoot outside the famous basilica. The photographer noticed the two archbishops donning colorful attire, and a clergyman with a collar. Slowly, he followed them to the steps of the church, his camera rolling. The rest of the crew followed and briefly surrounded them.

"No pictures, please," said Giovanni, but it was too late. As the lights flashed briefly blinding the archbishops, the monsignor immediately began a sprint to the medieval stone fence at the edge of the property. He climbed the stones and leaned against a protective iron railing. Beyond was the Paris skyline, and below a thirty-meter precipice of jagged rocks, twigs, and stone. Quickly balancing himself on top of the railing as if he were a diver preparing a back flip, Monsignor Gauthier faced the archbishops hot in pursuit. He extended his hands as if he were on his own cross. The monsignor threw himself backward off the cliff and landed head-first onto the rocks below, severing his spine and breaking his neck. He was pronounced dead at the scene.

Arriving too late to stop the monsignor from plunging, Archbishop Lajolo pulled out his cellular phone and called his office to report the event. Immediately the television crew swarmed around him and Archbishop Clement. A microphone in one hand, one cameraman began to ask them questions.

"No comment," Archbishop Lajolo said as they tried to make their way to the limousine. Unfortunately for them, the police arrived and prevented their escape. Archbishop Clement relented and told reporters, "Father Gauthier was suffering from severe depression. Unfortunately we didn't realize how bad his condition was."

"Archbishop, for a priest to commit suicide, a sin against the Church in front of the basilica, was he mocking the Church?"

"Anything is possible when one is depressed."

"Did you hear what the monsignor was saying as he ran away?" asked the cameraman.

"I didn't hear him say anything," replied Archbishop Clement.

"I understand he was a priest at the Cathedral at Reims."

"Yes," replied Clement. "No more questions please. Can't you see we're very upset?" And he left. The cameraman Jacques transformed himself into a news reporter and gave his camera to his colleague. The networks and the cable shows would pay big bucks for the interview and the wrap up. The signal was given to start the camera rolling, and Jacques began his coverage of the event.

> We have just witnessed a priest commit suicide in front of the famous Basilica Sacre de Coeur in the village of Montmartre. The priest was Father Gauthier from the Cathedral at Reims. He was visiting the basilica today with the Archbishop of Paris Clement and the Archbishop Giovanni Lajolo, the Vatican's top foreign policy adviser. A few minutes ago, the television crew began filming the Church officials as they walked to the basilica. Inexplicably, Father Gauthier broke ranks and ran to the stone fence. The priest climbed to the top of the iron railing embedded in the stone, turned to face us, and slowly raised his arms as if he were attached to a cross. Then he fell backward to a certain death. Stay tuned for updates. This is Jacques Giroux reporting from Channel 159. Au revoir.

In just minutes, the wire services were all over the story. Film footage depicting the suicide was shown on television screens every hour on the hour. The "story of the day" was also featured on the Web.

This is William Bachelor reporting for the BBC with Jacques Giroux. Jacques, you were at the scene when the suicide occurred. What did you think was happening when the priest, Monsignor Gauthier, climbed onto the stone barrier?

I thought he wanted to look at the Eiffel Tower.

One of your sound videos shows the archbishops running after the priest yelling stop. What did you make of that?

I don't know. It's weird. From the outset, the archbishops appeared to be uncomfortable with our presence.

Thank you, Jacques. The Vatican's office reported to us that Monsignor Gauthier was suffering from depression, but they offered no further comment. The police are investigating. This has been a presentation from the BBC. Stay tuned to your local news at the top of the hour.

Moscow Command Center

"Yes, I have seen the footage," said Igor, yelling into his cellular. We are doing everything technically that we can to block all satellite relays to the ISS. The problem is there are too many satellites with too many network signals."

Only minutes before he heard this news, Igor, pretending to be Father Gauthier, responded to Andre's e-mail. Unfortunately for Igor, Father Gauthier had been dead two hours before Igor hit the computer send button. He cursed himself on his bad timing and rotten luck.

ISS, Space

The effects of the Valium began to wane.

"Sanjay, how long do you intend to keep me under house arrest? Have you forgotten the shuttle will be docking in a few days?" Sanjay unlocked the cuffs on Andre and removed them. A news flash from CNN's interactive Web site caught his eye.

"Alexander, Ari, look at the monitor," Sanjay yelled. "And turn up the volume."

> This is CNN reporting at the Basilica Sacre Coeur. At 1:17 PM, a priest committed suicide by throwing himself backward over the precipice of a thirty-meter drop. His name was Father Gauthier from Reims. The monsignor had just arrived in a Vatican car with the eminent Archbishop Dominique Clement of Paris and Giovanni Lajolo, the Vatican's top foreign policy official. They approached the steps of the basilica, when a local television crew actually filmed the suicide. The archbishop of Paris said that the monsignor had been depressed.

> A new development has come to our attention. Inside Father Gauthier's coat was an airline ticket to La Paz, Bolivia. He was departing this evening. Apparently, the archbishops had planned to accompany the monsignor to the airport. CNN discovered the trip plans were made only today through the Vatican's travel agency. Police are still investigating. And now a short commercial break.

Trying to contain his tears, Andre said, "This is unbelievable. Suicide is against everything Father Gauthier stood for. Why would he deny himself salvation?"

"Andre," Sanjay still controlled the laptop. "You've got an e-mail, a reply from Father Gauthier."

"I told you he'd reply. What did he say?"

"Father Gauthier asked for Andre's permission to inform his superiors," Sanjay said.

"CNN reported Father Gauthier died two hours ago. When was this e-mail time stamped?" Ari asked.

"Thirty-five minutes ago," Sanjay replied. "Dead men don't send e-mails."

"Listen," Ari interrupted.

> Police have discovered that Father Gauthier was on route to La Paz, Bolivia. The reservations were one way and booked

by the Vatican travel agency, strongly suggesting he was being transferred. A Vatican spokesman said that the monsignor was looking forward to his new role in South America.

"Father Gauthier never mentioned he was leaving France. I would have known," Andre insisted.

Stay tuned for more on this suicide. In other Vatican news, in a press release issued today, an agreement was reached between the Eastern Church, the Russian government, and the Vatican to return to the Vatican all Vatican properties that were confiscated under the previous communist regimes. John Blair, reporting from CNN International.

"I think we can figure this out, Andre," Ari said. "Someone in the Church gained access to Yuri's e-mail, brought it to the attention of the Russian government, a deal was struck—property for silence. The fallout led to Yuri's arrest, and to Father Gauthier's immediate transfer and likely disappearance in Bolivia. Because he couldn't warn Andre by phone or e-mail, he decided to commit a suicide that would be captured on film and shown on the Internet. He knew the Russians wouldn't have time to block the story on the Internet. We have to get off the ISS, or we're all going to be killed. It's easier to kill us all, especially if they make it look like a space accident."

"The shuttle," Sanjay said.

"It's probably wired to explode when it docks at the ISS," Ari said.

"Ari's right," Alexander said. "We have no choice but to leave."

"Alexander, I am sorry. Ari, Sanjay. I've put our lives in danger. Father Gauthier is dead ... and maybe your brother, Yuri. This is my fault."

"Andre, I have to believe there is a chance we can save Yuri. We can't bring back Father Gauthier, but we can make sure he didn't die in vain."

"We haven't given the Russians any reason to suspect that we know their game," Sanjay said. "Andre, can you check the heat-resistant tiles on the escape capsule? I'll work on the coordinates and a place to land the capsule."

Moscow Command Center

Igor was pacing the floor of the windowless tech center. His cell phone rang.

"Hello, Boris. We didn't have time to block the network news. Of course, they know he died. The Frenchman is already receiving e-mails of condolences from his friends at the academy. I let those e-mails through because I don't want to arouse suspicion. He hasn't replied to any yet. Andre may know that Yuri was arrested … and now that his priest has died, he may be suspicious. He may have told the others about the e-mail. He may have even figured out that his priest couldn't have sent the last e-mail because he was already dead. We'll be monitoring them very carefully, Boris. Goodbye."

Igor took a puff from his cigarette and exhaled. Only three more days until the supply ship was scheduled to arrive at the ISS docking station. An explosive device embedded in the wall of the visiting shuttle was set to explode when the shuttle locked into the station, blowing up the shuttle and the ISS. There was always the risk the shuttle lift would be delayed due to inclement weather, or by a delay in the Pakistani nuclear-missile launch scheduled for tomorrow.

"Igor," Ivan said, "a new e-mail is coming from the ISS. It's from the Israeli to his wife." Igor walked over to Ivan's computer station.

Dearest Rachel,

I am so looking forward to seeing you and the children. Is the baby kicking? The supply ship is scheduled to dock on Friday and depart on Saturday for Russia? You may have heard about the French priest who committed suicide on national television. He was Andre's priest, and they were very close. He is grieving, but he doesn't want to talk much about it. Most of the time I am bedridden, but occasionally I have spurts of energy.

I've been listening to Sanjay's mp3 player. I would like to suggest that your father finally replace some of the Sinatra,

Tony Bennett, and Dean Martin recordings on his jukebox and replace them with these songs....

I'm sorry I can't call for David's birthday party tomorrow. The phones are still down. And Rachel, if for some reason I don't make it back to earth, please scatter my ashes in the Negev. See you soon in Shdema.

Love,
Ari

"Jumpin' Jack Flash, it's a gas, gas, gas. Ivan, did I ever tell you I saw the Stones perform in Moscow in 1998. They were great."

"Should I send this through?" Ivan asked.

"Absolutely. The Israeli and I like some of the same music. It's harmless. Send it through."

Chapter 37
TO THE PROMISED LAND

July 20, 2007
ISS, Space

It was just after midnight. "Thank you Big Brother," Ari said sarcastically. He had been on pins and needles since sending his e-mail to Rachel, hoping the Russians would let it through. And they did allow it through, as well as her reply. From Rachel's response, Ari knew she understood. He was confident she would alert her father, Meir, who would alert Israeli intelligence. If anyone could decipher the meaning of his song titles, it was the Mossad.

Dear Ari,

The kids and I are so excited to see you. My pregnancy is going well. What ever it takes we will get you better. Meir is making his best chicken soup for you, and you know that heals everything. I presented to him your song list. Dad won't budge on Sinatra, but he is at least open to the idea of updating his jukebox music collection. He suggests you burn a CD of those songs, and he will listen to them on your return to Shdema.

Love, Rachel

Moscow Command Center

It was 2 AM. Ivan had just poured himself another cup of black coffee and slouched into his swivel chair. Only one hour to go before he was relieved. Ivan was receiving satellite feeds into monitors from the ISS, 24/7.

"Igor, the Frenchman is outside performing unscheduled maintenance on the escape capsule." Ivan observed Andre's slow-motion movements as the Frenchman checked the heat shields. Igor, also watching, lit up a cigarette and inhaled deeply before exhaling.

"Igor, a wire from the control center, sent by the ISS."

Attention Command Center,

The ISS has been hit by space junk that punctured a hole nearly three centimeters wide ... systems on board are unstable ... in our space suits until normal systems are restored ... man outside trying to fix the problem.

Sanjay

"Ivan, my gut feeling is they're planning to ditch the ISS and escape on the emergency capsule."

"The escape capsule is programmed to take them to Russia," Ivan noted.

"They can easily disengage the program and land the capsule elsewhere."

"Where would they go, Igor?"

"Bring up the Israeli's e-mail Ivan." Where the hell is Shdema?" Ivan quickly used his search engine.

"Shdema is a missile range in southern Israel." Enraged, Igor threw his cigarette on the floor and uttered a few profanities. From his chair, Ivan quickly extended his foot to put out the burning cigarette.

"Could the music titles be some kind of code," Ivan said. "Should we alert Boris?"

"Not yet, Igor. Check out the music titles on your search engine. Let's watch the situation before we get Boris upset." Igor knew that

Boris would most certainly demote him if the Israeli's e-mail was a coded message. It was only 3 AM. There was time to think and observe. Igor lit another cigarette, his eyes riveted on the monitors.

Igor's head began to throb, the beginning of another migraine. He quickly popped two aspirin from a bottle nearby and closed his eyes for a few minutes. He fell asleep, but only briefly.

"Igor, these musical titles are definitely sequential. 'I'll be Watching You,' 'Sea Cruise,' 'When the Rain Comes.' Did you know the letters in rain can spell Iran, when Iran comes? There's 'What's Your Name.' 'When You Wish' is incomplete without 'Upon a Star.' Maui Hai, no such title, but there is a 'Bali Hai,' a song called 'Rocket Man' and 'Help,' and 'New Kid in Town.' Do you think you should call Boris?"

"No, this could all be circumstantial." Igor was lying to himself, and Ivan knew it, too.

Jerusalem, Israel

It was 4:00 AM when Mossad agents Shimon Levi and Ariel Garon arrived at the prime minister's home. The process that led to this meeting began a few hours earlier, when Rachel called her father, who in turn called Shimon Levi.

"Good evening Mr. Prime Minister."

"Good evening. What do you have?"

"Coded information from an e-mail sent by Ari Ben Ora," Shimon replied.

"Ari Ben Ora is scheduled to land in Russia on Friday. We're sending a medical team to fly him back," the prime minister said.

"I think he'll be leaving before then, Mr. Prime Minister, with the rest of the crew. I think they believe their lives are in danger."

"From what?" the prime minister asked.

"The Russians. For three days the ISS has had no phone service. Ari obviously believes his e-mail has been compromised, and that's why he responded in code."

"Show me his e-mail."

"Ari's use of a question mark at the end of the first sentence casts doubt that he will be returning Friday. His son David does not have a birthday today, and as you know ...."

"Jews don't scatter their ashes in the Negev," the prime minister interjected. "They plan to land the capsule in Shdema."

"Yes, Mr. Prime Minister, but their window of opportunity is narrow. Scheduled for tomorrow at 10:00 AM is the Pakistani nuclear-missile test. We believe Ari and the others can avoid the launch by at least two hours—if they leave no later than 6:00 AM."

"They could leave on Thursday," the prime minister noted.

"Mr. Prime Minister, we think they created an incident that compromised the life-support systems on the ISS. The Israeli Space Agency earlier affirmed via satellite communication a sudden loss of atmospheric pressure on the ISS. That means they're wearing their space suits. We think they're ready to leave on the escape capsule," Shimon responded.

"Mr. Prime Minister," Ariel said, "we have to consider the possibility that Ari and the others could perish on the descent. Therefore, we should pay particular attention to the rest of the e-mail. Arnold's Deli doesn't have a jukebox, never did. We believe the song titles reveal a sequential message. The first title is 'Every Breath You Take' and is followed by the lyrics 'every move you make, I'll be watching you.' We believe the message indicates the ISS is being watched. The second song title 'When the Rain Comes' is from a popular lyric from the popular song 'Rain' and is code for 'when I-ran comes.' The third title, 'Sea Cruise,' suggests a connection with the sea, and the fourth is 'Jumpin' Jack Flash it's a gas, gas, gas' suggests a link to petroleum. The next listed, Maui Hai, is code for 'Bali Hai,' from the movie *South Pacific*."

"A Russian connection to Iran and sea and Bali and petroleum. What do you make of that?" the prime minister queried.

"Iranian oil tankers cruise to Bali to deliver petroleum, which is refined into gasoline. We think Ari wants us to focus on a particular Iranian tanker. He prompts us to identify the name of this tanker with the musical clue in the title that asks the question 'What's your name?' Part of the name is provided by omission. The next song title 'When You Wish' is incomplete, missing 'Upon a Star.' The tanker's name contains the word 'star.' The following clue is in the lyric 'I think it's gonna be a long, long time' from the song 'Rocket Man,' which suggests that this particular Iranian tanker with the name Star has a rocket aboard."

"What's the next title?" the prime minister asked.

"'Help,'" Shimon replied, "suggesting the Iranians received help with this rocket. The next musical title is 'New Kid in Town,'" Shimon said, "strongly suggests that Iran with Russia's assistance may be able to launch a nuclear missile from this oil tanker. When Iran launches that missile, they will be the 'new kid in town,' code for the newest member of the world's nuclear club."

"Does Ari have any idea when or where this launch will happen?"

"No."

"Have you identified the Iranian oil tanker, Shimon?"

"We think we have, the *Shahab* or *Shooting Star*. It sits in the harbor at Bali."

"'Bali Hai.' Anything more in his e-mail?" asked the prime minister.

"Yes, Mr. Prime Minister," replied Ariel. "Ari's e-mail mentioned the televised suicide of the French priest. There's a connection, but we haven't established it yet."

"Thank you, gentlemen, for a job well done, and I must ready myself for an emergency cabinet meeting in one hour." The prime minister escorted Shimon and Ariel to the door. It was 5 AM, and the sun was beginning to rise.

Moscow Command Center

Igor looked at his watch: 5:05 AM. He poured himself another cup of coffee, which he drank as he paced the floor and watched live satellite video feeds from the ISS. Ivan remained on duty.

"Igor, this just came in from the ISS."

Attention ground control:

we cannot repair breach ... shutting down all systems .... all crew members are preparing to disengage and board space capsule for 6:00 AM departure .... expected arrival in Russia, 9:00 AM.

Sanjay

"I believe your assessment is correct, Igor. They do plan to land in Israel. You must tell Boris what happened."

"Yes, of course. Ivan, would you get me some fresh coffee please before I call him." Ivan walked to the coffeepot, poured two cups, and came back. "Ivan, print me a copy of the Israeli's e-mail and his wife's reply." Ivan started the printer and turned in his swivel chair. Igor did not want Boris to discover the e-mails. Ivan, regrettably, stood in the way. With a sleight of hand, Igor quickly dispensed a fatal dosage of tasteless and untraceable poison into Ivan's coffee. His KGB training came in handy after all.

"This is good coffee," Igor said, saluting Ivan with his cup. Instinctively, Ivan lifted his cup and took a swallow. "Here are the printouts, Igor."

"Thank you." Ivan's eyelids became heavy, and he lost consciousness. Igor called the medics. They came almost immediately and wheeled him away on a stretcher to the infirmary. With Ivan gone, Igor worked feverishly to purge the e-mail from the hard drive. He called Boris.

"Hello, Boris, this is Igor." Of course I am aware ... and I've lost Ivan, I don't know. He passed out, and the medics took him away on a stretcher. What's my assessment? I don't think they're coming to Russia, but if they do, reprogram their flight plan to take them over Kazakhstan. It's easier to kill them in space. Kazakhstan takes them over Pakistan. A well-timed Pakistani launch into the atmosphere will nuke them. Can you do that, Boris? If you can, tomorrow's papers will read something like this: Space capsule and its crew vaporized in nuclear-charged atmosphere ... nuked in a no fly zone."

"Igor, that's a great contingency plan. But you don't think they're flying to Russia."

"No, Boris. I think they're trying to get into Israel."

ISS Capsule

The time was 5:45 AM. Harnessed into their seats, each had brought a duffle bag containing a survival kit and other personal items. Ari and Alexander, fragile from radiation sickness, were under no delusions about the difficult physical challenges of a descent, the constant tossing and turning in the maneuvers. Andre was the designated pilot. Sanjay handed him the flight coordinates. He turned on the engines and activated computer flight control for stage one to power the craft. Later, during stage two, the reentry phase into earth's atmosphere, Andre's skills would be further tested in a precipitous fall at velocities twenty times faster than the speed of sound. Timely backward flying maneuvers and engine burns to decrease velocity were required. The heat shields had to function perfectly to protect the crew from incineration. In stage three and one hour of flight time remaining, Andre would disengage the computer flight plan to the Russian steppes and assume manual piloting operations of spins, turns, and final fuel burns to slow his descent to a desired landing speed of 321 km/h, or 200 mph.

"Everybody harnessed in," said Sanjay. "We're going to the Promised Land."

Andre began, "Commencing countdown 10-9-8-7-6-5-4-3-2-1."

Jerusalem, Israel

The Israeli cabinet convened at 6:00 AM for the emergency session. Prime Minister Olmert, looking somber and sleep deprived, addressed the group.

"The first order of business is to inform you that Ari Ben Ora and the others have evacuated the ISS and are flying to Israel in the escape capsule. God willing they will arrive safely. Using coded messages, Ari was able to communicate reliable evidence that Iran, with Russian and Pakistani assistance, is planning to test its first nuclear missile in the South Pacific under the camouflage of an oil tanker called the *Shahab*. The tanker sits in port at Bali. We believe that when the tanker leaves port and reaches the open sea, they will launch this missile." The prime minister was interrupted when an aide walked in and whispered something in his ear.

"Distribute them please, and speak freely, Benjamin."

"This is a report faxed from our embassy in Paris," Benjamin continued. "A young French Moroccan Jew by the name of Chai Tanger came to our embassy very early this morning. You may recall the name Monsignor Gauthier, the priest who committed suicide before a television crew in Paris yesterday. Monsignor Gauthier was a mentor to Andre Dubois, the French citizen on the ISS. Mr. Tanger is a waiter at the Café Viola in Reims, France, and was serving coffee to the monsignor, who was waiting for a taxi to take him to our embassy in Paris. Before the taxi arrived, he departed in a Vatican limousine. He left his windbreaker with Mr. Tanger. Later, after the suicide, Mr. Tanger discovered an envelope in the inside pocket of the windbreaker that contained the e-mail in your handouts. It was sent to Father Gauthier from Andre on the ISS. The e-mail was authored by a Russian intelligence officer and e-mailed to his brother on the ISS. Andre intercepted the communication, and sent it to the priest. Everybody take a few minutes to read this e-mail."

Moscow Command Center

Igor lit another cigarette, his tenth since he furtively laced Ivan's coffee with the lethal powder. The medical team had informed him Ivan had slipped into a coma. With each grunting inhale and exhale, Igor smoked each cigarette down to his nicotine-stained fingers before disposing his leftover butts hurriedly and sometimes angrily into the ashtray or onto the floor. Igor's eyes constantly watched the monitors. The space capsule was ninety minutes into flight. The time was 7:28 AM. The phone rang.

"The Pakistani authorities have been most agreeable and moved up their unannounced launch schedule to 8:00 AM."

"What's their cover?"

"The Pakistan government will say the launch codes were entered incorrectly. Igor, the returning capsule should incinerate in the atmosphere whether they fly to Russia or to Israel."

"Excellent news," responded Igor.

"By the way Igor, what's the latest on Ivan's condition?"

"Poor man's still in a coma."

"So strange for a man so young, don't you think?"

"Yes, very unfortunate. I certainly hope he makes a full recovery," Igor added.

"As do I," responded Boris. "He's a good man. Let's be in touch near the top of the hour."

ISS Capsule

His mobility ever restricted by his protective suit, Sanjay turned his head and shoulder to the left to check on Alexander and Ari, who had fallen in and out of consciousness during the flight. "Ari, Alexander, talk to me." No response yet, but he could see they were breathing. The time was 7:52 AM.

"We're entering earth's atmosphere and our heat shields are still intact," Andre said to Sanjay. "The computer flight controls are sensing the atmospheric change and signaling to us that the backward fly maneuver is about to begin. And that will be followed by the final engine burn of remaining rocket-fuel before our final descent. I have set the coordinates for the Shdema landing and will turn the capsule's direction thirty-two degrees south. After the engine burn, we'll go to manual override and take this puppy into Israel." Suddenly there was radio contact.

"This is RSA ground control to ISS capsule. Do you hear?"

"Affirmative," responded Andre.

"Who is piloting?"

"Andre Dubois," Sanjay said.

"This is to inform you, Andre, that your capsule has been rerouted to land at the airstrip north of Kazakhstan."

"Why?" asked Andre.

"We've been told there are wind gusts up to sixty kilometers on the steppes."

"Anything we have to do?" asked Andre.

"No, it's already in the computer, just a heads up to avoid confusion. Have a safe landing."

"Thanks, over and out."

Andre turned to Sanjay after ending communication with ground control. "That route takes us over Pakistan. Sanjay, I don't believe in coincidence. The Russians have to be onto us. We know they want to kill us, and on the ground, that will be difficult for them to pull off without arousing suspicion. What better place is there to destroy us than over Pakistan?"

"How would they do that, Andre?"

"All the Russians have to do is have the Pakistanis launch two hours early."

"Can we reroute our flight to avoid flying over Pakistan?"

"Not entirely, but I can try to reposition the capsule as our fuel will allow." With the backward fly maneuver completed, Andre turned on the switch that immediately disengaged the computer guidance control of the capsule and stopped the fuel burn. "We'll descend with a little more velocity and on a flatter curve. There's a good chance we'll undershoot Israel and land in the Mediterranean." Suddenly there was radio noise from mission control. Andre quickly shut off the radio.

Moscow Command Center

Igor discovered another pack of cigarettes in Ivan's drawer. Menthols were not Igor's favorite, but they would have to do. He took two deep puffs before he answered his phone.

"Igor," said Boris, "your instincts were correct. They changed their flight path immediately after mission control radioed them in. Mission control confirmed an alternate landing site. They can't get far enough away to avoid the nuclear wind blast from the detonation. In approximately twenty-five minutes the capsule should be vaporized, decompressed, and torn to shreds. It's 8 AM. We've hooked you into a split video feed so you can also watch the missile launch." Igor went into coughing spasms. "Are you all right?" asked Boris.

"Yes, yes, yes," Igor replied impatiently.

"Igor, the Iranian tanker sits in port waiting for our clearance before setting out to sea. I wish I were a fly on the wall of the Israeli Knesset when Iran launches its first nuclear missile."

"Actually, Boris, Russian technicians are preparing the launch, and Pakistan prepared the bomb."

"Immaterial, Igor, it's only the perception that's relevant, not the truth. We want Iran to receive the credit on this one." Igor mockingly but silently laughed. Iran was likely to receive an unwelcome visit from the Israelis. Igor no longer harbored any doubts, and by this time, Israeli intelligence had connected the dots.

He puffed on the menthol and decided he had enough. He put out the cigarette and tossed the remaining pack in the garbage can.

But he thought it over and retrieved the pack as the launch process began. Engulfed by billows of rocket-fuel exhaust, the nuclear missile ascended straight up toward the blue sky above the surrounding desert, slowly at first but gradually picking up speed.

"Igor, mark my words. For the next forty-eight hours, the media will have a field day looking for the answers and spawning conspiracy theories to explain this nuclear accident. Then this story will be dwarfed by the following headlines: 'Iran withdraws from the NPT, and from a tanker on the Indian Ocean conducts its first successful nuclear launch on a Shahab 3 missile.' Before I forget, Igor, the Kremlin wants me to complete an audit of your department by next week. We'll need to see all the monitored e-mails as part of a review process. I want to visit Ivan as well."

"Yes of course. I look forward to your visit, Boris," and he hung up the phone. *Not even a moment to wallow in self-pity*, he thought. The damn phone rang again.

"This is Igor."

"Hello, this is Dr. Aaskov. I have good news. Ivan has regained consciousness, although he suffered a minor stroke. His memory is impaired, and he has no recollection of passing out."

"Will his memory come back?"

"Maybe it will in time."

"Thank you, Dr. Aaskov. Be sure to tell Ivan I'll be over to see him shortly."

"It's too soon, Igor, perhaps in a day or two." Igor was feeling like he'd been handed a second lease on life. The potency of the lethal powder he had introduced into Ivan's bloodstream had dissipated with the passing years; it was still strong enough to cause a stroke but not to take a life. Nothing in life was ever certain except death and lousy menthol cigarettes.

Jerusalem, Israel

"Tzipi," Defense Minister Peretz said, "the Iranian tanker is out of strike range. Even if it were within range I would recommend against an air strike. I want the Iranians to detonate their nuclear bomb."

The dovish Shimon Peres replied, "Amir's right. You all know that I have been quoted as saying that Israel will not be the first country in the Middle East to introduce nuclear weapons. With Iran's assistance, Israel will be the second."

Defense Minister Peretz weighed in. "In response to an Iranian nuclear launch, I am recommending that we implement Operation Jericho, the planned coordination of surface-to-surface strikes, air-to-surface missile strikes, and submarine-launched missile strikes utilizing bunker bombers and, if necessary, Jericho III missiles. We have identified twenty Iranian nuclear targets. The first taken out will be the facility at Natanz, followed by Bushehr, Arak, and so on."

"Amir, the Jericho III is a nuclear-tipped missile. How would the Iranians respond to a nuclear attack on their facilities?" asked Foreign Minister Livni.

"With their arsenal of Shahab 3 and 4 missiles possibly carrying chemical or biological agents," Aretz responded. "It will be a test for our Arrow anti-missile deterrence system. The Iranians can no longer depend on Hezbollah to open a southern front. With the international forces patrolling, Hezbollah will no longer find it so easy to shoot off rockets, and the Lebanese government won't tolerate the destruction of their infrastructure again. Syria will do nothing. They have too much to lose."

"The majority of our citizens," Olmert said, "have been provided with gas masks and protection kits with antidotes to the chemical agents Sarin and VX, and civil-defense workers have been inoculated against smallpox and anthrax. The new apartments have safe rooms to seal out poisons, and there are accessible bomb shelters. A full-scale chemical or biological attack by Iran shouldn't kill that many Israelis, but Palestinians could perish by the tens of thousands."

"Don't we have to warn Abu Mazen?" asked Foreign Minister Livni.

"That would only start a panic in the Palestinian territories and alert the Iranians," the prime minister said. "If the mullahs scrub the test, we forfeit our pretext to take out those nuclear facilities, and taking them out can bring about positive change to the region. With Iranian prestige on the line and with no remaining nuclear option, the mullahs can be exposed for the frauds they are. Iran's leaders will appear weak in the eyes of the Arab world and be ripe for overthrow."

"What if the Iranians have a second nuclear option?" Livni queried.

"The consensus among us is that they don't, but consider the alternative, Tzipi. To do nothing is to accept an Iranian nuclear noose around our neck. How will Israelis handle the pressure? Perhaps the threat of our nuclear annihilation will cause an Israeli stampede out of Israel and back to Russia as the e-mail alleges. Who among us can dispute that virtually all of Israel's population in the north is suffering post-traumatic symptoms caused by the rocket attacks last year. Does anybody here believe that investment capital into Israel will continue from the United States? It will dry up. In my judgment, Israel will barely survive in an atmosphere that threatens its extinction."

"What do you think the Americans and Russians will do?" asked Foreign Minister Livni.

"The Americans will support us, and the Russians will stay on the sidelines. Undoubtedly, the international community will publicly condemn us but privately praise us, as they did in 1981 when we destroyed the Iraqi reactor. Under international law, Israel has a very good legal case. The World Court considers the threat or use of nuclear weapons under nearly all circumstances to be illegal, except for defensive purposes and when the survival of the state is at risk. By its own definition, a contained strike against Iran's nuclear plants meets that standard. Iran has signaled intent by its threats to 'wipe Israel off the map.' A nuclear test can easily be construed as a means to that end. Does anyone disagree? Please speak up now." There were none.

The prime minister looked at his watch. "It's almost 8:00 AM. There's a helicopter on the roof waiting to take me to Shdema."

Moscow Command Center

At 8:26 AM, Pakistan's nuclear-armed missile reached its zenith at 40 km and detonated at a yield of 10 kilotons, creating an energy burst of blinding light, thermal heat, and radiation. That was followed by a deafening sound, a huge fireball, and powerful winds. The nuclear blast emitted ionizing radiation for hundreds of miles. The heat generated from the fireball moved outward and created systems of overpressures powerful enough to collapse concrete structures had there been any.

The explosion disrupted the command center's communication system. Monitors went blank, and the lights went out. When the electricity was restored, the capsule had disappeared from the screen. Igor calculated the capsule's terminal velocity and the rate of its fall at nearly 200 miles per hour, placing the capsule at approximately 80 kilometers above the burgeoning mushroom cloud. By his estimation, it was not far enough away to escape destruction from a nuclear-charged atmosphere. Just the peeling of a heat-resistant tile or two on the capsule's underbelly would create a fiery tomb for those inside. But for the moment, he lacked certainty and felt cheated.

On the Mediterranean Sea

The capsule landed very hard on it first attempt before skidding to a stop, its attached parachute thrashing in the wind. Andre was surprised to be alive, surprised that he had survived the tumultuous wind shears and tornado-like winds that whipped the capsule around like a ball on a string as the capsule descended into the nuclear hurricane. He was surprised the capsule was still intact and didn't burn in the atmosphere. But he was not surprised that he undershot the Negev airstrip and landed in the Mediterranean Sea. Andre unbuckled his seat harness. Next to him was Sanjay, slumped over in his seat. Ari and Alexander had fallen into total unconsciousness.

"Alexander, Ari, Sanjay, wake up." He shook Sanjay's shoulder before taking his pulse. There was none. Then he saw the blood on the console. Sanjay's seat harness had broken apart during the landing. He had taken a hit to the head and died instantly. There was movement in the back. Ari and Alexander were still alive.

"Ari, Alexander, can you hear me?"

"Yes," said Ari.

"Me, too," said Alexander.

"Ari, when do you think the Israeli rescue unit will arrive?"

"Where are we?" Ari asked.

"Off the coast of Haifa, within thirty nautical miles," Andre replied.

"We're in international waters; the Russians could get to us first," said Alexander. "If that happens, we'll be sitting ducks stuck in these space suits. Why is Sanjay so quiet?"

"Sanjay's dead. I should have told you first. He was thrown against the console when his seat harness broke apart."

"Oh, my God!" said Ari.

"Andre, when did you last speak to him?" Alexander asked.

"It was just before the detonation, and then came the wind blasts. I don't know when he struck his head, but let's take solace that he didn't suffer. Crap, where is the Israeli rescue team? Ari, are you certain your wife understood your e-mail?"

"Yes I'm certain. I don't remember a blast, but satellites and communication systems can be degraded by electromagnetic pulses from the blast. We may have temporarily disappeared from the radar screen, although it looks later than mid-morning; it's 5:00 PM by my watch. We were scheduled to land a little after 9:00 AM, but the sun is in the western sky. Any other theories?"

"The probable explanation is that we all blacked out on landing, and we've been floating here for nearly eight hours. But that doesn't make sense either. Somebody should have rescued us. The only other explanation I can think of is that we remained in the atmosphere for those additional hours. The force of reverse wind shears created by the nuclear detonation must have been more powerful than earth's gravitational pull. I hope that's not the case, because that would have exposed us to hours of radiation," Andre noted.

"Ari, can we get an Israeli radio signal out here?" Alexander asked.

"Should be able to, Andre. Tune to 960 frequency." Andre turned the radio on, but there was nothing on 960.

"Try another frequency."

Andre carefully turned the radio dial through the static noises. "I found one."

The Great Arab revolt shows no sign of abating in spite of the passage of the White Paper in our British House of Commons this May with a vote of 268 to 17. Among those notables voting against its passage was Winston Churchill, claiming the White

Paper was contrary to the Balfour Declaration of 1917. This is Charles Andrews signing off from British Radio in Jerusalem. This concludes our June 20 evening show. Please tune in tomorrow night at the Sabbath's conclusion for a discussion of last year's Evian Conference in Paris. Good evening.

"The Evian conference was an international conference sponsored by FDR in the summer of 1938 to address the problem of Jews trapped in Germany and Austria. The Nazi government was overjoyed, stating the Conference exposed the hypocrisy of those countries that criticized Germany's treatment of its Jews when in fact none of those countries would take them," Ari stated.

Andre turned the dial, desperate to find another station. He found one from Beirut broadcasting in Arabic. They listened for a few minutes. Only Ari understood the full text.

"The Arabic broadcast is a tirade directed at the British, accusing the British of double dealing," Ari said. "I am beginning to wonder if we're still in the twenty-first century. There are no jets flying overhead, and no rescue teams, and no plausible explanation for the missing eight hours."

"Well, there's always Einstein's theory of relativity to consider," Andre said. "With the powerful gravitational field we experienced over Pakistan, the clock ticks more slowly, and what of the black holes that supposedly suck in light and everything around them?"

"Black holes are too fleeting, even for light to pass, and too tiny for a human to get through, let alone a space capsule. Even if it were possible for the capsule to pass through the black hole, its gravitational field would have crushed us to pieces," Ari responded.

"But what if sufficient antigravity or negative energy were created from the nuclear explosion that negated the gravitational field and left a portal opening wide and long enough for us to get through?" Andre asked.

"By the looks of things, we may have plenty of time to discuss these theories," Ari suggested. "I say we get out of these space suits, bury Sanjay at sea, change into our civilian clothes, inflate the rubber raft, and paddle to the coast. All our personal items can be stored in the duffle bag. How much food and water do we have, Alexander?"

"Three days' worth."

"That should be sufficient. The shortest route is to Israel, but if we are in the year 1939, there is no Israel, just a British blockade of Palestine. Lebanon, which is under the French Mandate, should be easier to slip into, especially since Andre is a French citizen."

"Ari," Andre noted, "both you and Alexander seemed to have recovered, your radiation symptoms seems to have disappeared. It's amazing. If we are back in time, neither of you have been exposed to radiation."

"It could be the ocean air of the Mediterranean," Ari replied.

"Or the work of God," Alexander said

After shedding their protective suits, each took a few minutes to jump into the warm waters of the Mediterranean, frolicking in its warm saltwater. After putting on their new clothes, they slid down the starboard side of the capsule's wing and into the raft. Ari carried the duffle bag that contained batteries, flashlights, the electronics, and a micro-Uzi. They said their last goodbyes to Sanjay, and with paddles in hand, shoved off the sinking capsule. There was still two hours left of daylight. Ari reached into the duffle bag, pulled out the Uzi, and loaded it with a magazine.

The sun had long disappeared, but the three-quarters moon lit up the night sky. On the eastern horizon was a silhouette of a fishing boat heading toward them. Over the engine noise, one of the Arab fishermen called out in Arabic.

"They're asking if we need help," Ari said. "Andre, try responding in French."

"Yes, we need help," Andre said. The Arabs understood. When the fishing boat was only a rope's throw away, one of the fishermen tossed a line to the raft, and Andre connected it to a metal loop fastened to the bow.

"We will tow you into Beirut," the Arab fisherman said.

"Merci. What day is today's date please?"

"Friday, August 19." Andre was afraid to ask him the year. They left space on Wednesday, July 20, 2007, for what should have been a two-hour flight. They landed in August, year uncertain.

"Did you notice the year imprinted on the boat's bow—1935?"Andre asked his crewmates.

Throughout the wee hours of the morning, each took turns sleeping as the fishing boat towed them to shore. Ari kept the loaded gun nearby just in case. They were awake before dawn and saw other fishing boats going out to sea. Ari took a few drinks of water from his canteen and said. "When we cross the border into Palestine, we'll need identification papers. My grandfather told me how he did it when he came into Palestine."

"But he came from the Soviet Union, Ari, and we're stateless," Andre professed.

"We'll tell them we're Jews who had joined the French Foreign Legion in order to sneak into Palestine. I speak Hebrew. They'll believe us. Except for an occasional missionary, only Jews risk their lives to get into Palestine. Look, the lights on the shore, that's Beirut."

Just after dawn, the fishing boat pulled into Beirut's harbor. Andre waved goodbye to the Lebanese fisherman and threw back the towline. Ari insisted he was strong enough to carry the duffle bag. The three walked to the harbor's commercial district. Food vendors were setting up for another day of negotiation. Ari noticed a pawnshop had just opened its doors for business.

"We need money for real food." He pulled off his 14-karat wedding band and gave it to Andre to sell to the pawnbroker. Andre came back with twenty dollars of French currency.

"Remember, if this is 1939, twenty dollars will go a long way," Ari said.

"There's a café across the street," Ari noticed. "How does the idea of strong coffee and breakfast sound?" They crossed the street to the café and sat at an outdoor table on the street side. It had been a long time since they were served real poached eggs with hollandaise sauce, and they feasted on sweet bread, orange juice, and Turkish coffee. Three meals for three dollars, including the tip, was affirmation they were in another time. A truck stopped in front of the cafe and dropped off its bundled newspapers. Andre ran to get a copy of the Friday, August 19, 1939, morning edition of the *Beirut Times*. Behind the truck was a taxi waiting to take his place in front of the café. Ari had an idea.

"Andre, ask the cab driver how much the fare is to An Naqurah."
Andre walked over to the Lebanese driver to inquire. He walked back.
"We're still a little short."

"Andre, tell him we will accept his fare and would like to offer him
breakfast before we leave. Give the money to Alexander. You and I will
be going to the bank across the street to cash a check."

"What check?"

"That's a German Import Export bank across the street. There's a
swastika on top of the entrance." I'm going to rob it. Do you want to
help me, Andre?"

Under the tablecloth, Ari pulled out his miniature Uzi from the
duffle bag and stuck it in the sleeve of his windbreaker resting on his
lap. Andre was ecstatic and eagerly consented. The plan was hatched.
Andre walked back to the cab, and the driver graciously accepted the
offer. He pulled into the space and turned off his engine. The driver
shook hands with Andre and walked over to the café.

"Al Salaam a'alaykum, I am Mohammed."

"And a good day to you. Do you speak English, Mohammed?"
asked Ari.

"Yes, a little, but I understand better than I speak."

"Please sit down Mohammed and join our friend Alexander. Order
breakfast, and when we return, we'll have you drive us to An Naqurah,
cash in advance." Andre and Ari walked across the street.

"Andre, demand twenty thousand from the bank teller, two
thousand in francs and eighteen thousand in English pounds. Inform
the teller I have a loaded gun and will shoot to kill. When you have
the money, turn around slowly and walk away. Be careful not to block
my vision."

Andre walked in first and stood in line at the bank window. Ari
sat on a chair and picked up a Nazi propaganda magazine with his
left hand; his right hand rested on the sleeve of his jacket that was
across his lap. Out of the corner of his eye, he saw a German security
officer paying attention to him. Ari's designer jeans might have made
him stand out. Only one person stood in front of Andre. The German
officer began walking slowly toward Ari, and stopped in front of him.

"Sprechen Sie Deutsch or Francais?"

"No Tatalalm Arabic," replied Ari.

"Strange that you don't look Lebanese. May I see some identification." The German spoke Arabic. Ari nodded his head. Andre was facing the teller.

"Na'am," Ari nodded and feigned slightly as if to reach for his pocket with his left hand while the end of his Uzi slammed into the crotch of the German who immediately doubled over in pain from the jolt.

Speaking in Arabic Ari said, "Drop your weapon." Aware the security officer had dropped his weapon, the teller anxiously followed Andre's instructions and passed the currency under the window. The teller discreetly activated a silent button that alerted two other German officers who were in the back.

Focused on Ari, the other bank patrons didn't even notice Andre walk out of the bank. Bank patrons watched him as he retrieved the officer's Lugar, and stuck it in his pants. Ari's parting words were "Sheihiye lecha yom na'imand." Andre walked quickly as he crossed the street. Ari walked backward. No sooner had they reached the café than the three security officers ran out of the bank, blasting away with their pistols. Untouched, Ari hit the ground and fired off a round. The Germans went down. Two appeared dead, and one wounded.

Mohammed was chewing his food when he saw the Germans get picked off. "Mohammed, it's time to go now." Alexander grabbed him by his arm, and the cab driver offered no resistance. They all reached the parked cab at the same time. The two bank robbers got in the back, and Alexander sat next to the driver. Mohammed started the engine and sped off.

"Mohammed, drive us to the Palestine border," Ari said in Arabic.

"You are Jews?"

"Not all of us," Andre said. "You will not be hurt if you just take us to the border."

"That machine gun you used. I've never seen it before, small like a handgun. May I ask what the weapon is called?" asked Mohammed.

"It's called an Uzi, after its inventor."

"I've never heard of that name," he replied.

"Mohammed, if you can take the back roads and avoid French patrols, I will quadruple your fare," Ari offered.

"Yes, I can do that. We can be at the border in less than two hours." Mohammed drove his cab over dirt roads and side streets for nearly two hours, avoiding the major roads. Mohammed slowed the cab to a stop on a bumpy dirt road leading to a bluff.

"At the top of the hill you can see the border two miles away." Ari looked at his watch, the time was noon.

Chapter 38
ESCAPE TO CANAAN

August 19, 1939
At the Border

"I've never seen a watch like yours. It shows the time, the day, and month all lit up and blinking like a neon sign. I will accept that as payment," Mohammed proffered to Ari.

"Thanks, but no thanks. This digital watch was my birthday gift from my wife. Mohammed, drive slowly to the top of the bluff and stop. I want to take a look." Mohammed placed the car in first gear and slowly stepped on the accelerator while releasing the clutch. At the summit, they looked south. The dirt road meandered down a rather steep hill until it merged with a two-lane paved road less than two miles from the border. Ari pulled out binoculars and watched the British patrol near the border station. He counted five soldiers, three sitting in an open military vehicle and two outside checking cars and mule-drawn carriages.

"Mohammed, this is where we part company. Take these two full canteens of water and don't forget your cigarettes on the front seat."

"Are you going to steal my car?" asked an excitable Mohammed in fluent Arabic.

"No," Ari replied. "I'm going to buy your car from you. What model year is your Citroen Traction?"

"1934."

"How much do you want?"

"One thousand francs, you promised to quadruple my fare." Mohammed was prepared to negotiate. Ari shook his head.

"How does two thousand francs sound?"

"Did you say two thousand?"

"Andre, give him the francs."

"Thank you so," Mohammed exclaimed. "My wife and children thank you. May Allah be with you and help you get into Palestine. Thank you." He took several steps backward and slightly bowed his head before he began to trot to the nearest Lebanese town.

Beirut, Lebanon

Hans was bleeding profusely from the wound in his thigh, but he crawled back into the bank. Sirens were audible. The French police and a medical team were on their way to the scene.

"Fraulein, send this message to Berlin." Hans began dictation.

> To Minister of Foreign Affairs:
> Joachim Von Ribbentrop
> Minister Von Ribbentrop:
>
> The Third Reich Import Export bank was robbed of eighteen thousand British pounds and two thousand francs at 10:00 AM local time on August 19. I am wounded above my thigh, but Heinrich and Adolph were killed. We were in pursuit when we went down from a hail of bullets fired from their machine gun, which was no larger than the size of a pistol—no more than ten inches in length but with enormous firepower, at least twenty rounds in less than a second … far superior to any weapon in its class than I have ever seen. We didn't have a chance to fire our pistols again.
>
> Officer Hans Schmorde

The French police arrived and roped off the crime scene. They gathered empty shell casings. Investigators, pencils in hand, walked up and down the street looking for witnesses to the shooting. The medical unit arrived minutes later, picked up the dead bodies, and followed the blood trail into the bank. They began working on Hans, who was prostrate on the floor.

"You're lucky the bullet went completely through," said one of the medics. "Other then a slight limp, you should make a full recovery." They began to dress the wound. Inspector Chevalier came in and bent down to Hans.

"Monsieur Schmorde, I am Inspector Chevalier. I was told you were a witness to the robbery and shootings."

"I noticed a man sitting. His attire seemed totally out of character. His clothes were very stylish, perhaps American. He spoke a different dialect of Arabic. I asked him to present his identification papers."

"Monsieur, you are not a French police officer. You are a bank guard and do not have the right to ask for identification. Please continue."

"Underneath his jacket he held an automatic weapon on me, and I gave up my gun to him."

"What kind of automatic weapon?"

"It was a small machine gun, not much bigger than my Lugar with no forward handgrip. But it had more firepower than any submachine gun in the German army."

"Could you tell anything from his looks?"

"He didn't look like an Arab. He was middle-aged, about 5'10" and had dark wavy hair."

"Could you recognize him again if you saw him?"

"Yes. He may have been a Jew, because he spoke Hebrew, so said one of the bank customers."

"What did he say in Hebrew?"

"I was told, 'have a nice day.'" Chevalier put aside his notepad and pencil and pulled something out of his inside pocket. "Let me show you something, Schmorde, the shell casings from the weapon that killed your comrades and almost killed you. These shell casings are of lighter weight than I am used to seeing, and like all casings, they have identification imprints."

"The imprint is in Hebrew. It reads made by Israeli Defense Industries. If there's nothing else, Schmorde, I will question the teller about the other suspect. I wish you a speedy recovery."

"He spoke perfect French, sir. He appeared to be a gentleman."

"Did he look Jewish?" Chevalier asked.

"Not a single bit. He was very Parisian, with light brown hair and soft facial features. He only asked for twenty thousand—eighteen thousand in English pounds and two thousand francs."

"Thank you Max," Chevalier said and left the bank. His investigators were interrogating the waiter at the café. Chevalier walked over.

"Captain, this waiter served breakfast to the suspects. The three were eating here and invited the cab driver to have breakfast. Two left for the bank."

"So we're looking for three people in a white Citroen cab. Probably heading south to Palestine. Capture them alive if possible. One more thing, Pierre, offer 100 francs as a reward for any solid information on these three. Print up flyers and distribute them around the harbor as well."

At the Border

Mohammed soon ran out of breath and slowed to a normal walk. No longer did he hear the engine of his cab. He decided there was plenty of walking daylight left to catch the next bus to Beirut from An Naqurah. So Mohammed turned around and returned to the top of the hill above the British check point, just to see if his passengers were shrewd enough to cross the border. At the top of the bluff, he found a comfortable spot next to a tree where he could sit and have a great view of the border station.

Andre drove, and Alexander sat in the backseat. Ari had positioned himself on the rear bumper, crouched down and holding onto the wheel cover with his left hand, and his reloaded Uzi with his right hand. Andre slowly drove the Citroen to the border station, where two British soldiers, one on each side of the car, approached.

"Your papers please," the officer said to Andre. In a split second Ari jumped off the vehicle and pointed his Uzi at the British officer on the passenger side. The officer on Andre's side, distracted by Ari, didn't see Alexander draw the German Lugar on him until it was too late.

"Both of you drop your guns and no one gets hurt," Ari said. Alerted, the three remaining British soldiers quickly assumed firing position behind the open doors of their vehicle. Using his British hostage for cover, Ari retrieved the officer's gun. With his hostage in front of him, Alexander walked carefully toward the other officers. Ari began ranting in fluent Hebrew, and then spoke in English.

"We simply want to get into Palestine. Now throw down your weapons." The soldiers did nothing. Still walking behind his hostage, Ari fired his Uzi, shooting out the two front tires of the soldiers' vehicle.

"Drop your weapons now," Ari demanded. The British soldiers were stunned at the rapid firepower from the pistol-sized weapon. They dropped their weapons and reached their hands toward the sky. Ari waved Andre through the gate.

"Pick up their guns and put them in the trunk." Ari threw the British hostages a tool kit from the trunk of the cab. "You," pointing to one of the British officers, "put your plates on our car. Alexander, go in the station and destroy their telecommunications equipment." Andre, retrieved the British weapons and placed them in the trunk, and in a few minutes, the three got back in the cab and escaped into Palestine.

"Fantastic," said Mohammed, clapping his hands in delight over the outcome and unaware he wasn't the only one watching the suspects get away. From the top of the bluff, a French patrol arrived in time to see the British guards put down their weapons and put up their hands. The captain had just called Chevalier and reported how the suspects crossed into British Palestine when he heard the sound of hand clapping from a man sitting by a tree.

"Stay where you are." Mohammed cringed when he heard those words. "Search him." In less than a minute, Mohammed was surrounded by French police who immediately conducted a body search on him. They pulled his wallet from his rear pocket and an opened pack of cigarettes from his front pant pocket.

"Captain, he's the taxi driver." The searching officer handed Mohammed's wallet to his captain.

"They stole my car," Mohammed pleaded.

"Then why were you applauding their getaway?"

"Because I hate the British more than I love my car," Mohammed replied. It was the right answer.

"I'm not too fond of them either. We have to ask you some questions, Mohammed."

"Captain, may I first have one of my cigarettes?"

"Of course. Give the man his cigarettes."

"Would you like one?" Mohammed asked.

"No, I have my own thank you," the captain replied, repulsed at the thought of sharing cigarettes with an Arab. Mohammed squeezed one unfiltered cigarette from the pack and removed a matchbook kept under the cigarette wrapping. Once again he was in control of the cigarette pack that held the 2,000 francs. Mohammed stuck the match and lit up his cigarette. He savored each puff, knowing that this was the last cigarette he would smoke until he was free of this interrogation.

"When I asked if they were Jews, the fair-haired one said in French, 'not all of us.' The one I had breakfast with I think was Russian, and the one carrying the machine gun spoke a different kind of Arabic."

"What can you tell me about this machine gun?"

"Lightweight, nimble, small with lots of firepower—a machine gun you could hold and fire with one hand. He called it an Uzi, named after its inventor." The captain was busy writing.

"Anything else?" asked the captain.

"The one carrying the gun … his watch lit up like a neon sign, flashing the time, the day, and date, each in its own small circle within the watch face. I've never seen a watch like that before. He called it a digital watch, a birthday gift from his wife. Have you ever seen such a watch?" The captain didn't answer.

"Mohammed, this police report will serve as evidentiary proof of your stolen vehicle, and I hope you have insurance so you can submit a claim."

"Yes, Captain, French insurance." The captain walked away and placed a call to Chevalier.

"Thank you, Captain," Inspector Chevalier replied. "Send me your report. You can release him now. We know where to find him if we need him. Operator, connect me to Inspector Stuart in Jerusalem."

Beirut, Lebanon

"Inspector Stuart, this is Inspector Chevalier in Beirut."

"Hello, Inspector Chevalier. And what do I owe the pleasure of this call?"

"Unfortunately, it's not a pleasure call. We've had a robbery in Beirut. The German Import Export Bank was held up; two guards were killed and one wounded. These criminals surprised the British patrol at the border crossing south of An Nayurah and drove into Palestine. None of your patrol was injured."

"Can you hold the line Inspector? Rodney, call into the border station at An Nayurah."

"Thank you. Please continue."

"The three are driving a white 1936 Citroen cab. Two witnesses swear the weapon used in the shooting was a miniature submachine gun no larger than a pistol and fired a twenty-round magazine within a second."

"That's impossible," the Englishman said.

"This miniature gun was named after its inventor, Uzi."

"That's a Hebrew name."

"There's more," said Chevalier, "the shell casings we found were imprinted in Hebrew for Israeli Defense Industries."

"Inspector Chevalier, we have excellent informants in Palestine, and we know what the Zionists are capable of doing. They are not capable of manufacturing machine guns and ammunition. A Citroen cab will be easy to spot, and we will find these criminals and extradite them to Beirut. Can you describe them for me?"

"One was described as fair complexioned, very French, not at all Semitic. He took the money from the teller. The shooter spoke Hebrew and wore very stylish jeans and a shirt. He had darker hair, in his early forties, we think. The third was younger, tall with light brown hair, and reported to speak English with a Russian accent. That's all we know."

"What was their take from the bank?"

"Eighteen thousand English pounds, and two thousand francs," the Frenchman said."

"That's not so much."

"My gut feeling," Chevalier noted, "is that this crime was not so much for money as it was for retribution against the Germans."

"You may be onto something Inspector," Stuart noted. "We'll pass this information along to all local authorities. I'll keep you informed, Inspector Chevalier."

"Thank you, Inspector Stuart. Goodbye."

"Cheerio."

"No communication at the border station, Inspector," said Rodney as he waited anxiously for the inspector to end his phone conversation.

"Rodney, issue an all points bulletin. Three men who robbed a Beirut bank and murdered two guards entered Palestine today at the border crossing at An Naqurah. They were last seen driving a white Citroen cab. They're considered armed and very dangerous. Offer a thousand pound reward."

Kibbutz Maabarot

"We don't care if you're an animist, atheist, communist, socialist, or even religious, but we don't like Nazis or fascists. Welcome to Maabarot," Yitzhak said. Located near the old road from Petah Tikva to Haifa on the Sharon Plain was the Kibbutz Maabarot, founded in 1924 by several hundred socialist Jews from Eastern Europe. The land for the kibbutz was originally sold to the Jewish National Fund by Arab owners. Ari remembered the kibbutz was a short drive from the Lebanese border. He had once visited the kibbutz as a child. "I suggest you let us hide your automobile before the British find you," Yitzhak exclaimed.

"So you know," said Ari.

"Word travels fast in Palestine. You speak excellent Hebrew. What is your name?"

"Ari Ben Ora. This is Alexander and Andre. Alexander and I are from Russia, and Andre is from France.

"A Russian with a Hebrew name," Yitzhak said.

"Yitzhak, we need some papers and identification. Can you help us?"

"Then we become accessories to your crime."

"I would like a chance to explain," Ari said.

"We can discuss this at dinner. You and your friends can change in the cabin off to your left. Dinner will be served in the main building behind me in an hour."

"Thank you for hospitality, Yitzhak, and please take the car keys. We won't need this vehicle anymore. It has military plates on it and British weapons in the trunk. All I ask is that you drive us into Jerusalem." Yitzhak took the keys.

"In the morning; tonight you'll spend with us." The cabin contained six makeshift cots and a bathroom and shower. They each staked a bed. Andre divided the money into three columns on the bed.

"I think when we get to the city we should split up," Andre suggested. "The Brits will be looking for a threesome." Ari removed his watch, stuffed his share of the money inside the tightened watchband, and placed it in the inside of his windbreaker pocket. He removed the ammunition clip from the Uzi and stuck the gun under the mattress.

"This is enough money for room and board for at least two years," Ari said. Andre and Alexander took their share and stuffed it into their pockets. An hour later, they walked into the dining room filled with rows of enough tables and chairs to accommodate several hundred people.

"Ari, Alex, and Andre, come and join us. I'd like you to meet Miriam, Abe, Sharon, and David." They exchanged greetings and shook hands.

"We don't have a kosher kitchen," Yitzhak said. "I hope that's not a problem."

"We're fine," Ari responded in Hebrew.

"Alex and Andre don't speak Hebrew," Yitzhak announced. "Tonight we speak English."

"How did you all manage to sneak into Palestine, Alex?" Miriam asked.

"Through Lebanon. We deserted the French Foreign Legion to get to Palestine."

"So you didn't know each other before the Legion?" asked Abe.

"Alex and I knew each other in Russia. Andre is from France."

"I see. The three of you are Zionists committed to the establishment of a Jewish state," Miriam said.

"Yes," Ari responded, "it is very difficult being a Jew in the Soviet Union."

"What is it like to be a Jew in France, Andre?" David asked. Andre took a moment to gather his thoughts.

"Well, we don't have pogroms in France, but resentment against Jews is endemic in France. Many French believe the Jews are treacherous and wield enormous influence, especially the Rothschild banking family."

"The Rothschilds have done great things in Palestine, like sponsoring the Palestine Electric Corporation and helping with Jewish resettlement," Yitzhak claimed.

"Alexander, what did you do before you joined the legion?" Miriam wanted to know.

"Once upon a time I taught physics, math, and science."

"I teach math and the sciences to the children," she responded, her face flush.

"That's wonderful," Alexander responded, sensing the positive body language between them. Miriam was a dark-haired beauty with large green eyes. Yitzhak also picked up on their mutual attraction and suggested that Alex sit in on Miriam's physics class the next day.

"If it is fine with the teacher." Miriam nodded, but avoided eye contact this time.

"Alex, we must get to Jerusalem tomorrow," Andre reminded him.

"Don't worry, we'll drive you to Jerusalem in the afternoon," Yitzhak said. "And Andre what did you do before joining the Legion?"

"I was an aviator."

"Excellent," Yitzhak responded. "One day we Jews will have our own country with an air force, and pilots like you will be needed to train others."

"And what of the Palestinian Arabs Yitzhak, will they be part of our country?" Andre asked.

"An excellent question, Andre. On the political left, there are those who advocate a bi-national state for Arabs and Jews, but many more in the political center want at least a separate Jewish state within Palestine. And there are powerful people on the right who support transferring the Arab population out of Palestine. What do you think Andre?"

"I think Jews and Arabs should live together in peace."

"That is something we should all aspire to," Yitzhak said. "Our guests have briefly told us where they came from. What some of you may not know is that they are being sought by the British authorities. Earlier today, our guests held up a German bank in Beirut."

"I did hear that on the radio. Two Germans were killed, and a third wounded," David said.

"I shot in self-defense," Ari admitted.

"Let's show our guests some gratitude. They brought us a cache of British weapons and a vehicle with British military plates," Yitzhak said. "I have no problem with you killing Nazis or taking their money. It's a small pittance compared to what they've stolen from Europe's Jews." Yitzhak took a pencil from his pocket and began writing on the paper napkin.

"Ari, contact this person as soon as you arrive in Jerusalem. His name is David Ben-Gurion. He has organized an effective Jewish fighting force known as the Haganah. He can help you."

"Thank you," Ari said.

"Ben-Gurion believes war in Europe is inevitable," Sharon said. "Hitler's luck is bound to run out. He's surrounded by the two largest armies in the world—the French and the Soviet Union—and the British have the strongest navy. We Jews have to hope first that the Germans lose the war, and then that the Brits leave Palestine to the Jews. And if they do, then we have to hope we can survive the Arab onslaught. If only we could get the British to reverse the White Paper and lift their quotas on Jewish immigration. There are so many Jews in Europe who would gladly come to Palestine now. Ari, do you think war in Europe is inevitable."

"I do. Hitler will settle for nothing less. The allies have set a bad precedent by appeasing him, first handing him Czechoslovakia and now Austria. I wouldn't be a bit surprised if Stalin made a deal with Hitler to carve up Poland."

"I beg to differ," David said. "Not only do Hitler and Stalin detest each other, but they are ideologically at war."

"But war can make for strange bedfellows," Yitzhak noted. "Enough war talk. Let's finish eating so I can show our guests Maabarot before the sun goes down. In the morning, David will take your pictures and provide you with forged identity cards. They're as good as real."

181

"I can't thank you enough," Ari said.

David and Sharon, the newlyweds, held hands as they followed behind Yitzhak, Ari, and Andre. Off to the side, Miriam walked with Alexander. Yitzhak explained that most all the food consumed was raised on the kibbutz, including the lettuce, tomatoes, beets, and chickens. Fresh fish came in from the coastal city of Netanya, about a thirty-minute drive. Maabarot's export crop was cotton.

When the sun went down, they returned to the guest cabin. Tonight, like previous nights, men and women from Maabarot would be taking turns patrolling the grounds to warn of any impending danger.

Chapter 39
ALL ROADS PASS THROUGH JERUSALEM

August 20, 1939
Kibbutz Maabarot

The next morning the guests were awakened by the sound of chickens and the clatter of pots and pans from the kitchen. The aroma of coffee permeated the air. Alexander made an announcement.

"Andre's right," Alexander said. "We should split up immediately. The British police have our descriptions and will be on the lookout for three men. For the time being, I'll stay here and help teach math and science classes. Miriam said she could use another instructor."

"I think you have a crush on the young teacher," Andre said.

"She's breathtaking, and why I shouldn't I stay here? There's nothing for me in a Stalinist Russia. In two years, the Soviet Union will be decimated by the German armed forces. Remember, the Germans never were able to reach Palestine. The British stopped the Krauts in Egypt."

"He's right," Ari noted.

"As soon as I can," Andre said, "I'm going to fly back to France. The Battle of France is next May, and I'm the only Frenchman who knows the German invasion plans. I might be able to stop Hitler."

"Maybe Hitler can be stopped before the Battle of France," Ari said. "We can provide bits and pieces of information to the British High Commissioner in Jerusalem that only the German High Command would be privy to, like invasion dates. As Andre correctly stated, we're the only ones on the planet who know Hitler's diabolical plans."

"It's worth a try."

"I agree," Alexander said.

"In return for information, I will expect the British to lift the blockade, reopen Palestine to Europe's Jews, and be in compliance with their obligations under the Palestine Mandate.

"Ari, even if the British reopen Palestine to the Jews, after September 1, World War II begins. Hitler invades and occupies Poland. He won't let the Jews out of Europe," Andre insisted.

"We can't be certain. He didn't have that choice the first time around. It might suit his purposes to let some of them out, especially if we can get Pope Pius to intercede."

"September 1 is only twelve days away," Alexander noted.

Beirut, Lebanon

The day after the robbery, Hans returned to work on crutches. Chevalier told him the investigation would remain open, but the suspects had slipped across the border into Palestine.

"Fraulein please take the following dictation and send it to Berlin."

Minister of Foreign Affairs:
Joachim Von Ribbentrop

Minister Von Ribbentrop:

The evidence is undeniable: the perpetuators of the robbery were Jews. French authorities failed to apprehend the fugitives before they entered Palestine. The shell casings have Hebrew imprints.

Yours truly,
Officer Schmorde

Hans was at the bank when he received a reply from Minister of Foreign Affairs Ribbentrop.

Officer Schmorde,

The Führer had a temper tantrum when he learned that Zionists were responsible and refused to believe that Jews wield such weapons. Haj Amin al Husseini, the Grand Mufti of Jerusalem and the German Consul in Jerusalem have been alerted to this situation.

Yours truly,
Joachim Von Ribbentrop
Minister of Foreign Affairs

Kibbutz Maabarot

"That's wonderful news," Yitzhak said when he heard that Alexander was staying on. "Miriam told me your knowledge of math and physics is excellent."

"Thank you, Yitzhak. Math and science are easy for me. I'm not sure that learning Hebrew will be so easy."

"The kids understand English and Russian, but they'll talk back to you in Hebrew. That's how you learn the language. Well, I think it's time for me to take your friends to Jerusalem."

Alexander gave both Ari and Andre a hug. Yitzhak drove up in a 1936 Packard, spewing up dust from the dirt road. He got out of the car and opened the rear passenger door behind the driver's seat. He removed the bolts that secured the rear seat. Into that concealed space, Ari dropped his duffle bag. Yitzhak screwed the bolts back on and handed them their forged British legal certificates.

"You must have friends in high places," Ari posited.

"Only one, Captain Wingate, but last May he was transferred to Britain and forbidden to return to Palestine. The captain was an excellent tactician, and military intelligence officer. During the Arab revolt of 1936, Jews were being slaughtered by Arab Palestinians led by the Grand Mufti of Jerusalem. Wingate learned Hebrew and trained the Jewish fighting brigade, the Haganah, to fight the Arabs. "

Ari knew the history of Charles Wingate. Moshe Dayan, the one-eyed hero of the Six-Day War, gave credit to Wingate for developing the Haganah into the formidable fighting force that defeated the Arab invasion in Israel's 1948 War of Independence. His support for a Jewish state in Palestine remained steadfast, even when his government's policy wasn't. His enemies slurred him with innuendos and accused him falsely of being Jewish, but as Yitzhak testified, he was simply a Christian who believed the Jews should be restored to Palestine.

When they arrived in Jerusalem, Yitzhak drove by the Jewish Agency. Several British officers were checking papers and interrogating several men in front of the Agency.

"I recognize two of the Brits from the border patrol," Andre said.

"The British are looking for you," Yitzhak said. "You better stay away from the Jewish Agency. Any place I can drop you off."

"Arnold's Deli," Ari said. "I was told if I made it Palestine I should go to Arnold's."

"Arnold's is just around the corner." When he arrived at the restaurant, Yitzhak pulled the car to a stop. Andre and Ari got out. Yitzhak removed the bolts in the back seat, and Ari took his duffle bag. They shook Yitzhak's hand. "Ari, remember to call Ben-Gurion." Ari nodded. Yitzhak stepped on the gas and drove to the Jewish Agency. He parked his car on the street and walked in.

"Hello, Yitzhak," Shlomo said.

"Shalom," Yitzhak carried a large envelope. "These are pictures of the men I want you to watch. I just dropped them off at Arnold's Deli."

"Who are they?"

"They're two of the three fugitives the British are hunting."

"Where's the third one?"

"Teaching math and science at Maabarot," Yitzhak replied.

"These are the guys who robbed the German bank in Beirut and killed a couple of Germans."

"That's right. This one is Ari, who speaks fluent Hebrew. He says he's from Russia, but his Hebrew tells me he's a Sabra. The other speaks no Hebrew. He's French."

Arnold's Deli, Jerusalem

Ari placed the duffle bag at his feet and stood before the entrance to Arnold's.

"I met my wife at this restaurant when I waited tables. Her grandfather Arnold started the business."

Ari threw the duffle bag over his shoulder, and they walked into the restaurant. A teenage boy was there to greet them.

"Would you like a booth or a table?"

"A booth is fine." Ari nodded and looked around the restaurant. Except for the furnishings, Arnold's didn't look much different than he remembered.

"What's your name?" Ari asked.

"David."

"You must be Arnold's son."

"Yes."

"It's a pleasure to meet you, David. My name is Ari, and this is my friend, Andre. He doesn't speak Hebrew, but he speaks Russian and English."

"Our menus are printed in all three languages."

"I know," Ari replied. "Is your baked half chicken still good?"

"Excellent. It comes with lentil soup." Andre nodded.

"We'll order two of your chicken dinners with two glasses of ice tea." David wrote down the orders and walked to the kitchen.

"Andre, what do you remember in the eight months between the German invasion of Poland and the Battle of France?"

"Not much. I remember from my history class the time between the battles was called the 'phony war' or 'sitzkrieg'."

"We know that Stalin invaded Poland a short time after Hitler did, and signed a nonaggression pact with Germany, but I don't remember the dates," Ari revealed.

"I remember the date the nonaggression pact was signed, August 23, 1939."

"Are you certain, Andre?"

"Yes. Too bad we can't access the Internet," Andre noted.

"That's okay. I have the next best thing: an encyclopedia download in my documents file, if my laptop still works."

"Your Uzi still works. We should find a really secure place to store our property and see if our laptops still work. I wouldn't be comfortable storing our electronics in a rented room."

"I agree." Ari thought for a moment. "Andre, where do you put your important papers, like your passport?"

"I put them in a safe deposit box at a bank."

"Exactly. Today is Saturday, the Jewish Sabbath, and the banks are closed. Tomorrow at noon let's meet at the lobby of the Anglo-Palestine Bank. It's on the way to the Old City. We'll walk by the branch after we finish eating,"Ari exclaimed.

"It makes perfect sense Ari. Every bank has a private room next to the vault. We can place our valuables in a large box, take the box to the room, lock the door, boot up our laptops, and hope they still function."

"Today, let's find a room to rent," Ari suggested. "Follow me down Jaffa Road to the Old City. We'll pass the bank, the King David Hotel, and enter the Old City of Jerusalem through the Jaffa Gate. You should be able to find a room in either the Jewish, Armenian, or Christian Quarters. Stay out of the Muslim Quarter."

"The Christian Quarter is the site of the Holy Church of the Sepulcher," Andre noted.

"Yes, next to the archbishop's residence," Ari added.

David returned with two glasses of ice tea, the lentil soup, and a basket of bread.

"Your dinners should be out in a few minutes."

"Thank you, David. The soup is very good." David smiled and graciously left to attend to other patrons. A few minutes later, he returned with two piping hot plates of chicken and vegetables. When they finished eating, Ari paid the bill and left a nice tip for David, his future father-in-law's affable brother, who wouldn't survive Israel's War of Independence. Ari wanted to change that, but he didn't know if he could. He didn't even know if history would repeat itself. The two fugitives began their journey down Jaffa Road.

Chapter 40
TAKING OFFENSE

August 21, 1939
The Anglo Palestine Bank

The Anglo-Palestine Bank was founded in London in 1902 by Zionists who wanted to establish banking in Ottoman-controlled Palestine. The bank's first branch in Palestine opened in the city of Jaffa. Ari and Andre walked into the Jerusalem branch of the bank, showed their identification papers, and paid in advance for a one-year rental of the largest safe deposit box; they received two sets of keys. Alexander was designated as contingent beneficiary in the event of their demises.

They took their box to a private room and quickly moved the contents from the duffle bag into the box, including the money, Uzi, laptops, cellular phones, iPod, and digital watches. After the contents were placed in the deposit box, they returned to the bank vault for lock up. Ari left the bank first. Andre followed at a distance.

Micah, a Haganah foot soldier, assigned to the Jewish Quarter first spotted Ari leaving the Old City. He was trailing Ari from across the street pretending to read the paper. Micah radioed in to Shlomo, who was on his motorized scooter. They watched Andre and Ari venture into the lobby of the Anglo-Palestine Bank. After they secured their property, Andre and Ari went their separate ways.

"Doesn't look like they robbed this bank," Shlomo said. "Whatever they had in that duffle bag is locked within that bank vault. I'll watch the Frenchman." Micah continued to follow Ari from a safe distance.

Ari stopped at Neiman's dry goods store before he returned to his room in the Jewish Quarter.

The King David Hotel

Later that afternoon, Ari left his room, wearing new pants and shirt, and strolled through the Jaffa Gate to the King David Hotel on Jaffa Road. Not far behind was Dov, another Haganah foot soldier. When Ari arrived, he walked through the lobby to the gift shop and bought a *Palestine Post*. He sat in the lobby for a few minutes, read the paper, and then rose from his chair and walked to the hotel courtesy phone. He dialed the hotel operator and asked to be connected to the British Government House.

"Please stay on the line, and I will connect you." After a few rings, Ari was connected.

"British Government House, who can I direct your call to?"

"I have information concerning the Beirut bank robbers you're looking for."

"What sort of information?"

"I know who they are and where they are."

"Please hold for Inspector Stuart."

"Inspector, another bloke calling for the reward, line one."

"This is Inspector Stuart."

"Inspector Stuart, I have information about the three men you're looking for."

"And what is your name sir?" Ari thought for a moment.

"Benjamin Baron."

"All right Mr. Baron. Tell me what you know."

"I am one of the three fugitives you're looking for. In fact, the robbery was my idea."

"Is that so Mr. Baron? I guess you're not calling for the reward money. You are aware that three German guards were shot at the scene; two of them were killed."

"Yes."

"You must be quite a good shot Mr. Baron, to be able to take down three guards."

"I had an unfair advantage, Inspector. I had a better weapon." *The correct answer*, the inspector thought.

"And what do you call your weapon, Mr. Baron?"

"An Uzi." Bingo! The inspector waved his other hand to signal to the other officers that this was no crank call.

"Please continue, Mr. Baron."

"Inspector, I believe you know the rest of the story. We surprised your patrol and crossed into Palestine."

"Let me say, Mr. Baron, I have taken dozens of crank calls. Yours appears to be very genuine. If you and the others surrender and return the stolen money, I would say there is an excellent chance we can charge you with a lesser crime, perhaps just illegal entry into Palestine. Because we have no extradition treaty with the French in Lebanon, we cannot try you for murder in Palestine. If, on the other hand, you refuse to turn yourself in, we will eventually find you and hand you over to the French authorities in Beirut."

"I think I'll take my chances on the run. And for the record, I didn't enter Palestine illegally. As a Jew, I am entitled to come to Palestine under the Palestine Mandate. What is illegal is your noncompliance with the Mandate and the British White Paper policy that keeps Jews out of Palestine."

"Take it up with the League of Nations. Mr. Baron, obviously you're an intelligent man. You must be calling for another reason. I think you want a deal, and maybe there is one. I would like to see your Uzi."

"I do want a deal, Inspector, but I have something more valuable to offer you than my miniature machine gun. I have information."

"Fair enough, Mr. Baron. Let me be the judge of that."

"Listen very carefully, Inspector. In two days, on August 23, representatives from Germany and the Soviet Union will announce they have signed a nonaggression pact."

"Is that so? How did you come across this information, Mr. Baron?

"That's my business. What is important is that you tell Sir Harold MacMichael." The line went dead. The inspector dialed the operator.

"Put me through to the commissioner." He tapped his fingers on the desk until he was connected.

"Good afternoon Commissioner. This is Inspector Stuart. I've just had the most interesting call."

The Church of the Holy Sepulcher

Andre stepped carefully on the cobblestones that adorned the courtyard of the Church of the Holy Sepulcher. Grand by any scale, and commissioned by Constantine in the fourth century, the church was constructed with huge blocks of medieval stone and surrounded by Roman columns.

Andre entered. The church was reportedly built on Calvary Hill, the location of Christ's Crucifixion and burial chamber. The custody of the most revered church in Christendom was zealously divided among the Christian denominations including the Syrian, Coptic, Greek Orthodox, Armenian Apostolic, and Roman Catholic; each had chapels within the compound. Andre felt he was on hallowed ground as he walked past the Stone of Unction, where Christ's body was reportedly anointed for burial. Ahead and to the right of the stairway was his destination, the Catholic Chapel of the Nailing Cross. He entered the chapel. Candles and flowers in vases were placed near the wood kneeling benches on top of a beautifully woven rug and travertine tile. For a brief moment, he was the only parishioner in the chapel. Two others walked to the pew, knelt, and bowed their heads. Andre also knelt to pray, crossed himself, and then walked directly to the confessional booth. The priest followed Andre into the booth and sat on the other side of the curtain.

"In the name of the Father, and of the Son, and the Holy Spirit, Amen," Andre began. After the priest responded in Latin with a short prayer, Andre said.

"Bless me Father for I have sinned."

"Tell me your sins?"

"Bank robbery," Andre replied.

"Tell me what happened?"

"Father, a few days ago I survived a plane crash into the Mediterranean. There were four of us, but only three survived. We were towed into Beirut by Arab fishermen. We robbed a German bank.

My accomplice killed the German guards who pursued us. Then we escaped into Palestine."

"Where did you come from originally?"

"France."

"Did you commit this robbery because you had no money?"

"Partially. I also acted out of anger. Father, I bring information for the archbishop."

"Continue, my son."

"Hitler intends to sign a nonaggression pact with Stalin on August 23. On September 1, Hitler's armies will commence a full assault and occupation of Poland. I think the archbishop would like to know. Please forgive my sins and accept this small token for the Church," and the penitent passed a hundred-pound note under the curtain.

"I will pass this information on to the archbishop." The priest crossed himself. "God, the Father of Mercies, through the death and resurrection of His Son, has reconciled the world to Himself and sent the Holy Spirit among us for forgiveness of sins; through the ministry of the Church, may God give you pardon and peace, and I accept your penance and absolve you from your sins in the name of the Father, and of the Son, and of the Holy Spirit."

"Thank you Father. Amen." Andre crossed himself and left the chapel.

Chapter 41
WHEN TOMORROW COMES

August 22, 1939
Beirut, Lebanon

"Inspector Chevalier, there is a call for you from the British Government House, an Inspector Stuart."

"I'll take the call, Maurice. Good morning Inspector."

"Good morning. I just wanted to update you. I received a call yesterday from a chap I believe was one of the fugitives. He calls himself Benjamin Baron, likely fictitious, but his recollection of events was unmistakable, and he referred to his weapon as the Uzi."

"Very interesting," Chevalier noted. "What else did Mr. Baron say?"

"Certainly not that he was going to surrender. He gratuitously offered me information about a Hitler and Stalin appeasement of sorts, going down tomorrow. Well, we'll know soon enough; it's supposedly just a day away."

"Inspector Stuart, I'm expecting a call from German Finance Minister Ribbentrop today regarding the status of the investigation."

"If I may make a suggestion, Chevalier, I wouldn't mention any of this conjecture to Ribbentrop. If, indeed, Mr. Baron is onto something, we certainly don't want the Germans to know."

"Inspector Stuart, you will have my complete cooperation in this matter."

"Jolly well. We'll talk tomorrow, I presume. Goodbye."

Kibbutz Maabarot

At the kibbutz, there were few secrets, and Alexander and Miriam's budding relationship was not one of them. Shlomo had just arrived at Maabarot, not only to collect and drive back to Jerusalem the made-over Citroen—now sprayed with several layers of black body paint courtesy of a few artistic kibbutzniks—but to update Yitzhak on the surveillance. Shlomo was no stranger to Maabarot, having joined Yitzhak and the Romanian members of the Left Wing Young Guard Zionists as the first settlement group at the kibbutz.

At age forty, Shlomo's hair began to recede and turn prematurely white above his suntanned leathery face and his blue eyes; it made him look ten years older. Although not a tall man, he carried a muscular frame. He had been among those who survived and drained the malaria-infested swamps, tilled the soil, and made the desert bountiful.

Like Yitzhak, he had witnessed the British, formerly allies with the Haganah during the three-year Arab revolt, gain favor among the Arabs by arresting Haganah members who challenged Britain's legal right to halt Jewish immigration and openly defy the League of Nations Palestine Mandate.

"Yitzhak, have you noticed anything suspicious about Alexander?" Shlomo asked.

"Not a thing. He is an excellent teacher. He's learning Hebrew quickly, and the children both like and respect him."

"I'd like to meet him."

"Let's walk to the classroom," Yitzhak suggested. Yitzhak was narrow of build, and six feet tall with Einstein-like hair. He looked more than seven inches taller than Shlomo as they walked to the schoolroom. "Miriam, you remember Shlomo."

"Yes," and she smiled and offered a hug to the Jerusalemite who eagerly accepted and reciprocated.

"Alex, let me introduce you to a dear friend of mine, Shlomo." They shook hands and exchanged greetings. "Alex, I've asked Shlomo to keep an eye on Ari and Andre while they're in Jerusalem."

"Your friends have taken rooms in the Old City," Shlomo said. "Ari moved into the Jewish Quarter, and Andre, the Christian Quarter. Yesterday, they met at the Anglo-Palestine Bank. Later Ari placed a call from the King David Hotel to the British Government House, while Andre went to confession at the Catholic Chapel in the Church of the Holy Sepulcher. If you are who you say you are, why is a fugitive on the run calling the British authorities? And what is a Zionist doing in a confessional booth?"

"If Zionism is defined as working on the behalf of a Jewish state in Palestine, the three of us our Zionists; but we're not all Jewish. Yitzhak said that everyone except fascists were welcome at Maabarot."

"That I did," Yitzhak admitted.

"Are you Jewish?" Shlomo asked.

"No, I'm an evangelical Christian."

"Is Ari Jewish?"

"Yes."

"And Andre is Catholic?"

"Yes."

"But you claim to be Zionists. Alex, you have five minutes to prove to me you're a Zionist, otherwise Ari and Andre will receive an unwelcome visit from my men."

"You want proof that I'm a Zionist. I will give you proof, but you have to promise me that henceforth, you and your Haganah will stay out of our affairs." Shlomo and Yitzhak looked at each other. Yitzhak broke the silence.

"We give you our word," said Yitzhak.

"And I give you mine," Miriam said.

"Tomorrow you, and the rest of the world, will be shocked to hear that Germany and the Soviet Union have signed a nonaggression pact."

"And that is what Ari told the British today?" Shomo asked.

"Yes, this is the beginning of a campaign to leak information to the British about Hitler. In return, we are asking for a change in British policy concerning Palestine, specifically a British retraction of the White Paper and a recommitment to their obligations under the Palestine Mandate."

Alex's audience was stunned. Yitzhak's first thought was how was it possible that these three men of mystery were privy to the secrets of Hitler and Stalin. Or were they?

"And is Andre reaching out to Jerusalem's archbishop?" Shlomo asked.

"I believe he is," Alexander replied.

"Yitzhak, I think we can wait a day to verify. What do you think?"

"Shlomo, we've been waiting over nineteen hundred years, what's another day?"

Chapter 42

YESTERDAY AND TODAY

August 24, 1939
Arnold's Deli, Jerusalem

News of the Stalin-Hitler pact sent shockwaves across four continents. Millions of Poles awakened to the reality that their country was likely to face a German invasion from the west and a Soviet invasion from the east. After acquiring Czechoslovakia and Austria without firing a shot, Hitler began orchestrating a campaign against Poland, demanding the free city of Gdansk sever its external affairs with Poland and be incorporated into the German empire. Tucked between the Nazis and the Soviet Union, Poland's ability to mount a defense against an invasion was dubious at best.

The British Government House

"Inspector Stuart, I have a call for you from Inspector Chevalier of the Beirut Police," said Officer Winfrey.

"I'll take it. Hello, Chevalier. How is Beirut?"

"Very nervous, Inspector. World events seem to be overwhelming us. Very impressive that Britain formalized its alliance with Poland."

"Had we not done that yesterday, Captain, I fear German troops would have already marched into Poland."

"Inspector Stuart, our Mr. Baron is a pretty good informant I'd say."

"Yes, he has earned my respect. I suspect I will be hearing from him soon. He wants something."

"Do you still plan to arrest him?" Chevalier asked.

"No. As you suggested, the world has changed in these few days. He may have done England and France a favor by killing two Germans and incapacitating a third. I almost forgot to ask you about your conversation with the German foreign affairs minister."

"I told him I had nothing new to report. He said Hitler wouldn't rest until those Jews were brought to justice. Isn't there a German colony in Jerusalem?"

"Yes, Captain, and a German consulate. No doubt the Nazis have spies all over Jerusalem."

"Nazis have spies everywhere," Chevalier replied.

"Exactly. We wouldn't want anything to happen to our informant. Can I suggest we keep this between ourselves until I know more?"

"Absolutely," Chevalier replied. Stuart heard a knock on his door.

"Inspector Chevalier, sorry to cut you short, but I must attend to some immediate business, and I do promise to keep you informed. Goodbye." Sir Harold closed the door behind him and sat down. "Good morning, Commissioner. Can I offer you some tea and crumpets?"

"Thank you Inspector." The commissioner poured himself a cup, and popped a crumpet in his mouth.

"Inspector, I took the liberty to notify London. They were very impressed with Mr. Baron's information. Do you expect to hear from him soon?"

"Yes, Commissioner. He wants something from us."

Officer Winfrey knocked on the door.

"Begging your pardon Inspector, the chap Ben Baron is on the line."

"I'll take the call," Sir Harold interceded.

"Good morning, Mr. Baron. I am Sir Harold MacMichael, the British High Commissioner of Palestine. I want to personally thank you for the information you provided Her Majesty's government. Obviously, we may have differences regarding the future of Palestine, but we are united in stopping the Germans from ever setting foot here."

"Commissioner, I'll be brief. Hitler has made up his mind about Poland. He will attack at daybreak on September 1."

"Mr. Baron, the British Foreign Office is toiling around the clock to reach some kind of accommodation between the Germans and the Poles."

"Commissioner, Hitler will demand that a Polish emissary with full powers arrive in Berlin immediately. He plans to make negotiations fail, blame the Polish government for the failure, and drive a wedge between the British, French, and the Poles." Sir Harold was stunned and pondered how this fugitive in Jerusalem could be privy to the most secretive negotiations between London and Berlin.

"Mr. Baron, I give you my word as a British officer and a gentleman that we are no longer interested in pressing any charges against you or your friends. Furthermore, it is within my power to bestow on you residency rights to Palestine. Mr. Baron, I consider you an asset and friend of the British Empire."

"Commissioner, I am an asset to the Commonwealth, but I am not a friend. In return for my continued information, I demand the British Empire immediately rescind its illegal White Paper policy and recommit to fulfilling its obligations under the terms and conditions of the Palestine Mandate by lifting the blockade and removing all quotas on Jewish immigration into Palestine."

"Mr. Baron, the Palestine Mandate was signed in 1922—before Hitler took power. I certainly empathize with the plight of the Jews, but Great Britain is in a very precarious position with the Arabs right now. The Commonwealth has to maintain control of both the Suez Canal and Arabian petroleum if we are to keep the Nazis out of Palestine, or would you prefer Germany as mandatory of Palestine? The Nazis are inciting the Arabs to revolt against the British, and we are trying to control the situation. Still, I will convey your request to the British Foreign Office. Call me after September 1, Mr. Baron. For God's sake, I hope you're wrong about Hitler."

"I wish I were, Commissioner."

Chapter 43

SEE YOU IN SEPTEMBER

August 30, 1939
Jaffa Road, Jerusalem

Ari walked into the bank at 10:00 AM on this Friday and signed and dated the register. He was escorted by a bank officer to the vault. When both his key and the bank's key were inserted, Ari removed his box from the vault and carried it to a secure room. He locked the door, sat down, and placed the box on the table. Ari lifted the lid and removed the laptop, having already scanned the wall for an outlet. And there it was, destined to be around for at least another seventy years—the three pronged outlet to charge the laptop's battery, he hoped. Connecting the adaptor, Ari plugged the extension chord into the outlet and heard the familiar beep. The sound was music to his ears; the electrical charge was working.

When the charge was complete, Ari moved his mouse on a document he downloaded before his trip in space: the encyclopedia. He defined his search to the chronology of World War II in Europe, specifically incidents from September 1, 1939, the German invasion of Poland, and May 10, 1940, the date the Germans invaded France.

Ari believed he had only two opportunities to defeat the Germans and change history before Hitler would massacre millions of people. The first opportunity represented the easiest chance to end the war quickly. Ari knew that between September 1 and September 20, Germany's best troops, and all of their tanks and planes, would be used in the invasion of Poland, leaving Germany's border with France almost bare. Ari recalled that prior to the invasion of Poland, Hitler assured his generals that France wouldn't have the stomach to attack Germany's rather defenseless border. He was right. The German generals affirmed as much in their postwar commentary during the Nuremberg trials.

Ari perused the documents, jotting down notes and dates. Drawing from his experience as an Israeli tank commander, he created a spreadsheet titled "See You in September," from a song on Sanjay's iPod and very fitting for a surprise September tank assault on the German Ruhr while the German troops were occupied in Poland. Ari's tanks needed air cover.

Arnold's Deli, Jerusalem

Andre and Ari had scheduled to meet each Friday at Arnold's for lunch. Ari arrived and was greeted by an attractive waitress, a recent émigré from Lithuania. Dora's hair was auburn, and her eyes green. Ari guessed she was barely north of twenty, but then he didn't know how old he was anymore. She had an engaging smile and a dimple beneath her right cheek, and instantaneously he thought of Rachel. Ari kept looking at her, and she noticed.

During the last two weeks, he had little time to grieve over the loss of his family and the life he knew in Israel. Even if he hadn't gone back in time, Ari's life expectancy would likely be shortened due to his radiation sickness. Instead, he was in 1939, in a healthy strong body free of radiation, with a chance to save the Jews from extermination, and perhaps tens of millions of others from death and destruction.

Andre arrived and sat down. Ari asked him if he had ever studied the European air war during World War II.

"Yes at the French Air Force Academy," Andre replied. Ari revealed his battle plan and the need to have air support for his tank assault over the Rhine and into the Ruhr.

"Andre, I've charged my laptop and created a spreadsheet for the tank assault called 'See You in September.'"

"How appropriate," Andre noted.

"Boot up my laptop and log on." He scribbled his password and user name on a napkin. "Go to documents, encyclopedia, World War II for any information you need, including testimony on troop movements from the German generals at Nuremberg. Access 'See

You in September.' Feel free to integrate your tactical air plan into the document, and back it up with the memory stick."

"Ari, how are you going to sell this to the British? The German invasion is in only two days."

"I've already tipped off the British, but in all probability, we won't convince the Allies to attack Germany in the next three weeks."

"What is the purpose of creating an Allied attack plan if the Allies have no intention of attacking?" Andre queried.

"Because I plan to show 'See You in September' to the commissioner to establish complete credibility for what I believe will be our only other opportunity to defeat Hitler."

"The Battle of France," Andre said.

"Exactly,' Ari replied. Dora walked to the table.

"Have you gentlemen decided?" Dora asked.

"Corn beef on rye, with coffee please," Ari said.

"I'll have the same, and a coffee to go," Andre said.

"Did you want yours to go?" she asked Ari.

"No, I am staying here."

"Good," Dora said and walked to the kitchen.

"Ari, I think she likes you." Ari could tell that Andre was energized by the possibility of defeating Hitler—and to avenge his country's World War II defeat. Still, Ari was concerned. He simply didn't know if history could be changed; but he would soon have a test case. The British passenger ship *Athenia* would be torpedoed and sunk by a German submarine at 9:00 PM on September 3, the very day Great Britain declared war on Germany. History could be changed if the passenger ship stayed in port. Ari decided to call Sir Harold and warn him of the German submarine.

Chapter 44
A MESSAGE FROM MICHAEL

August 31, 1939
The Church of the Holy Sepulcher

Andre entered the confessional booth in the Catholic Chapel at the Holy Sepulcher.

"Bless the Poles, Father. Tomorrow Hitler invades Poland."

"Yes, I will pray for them. I have no reason to doubt you. What is your name my son?

"Andre Dubois."

"Andre, I am Father Michael," and he slid an envelope under the separation curtain.

"What is this Father?"

"An invitation Andre. Archbishop Luigi Barlassina will be honored by your presence at his rectory. Dinner is at 7:00 PM."

"Father, please tell the archbishop the honor is mine. I must be going, Father." Andre crossed himself as Father Michael began to pray for the Poles.

Café Arens, Jerusalem

Café Arens, located at the intersection of King George and Ben Yehuda, was a popular eatery in downtown Jerusalem and west of the Old City. Yitzhak drove down from Maabarot early in the morning to make a stop at the hardware store and visit with Shlomo for a late lunch. The streets were quiet on this Sabbath, and the café was officially closed. The proprietors had provided Shlomo with a key, and hummus sandwiches were ready in the refrigerator. Shlomo boiled a pot of hot water for tea. Yitzhak entered through the back door.

"Shalom," Shlomo said as he poured two cups of tea.

"Shalom," Yitzhak replied. "Alexander's information was exact regarding the Hitler-Stalin pact."

"Yes, he was indeed the bearer of bad news."

"What have you got on Ari and Andre?" Yitzhak asked.

"Ari placed another call to the British Government House on Monday, and visited the Anglo-Palestine Bank this morning for two hours. Then he met Andre at Arnold's."

"When I drove them to Jerusalem, Arnold's is where they went."

"Andre didn't stay long. He ate his lunch on his way to the Anglo-Palestine Bank. He was there for three hours. Ari lingered for another thirty minutes at Arnold's, talking to the waitress and eventually returned to his room in the Old City. Between the two of them, they spent five hours at the bank today. When you drove them to Jerusalem, Ari was shouldering a large duffle bag. Did you ever see what was in that duffle bag, Yitzhak?"

"No. I assumed he was carrying the stolen money and some guns. I would place the money and the guns in a safe deposit box, too."

"But what could they be doing at the bank for several hours at a time?" Shlomo asked.

"Obviously they want privacy," Yitzhak said.

"And a bank can provide that privacy."

The Rectory

Situated behind the Church of the Holy Sepulcher was the rectory, an administrative building of the archdiocese and the home of the Latin Patriarch of Jerusalem, also known as the Archbishop of Jerusalem Luigi Barlassina, an Italian appointee. Andre arrived a few minutes early and soon discovered he would be the archbishop's only dinner guest. A church employee escorted him to the dining room, where he was politely seated at an elegant table with formal settings of silverware, china, and crystal on top of a beautifully embroidered silk tablecloth. Andre was seated at one end of elongated table. At the top of the hour, the archbishop made his entrance. Andre quickly stood up and kissed the archbishop's hand.

"Sit down my son," said the archbishop. "I hope you like veal."

"Veal is a favorite of mine."

"Please take some bread and wine, Andre. The vineyards in Palestine are really quite good, started by the Rothschild banking family. It's not like the French wines we're used to Andre, but I think you'll find it to your liking, especially if you like your wine dry. Father Michael has told me that you and two others survived a plane crash at sea and were towed into Beirut. You robbed a German bank and two people were killed; one was wounded."

"Regrettably," Andre said.

"Was Beirut your destination?"

"The truth is Archbishop, that Israel, excuse me, or rather Palestine was our destination."

"That's an unusual slip of the tongue, especially for a French Catholic. You are Catholic?"

"Yes, I was baptized in Reims, France."

"Then you must have learned ancient Israel ceased to exist in 70 CE. The Zionists want to recreate another Israel in Palestine, but the Vatican's position is unequivocally opposed to this idea. This is unlike the duplicitous British, who depend on perfidy in their dealings with the Jews, making promises they don't intend to keep. As you can attest, there is no love lost between me and the British. For years they've lobbied the pontiff to replace me. Andre, how is that you came to know of the Stalin-Hitler pact?" Andre finished swallowing a piece of bread and replied.

"I have a source."

"In the Kremlin or Gestapo?" the archbishop asked.

"With all due respect Archbishop, I'd rather not go down that road."

"I understand, Andre. Even within the walls of the Vatican one has to be careful. You told Father Michael of Hitler's plans to invade Poland tomorrow. Pius has received the same information. War is unavoidable now."

"Archbishop, what the Vatican may not know is that Stalin's army is going to join the fight on Hitler's side. The Red Army plans to invade

Poland on September 17 on a pretext their intrusion is necessary to preserve law and order at their border." Two waiters came through the kitchen doors carrying trays of the main course. One waiter served the entrees, while the other refilled the wine cups. The Archbishop thanked them, and the servants returned to the kitchen. After they returned to the kitchen, Andre continued. "After Poland is destroyed, Molotov and Ribbentrop intend to sign an official agreement called the German-Soviet Boundary and Friendship Treaty, which defines each country's sphere of influence. Hitler gets most of Poland, and Stalin, the big winner, gets control of the Baltic nations Lithuania, Latvia, and Estonia. Millions of Catholics will be indoctrinated and subjugated to Stalin's perverse and godless communism. Those who aren't will have Hitler to contend with and their misfortunes of being born as Slavs or Jews. Hitler's troops have orders to round up and murder thousands of Polish priests." Andre paused and methodically cut his veal into bite-size portions.

"Andre, instead of coming to Palestine, you could have provided this information to the French government."

"Hitler has sympathizers in France, even in the government," Andre replied.

"Andre, are you so certain that I am not a sympathizer? I once admired Hitler in the early thirties when Cardinal Pacelli, now our pontiff, signed the Concordat."

"And why did you admire Hitler?"

"I believed him when he promised to keep the communists out of Europe. But now I know he is a liar and an evil man."

"Archbishop, I implore you to beseech Pius. The Holy See is the only one with the power to challenge Hitler. As a Catholic, I appeal to you to do what you can to influence the pontiff to withdraw from this Concordat and excommunicate Hitler. Otherwise, this Concordat is destined to be a permanent stain on our Church and be forever affixed to the atrocities of the Third Reich. The Pope still has influence among many German officers. He can make them choose between Hitler and God. It's a risk worth taking, because these German officers will be the last generation of Germans nurtured on Christian values. After them is Hitler Youth."

"Andre, I believe you came to Palestine because you believed the shortest distance to Vatican City is through Jerusalem."

"Is that true, Archbishop?" The archbishop didn't answer. When Andre finished eating, he rose from the table, and kneeled on his left knee to kiss the archbishop's hand.

"I must be going. Thank you for graciousness and hospitality, Archbishop Barlassina."

"The pleasure was mine. Will Father Michael see you again?"

"Yes, of course."

Chapter 45

CHEATING HISTORY

September 1, 1939
Jewish Quarter, Old City of Jerusalem

In the wee hours of the morning, one and a half million German troops had assembled on the Polish border. Threats of retaliation from the British and the French went unheeded. An hour before dawn, the order was given from the German High Command. German infantry and tank divisions poured across the entire Polish border, unleashing a military assault unlike any the world had ever seen. It was called the blitzkrieg.

Andre awakened this morning to voices from tenants occupying adjacent rooms. The early risers had heard the war news on the radio. Ari recalled that, on September 3, England and France would convey their final ultimatum to Hitler: withdraw from Poland immediately. Hitler refused, and England and France declared war on Germany. World War II would begin, not on land but at sea. German submarines, known as U-boats, immediately began to target English merchant ships, but on the night of September 3, the day England declared war on Germany, 250 miles northwest of Ireland, a German submarine captain carelessly fired on the passenger ship *Athenia,* killing 128 of its 1,100 passengers. Twenty-eight Americans, including women and children, were among the dead. It was an egregious error and violation of international law and a public relations nightmare for the Nazis. To save face, Hitler ordered the German press to accuse the British Navy of sinking its own ship, claiming that Prime Minister Churchill did so to draw the United States into the war. It wasn't until the Nuremberg trials that the Germans admitted to the cover-up. Still, the attack was not planned by the German High Command, and Hitler knew nothing about the attack until after the fact.

But that was all old history. Ari realized he had a chance to create a new history and save the lives of 128 innocent people. Surely there would be time to warn the British to turn the *Athenia* back to port before it was too late, even though Ari had to wait two days until a state of war existed between Germany and Great Britain.

Chapter 46
LAST CHANCE TO TURN AROUND

September 3, 1939
King David Hotel, Jerusalem

On the go, Ari grabbed a quick coffee from a vendor in the Jewish Quarter. At 8:00 AM he entered the lobby at the King David Hotel, walked to the public phones, and dialed the hotel operator. "The British Government House please." Ari looked around. The hotel lobby was busy today. Ari overheard conversations in Hebrew and English about the German invasion of Poland. Officer Winfrey answered, and, as usual, Ari spoke in low tones.

"Good Morning, Major Winfrey. This is Mr. Baron. I believe Sir Harold is expecting my call."

"Sir Harold is in Cairo until tomorrow. May I take a message?" This was unexpected, and Ari was displeased.

"Put me through then to Inspector Stuart."

"I regret to inform you the inspector is in the field today at Jaffa."

"When is he expected to return?"

"Tomorrow also," Winfrey replied.

"Winfrey, can you get a message to Sir Harold?"

"Yes, of course." Ari grew cautious, not wanting to risk his cover. Wires could be intercepted, and spies were everywhere in Cairo.

"The message is that British passenger ships off the coast of England are in great danger from German U-boats, especially those on the high seas at night. All of Her Majesty's passenger ships need to return to the nearest port." Ari paused for Winfrey to write his notes and then continued. "There is a preponderance of German U-boats in the Atlantic off the coast of England, and although German sea captains have been instructed not to interfere with Her Majesty's passenger ships, there are German captains eager for a kill—valor before discretion. That is the message, and it should be heeded."

"Mr. Baron, need I remind you we are not yet in a state of war with the Germans." Ari looked at his watch. Winfrey was right. Britain's declaration of war was official at 11 AM British time, in less than an hour. "Until the British Empire is officially at war, I am unable to send this message."

"But you will send this message if war is declared today?"

"Mr. Baron, I will transmit this message when Great Britain is officially at war with Germany, but not before."

"Thank you, Major Winfrey."

"Thank you, Mr. Baron, and between you and me, I don't think you'll have that long to wait. Have a nice day, Mr. Baron."

"Goodbye, Major." Ari placed the phone on its cradle, exited through the lobby doors, and took a left on the cobblestone walkway down Jaffa Road that led to the bank. His IDF training had taught him that a great tank commander must always anticipate and prepare. Ari's war room was at the bank, and there he planned what he aspired to be his winning strategy for his inevitable showdown with Sir Harold and Inspector Stuart.

Cairo, Egypt

Hitler rejected Great Britain's final offer, and at 11:00 AM, Great Britain and France declared war on Germany. Sir Harold's all-day meeting was to coordinate a defensive strategy with the British High Commissioner of Egypt, especially regarding the Mediterranean ports and the Suez Canal. The meeting didn't conclude until dinner was over at 8:00 PM Cairo time, 6:00 PM London time. Sir Harold received the wire transmission from Winfrey at the behest of Mr. Baron but dismissed the warning as too nonspecific. He concluded that such an attack was highly unlikely and would only demean Hitler's reputation. For the moment, the British High Commissioner was more concerned about the British tonnage that was being sunk by German U-boats on the first day of the war.

Chapter 47
HISTORY REPEATS

September 4, 1939
King David Hotel, Jerusalem

At the hotel bookstore, Ari scanned the front page of several newspapers on the rack. Splashed on each front page was the headline story, the French and British Empires had declared war on Hitler's Third Reich, and below that headline in bold print was another: the ocean liner *Athenia* had been torpedoed and sunk with a death toll of 128.

Ari's first attempt to change the course of history had been futile. It should have been easy to save the *Athenia*. Disappointed, Ari searched philosophically for answers. The rhetorical question would remain unanswered. Could he or anybody for that matter change the course of history, or was the die already cast? And if history couldn't be changed, then whatever brought him to this place at this time perpetuated a most cruel hoax. Enough of this self- doubt, he decided. It was time to place the call.

"Major Winfrey here, can I help you?"

"Good morning, Major Winfrey, this is Mr. Baron."

"Please hold the line."

"Mr. Baron, you knew," Sir Harold said.

"Knew what?"

"You tried to warn me about the *Athenia*." Ari chose not to answer the question.

"Sir Harold, to the best of my knowledge, the order to fire on the *Athenia* was made by the captain on the U-boat. My sources informed me that there were trigger-happy sea captains lurking beneath the waves around the British Isles. The German Navy is falling behind in its competition with the army and wanted to prove itself. I tried to alert you to this."

"Enough said about the *Athenia*. Do you have other information to share with me Mr. Baron?"

"I do if the British government is prepared to lift the blockade and the immigration quota."

"Yes, Mr. Baron. Effective tomorrow, I have authorized a temporary stay of Her Majesty's policies in Palestine. It will be published in tomorrow's edition of the *Palestine Post*. What you won't read is that my government is working with the Swiss to ease the crisis for Poland's Jews. Hitler may consider letting a considerable number of Jews emigrate to Palestine. We will try to get as many out as we can when the situation in Poland stabilizes. Mr. Baron, I hope you realize that this accommodation will create considerable friction between Her Majesty's government and the region's Arabs, and that will surely play into Hitler's hands."

"I assure you, Commissioner, your Arab inconvenience will be trifle compared to what Great Britain stands to gain. We need to meet, Sir Harold."

"An excellent idea, Mr. Baron. Do you have a place and time in mind?"

"This Friday. I will call you with details."

"Please do. I am looking so forward to meeting you."

Ari window-shopped on Jaffa Road as he made his way back to the Old City. He noticed a reflection of a man trailing him from across the street. He was wearing sunglasses and chatting on a walkie-talkie. Ari caught a quick glimpse before the man disappeared into a crowd. Ari walked into the store and purchased a brown suitcase with a zipper compartment on its outside.

King David Hotel

Micah had followed Ari from the time he left his room in the Jewish Quarter through the Jaffa Gate to the King David. From a safe distance, he observed Ari place the phone call in the lobby, approach the front desk reservations clerk, and pay the clerk with British currency. As Ari left the hotel, Micah called Dov.

"Hello, Dov, our subject may have reserved a room at the King David. He's leaving now. Have to go." A few minutes later, from the shadows of a side street, Micah called again on his walkie-talkie. "Our suspect purchased a suitcase from Leonard's Luggage. He's returning to the Jewish Quarter. I'll follow him to the gate, and then you take over. Shalom."

Chapter 48
HIGH TEA AT THE KING DAVID

September 7, 1939
King David Hotel, Jerusalem

On Friday morning, Ari took a taxi from the Old City to the Anglo-Palestine Bank. He arrived at the King David at 1:00 PM carrying a heavy suitcase. A bellhop offered to carry his suitcase, but Ari politely declined and made his way to the lobby telephone. The operator connected him to Winfrey, who connected him to the commissioner. Ari provided instructions for Sir Harold to be in the King David lobby at 4:00 PM. Then he placed a call to Arnold's Deli. Dora answered the telephone.

"Hi, Dora, this is Ari. Do you remember me?"

"Yes, I do remember, Ari. Andre is here waiting for you."

"Dora, may I speak with him?"

"Of course. Andre, Ari is on the phone." Andre walked into the kitchen.

"Hello, Ari."

"Hello, Andre. I need your help." A few minutes later Ari hung up the phone and walked to the front desk.

"May I help you?" asked the reservation clerk. Ari showed him the receipt for the one-night rental for the two connecting rooms.

"Rooms 333 and 335," said the desk clerk, and he handed Ari the room keys. "Do you need help with your luggage?"

"No, thanks, just one suitcase."

"Mr. Davis, the staff of the King David cordially invites you to join us in the lobby for high tea this evening."

216

"Thank you." Ari accepted the keys, then walked to the hotel gift shop and purchased the late edition of the *Palestine Post* before taking the elevator to his room on the third floor. Ari read the headlines. In less than a week, the German Army had already crossed the Vistula River, and the war fallout had not even escaped Jerusalem. Sir Harold wasted no time expelling the German diplomats and interning their spies within the confines of Jerusalem's German Colony.

As for the man who trailed him yesterday, Ari reasoned he was likely Haganah, and that discomfited him. Sooner or later, Ari believed, he would be in the sights of those watching Haganah watch.

At 2:00 PM, Ari was setting up in room 333 when he heard a knock on the door of room 335. The two rooms were connected by interior doors. Ari walked into room 335, looked through the peephole at the entry door, and let his visitor in.

"Thanks for coming on such short notice," Ari said. "I couldn't get into specifics on the phone." Andre noticed cable wires running underneath the interior door and into the adjoining room, where they were camouflaged behind the dresser. On top of the dresser was the portable laptop printer. "We're about to roll out 'Operation See You in September'," Ari said. "I know it's a long shot, but it's worth a try."

"But you're giving up your cover to the British," Andre complained.

"But you're not. Hitler's armies just crossed the Vistula River in Poland. Events are moving fast. The British have lifted the blockade around Palestine and suspended quotas on Jewish immigration."

"That's great news. But Ari, where will your Jews come from? The Jews in France and Italy still think they're safe."

"Poland. The Swiss have informed the British that Hitler is not opposed to the idea of Polish Jews immigrating to Palestine. Hitler realizes that sending Jews to Palestine will only anger the Arabs and create problems for the British, maybe even trigger the Arabs to align with Germany against the British. Remember your history; Hitler's genocide against the Jews doesn't commence until the summer of 1941—after he invaded the Soviet Union. In 1940 and 1941, Hitler was busy rounding up 400,000 Jews for the Warsaw Ghetto. If Palestine stays open, there's a chance for them to get out. And their chance for freedom only improves if we can get the Allies to attack Hitler within the next ten days."

"I see your point, Ari. If the French and British attack Germany's weak defenses along the Rhine and destroy their armaments industry in the Ruhr, Hitler will have to move most of his troops out of Poland—before he gets to conquer Poland."

"This is the opportunity for those German generals who oppose Hitler to overthrow him, and the war in Europe may cease. It's possible that Stalin could still invade Poland as the Germans evacuate, but I don't believe he will. The Germans don't want the Russians at their border, and the French and English fleets could easily blockade the Russian ports. By the way, how was your meeting with the Archbishop?"

"I think it went well."

"Good. When Sir Harold arrives in the lobby, I have instructed a bellboy to tell him that a Mr. Baron will be at the third floor foyer, but I will be in the lobby when he arrives and ride up with him to make certain we're alone when we get off."

"At which time you'll introduce yourself and invite him to room 333," Andre said.

"Yes, Andre. You can operate the laptop in 335, and print out two hard copies of 'See You in September' after I activate my cellular ring tone and say clear."

"The commissioner will think you're talking with someone."

"Yes, and he'll immediately be distracted by the sound of the printer."

"We'll go over the attack plans, and I will urge the commissioner to launch this offensive within the next ten days if possible. When he leaves the room, you come in and help me pack up the laptop, printer, cellular phone, and Uzi into this suitcase and return to your room. I'll close the connecting door. In fifteen minutes I will walk out of my room and go to the lobby for high tea. It's probable that British agents are all over this hotel, and when they see me in the hotel lobby, they may pick the lock to this room."

"When should I leave the room?" Andre inquired.

"Right after me. Call the front desk for a bellman and reserve a taxi. Have him carry your suitcase directly to the taxi and proceed to the bank. It closes at sundown. Do you still have your handgun on you?"

"Always when I walk the streets of Jerusalem," Andre replied. "Once your cover is blown, the British will follow you."

"Yes, they will, which means I have to drop out of Arnold's on Friday."

"Okay, but we still need to communicate," Andre insisted.

"We'll leave notes in the safe deposit box." Ari looked at his watch. The time was 3:35 PM. He left his room and went down to the lobby.

British Government House

"Inspector Stuart, you have a call from an Inspector Chevalier," Winfrey reported.

"Thank you Winfrey. Hello, Chevalier, how are you?"

"Bonjour, Inspector Stuart, I am fine, except we are at war against the Germans again. How did it come to this? Inspector, please forgive the question. I have to tell you that when we declared war on Hitler, we immediately closed down the German Import Bank and sent their employees back to Berlin. That's not the end of the story. Later that day, I receive a transmittal from Ribbentrop warning me not to close this case. He reminded me that there will be consequences if justice is not served. He said there will be a time when our countries are no longer in a state of war. Can you believe, Inspector, that this warmonger is talking about justice?"

"That is simply amazing. May I share your story with Sir Harold?"

"Yes, and with the informer when you meet him."

"If I am lucky enough to hear from him again, Inspector Chevalier. My guess is that our informer is on the run from the Kremlin, probably one of the few remaining Trotskyites that Stalin hasn't had murdered."

"In Russia, but France is overrun with the Jewish communists," the Frenchman replied.

"So I've heard, and they're here in Palestine as well. If I hear from this chap I will call you immediately."

"Thank you, Inspector, and let us hope the Huns come to their senses before we are forced to destroy them again. Au revoir."

"Thanks for the ring." Sir Harold knocked on his door.

"Come in Commissioner." Sir Harold opened the door and said. "Shall we go, Inspector? Godfrey's waiting."

"Yes, of course." The two officers walked by the two British guards posted on each side of flowerpots of perennials.

"Sir Harold, we found no record of Ben Baron registered at the King David."

"Of course not, Inspector. Whoever Mr. Baron is, he is not stupid. Did you dispatch our agents to the hotel?"

"They're in place."

"Good afternoon, Sir Harold. Good afternoon, Inspector," the chauffer said.

"Good afternoon, Godfrey. To the King David please," Sir Harold requested.

"Yes, Sir, an excellent choice for high tea, if I may say so."

King David Hotel, Jerusalem

Nigel Bennett, photographer and journalist from the right wing–leaning British tabloid *The Daily Mail*, had missed his first-ever Jerusalem sunrise. He even slept through the poolside breakfast buffet, and when his eyes finally opened, it was almost mid-afternoon. Nigel got himself out of bed, and after a shower and a clean shave, he was hungry for fish and chips. Only yesterday Archibald Stanley, his editor, had earnestly dispatched Nigel to Palestine by way of Malta and Cairo, but he arrived ten hours late and not until the wee hours of the morning. His assignment was to write a story for his Nazi-leaning editor on the British government's abusive crackdown of Jerusalem's once-proud German Colony. It had been established as a religious colony late in the late nineteenth century, but was now regarded as a haven for Nazi spies, unjustly according to Stanley. Nigel decided that story could wait until tomorrow. He was washing down his basket of fish and chips with beer when he noticed the arrival of two uniformed British officers.

"Pardon me," he asked the waitress. "Do you know any of those English officers walking in?"

"Sure, the taller one is Sir Harold MacMichael, the British High Commissioner."

"Thank you, dear," said Nigel. He watched as a bellhop approached the two Brits and gave Sir Harold a written message. The officers separated; the shorter officer walked to the bar, and Sir Harold walked to the elevator. Nigel observed the inspector sit on a bar stool and speak inaudibly into his walkie-talkie. Nigel quickly turned his focus to Sir Harold, waiting patiently for the elevator doors to open. He attached no significance to the other man waiting, and Ari's presence would have gone unnoticed had Nigel not quickly taken two pictures of Sir Harold with his new f4.5 lens Japanese-made wristwatch camera.

Dov was also present in the lobby when the British officers arrived. Earlier he had followed Ari on his motor scooter as Ari taxied from the Jewish Quarter to the Anglo-Palestine Bank and then to the King David Hotel. Dov was in the lobby when Andre arrived and followed him, radioing in his position. He followed Andre to room 335, and nonchalantly passed by the Frenchman. To maintain his cover, Dov quickly entered a room with the door ajar. The cleaning crew was tidying up.

"This doesn't look like my room."

"And you don't look like the Englishman who just left," the maid stated. "What is your room, Sir?"

"Room 441," Dov replied.

"This is room 331."

"I believe I got off on the wrong floor. Pardon the intrusion."

"Sir, it happens all the time." That gave Dov enough time to escape downstairs unnoticed. Micah was already sitting in an easy chair in the lobby, his face nearly covered by the *Palestine Post*. Dov continued to maintain surveillance outside.

Nigel wasn't the only one watching. Micah watched as Ari entered the elevator with the commissioner. As a matter of courtesy, the elevator operator waited momentarily for other guests. None came. The elevator doors closed, and the elevator ascended. Micah called in.

"Any sign of Andre?" Shlomo asked.

"No sign," Micah replied. "As far as I know, he's still in room 335. Shlomo, are you certain our subjects are not British agents?"

"Yes," Shlomo replied.

"How can you be so sure?"

"A British spy would not have chosen to be seen in public."

"Are you saying Ari wanted us to see him? Then he knows he's being followed."

"Yes," Shlomo replied.

"Why?"

"Micah, Ari wants us to connect the dots. His meeting with Sir Harold has everything to do with what you'll read about in tomorrow's *Post*: the end of the White Paper. We just got word from the Jewish Agency. The British are lifting the blockade and ending Jewish immigration quotas."

"Shlomo, how was Ari able to persuade the British when all the other Jews in the world failed?"

"God only knows, Micah. Your orders are still to be vigilant, and there is to be no interference unless either of our subjects is in clear and present danger. The Arabs will not take this news lightly."

The elevator doors opened to the third-floor foyer. Ari exited first. Sir Harold stood rigidly by the foyer, his gun holstered, while Ari walked toward his room and unlocked the door. Then he said, "I did you British and the French a favor in Beirut."

"You certainly did, Mr. Baron. The difference is that we British appreciate favors; the French take them for granted. May I join you, Mr. Baron?" They shook hands, and Ari closed the door behind him. Sir Harold quickly glanced around the room and noticed the portable printer. "What is this device Mr. Baron?"

"A telegraph," Ari replied.

"It's quite different."

"This one is state of the art, portable, translates Morse code to English."

"Is that so? May I see a demonstration?"

"Sir Harold, please take a seat on the sofa. I invited you to meet with me with full knowledge that by doing so I've compromised my identity and taken on great personal risk. I'm already being watched by the Jewish resistance."

"I thought you were the Jewish resistance, Mr. Baron." Ari sat on the chair across from him.

"I'm not the Haganah, but our objectives are the same: the establishment of a promised Jewish homeland in Palestine. Must I remind you, Sir Harold, the British White Paper was a violation of the Palestinian Mandate, which guarantees the Jewish people a Jewish homeland in Palestine west of the Jordan River. The British Empire willingly accepted The League of Nations Mandate for Palestine with its terms and conditions, but your government is subverting the Mandate, instead of adhering to it. That is illegal, Sir, and morally reprehensible."

"The Palestine Mandate is a World War I relic," the commissioner responded. "Since 1922, Her Majesty's government has assisted in the resettlement of over 300,000 Jews into Palestine, bringing the current Jewish population to almost 450,000, but the Jews are still a minority within Palestine. The Arab population of Palestine is over 900,000, and they do not want to be part of a Jewish state. In 1936, the Peel Commission report recommended the partitioning of Jewish Palestine into a Jewish and Arab state. Unfortunately, the Arabs wouldn't even accept a smaller Jewish state in Palestine."

"It wasn't their decision to make, nor was it yours to override the Mandate, Commissioner. You British act as if Palestine is your private property."

"Mr. Baron, if it weren't for the valor of thousands of British soldiers who lost their lives in the last war, Palestine would still be part of the Turkish Empire. Of course, we have a vested interest. Look, Baron, the Arabs are every bit as nationalistic as the Jews, and the Peel report was an attempt at reconciliation. The obvious choice was to create two states along the population zones."

"The Arabs would have received three-quarters of the land in Palestine west of the Jordan River," Ari declared.

"Because there are more of them, did you know many of the Jewish leaders would have accepted the smaller state?"

"Yes, I know."

"The truth is, Baron, we ran out of other options with Hitler on the scene."

"I disagree, Commissioner. Do you recall that the League of Nations set precedent and supervised a successful ethnic population exchange at the conclusion of the 1922 Greco-Turkish War?"

"I do recall," Sir Harold said. "In eighteen months 1,300,000 Greek nationals of the Orthodox religion, who were residing in Turkey, were under League of Nation orders to relocate to Greece, and that 400,000 Turkish nationals living in Greece and of the Muslim religion were under orders to move to Turkey. By the spring of 1923, the exchange was completed, an amazing accomplishment."

"That was your other option, Commissioner. Did you British need seventeen years to realize that Arabs wouldn't accept a Jewish state in Palestine? You had seventeen years to do what the League of Nations did in seventeen months: separate ethnic groups who had grievances against the other. Seventeen years is more than enough time for the British to move Arabs across the Jordan River to the Arab division of the Mandate, Transjordan, which no longer allows residency to Jews."

"Mr. Baron, we can't cry over spilled milk. What's done is done. Today I've ordered a suspension of the White Paper. Tomorrow the sea blockade will be lifted for Jews to come into Palestine."

"Poland's Jews are about to suffer unimaginable indignities at the hands of the Nazis. Get them to Palestine, Sir Harold, and let the Jews be a majority in their own land. In return, I will help you defeat Hitler."

"Mr. Baron, transporting the Arabs across the Jordan River is out of the question. The Chamberlain government is most concerned with maintaining good relations with the Arabs. Strategic interests are involved, and Arabia has vast reserves of petroleum. Perhaps the Jews may have more luck with Britain's next government."

"Commissioner, I am under no obligation to assist you in the war effort."

"And I am under no obligation to lift the blockade or work with the Swiss delegation to get Jews out of Poland. I pay a price, too, Mr. Baron. Tomorrow I will be accused by the Arabs of committing treachery and perfidy, and I may have to divert valuable and limited resources to stave off another Arab revolt."

Andre sat cross-legged on the floor on the other side of the door, eavesdropping and waiting for Ari to activate the ring tone on his cellular phone. Sensing that Ari and Sir Harold had reached an impasse, Andre took the initiative. On his laptop Andre entered the print command and listened for the purring sound of the printer.

"A transmittal," Sir Harold said enthusiastically. He saw each page fall into the tray, and while his attention was diverted, Ari quickly removed the cellular phone from his jacket pocket and activated the ring tone. The ring was loud enough to catch Sir Harold's attention, and he turned around. Ari held the portable phone to his ear, pretending to answer a call. He uttered a soft yes before disengaging the call and pointing the cellular at Sir Harold.

"Is that how you communicate? A wireless phone, may I see it?"

"Not before I see you," Ari replied.

"What on earth are you talking about?" Ari quickly touched a few buttons. He watched Sir Harold stand in awe when the commissioner saw his picture in color on the phone screen and heard a replay of his voice.

"You recorded my voice and captured a moving picture of me from that little phone?"

"Yes, I did. My phone has a hidden camera and a microphone."

"Now I'm beginning to believe the rumors about your mini-submachine gun that fires a full magazine of ammunition in a second."

"The Uzi, a little under a second," Ari said. "Sir Harold, these printouts are very important." Ari handed him a printout.

" 'Operation See You In September.' Mind if I smoke?" Sir Harold didn't wait for answer. He lit one up and sat on the sofa. 'An Allied offensive against the German industrial center of the Ruhr must commence no later than September 19.' That's less than two weeks. Who sent you this, General Beck or General Halder? Don't look surprised Ari, British intelligence knows what German generals want to depose Hitler."

"Commissioner, the German generals share the following opinion. If Hitler's Germany does not collapse in 1939, it will be because the 110 French and British divisions took no action against Germany's 23 second rate and poorly trained divisions defending the German border.

Furthermore, the Siegfried line is unfinished, and the entire German Air Force and tank divisions are now engaged in Poland.

"The French and the British have 2,500 tanks against no German tanks and 3,000 aircraft against no German aircraft. Sir Harold, Great Britain and France are obligated by mutual treaties with Poland to attack Germany. It will never be easier than this."

"I agree with the assessment; however, the French government fears that Hitler will move his army and panzers rapidly back and send his planes to bomb French cities and factories," the commissioner said.

"It's not so easy for the Germans. The panzers have to be retrofitted, and that will require several months. And their army will be critically short of ammunition and raw materials by the end of the Polish campaign. With the British blockade from the sea, Hitler may not be in a position to wage war against France. If Hitler can hold onto power—and that is in doubt—he may come at France from the air, but the French have fighter planes."

"Mr. Baron, the French and the Germans know that French aircraft are inferior."

"True, but your British Spitfire is the best fighter plane in the world."

"We believe it is, Mr. Baron," Sir Harold responded proudly. "The War Department would have to approve the transfer."

"Commissioner, you must convince the War Department to fly over a squadron of Spitfires to help the French. An attack on Germany in the next few days may still convince Mussolini and Stalin to cancel their alliance with Hitler. Hitler has invited Stalin to invade Poland from the east. He's waiting to see if the Allies have the will to attack Germany. If they don't, Stalin is planning to send his troops into Poland in about ten days."

"An unpleasant development," the Commissioner noted.

"And a harbinger of worse things to come if the Allies miss this opportunity to strike and cripple German industry. Despite all of Hitler's talk of peace with France and England, when he is finished with Poland, he is coming after France. Somehow you must convince the French that it is in their best interest to launch an offensive war while the Allies have the advantage." Sir Harold looked at his watch.

"I'll see what I can do. But now I must be going. Can I ring you on your wireless Mr. Baron?"

"Sorry but it only works on a wireless connection," Ari replied.

"Amazing, your gadgets; it's like something I would envision from the future. And to be able to produce them under the nose of the world's scientific community is simply an astonishing feat. I'm glad we're on the same side Mr. Baron."

"I don't have much choice, do I Commissioner?"

"I suppose not."

"Mr. Baron, for your own protection, Inspector Stuart has dispatched a field of agents to watch you. I assure you they will be discreet."

"Commissioner, all that will accomplish is to draw unneeded attention to me."

"We certainly don't want to draw any attention toward you. You are, however, an asset to the Crown. One day you may even require our protection. We don't have a lot of time, and I need to ring London. Let's talk Monday. A pleasure meeting you, Mr. Baron." The two shook hands and Sir Harold left the room. As soon as the door closed, Ari and Andre commenced disconnecting the plugs and cables. In a few minutes the gear was packed in a suitcase. Ari left his hotel room and walked to the elevator. Six people stood in the foyer waiting to go down. Not surprising, Ari thought, it was Friday night high tea.

Ari was in the lobby drinking tea and nibbling on a scone when he saw Andre and a bellhop walk out of the lobby and into a taxi. Sir Harold, who had left the hotel, was immediately notified that the occupant of room 333 had left his room and was having tea. In minutes, British agents had picked the lock with instructions to only search and photograph. A few minutes later Stuart called Sir Harold.

"Nothing in the room, Sir, but there is a connecting door to the next room."

"Make certain no one is there before entering."

"Yes, Sir." Fifteen minutes later, another call came from Inspector Stuart.

"Both rooms are empty, Sir."

"Mr. Baron is very clever. He obviously had an accomplice remove all the contents. Inspector, Godfrey is waiting for you outside. Go home and enjoy your supper."

"Thank you, Sir. We will continue our watch on, Mr. Baron."

After high tea and some dinner, Ari went back to the room and double locked the door. It had been one heck of a day. Soon he fell asleep.

Chapter 49
A PICTURE IS WORTH A THOUSAND WORDS

September 12, 1939
London, England

Nigel Bennett walked into Stanley's office.

"When did you get back to London?" his editor asked.

"Late last night," Bennett replied. He dropped the story and his camera on Stanley's desk.

"Did you get good pictures?"

"I almost forgot," Nigel took off his wristwatch. "The first night I was at the King David, guess who walks into the lobby?"

"Moses?"

"Almost, the British High Commissioner. I snapped a few pictures of him. Can you use them?"

"Maybe, Sir Harold MacMichael is pretty controversial around here. Word is he persuaded the Chamberlain government to overturn the British White Paper as a reprieve for the Polish Jews. And it would be damn good strategy for the Germans to let the Polish Jews go to Palestine. It's good press for Hitler and creates problems for the British with the Arabs. It might slow the war rhetoric from 10 Downing Street if the empire faces a full-scale Arab revolt from Alexandria to Baghdad. I think we'll do an op-ed on that. Nigel, why don't you take the day off and rest up? I'll see that your negatives get developed."

Later that evening Archibald Stanley arranged to meet an envoy to the Spanish ambassador for cocktails. He gave the envoy an envelope containing an open unsigned letter and several of Nigel's photographs. The next day the envelope containing the letter and pictures was flown to Madrid, arriving the following day at the Berlin offices of Joseph Goebbels, the minister of propaganda of the Third Reich. At the end of the month the minister would make the usual deposit into Stanley's Swiss bank account.

September 12 passed, and the overwhelming French military force, including a British contingent, remained inactive along the French-German border—despite the treaties with Poland that obligated France to attack Germany. Ari heard the bad news from Sir Harold. The British High Commissioner was apologetic that the defeatist attitudes of the French generals commanding the world's largest standing army in 1939 lacked the will to fight; they preferred to huddle behind the Maginot Line, a defensive fortification of concrete, tunnels and bunkers along the French-German border.

Ari realized the chance to stop Hitler in September was, at the outset, a long shot. Ari was convinced his only other opportunity to stop Hitler prior to the Holocaust would be in May, at the pivotal Battle of France. Denying Hitler victory in France would deny him the real estate in the east he so coveted for his death camps. Without a French defeat, Hitler could not attack the Soviet Union, and the millions of Jews in the eastern states and the Soviet Union would remain beyond his grasp. There could also be redemption for Andre. The Battle of France was an opportunity to restore honor to France.

Chapter 50
A LITTLE LESS 'HOUSECLEANING'

October 1, 1939
Berlin, Germany

"It's been a great week for the Führer," said the German propaganda minister Joseph Goebbels.

"And a better week for Stalin," replied Foreign Minister Ribbentrop. At Hitler's prodding, Stalin's armies invaded eastern Poland on September 17, and on September 27, Warsaw finally surrendered to the Nazis. The former Polish government was exiled in London, and on September 28, the Soviet Union and Germany announced a new pact, the German-Soviet Boundary and Friendship Treaty that divided up Poland and returned to Stalin what had been lost in the last war: the Baltic States of Estonia, Latvia, and Lithuania.

"The Führer will take his revenge on Stalin at a more suitable time. Did you hear that Heydrich has been assigned to supervise German resettlement?"

"An excellent choice. He is ruthless and enjoys cruelty," responded Ribbentrop.

"Heydrich has a huge task resettling hundreds of thousands of Germans families from the Baltic States into former Polish territory annexed by the Reich. The living space will, of course, be provided by evicting half a million Jews and twice as many Poles, seizing their property and relocating them east of the Vistula River," Goebbels added.

"Speaking of Jews Herr Goebbels, I was fascinated to read your op-ed in today's edition of *Das Reich*."

"Yes I believe a German-Anglo alliance is still possible and necessary to counter the growing power of Japan and America."

"You even suggested that Germany exact some tribute from the World Jewish Congress for every Polish Jew who emigrates to Palestine."

"If the Führer agrees, the Reich stands to gain tens of millions in hard currency. An expulsion of Poland's Jews only burdens the British in the Middle East, making it more difficult to contain Arab uprisings. An Arab revolt throughout the Middle East would divert British resources from other colonies to quell the revolt, and may even encourage the present British government to seek a peace with Germany. If Britain makes peace, so will France; the Führer can prepare to crush the Soviet Union. But even if the British don't seek peace, Hitler would likely receive positive press for his humane policy of Jewish immigration during a time of war."

"That last sentence sounds quite familiar. I think I read it verbatim in the British paper, *The Daily Mail*," Ribbentrop mentioned.

"I didn't know you read the *Mail*, Herr Ribbentrop."

The previous night, Goebbels gave Stanley's letter to Hitler, who embraced the idea of Jewish expulsion for a price. The Führer had already been approached by the Swiss on behalf of the British. "Housecleaning," the code name for the future plan to eliminate the Jews, could wait. Poland had at least three million Jews. The Führer issued a secret directive: every month a maximum of twenty thousand Jews from the Warsaw Ghetto could buy their freedom to Palestine at a cost of a hundred marks a head, as long as twenty thousand additional Jews were found to take their place in the ghetto.

"Herr Ribbentrop, the Führer agrees that Palestine offers the Reich an immediate solution for the Jewish problem. Other options, like a compulsory resettlement to Madagascar, are being considered of course, but that would require French consent, which is unlikely until they are defeated. Palestine is the now the path of least resistance."

"Herr Goebbels, in your newspaper I came across a picture of Palestine's British high commissioner at the Jewish-owned King David Hotel in Jerusalem, an excellent photograph of him. May I ask who took his picture?"

"A freelance Swiss photographer," Goebbels lied. "Why?"

"You remember the Beirut robbery of the German Import Export Bank a few weeks ago?"

"Yes."

"I received a call this morning from the wounded guard. His name is Schmorde, and he's back in Germany. He is absolutely certain that the man standing next to the high commissioner in the photograph was the one who fired the hand-sized machine gun that killed the guards. I thought your photographer might know who this man is and why he was standing next to the most powerful British official in Palestine."

"I'll ask my source," Goebbels replied.

"In normal times I could rely on German spies, but the British have shut down the colony. Now I will have to use the Arabs to find out about this Jew."

"Jew?" Goebbels asked.

"Yes, this man's last words to Schmorde were in Hebrew, mockingly of course. I have been in contact with our Arab friend in Jerusalem and instructed him to apprehend this Jew, but not to kill him. I want to interrogate him in Germany."

"How will you smuggle him in?" Goebbels asked.

"The Greek and Turkish ships that are transporting the Jews to Palestine will be returning to the port of Odessa," the foreign minister replied.

"Herr Ribbentrop, when you are finished with this swine, what do you intend to do with him?"

"I'll let the wounded guard Schmorde decide his fate."

East Jerusalem

"Abdullah, Foreign Minister Ribbentrop is requesting a favor, one suitable to your experience." A smile crossed Abdullah's face, affirmation that he was still the Grand Mufti's favorite assassin. But for how much longer? Coming up too quickly in the ranks was Yousef, ten years his junior.

"What does he want?"

"Not a kill, Abdullah, just to capture a certain Jew. I'll have a photograph for you in a few days."

233

"Haj Amin, why should I do any favors for the Nazis? They are sending Jews to Palestine."

"Abdullah, when a Jew is killed or captured, you are doing us a favor. The Germans are acquiring money from the Jews, no different than our Arab landlords who have been selling land to Jews for decades."

Chapter 51
THE JOURNAL

October 5, 1939
Anglo-Palestine Bank, Jerusalem

Ari signed the bank register as he had done so often before in order to gain access to the safe deposit boxes and privacy of a room. Since meeting with the British high commissioner, he kept a journal and placed it in the safe deposit box in order to maintain communication with Andre. He noted the following entries.

> September 12
> Allies reject attack on Rhine. Our next and perhaps last opportunity to stop Hitler will be the Battle for France.
> Ari

> September 14
> Do not despair. It will be the Battle for France where Hitler meets his Waterloo. Let us prepare battle plans.
> Andre

> September 17
> Began to research epic battle, feel free to view new document "Battle for France."
> Ari

> October 3

I am also researching. At confession I revealed Nazi genocidal plans. A meeting with Archbishop Barlassina was cancelled. He was called to Rome.
Andre

October 5
That may be good news; perhaps Pius will withdraw from the Concordat and excommunicate Hitler.
Ari

Ari was followed into the bank by an undercover British officer, who witnessed his subject sign in under the name of Ari Ben Ora. The British officer walked outside to call in the information.

Chapter 52
THE MADAGASCAR PLAN

November 1, 1939
The Rectory

"Welcome, Andre," Archbishop Barlassina exclaimed. "I am pleased you were able to see me on such short notice. It's a beautiful morning in Jerusalem. Please sit and join me for coffee."

"Thank you, Archbishop."

"So much has changed in the world since we last met, and not for the better. I have just returned from Rome. While I was at the Vatican, I met with Pope Pius privately and told him of you, Andre. He is very appreciative of your efforts. Unfortunately, his holiness is not yet ready to test the faith of the German soldiers or withdraw from the Concordat."

"Archbishop, Hitler's SS units have initiated a racial genocide in Poland. Jewish civilians are digging their own graves before they are shot to death. Even the priests are not exempt."

"Yes, I know. Pius has received confirmation of at least a thousand Polish priests murdered by the SS in October. More were hauled off to internment camps."

"There is more," Andre said. "You will soon hear that Hitler has ordered the sick and disabled in Germany to be exterminated. Aktion T4, the name of this nefarious plan, is to eliminate life unworthy of life according to Hitler. Midwives, physicians, and hospital administrators will be required by law to report those who show symptoms of mental diseases, retardation, physical disorders, and deformities. Decisions will be rendered as to who will live and die either from injection, starvation, or poison gas. Relatives will be provided with falsified death certificates."

"Are the sick Jews?" the archbishop inquired.

"Not even Jews, German Christians. Pius can surely excommunicate Hitler now."

"I don't know, Andre. Hitler is very strong, and Mussolini, his lap dog, is only a few kilometers away from the Vatican. And there is the matter of the Polish Jews; twenty thousand have boarded ships from Odessa and are on their way to Palestine."

"Archbishop, I know for a fact that if Poland's Jews are not freed, Hitler will exterminate them."

"That is why the pontiff will not excommunicate Hitler. He is afraid the Führer will be so enraged that he will mercilessly murder Polish Catholics as well as the Jews. But as far as the Jews are concerned, they should be allowed to go anywhere—except Palestine. Andre, did you know that even before the Nazis, the German and the Polish governments were studying the feasibility of resettling their Jewish populations in the island of Madagascar, off the coast of Africa?"

"I didn't know."

"Ribbentrop will soon propose this very idea to the Vatican as part of an overall peace plan. Of course, Madagascar is a French colony, and this idea is not possible without French approval, not likely from the current French government. Let us pray for the Jews to survive but not to come to Palestine and become the majority."

"Would that be so horrible, Archbishop?"

"As a majority, the Jews would be in a position to demand their own state. There are Christian holy sites to consider, No, Andre. We cannot endorse a reconstituted Jewish state with Jerusalem as its capital. Remember, the Jews didn't support our Lord; therefore, they should not expect our support for a state. But enough of that. Even as we speak there are secret three-party negotiations though the Vatican to dispose of Hitler. You see, good Germans want to be rid of Hitler too."

"These negotiations will not bear any fruit."

"How can you be so certain Andre?"

"Before the good Germans ever consider giving up Hitler, they'll want guarantees they'll keep the conquered land, and the Allies will refuse."

"Andre, I will inform Pius of Hitler's extermination plans. God bless you and stay in touch." Andre kissed the archbishop's hand and walked away. Andre left the rectory and the Old City and walked to the Anglo-Palestine Bank. He signed in, removed the deposit box, and carried it to the private room. He locked the door, opened the box, and removed the journal for his posting.

Nov. 1
Concordat remains the Vatican policy. Archbishop not pleased that Polish Jews are coming to Palestine.
Andre

Andre booted up the laptop and searched for information concerning the Madagascar Plan. He found it, and the archbishop was right. Before Hitler, there was a plan to forcibly transport Europe's Jews to that island. And after Hitler, the plan was reconsidered when France was defeated, but was soon scrapped because Britain remained at war with Germany and the British still had the best navy. Andre wondered if Pius were planning on a French defeat and German takeover of Madagascar, so that Europe's Jews would find refuge in Madagascar instead of in Palestine. Could that explain the papal silence in the wake of mass killings of Polish priests? History confirmed that it was the German Christians and the local priests, not the Vatican, that protested so overwhelmingly against Hitler's wholesale killing of the sick and disabled that caused the Führer to publicly abandon his proposed policy. Andre imagined what good Germans may have accomplished if only they had protested as vehemently against Hitler's maltreatment of the Jews within their own country.

Andre left the bank. It was only a ten-minute walk to Arnold's and today was Friday. He didn't expect Ari, but there was always the chance that Alexander would venture down from Maabarot. When he entered Arnold's he was greeted by Dora.

"Shalom, Andre, where is your friend Ari today?" Andre shrugged. "Coffee?" she asked.

"Please, with a glass of water." A man sitting a few tables down began to walk toward him.

"Hello, Andre. My name is Shlomo, and I am a friend of Yitzhak's from Kibbutz Maabarot. May I sit for a few minutes?"

"Yes, of course." Shlomo sensed that Andre was discomfited by his presence.

"Andre, your friend Ari is in grave danger. The men that work for the Grand Mufti al Husseini are all over Jerusalem looking for him. We must find him."

"Can they identify Ari?"

"Ari's photograph was published in a German newspaper." Shlomo removed a folded news page from his jacket pocket and handed it to Andre. "This is the October 1 edition of *Das Reich*, Joseph Goebbels' newspaper. There is Ari's picture. The grand mufti is circulating this picture throughout Jerusalem and offering a reward for the one who finds him. I have a car outside."

"What are we waiting for?" asked Andre.

British Government House

Inspector Stuart impatiently rapped on the door but didn't wait for the perfunctory invitation to enter.

"Come in Inspector."

"Sorry for the abrupt intrusion, Sir Harold. You need to see these pictures."

"Where did you find this, Stuart?"

"In the Muslim Quarter. It's quite unfortunate Mr. Baron was photographed next to you, and apparently he was recognized. My Arab sources tell me the Nazis have ordered the mufti to kidnap him and smuggle him out of Palestine."

"Doubly unfortunate, for only ten minutes ago I was chatting with Baron. I did tell you his real name is Ari Ben Ora?"

"Yes."

"I prefer calling him Baron, sounds more British and since we have no record of him being born or registered in Palestine, he could be using several aliases," Sir Harold admitted.

"Begging your pardon, Commissioner, may I inquire into the nature of the conversation?"

"All I can say, Inspector, is that he made a fantastic prediction of an event that is supposed to occur in January that will change the course of the war. The specifics of that event I am now sworn to secrecy, the details of which I am forwarding to myself in a registered letter not to be opened until after that January date. In the meantime, Inspector, how many of our men are watching him?"

"Two right now, six more should be there within ten minutes."

"Where is he now?"

"He just left the King David and is walking toward the Jaffa Gate."

"Pick him up."

Jaffa Road, Jerusalem

"There's a revolver under the passenger seat," Shlomo said.

"I have one tucked in my pants," Andre responded. They exited through the kitchen and out the delivery door. Shlomo started the car and drove the vehicle east on Jaffa Road, passing the bank and headed in the direction of the Old City.

"Ari's not alone. A few of my men are close behind him," Shlomo said.

"How long have you been watching him?"

"Since you first arrived in Jerusalem. Ari caught on. He didn't tell you?"

"No."

"The three of you blasted your way out of Beirut into Palestine. We thought we better keep an eye on you."

"To set the record straight, I'm not Jewish."

"I figured that out when you went to confession, and a few days later met with the archbishop. Very impressive. Ari met with the high commissioner—also impressive considering neither one of you has a verifiable identity. Obviously you have something the archbishop and high commissioner value. I would guess it's information, and somehow you obtain that information from within the Anglo-Palestine Bank. We know both of you were somehow responsible for persuading the British to lift the blockade and reverse the White Paper policy."

"Whatever would make you come to that conclusion?" Andre asked.

"I knew shortly after Ari stood in full view with the high commissioner. The news came to the Jewish Agency that the high commissioner was lifting the blockade. We connected the dots. Because of you and Ari, Jews are coming into Palestine again. Twelve thousand Polish Jews last month. You two have ended the British White Paper policy, an accomplishment that had eluded world Jewry."

"Don't thank me Shlomo. Thank Ari. He was able to persuade the British. My discussions with the archbishop were of a different concern, and they have more to do with Europe than Palestine."

"But Andre, events in Europe have everything to do with Palestine." Shlomo reached for his walkie-talkie. "Micah, where is Ari?"

"Walking toward Jaffa Gate," Micah replied.

"Stay close to him. We're only a few minutes away."

"We found him Yousef. The Jew is coming into the Old City, through Jaffa Gate," Abdullah transmitted.

"Good, we just entered through the New Gate. I'll drive slowly and block the east entrance; you block the west entrance. Be cautious, he may be armed."

"We have twelve to his one," Abdullah said.

"We still need him alive. Shoot at his legs," Yousef commanded. Abdullah cringed at Yousef's condescending tone. Even young Mohammed, who was driving, smiled mockingly. Abdullah thought immediately of revenge. If he had a clean shot in the crossfire, he would take Yousef down and tell the mufti it was an accident.

Through the Jerusalem side of the Jaffa Gate entered an Arab woman riding a donkey who had just passed Ari. A black Citroen slowly followed and passed an Armenian street vendor pushing his two-wheeled wooden cart. Abdullah and his fighters reached the west entrance and saw the black Citroen stop. Someone was talking to Ari. Things went from bad to worse. Ari got in the Citroen just before Yousef's car arrived at the east entrance. Abdullah yelled in Arabic into his walkie-talkie. "He's in a black Citroen."

"Take the tires out," Yousef said. The Arab fighters came out of Yousef's car, firing away at the black Citroen. Bullets hit the engine, the tires, and the bumpers. In the excitement, the donkey reared its front legs and threw the Arab woman. She fell to her death, and the donkey took a fatal bullet and fell down on its side. The Armenian vendor hit the ground and crawled to the back of Citroen, his two-wheeler overturned with all the fruit and produce spilling out. Abdullah and his men got out of their car, but only got one round off. The British police had arrived and shot three dead including Mohammed. The two Arab gunmen positioned at the Tower of David began shooting at the British, who were pinned down. Abdullah and Saddam, using their car door as a defensive shield, also fired at the Brits. They had no idea that Micah and Dov were behind them. Two quick shots to the each of their heads finished off Abdullah and Saddam. Ari threw the Uzi behind the dead donkey and rolled out of the car until he reached the animal. Prostrate, he turned the Uzi on three of Yousef's fighters, who were trying to close the gap. They fell instantly. Yousef had never heard such rapid machine-gun fire like the one that riddled holes though three of his best fighters. He caught a glimpse of the tiny gun extended from Ari's hand above the dead mule. His two remaining fighters were bogged down in gunfire. He signaled for Nasir to retreat. The two made their way back to the car and quickly exited the Old City. Shlomo called for another car at the east entrance. Andre had taken a bullet. Once the shooting ended, Shlomo placed him on the two-wheeler and pushed it to the east entrance. Ari secured the east entrance and heard the sound of running footsteps.

"These are my men, Ari," Shlomo said." Micah and Dov ran down the steps of the tower past Ari. When the car arrived, Ari and Shlomo gently placed Andre on the backseat. He was bleeding from a chest wound.

"Take him to the hospital," Shlomo commanded. The car careened away. Andre's head rested on Ari's lap. Andre opened his eyes slowly and said hoarsely.

"Ari, promise me you'll save France from Hitler. Promise me."

"I promise you. We both will. We're going to get you to the hospital. Hang on."

A truck full of British soldiers sped through the New Gate to the north side of the Old City and stopped at the stairway leading up to the east side of the Tower of David. On ascending the stairs, they discovered the bodies of two dead Arabs lying next to their weapons. Bullet holes in the back of their heads suggested they had been trapped in the cross fire. The captain radioed in. "Inspector, all the Arabs accounted for are dead. Inclined to believe the final two fighters on the tower were taken out on the tower by non-British fire."

"Where is Baron?" Inspector Stuart demanded.

"Unknown, sir. Three men left in another vehicle at the east entrance. Our only witness, an Armenian food vendor, said one of the men was shot during the fight and wheeled out on his cart. There was an Arab woman, who was thrown off her mule. She died at the scene."

"Have the vendor brought in for further interrogation, and Captain, have your men check the hospitals for recent gunshot victims."

"Right away, Sir," the officer said.

"One more thing, Captain, what color was the Citroen?"

"It was a painted black on white Sir, but it's all shot up."

"Even so, tow it in."

Hadassah Hospital at Mount Scopus

Shimon drove. The hospital was only a five-minute drive. It seemed everything was always close in Jerusalem, your friends as well as your enemies. The Chevrolet screeched to a halt at the emergency entrance. Shlomo ran in and alerted the staff. They took Andre into the hospital by stretcher.

"We'll watch him," said Shlomo. Ari looked out the window. Every Israeli knew the story of the Hadassah medical convoy massacre. On April 13, 1948, an armored convoy of doctors, nurses, medical students, and administrative staff was ambushed by Arab forces. Seventy-seven of the group were killed. The hospital shut down but eventually reopened eight years after the Six-Day War of 1967. Most of its patients came from the Arab neighborhoods of East Jerusalem.

"Where are you taking me?" Ari asked.

"I don't think we've met. My name is Shlomo, and I'm a friend of Yitzhak's. Take a look at this, Ari." He handed Ari the news page from *Das Reich*.

"My God," Ari exclaimed when he saw his picture next to Sir Harold.

"You were recognized in Germany, and the Nazis ordered a hit on you through their Jerusalem proxy, the grand mufti. The Germans were naturally curious about your connection to Sir Harold. After all, you robbed a German bank and killed some guards at a time when there was no state of war. I would also speculate they have heard stories about your little machine gun, and I can attest it is unlike any gun I have ever seen," Shlomo said.

"It's yours. Take it apart and learn how to make more." Ari handed him the Uzi.

"Thanks. We're taking you to Maabarot. You're not safe in Jerusalem."

British Government House

"We found shell casings at the scene imprinted with an Israeli Defense Industries logo," Inspector Stuart said. "At about the same time a male gunshot victim was taken to Hadassah Hospital. He was in surgery when we arrived."

"Were you able to identify him?" asked Sir Harold.

"Yes Sir, Andre Dubois from Maabarot according to his papers. His papers were forged."

"A Frenchman from Maabarot, isn't that up near our border station, Inspector?"

"Indeed it is Sir Harold. He could very well be Baron's second accomplice in the Beirut robbery."

"Is the chap expected to survive?"

"Too soon to know," Stuart replied.

"Well, I hope he does since we've lost Baron," Sir Harold lamented.

"In my judgment not for long since the Arabs don't likely have him."

"How can you be so sure, Inspector?"

"I don't believe the mufti's men would have bothered to make a hospital stop."

"You make an excellent point, Inspector."

Maabarot, Palestine

They arrived in time for dinner. Ari and Alexander reunited and hugs were exchanged. Yitzhak and Miriam were all smiles. The separation seemed like years, but it was less than three months. Yitzhak happily proclaimed the population of Maabarot had grown by a third because the Jewish Agency had placed a number of recently arrived Polish orphans at the kibbutz. At the dinner table, Shlomo showed off Ari's photograph from the German paper and explained how that led to the Jaffa Gate shootout and Andre at the Hadassah Hospital.

British Government House

Inspector Stuart's intuition was right. The very next morning Ari placed a call to the high commissioner to notify him he was safe and out of Jerusalem. Sir Harold took an educated guess and said. "I trust you're safe in Maabarot Mr. Baron."

"I compliment you on your investigative work, Commissioner."

"Thank you Baron, or do you prefer being called Ari?"

"Touché."

"I would have expected that response from Mr. Dubois."

"How is Andre?"

"Mr. Dubois is still confined to his bed, but is making slow progress. I'll get right to the point Ari. Can I rely on Mr. Dubois as I have relied on you?"

"He won't be much help to you. I transported our communication apparatus here."

"Do you still stand by your prediction on January 10?"

"I do. Did you follow my instructions Commissioner?"

"Yes. I will take the unopened registered letter to London with me."

"Commissioner, I want to thank you for watching me in Jerusalem. Your men helped save my life."

"It's a life worth saving. Cheerio."

Berlin, Germany

On the following day, Ribbentrop received a wire that the mufti's Arab forces had failed in their attempt to capture the elusive one. His present condition and location could not be confirmed, but informants reported a gunshot victim was taken to Hadassah Hospital where British guards were posted. He continued to read.

> When our subject was walking alone under the Jaffa Gate two men approached in a car and offered him a ride. We commenced firing at the vehicle's engines and tires. Almost immediately British soldiers were on the scene engaging my men at the west entrance. Our subject possessed a hand-sized machine gun that fired off a full magazine of ammunition in only a second, killing three of my soldiers at the east entrance. Eventually, Haganah fighters from the Old City joined in the fight. Out of twelve Arab fighters, ten were killed.

On hearing the news, the Führer concluded the elusive Jew may have invented a mini-machine gun and sold it to the British in exchange for lifting the blockade and immigration quotas in Palestine. Ribbentrop, who always favored Madagascar for Jewish resettlement, asked the Führer what value there was to a British open-door policy to Palestine if nobody walks through the door. Hitler revealed to Ribbentrop that two days prior, the German economics minister met secretly in Mexico City with leaders of World Zionist Organization. An agreement was sealed that the Reich would begin to receive the equivalent in gold bullion of one hundred marks for each Jew the Nazis shipped off to Palestine. The millions of German marks would not only finance Germany's future wars, but also provide the opportunity to deplete world Jewry of its financial resources. He then reminded Ribbentrop that the cost in ammunition alone was staggering for the first 25,000 Jews that Himmler's armed SS shot to death, let alone the time consumed for digging their graves. Hitler ended the meeting in a conciliatory tone and assured his foreign minister the policy could change with different circumstances. Ribbentrop concurred and the meeting ended.

Palestine

With the arrival of more Polish Jews, the Palestinian Arab revolt
that had petered out a few months before reignited under the tutelage
of Grand Mufti Husseini. In mid-November, Arabs began to attack
Jewish settlements in the countryside as well as in the cities. Even
property wasn't spared. Rail lines and pipelines were blown up. The
British came down hard on the militant Arabs. Scores were arrested,
hanged or expelled, and hundreds were killed in skirmishes. As in the
last revolt, Jews and British soldiers also died but in lesser numbers.
Fearing arrest, the grand mufti fled Jerusalem.

None of this was lost on Sir Harold. The previous commissioner
was gunned down by Arabs in the holy town of Nazareth in 1937,
and by Christmas, Prime Minister Chamberlain had enough of the
Arab revolt. On December 23, Chamberlain placed a call to the
high commissioner notifying him that, effective January 1, the open-
door policy for Jewish immigration into Palestine would halt and be
replaced by the naval blockade. Sir Harold requested time to plead
his case for maintaining an open-door policy. He was granted a one-
hour meeting with the prime minister on December 26. On Christmas
Eve, he boarded a plane to London, with refueling stops in Cairo and
Casablanca. In his briefcase was the registered letter he wasn't supposed
to open until January 10.

Chapter 53
NEXT PLANE TO LONDON

December 26, 1939
10 Downing Street, London

"I certainly appreciate the gravity of your situation Commissioner, but if this Arab revolt isn't put down, the empire will soon face Arab rebellion throughout the entire region, from the Suez to Baghdad. We simply have to give in to the Arabs and reinstate the White Paper. What makes this situation all the more unbearable is that MI-6 has discovered the World Zionist Organization is transferring gold bullion valued in the hundreds of millions to German accounts in Mexico City for this Jewish immigration to Palestine. Simply ridding Germany and Poland of its Jews is not enough for Hitler. He wants all their money too."

"Mr. Prime Minister, as acute a problem as this, I don't believe Britain can afford to lose my informant. He wants no money, only that Britain fulfills its obligation under the Palestine Mandate. Had we the courage of his convictions, the Allies may have destroyed Hitler in September. His communications network is mobile and far more advanced than anything I've ever seen, evolutions ahead of Morse code. He communicates to Berlin from Jerusalem by wireless phone."

"How can you be certain that your informant spoke to someone in Berlin?" Chamberlain asked.

"I can attest that the wireless phone was able to record me and capture moving pictures of me in color." Sir Harold opened his suitcase. My informant, Mr. Baron, told me of an event that is going to happen on January 10. I recorded the details on a sheet of paper that I mailed to myself in this unopened letter."

"Let's read the letter now," Chamberlain said. Sir Harold took a letter opener from the briefcase, slit open the envelope and removed the letter. He gave it to the prime minister, who read aloud:

> On January 10, a German military plane will make an unscheduled landing in Belgium. On the plane will be a high-ranking Luftwaffe officer. In his briefcase, the Belgians will discover the German attack plans for France and the lower countries, prompting the German High Command to revise its attack plan.

"I am beginning to see your point of view Commissioner. Let's remain in a holding pattern in Palestine, at least until the tenth. May I keep the letter?"

"Absolutely, Mr. Prime Minister. I shall be flying back to Palestine in two days to welcome the New Year in Jerusalem. May 1940 be a better year than 1939."

"I certainly hope so," Chamberlain replied.

Chapter 54
LET THE RIVER RUN

January 11, 1940
British Government House, Jerusalem

The day after the prediction, Ari placed a call to Sir Harold. "Ari, you knew in advance about the Belgium plane landing. The point is that the war plans the Belgians found are very similar to the Shlieffen attack on the West in the last war, right flank through Belgium and Holland to the weakest part of the French Maginot Line, but instead of sweeping east to Paris as in Shlieffen's attack, Hitler wants to take the French coast first, trap the French armies, and isolate Britain. Interesting but not overly creative; still, there are just not that many options against the fortified Maginot Line, wouldn't you agree, Ari? What was the point of this charade? You seem to have a good feel for things military."

"To expect the unexpected when the German attack comes, remember my words Commissioner. Write them down please."

"I'm writing them. Speaking of Hitler, Ari, did you know that the Zionists are financing him?"

"What are you talking about Commissioner?"

"Hitler eventually got the idea that Jews with money would pay him to send the Jewish Poles to Palestine. He was right. I had to go to London and appeal to the prime minister to keep Palestine open. The prime minister would rather appease the Arabs and keep money out of Hitler's coffers. I'm telling you this because I don't know how long . …" Ari interrupted.

251

"It's simple, Commissioner. You British have to decide what is better for you: Nazi Germany's defeat or a protracted war that will forever remove the 'Great' out of Great Britain. You can't have it both ways." Ari ended the call. He was disturbed. It wasn't enough for Hitler to confiscate all the property from his Polish victims; he was bent on bankrupting world Jewry in the process.

In late September, when Ari began compiling information stored in his laptop to prepare a battle plan for France, he read about a German plane that was forced to land on a Belgium airfield on January 10, 1940, due to inclement weather. Sensing British resolve was weakening in the face of Arab retaliation, and with the knowledge that Hitler wouldn't move on the West until April, Ari revealed to Sir Harold the date of the German plane landing. He asked the commissioner to mail himself a letter containing that information, and to leave it sealed until January 11 as proof. Ari, cognizant that historical events were changed when Hitler let Jews out of Poland and the British let them into Palestine, was worried that his meddling might change the timeline of the war. So he was relieved when the plane landed in Belgium on January 10.

Ari surmised that history was still on track, like a powerful river current, bendable but not easy to stop. Ari had every intention to dam that river at the battle for France on May 10, but not before, maintaining critical silence even when the German Navy commenced operations for its occupation of neutral Denmark and Norway in early April. He imagined what an angry Sir Harold would say about Ari's intelligence failure.

Chapter 55
TWICE SAVED

January 15, 1940
Hadassah Hospital at Mount Scopus

Today Andre was informed that he would be discharged tomorrow. The doctors also told him that he almost died twice. The first time was from a bullet wound that pierced his chest and lodged only millimeters away from his heart; the second time was from bacterial pneumonia he contacted postsurgery. He was placed in a special unit of the hospital for four weeks until he fully recovered.

Inspector Stuart finally had his opportunity to question Andre, not to grind him but really to get a sense of who he was. Andre was weak but fully conscious when the British officer walked in.

"How do you do, Andre. My name is Inspector Stuart."

"Hello, Inspector," Andre replied in a weak voice.

"Andre, I would like to ask you a few questions about the shooting. I promise not to take long. The first question, were you shot inside the vehicle or outside the vehicle?"

"Outside. I was walking back to the Christian Quarter behind an Arab woman on her donkey when bullets started to fly. When I was hit, two men got out of a car and pulled me in. I must have passed out. When I regained consciousness I was at the hospital. If you find these men, I would like to thank them."

"Are you saying, Andre, that you were an innocent bystander who was at the wrong place at the wrong time?"

"I think so. Lately there have been a lot of gunfights on the streets of Jerusalem."

"Andre, does the name Ben Baron or Ari Ben Ora ring a bell?"

"No, Monsieur."

"I see you came to Jerusalem from the Maabarot Kibbutz. Andre, you're wearing a crucifix, but your registration certificate identifies you as a Hebrew. I know it's a personal question, but are you a Jew or a Christian?"

"I was a Jew, but now I'm a Christian. That's why I live in the Christian Quarter of the Old City. I practice Roman Catholicism."

"One last question, what kind of work do you do?"

"I taught French at the kibbutz. I have been looking for work in Jerusalem. My English is fair, but it would help if I were more fluent in Hebrew and Arabic."

"You've answered all my questions, Andre. If you ever need my assistance, call me at this number. I understand you're being released in the morning. Goodbye, and best of luck to you. Andre."

"Thank you." Inspector Stuart closed the door. Quietly he spoke to the guard, then drove back to the Government House to present his findings to Sir Harold.

Chapter 56
FAREWELL JERUSALEM

January 16, 1940
Hadassah Hospital at Mount Scopus

Hamid Saba pushed his wet mop around the floor of the vacated hospital room. Only yesterday he informed Yousef the patient would be released by 10:00 AM today. He hoped Yousef found this man. Hamid had worked for the hospital seven years and enjoyed his job on the cleaning crew. The Jewish doctors at the hospital had treated Arab patients as well as their Jewish ones. But Yousef threatened Hamid's family if he didn't obtain the identity of the gunshot victim. He was given Ari's picture, but he could never get close enough to get a look. British guards were posted round the clock. The name on his chart identified the patient simply as Jaffa, and hospital records were secured by lock and key. Hamid thought of a way he might be able to save his family. Last week, unexpectedly, Yousef came to Hamid's house during the dinner hour.

"Welcome, Yousef. Please come in," Hamid said. Yousef sat down and gorged on a leg of lamb in front of Hamid's wife and four children. Then he said, "You have good news for me, Hamid?"

"I do. On the eve of this patient's hospital discharge, I will know what time he leaves from my cleaning assignment schedule."

"You know his room number?" Yousef chewed with his mouth open.

"I know his room number. On the day before his discharge, I will tell you and you can follow him when he leaves. Watch the British, too, for they are certain to watch him. That is the best I can do, Yousef."

"For the sake of your family, I hope it is good enough." Yousef grabbed another piece of lamb and left.

Andre left his room in a wheelchair pushed by a hospital attendant. When the elevator doors opened to the first floor, Andre was very surprised to see Shlomo waiting for him. The attendant took Andre through the exit door as Shlomo walked along.

"I haven't seen the bill yet," Andre exclaimed.

"Your account has been settled," the attendant replied. The attendant stopped at the vehicle. He offered to assist Andre into the car, but Andre resisted.

"Let me try this myself," he said. He placed both hands on the arms of the wheelchair and boosted himself into Shlomo's car. The attendant closed the passenger door as the car sped away.

"How do you feel, Andre?"

"A little sore but not too bad," Andre responded. "I see you packed my suitcase. I don't remember giving you my room key, Shlomo."

"Your clothes, everything you need for Maabarot."

"I prefer to stay in Jerusalem," Andre protested.

"Andre, Jerusalem is not safe for you now. We were lucky to get Ari out."

"How is Ari?" Andre inquired.

"He's safe in Maabarot. Andre, the British discovered you're his accomplice, and that's why they've been watching you so closely. And don't think that hasn't gone unnoticed. The hospital treats Arab patients, has Arab employees, and contracts with Arab vendors. Any of them could easily be a pipeline to the mufti. He might have reason to believe your capture might lead him to Ari."

"Inspector Stuart caught me in a lie. He asked me if I knew an Ari Ben Ora, and I said no."

"The British expect to be lied to," Shlomo replied. "They're quite good at it themselves."

"I'll go with you to Maabarot, but not now," Andre exclaimed. "I've got a few things to attend to. Meet me in the alley behind the Holy Church of the Sepulcher at 6:00 PM."

"Where should I take you now?"

"To my room in the Old City."

"Andre, take the gun in the glove compartment. Be careful and I'll see you behind the church at 6:00."

It was an unusual convoy of drivers that proceeded through the New Gate into the Old City's Christian Quarter. In the lead position was Shlomo. Closely behind and mounted on a noisy Vespa were Dov and Micah, and in third position was a jeep filled with British soldiers dispatched to patrol Andre's neighborhood. Trailing the pack at a safe distance were the mufti's men, Yousef and Anwar, in a Ford wagon. Shlomo slowed to a stop, looked into his rearview mirror, and saw the British soldiers pull into the curb behind him. Andre slowly got out and began to gingerly walk to his room. Shlomo drove away. The Haganah boys rode slowly by, but took a hard right into the alley and brought the scooter to an abrupt halt. Dov dismounted and walked to his surveillance location, the Christian bookstore across from Andre's boardinghouse. That is when he noticed the camera flash from an old, beige Ford wagon parked at the tobacco shop next to the Christian bookstore. The driver left the wagon and ventured into the tobacco store, while the passenger with the camera drove away.

Dov continued walking until he reached the Christian bookstore. Not wanting to attract attention, he never left the store without purchasing a book. He followed his usual routine and sat by the window and began to read the book he selected. A few minutes later Micah drove his scooter up to the store, walked in, and sat down next to Dov.

"Dov, Andre's going to meet Shlomo behind his chapel at 6:00."

"Micah, I think we have a live one next door at the tobacco shop."

Precisely at 5:15 PM, Andre left his room and proceeded to walk Via Dolorosa. Two of the British officers followed him, twenty paces behind. Anwar was also on the move. Yousef had instructed him to follow the British at a safe distance. He was wearing a heavy jacket with bulging pockets. Watching this all play out were Dov and Micah. Dov walked out of the bookstore. It was a chilly evening. Micah threw Dov a sweater from the saddlebag and kick-started the scooter's engine. The noise of the engine briefly distracted Anwar. He turned around to see a man riding his scooter in the opposite direction; he didn't notice Dov crossing the street. Micah circled around and arrived at the chapel a few minutes before Andre and Anwar.

The Church of the Holy Sepulcher

"Yousef, I am calling you from within the Holy Church of the Sepulcher," Anwar said. "Yousef, the patient has entered the Chapel of the Nailing Cross, am requesting permission to go in. Yes, two of the British are guarding the entrance."

"Proceed with caution Anwar. Ahmed and I should be there in about twenty minutes." Anwar hid the walkie-talkie behind a statuette in the rotunda and removed his jacket.

The British performed a routine search on Anwar, checking his jacket pockets, but failing to find the knife sewn into lining of his sleeve. Anwar entered the chapel and sat in the third pew from the back, two pews in front of where Micah was sitting. Anwar glanced around and began counting. There were nine men and four women in the pews, but none looked like the man he was following. And then he heard the faint sounds of a conversation coming from the confessional. Anwar slid over on the bench as close to the confessional as he could, but was still unable to fathom the conversation.

"Andre, where have you been? The archbishop was asking for you."

"Father, I was shot at the Jaffa Gate and spent weeks recovering in the hospital."

"I remember hearing about that incident between the grand mufti's men and the British soldiers. I heard that an Arab woman died, but I had no idea you were caught in the crossfire."

"I wasn't exactly an innocent bystander, Father. I was trying to save my friend from the grand mufti's men. He was walking behind the Arab woman."

"I see."

"Yes, and now the mufti must know who I am. I am leaving Jerusalem and came to say goodbye."

"Where are you going Andre?"

"It's safer if you and the archbishop don't know. Bless me, Father."

"Bless you, my son."

Andre wanted to tell Father Michael the entire truth. That he had come from the future, that if France fell, there would be an Auschwitz, Treblinka and the other death camps. Millions of civilians gassed to death for being Jews or Slavs—after which their hair and gold fillings would be extracted and their bodies burned in ovens, leaving nothing but the residue of ashes to be blown like dust in the wind.

He wanted to tell Father Michael that the Jews would receive a tiny state in Palestine, that the Second Vatican Council was coming that would forever change the Church's relationship with the Jews, and that Pius XII would go down in history as "Hitler's Pope." Andre's dilemma was that the Vatican didn't share his sense of urgency, because none of these events had yet occurred. Certainly Jews and Poles were slaughtered, but Hitler's death camps would not be operational until 1942. And that would only happen if history didn't change. Some things were different this time around. The British kept Palestine open, and Hitler was permitting Polish Jews to emigrate to Palestine, and they were coming in by the thousands. Andre looked at his watch.

"Father, it's time for me to go. May I leave by the back exit?"

"Of course, Andre. I'll walk you to the door."

As they left the confessional booth and walked toward the pulpit, Anwar slithered quickly toward them carrying the folded jacket on his left arm while extending his right into the jacket sleeve. Father Michael abruptly halted when he felt the tip of the knife in his back. Anwar spoke quietly.

"Listen very carefully. Unless you do what I say, I will thrust the full blade of my knife into your priest." Andre nodded. "Priest, take us through the back door."

Micah was fortunate that he arrived before the British began searching for weapons at the chapel entrance. Otherwise they may have found his knife in his sheath tucked inside his belt loops. As Anwar moved forward, Micah pulled his blade from the sheath and, in a motion he had practiced repeatedly, threw his knife at Anwar. It hit its mark. The Arab uttered a deep groan as the knife lodged deep between his shoulders. He fell to the ground. Micah approached his victim and pulled out the knife.

"Both of you, out the back, now," Father Michael commanded.

Alerted by screams, the British policemen came running into the chapel. Father Michael calmed the worshippers, while one of the Brits radioed for a medical team. The other searched the chapel for Andre and Micah.

"Where is the man who was in the confessional?" asked the other British guard.

"He left through the back door with the young man who saved us from this one on the floor," Father Michael replied. The British policeman ran through the door and into the dark alley. First he heard the sound of a scooter engine fade into the distance, and then a gunshot. The policeman had barely turned around when he took two bullets to the chest and fell in the alley.

Amid the bedlam, Ahmed and Yousef were unnoticed as they quietly entered the chapel. Yousef shot the British radio operator, held a gun on Father Michael, and ordered the worshippers to keep their heads down while Ahmed followed the second policeman to the alley. Yousef knelt to attend to Anwar, who was barely alive.

"Yousef, I failed, but the priest may know where to find the hospital patient."

"I'm sure he does. Anwar, I can't take you with us ... and I can't leave you for the British."

"I understand," Anwar dutifully said.

"One day, Anwar, we'll meet in Paradise." With a quick twisting motion, Yousef broke Anwar's neck. "Ahmed, go to the car and meet me in the alley." Ahmed left by the front door. "Priest, lock up the chapel." Once again Yousef ordered the congregants to keep their heads down. Father Michael closed and locked both sets of doors, preventing the congregants from leaving the chapel. By the time the medical team and additional British forces arrived, Yousef and the priest were in the backseat of the van on the way to Arab East Jerusalem.

"Priest, what is your name?"

"Father Michael."

"You are the priest to the man who was in the hospital. What is this man's name?"

"As a priest, I am bound by the priest/penitent privilege. All conversations between a man or a woman and his or her priest are protected."

"We'll see about that," Yousef replied.

Chapter 57
A WAITING GAME

January 23, 1940
British Government House

"I thought last week was bad—two dead British policemen, a missing priest, and no leads." So lamented the British High Commissioner. Sir Harold was just informed the missing priest, Father Michael, was dead, his body was discovered in a dumpster off the side of the road in the Muslim Quarter of Old Jerusalem. He had been shot in the head after his torture; his fingernails had been ripped off, and several of his teeth had been removed. "Andre's in Maabarot," the commissioner said. "Ari called me. Andre is quite upset on hearing the news about Father Michael. Apparently he gave his priest and the archbishop some of the information we received."

"I don't understand these French Catholics and their need to confess. Talk to a priest about your amorous affairs or duplicitous business transactions, but some things are better left unsaid, especially when it's not obvious what side the priest is on in this war," Stuart said.

"Through his communication with the archbishop, Andre was hoping to persuade the pope to cancel the Concordat and excommunicate Hitler. We have to assume that the priest broke down under torture and revealed everything he knew," Sir Harold posited.

"And Hitler will believe he has a traitor in the High Command."

"Not necessarily, Inspector. Hitler may choose to believe the leak is from the Soviet side."

"I certainly hope so. There is some good news, Sir Harold. We've identified the dead man at the church as Anwar Said, one of the mufti's men."

"Issue an arrest warrant for the Grand Mufti Husseini. Do you know his present location, Inspector?"

"No, he moves around frequently, but we'll get him."

"And Inspector, as a precaution, send a platoon of our men to secure the perimeter around Maabarot."

"Yes, Sir. Begging your pardon, Sir, this arrangement with Mr. Baron, I mean Ari, is it all worth the ire of the Arabs?"

"You are referring to our open-door immigration policy for the Jews."

"Exactly, Sir, your order to suspend the White Paper."

"If the allies had followed Mr. Baron's conviction to attack the twenty or so lousy German divisions on the Rhine and Ruhr when Hitler's best armies were in Poland, this war may have been over. Now the Allies are forced to play a waiting game until Germany decides to attack with over 200 of its best and battle-tested divisions. Stuart, every bit of advance information that Mr. Baron has provided us has come to fruition. We need to know when and where the Germans are going to attack if we have any chance to win. And all that Mr. Baron requests is that we British be true our word and abide by the Palestinian Mandate. I think we're getting off cheap," Sir Harold quipped.

Chapter 58
WHO IS THE MOLE?

February 10, 1940
Berlin, Germany

At the behest of Ribbentrop, Hitler hastily called a meeting of his most trusted advisers. Attending were Minister of Propaganda Joseph Goebbels, Minister of the Interior Heinrich Himmler, Minister of Foreign Affairs Joachim Von Ribbentrop, Hitler's deputy Rudolph Hess, Luftwaffe commander Herman Goering, and Chief of the Jewish Office within the Third Reich Adolph Eichmann. When they were all seated the Führer spoke.

"All of you are familiar with the incident in Beirut last summer when two men robbed our bank and killed two of our guards. The surviving officer, Schmorde, has been able to confirm the identity of the second robber, a Frenchman named Andre Dubois. Before he fled to Syria, Grand Mufti Haj Amin al Husseini sent this photograph along with some important information. Our conclusion is that these men who slipped into Palestine from Beirut have been providing information to the British high commissioner and archbishop of Jerusalem. Husseini's men followed the Frenchman to his final confession."

"Did they kill the Frenchman?" asked Goering.

"No," replied Hitler. "He escaped, but Husseini extracted the information from the priest."

"Excuse me, Führer," said Eichmann. "I was under the impression these criminals were Jewish."

"At least this one appears not to be. There were four when their plane crashed on the Mediterranean Sea outside of Beirut. Three of the four survived the crash. Where the flight originated from the priest didn't know. Their rubber raft was towed into Beirut harbor by some Arab fishermen, and soon after, two of the three robbed the German bank. The Frenchman was at the cashier's window. The other, whom Schmorde identified from the photograph in *Das Reich*, surprised the three guards with an elusive hand-sized machine gun that killed two of the three guards. The fugitives hijacked a taxi and escaped into Palestine.

"This Frenchmen knew in advance the exact dates and conditions of Germany's Non-Aggression Pact with the Soviet Union; the dates when Germany would invade Poland; our plans to destroy the clergy, the nobility, and the Jews. He knew the Soviet invasion date into eastern Poland. He even knew about our extermination plans. He kept asking his priest if the Pope intends to test the faith of German Catholics, and warned that would be the last generation of Germans who will know Christ.

"There are thirty million Catholics in Germany, including myself and many of our finest officers. If Pius decides to oppose me, if he should cancel our Concordat and excommunicate me from the Church, thousands of German officers may turn against me. No army on earth is capable of bringing down the Third Reich, yet this one man could destroy it." Hitler regained his composure and changed the subject. "What if the British have discovered my invasion plans for France?"

"Führer, the mole could be in the Kremlin," Goebbels suggested.

"Wishful thinking, Herr Goebbels. As the Fuhrer stated, the Frenchman knew of the extermination plan," Ribbentrop countered.

"Stalin has spies in Berlin," Goebbels replied. "Hundreds of doctors and hospital administrators are involved with this program, and many are disgruntled with this policy. Any of them could have easily passed on the information to the Soviets. To conduct a witch hunt in the High Command will only demoralize and turn the generals against the Führer. We have no proof."

"Herr Goebbels is right," Hitler replied. "Herr Ribbentrop, at the conclusion of this meeting, I suggest you notify Molotov in Moscow, and tell him we suspect there is a mole in the Kremlin. Perhaps he can find the rat. Henceforth, no representatives of the Soviet government or military are to receive any advance information of future German military campaigns. Herr Eichmann, how many Polish Jews have emigrated to Palestine?"

"About a hundred thousand," Eichmann replied. "And that exchange has brought into the Reich Swiss currency equivalent to ten million German marks."

"How many Jews has the SS eliminated?"

"According to Herr Heydrich, approximately fifty thousand, mostly shot and buried in unidentified mass graves," Eichmann continued. "Mein Führer, I'm concerned that this unfettered Jewish immigration to Palestine will cost us the support of the Arabs."

"I'm not concerned about the Arabs," Hitler replied. "I have repeatedly told Husseini that when the British are out of Palestine, the Arabs can do their own 'housecleaning' of the Jews. I'm more concerned about the Vatican."

"Mein Führer," said Ribbentrop, "recently I have met with the Pope. It is true that he harbors much animosity toward the Third Reich. He views Germany's pact with Stalin a serious breach of the Concordat, and he is affronted by what he considers German brutality against the general population in Poland, especially the priests. Furthermore, Pius is vehemently opposed to sending European Jews to Palestine. In spite of this, it is my judgment that the Pope will not come out against you publicly."

"What makes you so certain about your conclusion, Herr Ribbentrop?" Hitler queried.

"Pius knows that without the resolve of the German National Socialist Party to rid Germany of its communists, the rest of Western Europe would have fallen to Stalin, who would have routed the Vatican and confiscated all church property as he did in Russia. Today, Pius cannot be blind to the millions of Soviet troops amassed along the borders of Poland, Finland, Lithuania, Estonia, and Latvia. Pius knows he needs a strong Germany to protect his Church."

"I hope your assessment is correct, Herr Ribbentrop. This meeting is adjourned."

"Heil Hitler," Goebbels said as he clicked his heels, rose from his chair, and extended his left arm in salute.

"Heil Hitler," said the remaining cabinet members as they rose and saluted.

Chapter 59
VIVA LA FRANCE

March 30, 1940
Kibbutz Maabarot

There were changes at Maabarot. Andre slowly regained his strength. Alexander and Miriam were married, and Ari took on the appearance of an observant Jew, incognito, sporting a full beard with dreadlocks and wearing dark garb. The Battle of France was only six weeks away, and he had to return to Jerusalem.

Andre was sickened when he heard that Father Michael had been tortured and killed by the mufti's men. He was also worried the mufti had extracted information and passed it on to the Germans. Andre was also despondent because his efforts to effect change at the Vatican appeared to be in vain. He decided it was time to leave Palestine and return to France. He appealed to Ari. "If I get to France, I have time to join the French Air Force before the Battle of France. With my knowledge of avionics and aerodynamics, I have a chance to instruct French pilots and improve their fighting capabilities. I don't belong in Palestine Ari. I'm not a Christian Zionist like Alexander. I'm a French Catholic, united with you to destroy Hitler before he destroys all of Europe. Will you help me get to Lebanon?"

"Yes, of course."

"I need French citizenship papers to enter Lebanon, and I need money for airfare to Paris."

"Tomorrow Yitzhak will take me to Jerusalem. I'll stop at the bank. He'll return with your francs. Daniel can get your French citizenship papers."

"When will you return from Jerusalem?"

"I don't know; hopefully, before the Battle of France on May 10."

"Ari, what if Hitler changes his invasion date?"

"Because of what Father Michael may have revealed under torture?" Ari asked.

"Yes," Andre said.

"We'll know next month. If Hitler is true to his timetable, the 'phony war' with Britain and France will come to an abrupt end with the German naval attack on Denmark and Norway."

"Will you warn the commissioner?" Andre asked.

"Absolutely not. Hitler's conquest of Denmark and Norway was a prelude to the Battle of France, and strategically provided Germany's ships and U-boats with unfettered access to the Atlantic sea lanes as well as airbases for striking England. For the superior British Navy, the loss of Denmark and Norway was a humiliating defeat and gave Hitler the confidence to attack France and the lower countries in May. The loss of these countries will be a reality check for the British and should improve my bargaining position with the commissioner."

"On the contrary, Ari. I can imagine you'll only lose credibility. I think he'll consider this an intelligence gaffe, your blunder."

"Not if I have a credible reason for not providing him with the advance information."

"And do you?"

"I think so."

"Well, I hope so. Ari, when this is all over and if I'm still alive, promise me you'll come to Paris. Alexander too."

"I promise I will. You'll have to ask Alexander."

"I will, and I will write you at Maabarot."

"You'll have to. We don't have e-mail anymore." Andre laughed and they embraced.

"See you at dinner tonight," Andre said.

The following morning Ari and Yitzhak drove the car to Jerusalem, and Daniel began creating new documents for Andre. Daniel supervised when Yitzhak was gone, and arranged for Omar, a Bedouin friend since his childhood, to escort Andre to Lebanon, riding on camels with six other Bedouin tribesmen. Bedouins regularly crossed between

Palestine and Lebanon, usually without interference from British or French authorities. Once in Lebanon, Andre could board a bus to the Lebanese airport. With the proper papers, Andre could board the long flight back to France that stopped for refueling in Cairo, Algiers, Rabat, and Lisbon before finally arriving in Paris.

Yitzhak drove into Jerusalem and remained in his parked car next to the bank while Ari exchanged two thousand British pounds into francs. After Ari gave Yitzhak the francs, he drove Ari to Arnold's. Arnold recently finished converting his garage behind the restaurant to a livable room with a bathroom, shower, and pullout bed. Originally his idea was to provide room and board to an immigrant in exchange for help in the kitchen. Ari would be that immigrant.

"Welcome Ari, it's a pleasure," Arnold said.

"The pleasure is mine, Mr. Goldstein."

"Call me Arnold, and I think you met David. This is my other son, Meir."

"Shalom," Meir said.

"Shalom," Ari said to both David and his future father-in-law, Meir.

"Ari, let me give you the keys to the apartment. When you get hungry come to the kitchen."

"Thank you." Ari opened the door to his room and put his suitcase down. He had returned to his room during that summer in 1982, when he waited tables at Arnold's. Memories of Rachel came back. Ari took a shower and changed clothes. When he was ready, Ari walked through the back door and into the kitchen. The fragrance of roasting coffee filled his senses and stimulated his appetite.

"How about I cook you up some lox and eggs Ari?" Arnold asked.

"Only if you let me help you in the kitchen," Ari said.

Chapter 60
THE WESER EXERCISE

April 9, 1940
Arnold's Deli, Jerusalem

From the office off the kitchen, Ari called Sir Harold at precisely 10:00 AM. "Ari, if you are calling to warn me about the German naval invasion of Denmark and Norway, you're too late, two hours late to be exact. Actually that's not accurate. The attack commenced two hours ago. Why didn't you call me yesterday or sooner?"

"Sir Harold, I didn't receive advance information of the attack, and neither did the Army High Command and general staff, not even Goering. This military action was planned secretly by the OKW and the German Navy." Andre decided to change tactics and shift responsibility to the British. "Commissioner, were there no visible signs, like German ship movements or troop mobilizations near the Danish and Norwegian ports that would hint of an attack on Norway or Denmark?"

"There were signs Ari. Not only did we ignore them, but so did the governments in Denmark and Norway. Both countries had recently signed nonaggression pacts with Germany and believed they were safe from attack. They were naive to think that Germany would honor such treaties, because Germany has no direct access to the Atlantic Ocean. In World War I, we were able to bottle up their navy by mining and patrolling the narrow North Sea from the coast of Norway to the Shetland Islands. Now the Germans can use the bases in Norway to secure their supply lines for raw materials and have total access to the Atlantic Ocean for their navy and U-boats."

"But the British still have superior naval forces," Ari contended.

"Of course we do, but the playing field has changed. Now the war will finally come to England, I regret to say. We'll have to fight hard and smart to kick the Krauts out of those countries. Ari, do you know when Hitler plans to attack France?"

"No, I'll phone you as soon as I know Commissioner."

Berlin, Germany

Hitler summoned a cabinet meeting. "I have great news," he began. "Admiral Raeder has informed me that Operation Weser Exercise has exceeded its objectives in its first day. The German Navy has seized strategic bases in both Denmark and Norway. We can be assured the British received no advance notice about this operation, because the Royal Navy was caught napping. Furthermore, Soviet foreign minister Molotov and Stalin have assured Herr Ribbentrop they have found the moles and are interrogating them. My directive still stands. Anyone caught providing the Soviets with information on any future German military campaign will be arrested and shot. Germany's nonaggression pact with the Soviet Union is not worth the paper it's written on. Let us win one front at a time, and not repeat the same mistake that cost Germany the first World War: fighting on two fronts at the same time. As soon as we're done in the west, I will unleash all the power of the Third Reich on the Soviet Union."

Chapter 61
DIRECTIVE 21

April 10, 1940
Arnold's Deli, Jerusalem

Unfortunately for Sir Harold, the British did not kick the Krauts out of Denmark and Norway during Hitler's Operation Weser, but not for lack of trying. By April 17, the Royal Navy grudgingly accepted the fact that the inferior German Navy, using the elements of surprise and trickery, was able to gain a strategic advantage against the Allies when the two Nordic countries fell.

While the British Navy and Royal Air Force were battling the German Navy and Luftwaffe, Ari, disguised as a Hasidic Jew, made frequent visits to the Anglo-Palestine Bank, signing in each time, removing his safe deposit box, and using the resources on his computer to research German and Allied tactics deployed at the Battle of France.

Ari drew on his experience as a tank commander to create a defensive plan for the Allied troops, whose success would depend on his ability to convince the Allied leaders to realign military assets along the front to stave off the inevitable German blitzkrieg through hilly forested terrain that was considered impenetrable.

Ari wasn't simply going to volunteer this information to the commissioner. On the contrary, he intended to bargain and force the British to pay a very stiff price. That negotiation would happen later. His immediate objective was to gratuitously offer the commissioner a credible copy of Hitler's Directive 21, which he discovered on his software encyclopedia. Directive 21 was Hitler's executive order to invade the Soviet Union in 1941.

The next day Ari caught a ride with Shlomo to Maabarot. The darkroom at Maabarot, the place where so many forged documents were created, was the perfect place for Ari to apply a touch of photolithography to his computer printout in order to make it appear authentic and contemporary.

Yitzhak returned Ari to Arnold's the following day. Dora watched him as he came into the kitchen. She had taken a romantic interest in Ari, although she didn't particularly care for the beard or the payis, the sidelocks. Still, she tried to persuade Ari to accompany her to the weekly social at the Jewish Agency. He put her off until June. Dora knew that Ari was hiding. He was very mysterious, and that made him more appealing to her.

Chapter 62
BACK TO THE MANDATE

April 14, 1940
British Government House

"So you're Alexander," Sir Harold rendered judgment as he sat behind his desk.

"Yes."

"Ari said you have something of interest for me." Alexander removed an envelope from his briefcase and handed it to Sir Harold.

"Please have a seat."

"Thank you." Alexander sat down.

"This is written in German," the commissioner noted. "My German is not very good, but Inspector Stuart is a linguist and speaks the language fluently." Sir Harold picked up the phone and requested the inspector's presence in his office.

"Do you understand German?" he asked his guest.

"Yes." There was a knock on the door.

"Come in, Inspector. Inspector Stuart, meet Alexander. He came down from Maabarot. Inspector, the document is written in German. Translate please." Stuart put on his bifocals and silently read.

"Sir Harold, may I be free to speak in front of our guest?"

"Quite all right; he understands German."

"Sir, this appears to be one of nine copies of Directive 21, issued and signed by Adolf Hitler, code named Operation Barbarossa, authorizing an invasion of the Soviet Union after the defeat of France and Great Britain."

"Is this document authentic?"

273

"I strongly suspect it is. It appears to be Hitler's signature."

"Thank you, Stuart. Please make several copies and get this off to London."

"Yes, Commissioner. Anything else?"

"One more thing: keep this between us and London. Nobody else at the Government House need be privy to this document."

"Understood, Commissioner," Stuart closed the door as he left.

"May I express my opinion, Sir Harold?" Alexander asked.

"Absolutely. I'm very interested in your opinion."

"If I were your prime minister, I would not immediately reveal this directive to Premier Stalin."

"You wouldn't?"

"No, Sir. I would present him this directive only after the Germans attack France. Stalin controls petroleum and other raw materials Hitler needs to continue his war effort. Stalin will gladly deprive Hitler of these war materials if he sees the Allies are holding their lines. Stalin knows what Hitler fears most of all."

"And what is that?"

"A war on two fronts. Give Stalin the document when you have the most leverage, and you get the most leverage when Hitler's offensive is derailed in France.

"I completely agree with your assessment, Alexander, but stopping Hitler may not be that easy."

"Easier when one knows the German attack plan," Alexander said.

"I've been waiting for those plans, Alexander, and I was hoping Ari gave them to you." Alexander rose from his chair and walked to the commissioner. From his briefcase Alexander removed a document and placed it on the glass top of the commissioner's desk. Sir Harold leaned forward in his chair and readjusted his glasses for reading.

"Alexander, you've just handed me a copy of the Palestine Mandate."

"Commissioner, the road to your victory in France begins with the Palestine Mandate. Shall we discuss its resolutions?"

"Fair enough," said Sir Harold, and he began to read aloud.

THE PALESTINE MANDATE
COUNCIL OF THE LEAGUE OF NATIONS

Whereas the Principal Allied Powers have agreed, for the purpose of giving effect to entrust a Mandatory selected by said Powers the administration of the territory of Palestine, which formerly belonged to the Turkish Empire, within such boundaries as may be fixed by them; and

Whereas the Principal Allied Powers have also agreed that the Mandatory should be responsible for putting into effect **the declaration originally made on November 2, 1917,** by the Government of his Britannic Majesty, and adopted by the said Powers, in favor of a the establishment in Palestine of a national home for the Jewish people, it clearly being understood that nothing should be done which might prejudice the civil and religious rights of existing non-Jewish communities in Palestine, or the rights and political status enjoyed by Jews in any other country; and

Whereas the Principal Allied Powers have selected his Britannic Majesty as the Mandatory for Palestine; and

Whereas the Mandate in respect of Palestine has been formulated in the following terms and submitted to the Council of the League for approval; and Whereas His Britannic Majesty has accepted the Mandate in respect of Palestine and undertaken to exercise it on behalf of the League of Nations in conformity with the following provisions and;

Whereas, it is provided that the degree of authority, control or administration to be exercised by the Mandatory, not having been previously agreed upon by Members of the League, shall be explicitly defined by the Council of the League of Nations; confirming the said Mandate, defines its terms as follows:

"Articles 1 and 2 affirm are reaffirmed in the preamble," Sir Harold noted.

"I agree. Continue please."

"Article 3, we British are to encourage local autonomy."

Article 4

An appropriate Jewish Agency shall be recognized as a public body for the purpose of advising and co-operating with the Administration of Palestine in such economic, social and other matters as may affect the establishment of a Jewish national home and the interests of the Jewish population in Palestine, and, subject always to the control of the Administration to assist and take part of the development of the country.

The Zionist organization, so long as its organization and constitution are in the opinion of the Mandatory appropriate, shall be recognized as such agency. It shall take steps in consultation with His Britannic's Majesty's Government to secure the co-operation of all Jews who are willing to assist in the establishment of a Jewish national home.

Article 5

The Mandatory shall be responsible for seeing that no Palestine territory shall be ceded or leased to, or in any way placed under the control of the Government of any foreign power.

"Yet, in 1923," Alexander noted, "the British Mandatory—without proper authority—ceded Palestine's Golan Heights to the French Mandate in Syria. A simple yes or no will suffice, Sir Harold."

"Yes."

"Continue, please."

Article 6

The Administration of Palestine, while insuring the rights of other sections of the population are not prejudiced, shall facilitate Jewish immigration under suitable conditions and shall encourage, in co-operation with the Jewish Agency referred to Article 4, close settlement by Jews on the land, including State lands and waste lands not required for public purposes.

Article 7

The Administration of Palestine shall be responsible for enacting a nationality law. There shall be included in this law provisions framed so as to facilitate the acquisition of Palestinian citizenship by Jews who take up their permanent residence in Palestine.

"Article 8 cancels the consular protection once granted by the Turks, and Article 9 guarantees equal justice under the law for natives and foreigners and recognition of local customs. Article 10 deals with extradition treaties, and Article 11 addresses public projects. Article 12, the Mandatory is entrusted with foreign relations and protection of Palestinian citizens abroad. Article 13 authorizes the Mandatory. Who is responsible to the League of Nations in all matters connected herewith, to preserve religious access to all the Holy sites and buildings for Jews, Christians and Muslims and affirms that nothing in the Mandate shall be construed as conferring upon the Mandate authority to interfere with Moslem shrines. Article 14 authorizes the Mandatory to appoint a special commission to address competing claims with respect to the Holy sites and submit reports and recommendations to the League of Nations. Articles 15 and 16 forbid discrimination and further guarantee individual religious rights and freedoms with respect to worship and education. Article 17 provides for locals to volunteer for local defense of the country. Article 18 addresses taxes, custom duties, and commercial practices with respect to Palestine, and Article 19 requires compliance with international law regarding trafficking in arms, drugs, etc. Article 20 addresses policies for general welfare and fighting disease, and Article 21 defines the law with respect to antiquities and archeological digs. Article 22 recognizes Hebrew, Arabic and English as the official languages of Palestine to be imprinted on currency and stamps, and Article 23 recognizes religious holidays as legal days for respective adherents. Article 24 is an annual performance report submitted to the Council to take a measure of the progress during the year in the carrying out of the Mandate. Article 25 provides the Mandatory with the consent of the League the right to withhold application to the Palestinian territories for a Jewish homeland east of the Jordan River. In September of 1922, the League of Nations agreed that Palestinian territories east of the Jordan River will be excluded from all provisions dealing with Jewish settlement. From that point on Britain administered the part west of the Jordan as Palestine and the part east of the Jordan River as Transjordan."

"So Jews weren't allowed to live on the Transjordan side of the river," Alexander clarified, "or on the Golan Heights in 1923, when it was ceded to the French."

"That's right. The Jews had to be expelled from the Golan Heights and Transjordan," Sir Harold replied.

"The Palestine Mandate was ratified by the League of Nations on July 24, 1922, and Articles 15 and 16 of this mandate expressly forbid discrimination based on religion or ethnicity."

"Indeed they do, Alexander, but as I previously mentioned, in September, 1922, the League of Nations excluded all the provisions dealing with Jewish settlement east of the Jordan River. After September, the Palestine Mandate was treated as two separate mandates, Palestine and Transjordan."

"Articles 15 and 16 impose a higher standard for Jews." Alexander insisted.

"Alexander, Arab tribes have no history of representative government, nor frankly do they want it. The British Empire needs to complete this oil pipeline from Iraq through Transjordan to the Palestinian seaports."

"The British Empire also needs to defeat Adolf Hitler."

"Precisely why Arabian petroleum is so important to us, Alexander. Article 26 addresses the legal process for solving disputes between any members of the League against the Mandatory regarding the interpretation of the Mandate or the application of its provisions.

Article 27 requires consent from the Council of the League of Nations in order to modify any terms of this mandate."

"Sir Harold, what consent did your government acquire from the Council to cede the Golan Heights to the French Mandate in 1923?"

"None," Sir Harold replied.

"So your government willingly and unilaterally violated Articles 5 and 27."

"Yes."

"I'll read to you what President Wilson of the United States cabled the British Cabinet on hearing of this illegal property transfer."

"I recall this response was quite unpleasant," Sir Harold said.

> The Zionist course depends on northern and eastern boundaries for a self-maintaining economic development of the country. This means on the north, Palestine must include the Litani River and the watersheds of the Hermon, and on the east it must include the plains of the Joulan and the Hauran. Narrower than this is a mutilation. ... I need not remind you that neither in this country nor in Paris has there been any opposition to the Zionist program, and to its realization the boundaries I have named are indispensable.

"Sir Harold, what was the council's position on Great Britain's Peel Commission recommendation that Palestine be partitioned in a Jewish and Arab state?"

"The Council was not consulted."

"And, did the Council approve the British White Paper in 1939, a policy that restricted Jewish immigration, barred land purchases, a disarmament of the Haganah, and a naval blockade of Palestine?"

"No approval. Officially Great Britain was admonished by the Council." Sir Harold retrieved a file from his desk, removed a letter, and began to read.

> The League Mandate Commission declares the White Paper Policy to be illegal, the policy set out in the White Paper is not in accordance with the interpretation which, in agreement the Mandatory Power and the Council, the Commission has placed upon the Palestine Mandate.

"Alexander, in the seventeen years that we British have been the Mandatory, we've had to deal constantly with Arab riots against Jewish immigration into Palestine. During the three-year Arab riots that began in 1936, the British government became entirely convinced that the Jews and Arabs had to separate within Palestine. The British Peel Commission report recommended abolishing the Mandate and creating two states within Palestine, one Jewish and one Arab. Unfortunately for the Jews, they are outnumbered three to one and would have received a small part of Palestine, but at least the Jews would have achieved a state."

"A state on only 5 percent of the original Palestinian territory with immigration quotas attached," Alexander noted.

"Still, many influential Jews accepted the idea of a two-state solution based on the report, but unfortunately the Arabs rejected it."

"Had the Arabs and the Jews accepted the two-state solution, how would the British have dealt with Arabs who resided on the Jewish side of Palestine and Jews domiciled on the Arab side Palestine?"

"By implementing a compulsory population transfer; we already did the math. A quarter of a million Arabs would be transferred to the Arab state in Palestine, and slightly over twelve hundred Jews to the Jewish state. And then we would have petitioned the League of Nations to terminate the Mandate in accordance with Article 28. Perhaps I should read the article verbatim.

Article 28

In the event of the termination of the Mandate hereby conferred upon the Mandatory, the Council of the League of Nations shall make such arrangements as may be deemed necessary for safeguarding in perpetuity, under guarantees of the League, the rights secured by Articles 13 and 14, and shall use its influence for securing, under the guarantee of the League, that the Government of Palestine will fully honor the financial obligations legitimately incurred by the Administration of Palestine during the period of the Mandate, including the rights of public servants to pensions or gratuities.

The present instrument shall be deposited in the original archives of the League of Nations and certified copies shall be forwarded to the Secretary-General of the League of Nations to all members of the League.

Dated in London the twenty fourth day of July, one thousand nine hundred and twenty two.

"I believe the Council of the League would have accepted our recommendations to terminate the Mandate in favor of a two-state solution, but of course that didn't happen. What did happen were Arab riots in Palestine and the increasing and menacing danger of Nazi Germany to the Middle East. We British had no choice but to prefer our national interests over an outdated document. Any country would. I hope that explains our position on the White Paper policy."

"I'm not here to judge you or the British Empire." Alexander handed Sir Harold another envelope. "If your prime minister agrees to all the terms in the letter of intent, the British government will be provided in advance the time, place, and the mode of the German attacks on Holland, Belgium, and France. That's a fair exchange, I'd say. A Jewish Palestine in exchange for defeating Hitler." Alexander began to read from his copy.

A. That Her Majesty's government acknowledges her White Paper policy to be in violation of Articles 27 of the Mandate and that said Paper has no legal standing in Great Britain.

B. That Her Majesty's government acknowledges the Mandatory's action to cede the Golan Heights in 1923 was illegal under Articles 5 and 27 of the Mandate, and at the conclusion of war with Germany, the Mandatory promises to remedy and reclaim the Golan Heights to the Palestine Mandate.

C. Beginning no later than thirty days after the conclusion of the war with Germany, Great Britain, as Mandatory, will support and agree to take the necessary steps to implement and conclude a compulsory transfer to Transjordan, or other countries of origin, only those Arabs who settled into Palestine after July 24, 1922, the effective date of Palestine Mandate, and that the Mandatory, if challenged on Article 26, will cite as precedent the 1922 League of Nations supervised and compulsory population transfer, during a span of eighteen months, of approximately 400,000 Greek Nationals of the Orthodox faith living in Moslem Turkey to Greece, and approximately 1,300,000 Turkish Nationals of the Moslem faith living in Greece to Turkey at the end of the three-year Greco-Turkish War.

"You're asking that Britain deport nearly half of the Arab population of Palestine," Sir Harold noted.

"I am only asking you to do what you said you would have done, Commissioner, had Palestine been partitioned into two states in 1936. Neither Article 6 nor 7 bestows on Arabs the right to citizenship in a Jewish national home, only 'that the rights of other sections of the population are not prejudiced.' By definition, these rights of the 'other sections of the population' should be limited to only those who have lived in Palestine before the Mandate." Sir Harold read on.

D. When the ratio of Jewish population within the Mandate can be counted 70 percent to 30 percent of the other population sections, then according to Article 28, the Mandatory will propose to the Council of the League of Nations a termination of said Mandate and the establishment of a Jewish homeland in all of Palestine west of the Jordan, except for matters concerning Articles 13 and 14, which remain under the supervision of the League of Nations.

E. A British troop withdrawal from Palestine shall commence the day after statehood is proclaimed and be completed within three months. Great Britain will continue its Mandate in Transjordan, Egypt, and Iraq for a minimum of two additional years and develop a model for economic cooperation and recognition of Palestine.

"Alexander, the Arabs aren't likely to accept a Jewish Palestine in two decades let alone in two years. Lest you forget, it is only the power of Britain that prevents the Egyptian Army and the British-trained Jordanian Legion, the best Arab fighting force, from occupying Palestine. And it is only the power of Britain that prevents Hitler from turning Jerusalem into another Warsaw Ghetto. As you request, I will immediately cable your proposal to the prime minister." Sir Harold rose from his chair. "Did I finally get to meet the third accomplice in the Beirut robbery?"

"Yes, Commissioner. I was held in reserve."

"Clever tactic," Sir Harold said.

"Sir Harold, please tell your prime minister our terms are non-negotiable. I would also urge him not to tarry. The invasion of France will commence within in two fortnights."

"That's doesn't leave the Allies much time. I'll need three days to get to London and back."

"Clear your calendar on your arrival day. I'll be in your office at 9:00 AM. Have the prime minister sign each of the three pages."

"When will I receive the German invasion plans?"

"After our meeting."

"And if the prime minister refuses to agree to your terms?"

"I think the better question to ask is if the prime minister is willing to sacrifice the British Empire over Palestine. Read your Bible Commissioner. Remember, if you want the blessing of God on your country, you must bless the Jewish people. Genesis 12:2–3. 'I will bless those who bless you and I will curse him who curses you.'"

"I don't read the Old Testament, Alexander, I'm not a Jew."

"Neither am I. See you in three days, Commissioner."

Chapter 63
SIGNED, SEALED, AND DELIVERED

April 17, 1940
British Government House

The whirlwind trip to London and back took a physical toll on Sir Harold, and he appeared fatigued and a bit ragged the morning he returned to work. Alexander was waiting for him by the information desk. "Come into my office Alexander." Alexander followed him in. He closed the door and handed Alexander a large manila envelope. "This is your signed copy."

Alexander reviewed the document before placing it in his briefcase and said, "Ari has the war plans. He's expecting you at the Café Arens."

"Are you coming, Alexander?"

"No, Commissioner, I have to get back to Maabarot. My wife is pregnant and due next month."

"Congratulations, Alexander. Do you and your family intend to remain in Palestine when the war is over?"

"I do. There is nothing left for me in a Stalinist Russia."

"Perhaps I can get you into England."

"Thank you, but I prefer to stay in Palestine."

"You may want to reconsider. After we British leave the region, the Arabs will likely make good on their promise to destroy the Jews in Palestine. You will have a child to think of."

"The Arabs will fail," Alexander responded, and walked out of the British Government House for the last time.

Café Arens, Jerusalem

Sir Harold was accompanied by an escort of four manned military vehicles, two in the lead position and two in the rear. Godfrey, his driver, parked in front of the café as the four military vehicles were deployed to divert vehicular and pedestrian traffic from the restaurant. Yitzhak met the commissioner as he entered the establishment. They walked to a private room where David Ben Gurion of the Jewish Agency was sitting at a table. Greetings were quickly exchanged. Sir Harold opened his briefcase and removed the two remaining originals signed by Prime Minister Neville Chamberlain. David Ben Gurion attached his signature to both originals and returned one to the commissioner. Ari entered the room.

"Is that you, Ari? Clever disguise, the beard and the sidelocks," Sir Harold noted. Ben Gurion rose from the table. He was a small man with a huge head of white hair, who would become Israel's first elected prime minister in 1948. Nothing would please Ari more than seeing Ben Gurion elected Israel's first prime minister in 1941.

"Goodbye, Commissioner, Ari," Ben Gurion said as he quickly collected his papers and exited through the back door. Ari sat at the table and pulled out a rolled-up map of central Europe from the inside of his jacket pocket. He spread the map out on the surface of the table.

"Commissioner, on May 10, German aircraft will commence bombing airbases in Belgium, Luxembourg, the Netherlands, and France. The Luftwaffe plan is to destroy the Allied aircraft on the ground, as it destroyed the Polish Air Force in September. Simultaneously, thousands of highly trained German paratroopers will coordinate to seize the key defensive river forts between Antwerp and Liege in Belgium." Ari took his pen and drew a line on the map between the two cities.

"But those forts are nearly impenetrable," Sir Harold opined. "Surely the Belgians can hold on until our reinforcements arrive."

"I wouldn't count on it. What would your next move be if you were the Allied command?"

"I would rush numerically superior forces, the French First, Seventh, and Ninth Armies with my nine British divisions to defend the Dyle

River from Antwerp and south along the Meuse to Sedan," Sir Harold replied.

"And use your best divisions."

"Yes."

"That's what the Germans are expecting in the open terrain of Belgium against their smaller but superior and battle-tested German army, one with far superior airpower, better mobility. It's a trap."

"How can it be a trap? The weakest link in the Maginot Line is through Belgium," Sir Harold insisted. "It's the old Von Schlieffen Plan from World War I." Ari took his pen and drew a line through the Ardennes, a mountainous, wooded region between France and Germany.

"The Germans are coming through Belgium, but with a much smaller force in order to draw out your best divisions into the Belgian open terrain, while the major German offensive is coming from the Ardennes forest. Can you imagine tanks and infantry lined up in three columns for a hundred miles all the way to Luxembourg?"

"That's ludicrous," Sir Harold replied. "The Ardennes is too mountainous and heavily wooded, impassable for tanks. That's why the French didn't build the Maginot Line there."

"That was true in 1918, but won't be in 1940. Commissioner, the German divisions will break through the Ardennes and trap your divisions in Belgium, after which the Germans will commence another offensive from Sedan and head straight for Paris. They could reach Dinant in two days, and if they do, the French government will have to abandon Paris, and the nine divisions of the British Army could very well be trapped in France."

"That would be a disaster," Sir Harold conceded.

"Commissioner, in order to stop Hitler, the Allies will need to transfer the bulk of their divisions and heavy weapons to the Ardennes. When German ground forces attack northern Belgium, pretend to rush to Belgium's defense but quickly retreat to defensive lines. You can slow them down, but expect the German offensive through Belgium to breach the Allied lines and head to the French coast."

"That's a variation of the Shlieffen Plan."

"Hitler doesn't want to sacrifice a lot of German soldiers in France in this war. He wants to conserve his troop strength for an attack on the Soviet Union. And by securing the English Channel, he believes he can get the British government to sue for peace once the French Army has capitulated."

"I think I'm beginning to see the bigger picture," Sir Harold said. "If the war doesn't go well for Hitler, won't his northern army be cut off?"

"Yes. Now the Germans will be moving with fast tanks, motorized infantry, and artillery supported by dive bombers that concentrate on the weak part of your defensive line. The Krauts call it blitzkrieg, and they think there's no defense against it. They're wrong. The tanks and motorized infantry often outrun their supply lines, and their flanks can be vulnerable to attack. German tanks can be destroyed by artillery and heavy guns, but you have to deploy and camouflage your best artillery at the Ardennes. Conceal and protect your fighter planes. Allied fighter planes need to be held in reserve to shoot down the German dive bombers that will precede the tank invasion through the Ardennes. German dive bombers are highly accurate and deafening, but slow; they're an easy target for your fighter planes." Sir Harold had been rapidly taking notes. He stopped momentarily to pour a glass of water from a pitcher and take a drink.

"How should the Allied tank units be deployed?"

"Defensively. The panzer divisions will be moving rapidly, and German tank commanders prefer not to fire on enemy targets while they are on the move. Deploy your tanks in strategic positions, preferably camouflaged and stationary, and hit the Germans broadside. The German tank commanders want you out in the open. Stay hidden in your fortified positions. Keep still and wait until they are in effective range. Movement of any kind is a mistake. A tank in motion cannot fire as effectively as one that is stationary. When German tanks are single file, concentrate all firepower on the lead tank. Tanks that follow can be easy targets because they have to slow down and bypass the lead tank before turning their cannon against an adversary. And lay hundreds of anti-tank mines at the road crossings. Commissioner, you've got three weeks. Remember, Hitler's gamble is to achieve a quick and decisive victory in France, not a war of attrition. He can't take on the Soviet Union if German troop fatalities are excessive. And if the war goes badly for Hitler, we can only hope the German High Command will remove Hitler from power, preferably by assassination."

"What then?" Sir Harold queried.

"Hopefully, there will be peace talks and an end to this war. The new German government will have to root out Nazism and get its house in order, withdraw from occupied territories, and provide restitution to its victims. Territorial claims will have to be settled through arbitration. The Allies will have to put pressure on Stalin to withdraw from all the territory his armies have occupied."

"The end of the war could be chaotic. Imagine, Ari, a postwar environment involving hundreds of thousands of displaced Jews and Poles trying to reclaim their homes."

"I can imagine," Ari said.

"How many Jews do you estimate would come to Palestine?"

"At least two million," Ari replied.

"Two million Jews in Palestine would constitute a majority."

"For a Jewish state," Ari said.

Chapter 64

Notes from the Journal of Sir Harold MacMichael, British High Commissioner of Palestine

July 20, 1941
British Government House

At dawn, and as Ari predicted, Hitler's attack on the West commenced along a 175-mile front between the North Sea to the Maginot Line. German armed forces in violation of their treaties crossed the borders into Holland, Belgium, and Luxembourg, relentlessly bombing the cities of Rotterdam, Amsterdam, and The Hague. As Ari said, Hitler's paratroopers quickly and relentlessly swooped down behind enemy lines and seized the vital bridges and Belgian defensive fortresses along the Meuse River.

Allied Command concurred with Ari's assessment not to commit the bulk of its forces to rush to the Flemish region to confront the German invaders, but to remain within their fortified positions along the border. Alternatively, the Allied plan was to feign a major attack into Belgium so the German High Command would erroneously believe the bulk of the Allied army, thirty-six divisions against twenty German divisions, would be committed to the defense of Holland and Belgium.

May 14, 1940

The Dutch armed forces surrendered, and with British assistance, the queen of Holland and her government fled to London. The Belgian Army fought well and slowed the German offensive, but without Allied reinforcements, grudgingly yielded ground to superior German forces and air power. The French retreat emboldened Hitler. Against the advice of his generals, the Führer commanded half of the northern army to disengage the Belgian and retreating French armies, breach the weakest link along the French defensive line in the north, and race to the channel. The remaining half was commanded to engage and flank to the south until the first units of the southern army broke through the Ardennes to complete encirclement.

During the retreat, French tanks strategically took positions behind anything that offered cover, including farmhouses, bluffs, and bushes, usually without air support, anti-tank, or anti-aircraft guns. The camouflaged tanks were very effective in picking off the tanks, especially when the German panzers were rapidly moving in single-file formation. Rather than slow their advance, German tank commanders often called on air support to take out the French tanks. In the previous three weeks, the French were able to camouflage several thousand gliders to look like fighter planes at targeted French airfields, while anti-tank weapons and anti-aircraft guns had been moved to the French side of the Ardennes.

In the first few days of the attack, Luftwaffe pilots destroyed the gliders and erroneously believed they had destroyed most of the French Air Force on the ground. However, the French fighter planes were held in reserve, concealed in above ground storage facilities adjacent to roads that could be used as runways.

And on May 14, the great German offensive broke through the heavily wooded Ardennes just as Ari had foretold. Never before had Allied forces witnessed such a concentration of armor, tanks, and motorized guns supported by dive bombers and fighter planes. The German juggernaut naturally flanked right to the north to set the trap for what the Germans believed were the bulk of the Allied armies between Belgium and the German Sixth, which had already breached the French lines. The German plan was to initiate a pincer move from the south, east, and west to destroy the French First, Seventh, and Ninth armies, along with the nine divisions of our British Expeditionary Force in Belgium, then break through Sedan and continue nonstop to Paris.

May 15, 1940

In their northern advance from the Ardennes, five of the seven panzer divisions began to encounter increasingly stiff resistance from the Allied forces. It was on this day that the German generals would realize that the First and the Seventh French armies, with heavy guns and hundreds of tanks in fortified positions, were not engaged in Belgium but stood between this offensive and the northern front. And it would be the following day when the German generals ruefully discovered that the French Ninth, with heavy weapons from the south, had encircled their rear and effectively blocked an easy escape back through the Ardennes.

When Hitler received the news, I was later told he became hysterical. The German High Command presented Hitler a plan to retreat. They suggested that two of the panzer divisions held in reserve on the German side of the Ardennes should be put into action to encircle the French Ninth during the panzer retreat. Hitler would have nothing of it. Believing there was no longer a substantial French Air Force, Hitler ordered all of the Luftwaffe in the northern front to attack the Allied positions along the French side of the Ardennes. Hitler's generals protested vehemently and reminded him of the nine top-notch British divisions still in the north that could cut off the German Sixth on the French coast.

May 16, 1940

In the early morning hours, scores of Luftwaffe pilots in the first wave of sorties to strafe and bomb the Allied positions couldn't believe their eyes. Wave after wave of French fighter planes appeared from all directions. Although no match for the German fighter planes, the German kill ratio was only two to one. Eight hundred French planes went down, but so did four hundred German planes, many from French anti-aircraft guns. The more mobile German forces became bogged down as tanks exchanged fire. Both sides were paying a heavy price in equipment and men. I was later informed that Hitler went crazy when his generals told him that the final offensive panzer drive through the Sedan to Paris was no longer a viable option.

May 17, 1940

Wave after wave of Luftwaffe bombers and dive bombers dotted the sky, but they were challenged by several hundred French aircraft. A German general would later admit the French had fooled them with painted gliders that appeared in the darkness of dawn to be French fighter aircraft. Again the German kill ratio was two to one. Germany lost 620 pilots and fighter airplanes. This was disastrous, more so when the German generals were informed that scores of British Spitfires, equal to the best German fighter planes, were strafing the German Sixth Army in Abbeville, France. Hitler was forced to send the German fighter planes back to the north. Along the Ardennes, three of the five panzer divisions had been destroyed or degraded. This time Hitler grudgingly gave into his generals and redeployed the two panzer divisions on the German side to help the remaining three panzer divisions to fight their way back into Germany.

May 20, 1940

In three days, the remnant of the German Southern Army fought its way back to Germany through the forest to regroup with only a third of its original force. Estimated German wounded and dead was approximately 300,000. Allied losses in the south were just under 400,000. While the French Ninth Army remained deployed between the Ardennes and Sedan, the First and Seventh armies marched north to join the nine British divisions.

Unfortunately for Hitler, the retreat through the Ardennes was slow and arduous due to the onset of rain and mud. His earlier decision to send half the Sixth Army through the French lines to Abbeville proved to be disastrous. The numerically superior Seventh Army and the British Army encircled the German Sixth Army, which was running out of petroleum and ammunition. The Allied Ninth Army regrouped with the Belgian divisions to form a defensive line along the Dyle. The closest German Army was in retreat, trekking its way through the Ardennes, and efforts to resupply the German Sixth from the air proved unsuccessful due to the presence of the British Spitfires.

May 28, 1940

General Haag surrendered his ten divisions of the German Sixth at Calais to the Allied Command. All German soldiers immediately became prisoners of war and were transferred to detention camps. Also captured was an assortment of German military hardware including tanks, and long-range weapons.

Reaction to Hitler's first defeat was swift throughout many of the world's capitals. Benito Mussolini did not invade southern France, as Hitler has prodded him to do. President Roosevelt was relieved, and the American Congress felt encouraged that America may still be able to stay out of this war. Most ecstatic was Premier Stalin, who most sincerely wanted Hitler to falter, especially after Britain's ambassador in Moscow delivered to Stalin Hitler's Directive 21, Operation Barbarossa, Germany's planned invasion of the Soviet Union in 1941. Several months later I learned an increasingly angered Hitler froze all Jewish emigration to Palestine and ordered the SS to shoot a thousand Jews to death every day until all of France is in German hands.

June 6, 1940

The Russian ambassador in London informed our newly elected prime minister Winston Churchill that Hitler was likely preparing for another major offensive into France. The German War Procurement Department increased its shipment order threefold for Romanian oil and twice for raw materials, signaling that Hitler was gearing up for an extended military campaign. The ambassador also informed Churchill that half of the German generals were fired or demoted, and Hitler, suspecting perfidy, ordered an internal investigation of all officers who knew of the German invasion plans. Infighting among his closest advisers was endemic, and except for Himmler and Goebbels, all others are viewed with suspicion.

June 7, 1940

I met with Ari today at the Café Arens and provided him a list of the high-ranking German officers Hitler displaced. Ari regretfully confirmed his sources were on that list but wouldn't give names. It seems likely that Ari will no longer be able to assist the Allied effort, but his contribution to date had been invaluable and immeasurable. It pains me that when historians write about this war, Ari Ben Ora will never be recognized, not only for his deft espionage but his brilliance and grasp of military tactics.

June 21, 1940

Germany is amassing twenty divisions along the Belgian border. Although another attack appears imminent, Hitler has already sacrificed a half a million of his best troops.

June 26, 1940

A bombshell. The German ambassador in Moscow is handed several letters by Foreign Minister Molotov, including the original communiqué of Directive 21. The German ambassador disavows any knowledge of the planned invasion of the Soviet Union. Molotov read aloud that "effective immediately, the Soviet Union withdraws from all treaty obligations with Germany," and suggested he catch the next plane to Berlin.

June 27, 1940

I learned later when Hitler became aware that Stalin had an original communiqué of the directive, he had a temper tantrum of epic proportions. He called for a meeting of his new general staff, including his new favorite, General Rommel.

The new situation was that Stalin amassed three million of his troops in eastern Poland. Rommel reminded Hitler of his own words that Germany should at all costs avoid a two-front war. He urged that, for the sake of future generations, Hitler should come to terms with France and Great Britain—even if it meant giving up Poland and other conquered territories. Rommel assured Hitler that Germany had adequate strength to repel a Soviet invasion, but only if the German divisions along the Belgian border were quickly moved to the east. Rommel didn't say explicitly, but Hitler read between the lines. For the good of the Fatherland, Hitler should step down. France and Britain would never agree to an accommodation with Germany unless Hitler and his gang of thugs were eliminated, including the entire Nazi apparatus. Rommel soon realized the Führer would never willingly give up his power. Hitler tried to convince his generals that a quick victory in France was still achievable. Rommel reminded him that oil and raw materials from the Soviet Union were no longer available for the German war effort, and if France didn't fall quickly, Germany would collapse. Again Rommel urged that Hitler make peace with the West and align with France and Britain against continued Soviet expansion. The Führer told Rommel and the others he would think about it and give them his decision in two days.

June 29, 1940

Hitler returned from Wolf's Lair, his mountain hideaway, and met with Rommel and his staff. Hitler noted most of the French armies were in the north of France, protected by the British Spitfires. Only one French Army without fighter planes is stretched between the Ardennes and Sedan. Three panzer divisions can easily break through to Paris. In the north, ten German divisions will attack along the Belgian line to draw the Allied forces away from the initial thrust from Sedan. It was Hitler's judgment that if Paris fell, the French would sue for peace. Rommel concurred the attack could succeed but that it required a transfer of divisions now stationed in Poland. This would leave a defenseless eastern border adjacent to the Soviet forces. Hitler reminded Rommel that the French border had been just as bare when Germany invaded Poland the previous year and the French did nothing. Rommel was silent but disagreed with Hitler's assessment. Russia and France were different countries. The Führer ordered the operation to commence no later than July 16 and adjourned the meeting.

July 14, 1940

Seven of the ten divisions that were stationed in Poland had now joined the two panzer divisions on the outskirts of Wiesbaden. Four of these divisions were instructed to proceed to Paris after the first attack into central Belgium flanked to the right to trap the Belgians and French armies in the north.

July 15, 1940

Without access to Ari's informants in Berlin, the Allied command guessed that the next attack would come from northern Belgium. They were wrong. The Germans broke through the line at Sedan. Engineers cleared mines and used pontoons to bridge the river crossings, creating a pathway for Rommel's tanks to push unimpeded to Paris. The German attack flanked right and cut off the Allies in the north. This time there were no French fighter planes to slow Rommel's panzers as he forged through central France.

July 16, 1940

For several weeks Churchill and Stalin were in secret negotiations. In exchange for opening up the second front against Germany, the Soviet dictator insisted on Allied assurances that the Baltic countries remain part of the Soviet Union after the war. Churchill gave no such assurances, reminding Stalin if France suddenly fell, and if the Soviet troops performed as poorly against the Germans as they did against the Finns, Hitler's armies would crush the Soviet forces. The easiest way to defeat Hitler was to force him to fight on two fronts simultaneously. Apparently Stalin was convinced. The day after Rommel's panzers rolled into Paris, Hitler ordered him to return with his troops to defend the homeland from a massive Soviet attack through Poland.

July 18, 1940

When Rommel reached Berlin, he was summoned to meet with Hitler. As Rommel walked into the meeting he drew his pistol from the holster and fired at close range into Hitler's forehead and blew his brains out. Rommel's men, with the help of the German police, began arresting and disarming the SS officers all over Germany. Before the end of the day, all of Hitler's cabinet—including Himmler, Hess, Ribbentrop, Eichmann,

Goering, and Goebbels—were located and assassinated. The military immediately assumed control of Germany, and through Swiss intermediaries, offered conditions to ending the war. The conditions began with a German offer to withdraw from all territories not included in the 1938 Munich Agreement, and a promise to root out all vestiges of Nazism from Germany. In exchange, there would be an immediate cease-fire and end to the war. Two days later, all parties had agreed to an immediate cease-fire.

July 29, 1940

The war in Europe officially ended. The exiled Polish government returned to Warsaw. Fearing retaliation from a French-German-Anglo alliance, Stalin's troops reluctantly withdrew from Poland and the Baltic States and returned to their post–World War I borders. Legal commissions were set up all over Germany and Eastern Europe to assist and handle the claims of the millions of displaced war refugees.

The task of restitution would be overwhelming and likely continue for years. No government in Europe even batted a disapproving eye when Her Majesty's government took the initiative to relocate the most downtrodden of Europe's victims, the Polish Jews, to Palestine.

December 31, 1941

With the largest Merchant-Marine fleet in Europe at her disposal, Great Britain was able to transport over one million Polish Jews to Palestine by the end of December 1941.

And during those seventeen months, the British Mandatory of Palestine, relying on both Ottoman and British census reports, was compelled by agreement to transfer over 400,000 Arabs who settled in Jewish Palestine after the date of the Mandate to Transjordan with just and fair monetary compensation. Palestine has achieved a Jewish majority of

1,400,000, compared to its Arab population of 800,000. On May 1, Palestine will reclaim its ancient name of Israel.

By early April, all British troops will have left Palestine for reassignment in Transjordan, Iraq, and Egypt, where Her Majesty's troops will remain for no longer than eighteen months. At that time, the Arabs will take charge of their own countries. I still hope that the new Arab countries will accept the Jewish state of Israel.

Chapter 65
A SPACE ODDITY

July 20, 2007
Moscow Command Center

Pakistan's nuclear launch and atmospheric detonation triggered a chain of electromagnetic pulses that crippled electronic systems throughout the Middle East and Asia. For nearly an hour, telephone and satellite communications were down, proof positive that humans were slaves to their own technology. Igor continued to stare into a monitor that looked more like a window to a Siberian snowstorm. He sat, his eyes glued, lighting one lousy menthol after the other. But eventually his phone rang and the systems recovered. Igor let the phone ring. It could only be Boris calling, and it didn't matter anymore; the worst of Igor's fears was now confirmed. Against all odds, the capsule had remained intact and landed in the Mediterranean Sea. He finally picked up the phone.

"We still have a chance to reach the capsule before the Israelis," Boris said excitedly. "We have a merchant ship close to the location, and the captain has just dispatched a hydrofoil and helicopter to the location."

"I think the capsule may be in Israeli territorial waters," Igor noted.

"We'll worry about that later. It's all about damage control right now, and that means getting to the crew, if they're still alive, before the Israelis do. There are explosives on the hydrofoil to sink the capsule."

"What will happen to the survivors?" Igor asked.

"After we interrogate them, they will be administered fatal doses of radiation pills. The press release will indicate they succumbed from radiation exposure during the nuclear fallout, and their corpses will be held on our ship to be reclaimed."

"What if the Israelis get there first?" Igor asked.

"If we don't get to the capsule, Putin will immediately scrub the Iranian nuclear launch, disarm the missile, and transport the warhead to our submarine."

"But the Israelis will discover the evidence of Russia's involvement," Igor appealed.

"Without conclusive evidence, they have nothing more than a conspiracy theory."

Igor couldn't contain himself. Maybe it was too little sleep or too much caffeine in his system, but Igor began laughing aloud into his phone. He had gone to great lengths to conceal an e-mail that no one in the Kremlin would even look for anymore.

"What's so funny?"

"Forgive me Boris, but this is reminiscent of a Hollywood movie chase scene with cops and robbers."

"Interesting observation, Igor, and who are the cops and who are the robbers?"

"We're the robbers, Boris. We're trying to hijack an economy. Do you actually think that Israel is going to cower to a nuclear Iran? Iran has no air force capable of penetrating Israeli air space and no guarantee that its missiles can either. On the other hand, Israel can launch nukes from submarines, from the air, and from the ground. So I ask you, Boris, how do you think Israel will respond if there is an Iranian nuclear test?"

"If Iran commences with the missile test, we believe Israel will not hesitate to destroy Iran's nuclear sites, even using battlefield nukes. Iran will throw a lot at Israel—chemical, biological, and conventional warheads—but the majority of Israelis should survive. Palestinians could die by the tens of thousands."

"What will Syria do?" Igor asked.

"We will tell Syria to sit out, and this time Hezbollah will be degraded by the UN force and Lebanese Army."

"Then where is Russia's payoff?"

"Igor, after Israel destroys the Iranian infrastructure, who is better positioned to rebuild Iran than Russia? If we can't steal one economy, we will rebuild another. That was always the plan. Either way, Russia obtains great profits and influence in the region. Look at your monitor, Igor, our helicopter is circling above the capsule."

ISS Capsule

The capsule rolled on the waves, and Sanjay quickly unbuckled his harness and looked across at Andre. "Andre, are you okay?"

"I think so, and you?

"A little shaken," Sanjay said. "Ari, Alexander, talk to me."

"I hear you," Alexander replied. "Ari's unconscious."

"Is he alive?" Andre asked.

"He's barely breathing." Suddenly they heard the approaching sound of the helicopter. Sanjay looked out. "It's a Russian 'copter." Alexander reached behind his seat.

"Andre, take the Uzi." The noisy helicopter hovered only fifty feet above the capsule. The Russian spoke into a loudspeaker.

"We're from the medical unit. We'll take you out one at a time to safety. How many of your crew survived?" Andre opened the hatch, pointed the gun, and fired two shots by the copter's broadside. The copter quickly moved out of range and radioed in for instructions, but it was too late. Israeli gunships and attack helicopters had arrived. The Russian helicopter headed for the safety of international waters, and the hydrofoil boat that could be sighted on the horizon was likewise instructed to return to the ship. Again they heard the sound of helicopters above the capsule, but these brandished the bright blue Star of David. Andre put down his gun.

"We are from Israel. How many of you are alive?" asked the Israeli on his loudspeaker.

Andre put up four fingers. One by one, they were raised from the capsule into a medical helicopter and flown to a military hospital in Haifa. Ari, still unconscious, was immediately hooked onto life support. The others were wrapped in blankets and given oxygen. A speedboat pulled alongside the capsule and a team of Mossad agents, including Shimon and Ariel, climbed down the hatch and removed the crew's personal items—including clothing, duffle bags, laptops, mp3 players, cell phones, and Ari's mini-Uzi—then sped back to their base at Haifa. Another group of agents aboard a second boat towed the capsule into Haifa harbor.

Shimon and Ariel docked at the Haifa base before media correspondents representing the news agencies descended on Haifa. One journalist began his broadcast with a question for the viewers.

> How could they have survived over Pakistan? We know that the crew had to leave the ISS because the station had been severely damaged by space debris, but somebody forgot to tell the Pakistanis that the space capsule would be entering their airspace during their nuclear launch. Just in ... prior to their rescue, a Russian 'copter attempted a rescue mission but yielded to the Israeli rescue teams in Israeli waters. As to the whereabouts of the crew, they were rushed to an undisclosed location by an Israeli' copter. John Roper reporting, CNN International.

Moscow Command Center

"What now?" Igor asked.
"This is now a matter for Foreign Affairs."

And with the ISS crew falling into Israeli hands, the deals Russia made, like dominoes, began to fall. The following day, a spokesman for the Kremlin reported negotiations with the Vatican concerning the transfer of property rights had ended without any significant progress. At a news conference two days later, the Russian and Pakistani ambassadors scrubbed the Russian nuclear-assistance program due to increased regional political instability. A week later, a Russian submarine surreptitiously pulled into the port city of Karachi, Pakistan, and returned the nuclear warhead.

Haifa, Israel

Into the wee hours of the morning, Ariel and Shimon sifted through hard drives, retrieving deleted e-mail and cellular-phone conversations. Starting with Andre's laptop, the two Mossad agents followed the electronic trail that began with Yuri in Moscow and ended with Ari's covert e-mail to Rachel.

"Shimon, Andre just received a new e-mail."

"Who sent it?"

"Michelle."

"That's his old flame. She's been living in Israel. What does she say?"

"She wants to see him," Ariel said.

"We can tell him at the hospital." Ariel noticed his partner's demeanor change.

"What did you find Shimon?"

"A manuscript. Ari penned a manuscript titled 'The Palestine Exchange.'"

"Provocative title, sounds like a novel," Ariel opined.

Chapter 66
BACK TO THE FUTURE

July 23, 2007
Haifa Military Hospital

Shimon was waiting to speak to Ari's neurologist, Dr. Wasserman, when he noticed an attractive but despondent woman and her two sad children leave Ari's hospital room. She wore her auburn hair in a ponytail.

"Mrs. Ben Ora," Shimon rose from his chair. "My name is Shimon Levi. I was part of the rescue team. How is your husband?"

"Mr. Levi, my husband is very weak from radiation sickness, but the doctors are optimistic he can still regenerate new tissue and recover. It might take a year or eighteen months."

"Isn't that good news, Mrs. Ben Ora?"

"Yes, but my husband didn't recognize his children. He has memory loss, probably caused by trauma to his head. Dr. Wasserman calls his condition retrograde amnesia."

"Then he must have recognized you."

"He did, but he thinks I'm someone else."

"Dora?" Shimon asked.

"Yes, how did you know that?" Rachel exclaimed.

"By the color of your hair and the dimple on your right cheek. Mrs. Ben Ora, meet me in the cafeteria in ten minutes. Right now I have to see Dr. Wasserman."

"I'll be there," she said.

"You can't just walk in there!" the receptionist yelled at Shimon. She followed him into Ari's room.

"I'm sorry, Doctor Wasserman. He just stormed in. Shall I call security?"

"How dare you walk in." Dr. Wasserman demanded.

"Your patient believes that Sanjay drowned during the capsule's landing, and Andre is in France. He calls his wife Dora."

"Yes, how did you know? Don't worry, he's sleeping now."

"Educated guess. My name is Shimon Levi, and I was part of the rescue team. We went through Ari's laptop and discovered he wrote himself and the other crew members into a manuscript. He's obviously suffering from his concussion."

"Nurse, tell the orderlies to bring in Sanjay Bushar. Ari, wake up." Dr. Wasserman gently squeezed his arm. Ari awakened but seemed impaired. "Ari, I'd like you to meet Shimon. He was one of the men who rescued you from the capsule." Ari made an effort to speak, but his voice was very weak.

"My pleasure to meet you, Ari," Shimon said and shook his hand. At that moment, Sanjay, with a smile on his face, was wheeled into the room.

"Sanjay, I thought you died," Ari responded at seeing his friend.

"No, we're all alive and at the hospital."

"Andre's here too?" Ari asked.

"Yes," Sanjay enthusiastically replied. Dr. Wasserman interrupted.

"Ari, Shimon and I are going to let you two chat for a few minutes. If you need us, just ring. Can you get me a copy of his manuscript?" the doctor asked Shimon.

"I can get you a copy soon. Dr. Wasserman, how would you feel if Ari read his own manuscript along with his personal e-mails from his kids, his wife, and mother?"

"It might help him come back to the future," the doctor agreed.

"I'll be seeing you soon, Dr. Wasserman."

Rachel was sipping coffee and the kids were eating. Shimon pulled up a seat.

"Mrs. Ben Ora, Dora is a character in Ari's manuscript."

"What are you talking about?" Rachel asked.

"While your husband was in space, he began writing a novel and wrote himself and his crewmates into his manuscript. Dora is a waitress he met at Arnold's restaurant in 1939."

"I was a waitress at Arnold's when I met Ari. My family owns the restaurant."

"I know. Dora is you. Ari drew on what was real to create his story, but his injury has obviously blurred his ability to distinguish one from the other. By debunking his storyline, perhaps Ari can recover his memory."

"How will you do that?"

"By introducing contrary evidence," Shimon replied. "In Ari's story, Sanjay died on impact when the capsule landed on the sea, and as we speak, Ari and Sanjay are engaged in conversation. Until he saw Sanjay with his own eyes, he believed his friend was dead and buried at sea."

"Shimon, did Ari give his novel a name?"

"He did, 'The Palestine Exchange.' And if you'll excuse me, I'm going to print a few copies of this manuscript. I want Ari to rediscover your e-mails and read his manuscript. Hopefully that will jog his memory."

"I want a copy."

"Absolutely," said Shimon and took the elevator upstairs to check on Alexander.

"How is he, Dr. Weiss?"

"Bruised, and weak from radiation, but his exposure was not in lethal amounts. I'm optimistic that, given enough time, he will fully recover."

"That's great news. Can I talk to him?" Shimon asked.

"No more than ten minutes this time," Dr. Weiss advised. Shimon slowly opened the door.

"Hello, Alexander. My name is Shimon, and I helped rescue you the other day. Dr. Weiss tells me he expects you to make a full recovery. Do you feel well enough to talk to me for a few minutes?"

"Yes, I think so."

"Thank you. Alexander, can you tell me how your troubles began on the ISS?"

"Our troubles started when my brother Yuri discovered that Moscow and Iran were plotting against Israel. Yuri worked at the Kremlin, and he sent me an encrypted e-mail describing the plot and suggested we warn the Israelis. His e-mail reached my inbox while I was sleeping and recuperating from radiation exposure. Later I discovered that Andre stole my password, logged into my laptop, and opened Yuri's e-mail. He replied to Yuri using my identity, transferred the e-mail to his inbox, deleted it from mine, and sent Yuri's e-mail to his priest."

"Why would Andre steal your e-mail?"

"He overheard conversations. A few days before, Sanjay's brother was vacationing in Indonesia and recognized a group of high-level Russian nuclear scientists. Alexander passed along that information to Yuri. Sanjay didn't inform Andre, because he thought that Andre might tell someone in the French government. We didn't know what was happening at the time."

"Tell me about Andre?"

"Andre is very nationalistic and not enamored with Israel."

"Tell me a Frenchman who is."

"It's personal. Andre's father was the French engineer who died in the Israeli bombing raid of Osirak in 1981. Andre was just a child at the time and that left him an orphan. His priest became a surrogate father to him, and when Andre discovered that e-mail, I think he was seeking advice from his priest."

"Perhaps his priest was also seeking advice from someone in the Church," the Israeli mentioned.

"And then there was his fiancée."

"Michelle?"

"She fell in love with an Israeli archeologist, broke his heart. I think his name was also Ari."

"I think I know of this archeologist," Shimon added. "What happened after you found the stolen e-mail?"

"We cuffed Andre. He admitted he sent the e-mail to his priest but refused to acknowledge any responsibility for Yuri's arrest; that is, until his priest committed suicide. When Father Gauthier threw himself from the cliffs at Montmartre in front of television cameras, he was sending us an unmistakable message: our lives were in danger because of what we knew, and our communications had been compromised by

Russian interdictors. And that was confirmed when Andre received an e-mail reply from Father Gauthier, but the registered time and date of that e-mail was several hours after his death."

"Someone other than the priest replied to his e-mail," Shimon noted.

"Yes, and fortunately the Russian technicians didn't have time to interdict the Internet news. A supply ship was due to arrive at the ISS in two days, probably rigged with explosives. In anticipation, we punctured an unfixable hole in the space station and radioed in that the station was hit by flying debris compromising life-support systems. This was our guise to abandon ship and return to Israel on the escape capsule.

"The return flight was preprogrammed to land at a Russian airstrip in the steppes, except Andre overrode the computer and assumed manual control to land in the Israeli Negev. Everything was going according to plan until the nuclear explosion knocked us off course. We were not informed Pakistan was going to launch at our position at the same time."

"At the request of the Russians, the earlier launch undoubtedly was orchestrated to incinerate you in the atmosphere. The Russians must be in a state of shock that any of you survived."

"It wasn't exactly their last attempt. Just before you arrived, Andre fired a few warning shots at the Russian helicopter." Dr. Weiss walked in.

"Alexander, I have to leave now. We'll talk later."

"Shimon, if Yuri's alive, please try to save him. He risked his life for Israel."

"Yes, he did. I'll do what I can, Alex."

Ariel Garon carried Andre's French-designed Prostar Laptop Core 2 as he meandered through the motley group of television journalists and crews who had coalesced around the hospital's portal. As he passed, Ariel couldn't help but hear the news reported in an amalgam of languages. News that all the crewmembers had survived and were being treated for various degrees of physical ailments, including radiation exposure and physical trauma, had yielded to even more explosive headlines about the near nuclear miss and headlines suggesting conspiracies. In one French newspaper, the front page began with "Conspiracy over Pakistan," and plastered on the front page of an Italian newspaper was the heading "What Went Wrong over Pakistan?" Overnight, countless blogs of conspiracy theories appeared on the Internet.

Ariel flashed his ID for security and took the stairs to meet Shimon in the basement cafeteria. During the last three days, the two Israelis interviewed Sanjay and Alexander, listened to every song on the mp3 player, deciphered all the cellular-phone calls, retrieved e-mails, and reprinted Ari's manuscript and Sanjay's diary. After lunch, Shimon and Ariel planned to interview Andre before submitting their final report to the Israeli prime minister. Sanjay's diary had been most revealing and helped establish a profile of the Frenchman.

"Not a bad chicken sandwich," Ariel said, not at all disturbed that Shimon sitting across from him had already finished his lunch. Ariel had taken a few bites when his phone rang. He looked at the caller ID and swallowed quickly.

"Shalom, Dr. Wasserman," Ariel answered.

"Ariel, we need you upstairs."

"What's the problem?"

"We have two French visitors demanding to see Andre."

"Be right there." Shimon overheard the entire conversation, and within three minutes, the two agents walked off the elevator on the ninth floor and approached the two Frenchmen. Dr. Wasserman had placed himself between the door and the disagreeable French agents. Shimon and Ariel approached the Frenchmen.

"How do you do? I am Shimon Levi and this is my partner, Ariel Garon. May we be of some assistance?"

"Merci, Monsieurs Levi and Garon. I am Antoine Giroux, adjutant to French ambassador Michel, and may I introduce Inspector Jean Gallant from Paris. The inspector has flown in from Paris as part of an ongoing investigation."

"Monsieurs," Inspector Gallant spoke calmly and confidently, "we are conducting an investigation of a priest who died under suspicious circumstances. Perhaps you may have seen his suicide on national television."

"Yes, I did," Shimon replied.

"Pardon, Monsieur Levi, I see you are carrying a French-manufactured laptop. I must assume this belongs to Andre Dubois."

"It does," Shimon replied.

"Excellent, we know that Andre and Monsignor Gauthier were very close. We are looking for a communication between them that may assist in our understanding of why a man of the cloth willfully defied God by committing suicide. Perhaps an act of a crazed individual, but nothing I discovered suggests that this priest was agonized. And to televise his own death suggests to me that there may be hidden meaning in his act, perhaps he was willing to die in order to save others, as our Savior had."

"Presently, Inspector, we Israelis are conducting our own investigation into the capsule landing. When our investigation is over and if Andre consents, we will be happy to consider your request. In the meantime, you might be better off to try to find the dead priest's laptop."

"Father Gauthier's laptop seems to have disappeared."

"That's too bad," Shimon responded.

"Monsieur Levi, I insist that you allow us to ask Andre a few questions."

"If Andre is willing. I'll ask him." The two Frenchmen watched the two agents walk in and close the door behind them.

"Good morning, Andre. I am Agent Shimon Levi and this is Agent Ariel Garon. On behalf of the Israeli government, I want to extend my appreciation. The warning shots you fired at the Russian helicopter certainly avoided what would have led to an international incident between our countries. And due to satellite interruption, the news agencies never knew. How are you feeling today?"

"How am I feeling? Excellent, well enough to go home—which is exactly what I want to do."

"We're fine with that. Dr. Wasserman says you're fine medically, and outside this door eagerly awaiting their turn to see you is the French adjutant to the ambassador and a Parisian police inspector."

"A police inspector?"

"Inspector Gallant is here to ask you questions about the death of your priest, Father Gauthier."

"Good, I have a lot say."

"I'm sure you do. The Russian government and Church officials will only deny your accusations. It'll be your word against theirs. They'll say you're mentally unbalanced from living in space."

"But I have e-mails to prove my case."

"The Israeli government has your e-mails, and unless there's an Iranian nuclear launch, the e-mails are unsubstantiated claims. Still, there's a bit of irony here. We might be able to use the threat of these e-mails to blackmail the Russians and Iranians into good behavior," Shimon noted.

"Please don't use the word 'we.' I'm not interested in Israel's welfare. I'm a citizen of France, an orphan whose father was killed from an unprovoked Israeli bombing raid at Osirak."

"Andre, your father wasn't supposed to be working that weekend. He made a decision to go to the reactor. No one else was there at the time of the bombing, and no one else died. I'm sorry for your loss, and I can understand why you don't like Israel. But in this situation, you are not an innocent man, though you might have a chance at some redemption."

"Unless you can bring Father Gauthier back to life, I will have no redemption in this life."

"We can't bring your priest back, but we might be able to get Alexander's brother Yuri out of prison, if that's important to you."

"Of course it is."

"Then tell the Frenchmen you know nothing, and let our government handle this situation. Will you agree to be silent until we can free Yuri?"

"I can agree to that."

"Andre," Ariel said, "An Israeli citizen by the name of Ari Davidson was recently killed by Hezbollah in the last war."

"The only Ari I know is Ari Ben Ora," Andre replied.

"He was an archaeologist at a dig near Ashkelon, Israel," Shimon said. There was a moment of silence. Andre took a deep breath.

"I believe he was in a relationship with my ex-fiancée. She must be devastated."

"Two days ago, your ex-fiancée, Michelle, sent you an e-mail. I took the liberty to read it because it's my job to go through all communications. Would you like to read her e-mail Andre?"

"I would." Shimon sat on the bed and opened the e-mail on Andre's laptop.

"Can I reply?" Andre asked after he read her message.

"I'd rather you not," Shimon said. "Your laptop is part of our investigation. Why don't you see her? I'll take you to Ashkelon whenever you want."

"I would like to go as soon as possible."

"Whenever you're ready, walk out your door. Ariel and I will be waiting for you." The two Mossad agents walked out of Andre's room.

"Gentlemen from France, Andre will see you now," Shimon said.

Chapter 67
GOOD SHABBAT

January 7, 2008
Arnold's Delicatessen

"Good Shabbat" is a peaceful, well-intended greeting Jews around the world extend to one another during the weekly Sabbath, from sundown Friday until Saturday night. On the Jewish Sabbath, there is typically little vehicular traffic and the majority of businesses close. On this particular Sabbath, Arnold's Deli, with windows shuttered, only appeared to be closed.

Shimon was no stranger to the restaurant. Only last month, on another Sabbath day, he was part of a quartet that broke out a blindfolded Marwan Barghouti from the Jerusalem detention center and brought him to this restaurant. Shimon parked his car next to the alley at the rear of the restaurant and walked to the back door. He began to hum a few lyrics to a song he remembered from Sanjay's mp3 player, an American war protest song from the Vietnam era. Shimon thought about how fitting the lyrics were to Ari and his manuscript.

> You may leave here for four days in space
> But when you return it's the same old place.

Whether it was four days, or two months, or even eight decades ago, Israel was in most ways the same old place, and in the same fight. There were Arab riots in the 1920s and the 1930s, followed by decades of war. Shimon knocked twice and the back door opened.

"Good Shabbat, Mrs. Ben Ora."

"Please call me Rachel. Please come in, Shimon."

"It's a pleasure to be invited to Ari's homecoming party. How is he doing?"

"Better. His therapy has achieved results. A few months ago, he didn't recognize any of his children or his mother. But now he does, although he forgets a few things now and then. Next year my dad is going to retire, and Ari and I will take over the restaurant."

"Is Ari here?"

"No, he'll be here soon."

"I hope one day Ari will complete and publish his novel," Shimon said.

"You liked it?" Rachel asked.

"I do, Rachel. In my judgment much of the world erroneously perceives Israel as a child of the Holocaust, either legitimate or illegitimate, but definitely a post–World War II creation of a post–World War II idea foisted on the Arab world by Zionists and legitimized by a newly formed and guilt-ridden United Nations.

"Ari's manuscript could introduce today's generation to the history of the 1922 League of Nations. 'The Palestinian Mandate' was actually the first road map to a two-state solution in Palestine, an Arab state in Palestine to the east of the Jordan River and a Jewish state in the Palestine west of the Jordan River."

"Shimon, tell me who cares to know about the Palestine Mandate? It's just another treaty that was breached and broken. History's filled with them."

"It's the message that resonates. Just as ethnic Turks were expelled from Greece in 1922, so should the 400,000 Arabs who had come into Jewish Palestine after the 1922 Mandate."

"Shimon, is your solution to expel the three million Palestinians living in the West Bank and Gaza?"

"It's too late now, but not so long ago compulsory population exchanges and transfers were considered civilized and acceptable behavior. After World War II, hundreds of thousands of Poles and Germans were forcibly relocated, millions after the Turkish and Greek Wars in 1922. I hope your husband publishes his novel."

"After we spent so much time getting Ari out of his novel. Come, Shimon, I want you to meet my other guests."

"In a moment. I see Meir in the kitchen. I'd like to say hello to him."

"Don't be too long. Ari's due to arrive any minute."

"Good Shabbat Meir."

"Good Shabbat Shimon."

"Meir, keep this between you and me. There are high-ranking Israelis who are not too happy that your son-in law and the others survived. They believe if the escape capsule perished over Pakistan, the Iranians would have proceeded with their nuclear-missile test and given Israel an excuse to destroy Iran's nuclear sites."

"With bunker bombs and battlefield nukes?" Meir asked.

"Yes the whole enchilada."

"What happens next?" Meir inquired.

"Your guess is as good as mine." Rachel burst into the kitchen, and took Shimon by the hand. All the lights were dimmed in the dining room.

"Shimon, you've met Alexander."

"Yes, of course. Hello, Alexander, nice to see you." They shook hands.

"Shimon, I want you to meet my brother Yuri and our mother Anna." Shimon was speechless. Suddenly, Anna stepped up to Shimon and gave him the kind of hug a mother gives to a son who had been lost and found.

"Shimon, I want to thank you for rescuing Yuri and reuniting our family."

"A lot of people worked hard to free Yuri and bring your family to Israel, not just me."

"Nonsense, my Alex knows you were the one."

"You saved my life," Yuri said. "How can I ever thank you?"

"Yuri, on behalf of Israel, I am thanking you for your courage and selflessness. After you get settled, call me. I'm sure we can find something challenging and worthy for you to do while you're staying in Israel. Take my card, please."

"Thank you." Yuri said. Shimon smiled and excused himself.

"Shimon," Sanjay said.

"I thought you left for India," said a surprised Shimon.

"I did. I came back for Ari's welcome home party. I brought my brother Yatin with me."

"You spotted the Russian nuclear scientists."

"It takes one to know one," Yatin blithely responded.

"Yes, it does," Shimon replied. "Well it's nice to make your acquaintance." Shimon noticed the striking woman with long, straight brown hair standing alone and tried desperately to meet her, but he was a little late. She was only alone momentarily, until Andre was at her side. They were speaking French.

"Everybody, quiet and freeze," Rachel commanded. "Lights out, they're coming in the front door." The front door opened to a dark room. Rachel's kids, Rebecca and David, came in first, followed by Ari's mother Sarah.

"Somebody, turn on a light," Ari requested. Instantly, light filled the room.

"WELCOME HOME, ARI."

POSTSCRIPT

The Palestine Exchange is a fictional story. However, many of the novel's events and characters are real. The following represents a timeline intended to help the reader distinguish between historical fact and fiction.

PREMODERN HISTORY

597–586 BCE: Destruction of Solomon's Temple leads to first exile and deportation of Jews from their native home of Judea to Babylon by King Nebuchadnezzar.

537 BCE: Jews return from exile to Judea and rebuild the Temple.

70 CE–135 CE: To prevent a rebirth of the Jewish nation, Roman legions destroyed the kingdom of Judea, razed Jerusalem including the Second Temple, and renamed the biblical land, Palestine in 135 CE. The Jews are sent on their second exile, dispersed among the various Roman provinces in the Middle East, North Africa, and Europe.

MODERN HISTORY

1517–1917: Palestine and most of the Middle East is under the control of the Ottoman Empire.

1917: November 2, the Balfour Declaration was a classified statement by the British government concerning the partition of the Ottoman Empire and stated unequivocal British support for a Jewish "national home" in Palestine.

1918: Post-World War I, Turkey cedes control of Palestine to the victorious Allies.

1920: The Allied-sponsored Sanremo Peace Conference convened from April 19 to 26 and reaffirmed the Balfour Declaration's tenet to reconstitute a Jewish national home in Palestine.

1922: The conference's decision to reconstitute a Jewish homeland in Palestine was ratified by the League of Nations on July 24.

1920–1948: The Mandate for Palestine, or the Palestine Mandate, was a territory that included modern-day Israel, the Gaza Strip, West Bank, and Jordan. After the conclusion of World War I and the dissolution of the Ottoman Empire, the League of Nations created and entrusted the Mandate to the British Empire to administer with the intention of creating a future national home for the Jewish people.

1923: The League of Nations partitioned Palestine east of the Jordan River to be administered separately as Transjordan, later to become the Arab state of Jordan in 1946.

1920, 1929, 1936–1939: Arabs riot against the Jews and British authorities in Palestine due to increased Jewish immigration and land purchases.

1936: The British-sponsored Peel Commission Report recommends Palestine be partitioned into two separate states, one Arab and one Jewish. The report recommended that the Mandate be abolished, except in a corridor surrounding Jerusalem and stretching to the Mediterranean Coast just south of Jaffa. It also recommended that the underlying land under the Mandate's authority be apportioned between an Arab and Jewish states, including the compulsory transfer of Jewish and Arab populations to their respective states. The report stated:

> A precedent is afforded by the exchange effected between the Greek and Turkish populations on the morrow of the Greco-

Turkish War of 1922. … Under the supervision of the League of Nations, Greek nationals residing in Turkey, non-Muslims, were required to move to Greece, Turkish nationals residing in Greece of the Muslim faith were required to move to Turkey. The compulsory population exchange was completed in the spring of 1923. No less than 1,300,000 Greeks and 400,000 Turks were transferred in less than eighteen months.

The recommendations of the Peel Commission Report were rejected by both Jews and Arabs.

1939: The British White Paper of May 17 abandoned the Mandate and the idea of partition in Palestine by endorsing the idea of a bi-national state, an independent state governed jointly by Jews and Arabs. Jewish immigration into Palestine was restricted, and the Haganah, the British-trained Jewish fighting force, was disarmed.

1939–1945: World War II killed tens of millions. Six million Jews died in German death camps.

1947: In April, Britain formally petitioned the United Nations to end the British Mandate in Palestine. The UN General Assembly set up a Special Committee on Palestine (UNESCOP), concurred to end the Mandate, and recommended that Palestine be partitioned into Jewish and Arab states. On November 29, the General Assembly passed the partition plan. UN Resolution 181 divided the area into three entities: a Jewish state, an Arab state, and an international zone around Jerusalem.

1948: At midnight May 14, the provisional government of Israel proclaimed the new state of Israel, after nearly two thousand years. President Truman extended immediate recognition of the provisional government. On May 15, Arab armies invaded the incipient Jewish state, and the first Arab-Israeli war began.

BRITISH-OCCUPIED PALESTINE
1939–1941

Kibbutz Maabarot was founded in 1925 and settled in 1933. Its current population is 850 kibbutzim. It is located in the Sharon plain, near the old road from Petah Tikvah to Haifa.

Sir Harold MacMichael, British High Commissioner to Palestine, 1938–1944.

Madagascar Plan: An idea that circulated among early twentieth-century European governments including Poland, France, and Germany before and during Hitler's Third Reich. The plan included a compulsory transfer of Europe's Jewish population to the French island of Madagascar, off the coast of east Africa.

Archbishop Luigi Barlassina: Archbishop to Jerusalem, 1920–1947.

Mohammed Amin al Husseini, Grand Mufti of Jerusalem, 1921, 1936, was a virulent anti-Semitic Palestinian religious leader opposed to the idea of a Jewish state in the British Mandate of Palestine. He engineered many of the Arab riots against the Jews and moderate Arabs of Palestine. In 1937, the British forced him into exile to Syria after Husseini sided with Adolf Hitler. From 1941 until the end of World War II, as Hitler's guest in Berlin, Husseini advocated the extermination of the Jews on radio broadcasts to the Middle East. At the end of the war, Husseini fled to Egypt. He was indicted for war crimes, but never prosecuted. Although he tried to return to Arab Jerusalem, King Hussein of Jordan denied him permission to return. Husseini died in exile in 1974. His nephew was Yasser Arafat.

About the Author

Stephen Lewis is a freelance writer who has a talent for interweaving history and fiction into 'thriller' novels. A recently retired stock broker, Stephen resides in Arizona with his wife, where he plans to write more exciting novels and books.

Printed in the United States
202079BV00003B/22-81/P